AMELIA
NORTH
and the
Worlds

Trevor Lilley

Quacks Books
7 Grape Lane
Petergate
York
Yo1 7hu

Some words of wisdom for those about to enter the worlds of Amelia North.

If you are deliberating over whether to read this book then let me help you to make up your mind. Within these pages lies the tale of how one girl is destined to save the twin worlds from their respective fates. Now that is quite a task, but not impossible; she's ten. It may be that one of the worlds has been made up for this story or it may be that it actually exists. Who really knows?

If you see an Amelia, it's unlikely she's the one in this story. But anything is possible if you want to believe it, so maybe you'd better look closely. Once or twice in proceedings, you will encounter characters - and they're not all human - that will have you wondering if they really are out there somewhere. There will be those who you will hope are purely a figment of the imagination whenever you hear a bump in the night. Right now the very idea of handing a quill to a meerkat sounds absurd doesn't it? I know, that's how I felt - but I've tried several times since the end of the beginning.

Next time you see a large horse chestnut tree, you'll probably be reminded of Chowk and perhaps you'll ponder the likelihood of ever going there yourself. The best place to start looking, let me assure you, would be at a crossroads and I wish you the best of luck. What goes on in Chowk? Maybe if the sleepy cat had asked the same question it might still be alive today. Talking of curiosity, what might you see next time you peer into the brass rimmed glass of a ship's porthole? Curious? You should be.

One thing I can say with a reasonable degree of certainty is that Pearls of Bog Rosemary won't work anymore. But I wonder, would you even know one if you saw one? I have read there are no connecting holes left open anyway. But should we necessarily believe everything we read? What's that you say? You might as well try talking to a firefly? Well it's funny you should say that as it happens. Anyway, as grown-ups everywhere ought to tell you, you can never be certain what you're eating. So don't try it; who knows where you might end up. It won't necessarily be anywhere pleasant.

Last of all, whenever you see a colourful character of a certain age walking down the street - maybe there's one living right next door - you should consider asking them if they know Da North. I think you'll find most of them do.

Enjoy the story, for that is what it is.

Trevor Dene Lilley

31st day of July 2014

Chapters

Prologue

One Hundred and Fifty Years Ago

Another month of torrential rain and people were talking of keeping records. Would the nineteenth century ever see a wetter summer? It showed no sign of stopping, none at all. That July the weather steadily worsened. In every town, hardy Northern folk turned up collars and toiled against the gloom in the hope that things would take a turn for the better. It was a miserable night to be out; rumblings of distant thunder signalled the start of an electric storm.

Out on a remote Yorkshire hillside the heavy rain lashed against the broad shoulders of a solitary worker. Pausing from his labours, he took off his hat to shake the water from the brim as he scanned the mine workings from the wheelhouse to the edge of the first spoil heap. He wanted to be sure that he was alone. This was important, too important for any mistakes and he was glad that the drumming of rain on the tin roofs masked his scraping and hammering. He reached forward again, but then recoiled, startled by a vision. A rain-soaked child clawed at the stone slab and traced bloodied fingers along the inscription the worker was chiselling. One moment she was there beside the slab and then she faded into the howling wind. Breathing deeply, he redoubled his efforts as lightning streaked across the sky and flooded the hillside with an eerie glow. It was heavy work and risky too. Had he been caught it would have been unforgivable by those who had grown to trust him with

The Stone's care and safekeeping and he would have been banished forever. At least he wouldn't have been killed for his wrongdoing. There had never been a single killing since time began where he came from, yet he'd heard of beer-fuelled murders here when miners cheated in drunken card games. He'd learned a lot in the few weeks he'd been visiting Mordechai Fearn, the teenage lead miner from Low Bishopside. Working in the light of a single candle melted onto the brim of his hat, a miner could spend his entire lifetime struggling to extract a meagre living. Along airless, twisting underground passageways, the miner's whole existence was played out in pursuit of a vein of the precious ore, for little reward. It was about time Mordechai Fearn enjoyed a share of the providence he deserved in his bleak life.

The worker wiped the sweat from his eyes and slotted the tools back into his bag, now saturated with the heavy rain. From a pocket deep inside his topcoat he took out a heavy parcel wrapped in waxed cloth. Fearful that his actions would be discovered he glanced around again, peering through the gloom. He was alone and he turned his attention once again to the parcel, delicately folding back the swathes of cloth. His dark features were immediately lit by a silvery glow, which gave a magical sparkle to the raindrops clinging to the brim of his hat. The Stone's mesmerising beauty held his gaze for long moments until he carefully wrapped it once again and placed it inside the wall, vowing it would be the last thing he would ever steal. With a supreme effort, he lifted the heavy slab and slotted it securely into place over the front of the recess in which the parcel was now hidden from view. Standing back to admire his work, he took a long drink from his water bottle and then replaced the stopper with a slap.

'Well, that's you safely away for now,' he whispered before taking up his bottle once more and draining it. Gathering up his bag, he hurried into the low tunnel in the hillside behind the wheelhouse. The moment he disappeared from view, the storm lashed out in one final, furious maelstrom as if chastising the worker for stealing The Stone. The rain gave way to a sudden barrage of hailstones, which pounded the mine workings and obliterated any trace of the worker's visit. A blinding surge of forked lightning smashed into a tree that erupted in flames and crashed to the ground right where he had been working moments earlier. It had been a lucky escape.

By the light of a candle, he picked his way along the network of passageways, sometimes stooping, sometimes crawling, until he passed through to his own world and made his way home to Futhark. Before he settled down to sleep for the night he pulled a leather writing case from the mantelpiece and read the letter he'd been writing to his new friend. He smiled affectionately at the uncanny similarity between their names. Satisfied that his explanations were clear he added one last passage:

Mordechai Fearn my dear friend,

I have taken a great risk because I want to do some good in your world, to ease the suffering and the difficulties faced by you and the miners around you. I have hidden a treasure of immense value in a place where you should be able to find it. As I write, I am filled with sadness because I know that when I visit you to present this letter it will be the last time we meet. The power to cross over from my world to yours is dwindling and will soon be lost forever. In the name of

secrecy, I cannot tell you the location of The Shining Stone,
your treasure, so I give you this clue:
Namesake's old providence lies behind Futhark on a whim.

Your dear friend,

Mordechai Fern

He placed his quill back into the inkwell at his desk, closed the book and leaned forward to blow out the candle. As he pushed back his chair ready to stand, he heard a knock at the door. He froze, paralysed with fear. Had he been found out? Once again, the knocker rapped insistently. Without a sound Fern tiptoed towards the door and hesitated, summoning the courage to open it. At the precise moment his fingers curled around the handle the door burst open as though kicked with a great force and he tumbled backwards into the room. Looking up he saw a tall elegantly dressed woman standing there with her two small children.

'Well Sanguinella, Henrietta, look who cowers before us,' she cooed. 'It is the thief who has taken The Shining Stone and would keep it from us. Mordechai Fern, your time in this world is at an end. You will tell me where you have taken The Stone and then you will be banished to spend a lifetime in Oblivion.' She spoke with a calm authority.

'Give you The Stone?' cried the man. 'I will never allow The Shining Stone to come into the possession of the Couch family as long as I live, do you understand me? Give The Stone to Desdemona Couch? I know what you are and what will become of our world with The Stone in your hands!' Mordechai Fern was fearful yet resolute as he spoke. The woman stepped closer until she was standing directly above him.

'Well so be it, fool. I will find The Shining Stone after you are dead!' she snarled as her face twisted into a petrifying sneer of the darkest malice, sending shockwaves of fear deep into his soul. Without even making contact with the stricken man, she reached out a hand as if to grip around his throat and then she squeezed the life out of him until he slumped to the floor, dead. Without a second glance, the woman swept out of the room followed by a smirking Sanguinella. Henrietta lingered for a moment to pick up Fern's letter from the desk and hide it in the pocket of her black dress. Tears of sadness welled in her eyes at her mother's cruelty as she looked down at the limp body on the floor, vowing to keep the letter a secret for at least the next hundred years.

Chapter 1

Early in the Twenty-First Century

It was the middle of summer and perfect weather for picnics beside the River Nidd. The hot sunshine was a welcome change in this part of Yorkshire. Ever since the start of the school holidays it had rained a little every day. But not today. Today was different and people had flocked to the riverbank with their picnic blankets to enjoy Sunday lunch in the fresh air, making the most of the beautiful Yorkshire countryside for once. Some were content to read newspapers, which slowly baked to a crisp in the heat. Others made daisy chains into crowns and necklaces. Dads rolled up trousers and shivered against the chilly river, probing around with fishing nets to catch sticklebacks. Mums made quick work of finishing the raspberry sorbet before it turned to mushy syrup in the bowl. It had been a laborious job pushing the mixture through the sieve with the back of a wooden spoon; there was no way the refreshing treat was going to be wasted! Life trickled along at a leisurely pace down there beside the river, which completely suited the mood of the day. A holiday, where the sound of buzzing insects and moving water added to the peacefulness rather than disturbing it.

Melie North was happier to be up the hill, surveying the scene from her peaceful vantage point. Chewing on a stalk of grass, she sat cross-legged against a sycamore hoping the improved weather would last. It was adventuring weather and Melie had been longing for adventure all summer. She liked it up here because it was busy down by the river. Down there children and grown-ups alike chased around noisily, barking dogs danced backwards and forwards fetching sticks and squawking ducks begged for crumbs around the picnic blankets. On the hill, Melie was away from the crowds and if it hadn't been for the butterflies, she'd have been completely alone. There were dozens of them flittering along the hedge and as she squinted against the sun, Melie wondered why the only ones that would go through the hole were the little Purple Hairstreaks. The others wouldn't go near. It was a big hole up there near the top of the hedge and as she counted the Hairstreaks going in she soon noticed they weren't coming back out. Why didn't they come back? On days like this there was time for Melie North to ponder over simple mysteries such as these. But the days that lay in store that summer for Melie, short for Amelia of course, would be quite different.

'Coming ready or not!' yelled Luke as he scanned the riverbanks with eagle eyes. It was the start of another game of hide and seek. 'Right you lot, here I come,' he whispered, as if setting a personal challenge to find them all in record time. It wouldn't take long. They were hopeless at hiding, especially Melie. 'I can see you, behind that tree!' Luke bellowed triumphantly. 'Yes, come on, it's you. Ginger hair. Come on A - me - li - a, are you receiving me? Game over!' He knew his friend wouldn't be able to resist his irksome enunciation of the syllables.

Luke was right; Melie flounced out from behind the Sycamore, first to be found as usual but laughing with good humour all the same. Finding good hiding places was not one of her strong points although she was good at most aspects of playing out. But not lighting campfires;

Melie struggled with that. Her fires never burned for long enough to toast a slice of bread on a stick, as the others were always quick to point out at Teasing Time. Yet it was generally accepted that what country skills Amelia North didn't excel at were hardly worth the bother. If they needed to win a conker fight, they could offer up their champion. Navigating scientifically by the stars? Yes. Following a deeply rooted instinct to trace the trail from here to there? Well that was just the tip of the iceberg. Her Da was always showing off about her to anyone who would listen in his Friday night local, The Half Dead Tree, in Exchange Street, Turley Holes.

'She's a wonder child of the natural world my Melie, just like her mother,' he'd announce between swigs of his preferred malt whisky. Scotch in the pub, Irish at home. 'She eats up country lore for breakfast. I'm sure she'll change the world one day!' It was only a hazy notion, lingering from somewhere in his youth, but Da really believed she would and it wasn't the whisky talking. He always left well before closing time, turning up the collar of his old blue linen jacket and waltzing off home with a surprisingly nimble gait for a man in his late forties.

Maybe she would change the world; she wasn't too keen on the way it was turning out anyway. Melie was happy to let progress run its course and she possessed enough common sense to avoid being swept along with the whimsical fads and fashions. Something deep inside kept her comfortably distanced from the all-consuming world of information technology. Luke and one or two of the Schultz kids found an escape in computer gaming from time to time when overwhelmed by the force of Melie's personality.

'She's got one on her again,' they'd sigh through gritted teeth before retiring to the gaming room in Schultzville, their large house next door to The Half Dead Tree.

Da wasn't Melie's only admirer. There was old Billy too, her friendly neighbour. He was nicknamed Welly by the three gangs of kids who lived round and about Powder Mill Fields. He was aptly named; his only footwear seemed to be one green welly and one black welly both turned down at the top. Welly Jackson lived in a crumbling old cottage dubbed the Eighth Wonder of the World by the kids. They reasoned it was only being prevented from falling down by miraculous intervention, hence the name. He was always around and at large generally minding his own business and bothering no one. Not many were invited into Welly's inner circle, so not many ever learned his real name. Melie North was one of a trusted handful scattered amongst the three gangs of kids and was the one to whom he had granted an audience that day.

'So what are you going to be getting up to this summer then Melie?' he asked as he twirled his salt and peppery beard, which had yellowed a bit with pipe smoke.

'Well, you know,' she sighed, 'a bit of this and a bit of that I reckon. A bit of adventuring and a bit of exploring I'm sure. A bit of something unusual for a change, that'd be nice.'

'Well that'll do for starters girl,' the old man chuckled as he reclined in his battered old armchair. 'But mind you remember all you've learned. There's not many your age who can read the countryside like you can. Don't you go and forget all that stuff. You'll need it one day, you'll see,' wheezed the old man in a strangely serious tone. Yes, it did seem strange the way he kept going on about country skills as if they were all that mattered in life and would make all the difference in the world. To Melie and the three gangs of kids, country lore was just something they did when playing down at the Powder Mill in the little woodland. Absorbing as this was and no matter how far into the imagination zone it swept you, it was just playing after all.

'Why so serious Billy?' Melie asked the crumply old warrior as she twirled his pocket watch round and round her finger on its silver chain. He rose from his armchair and caught the watch in mid twirl, then flumped back down sending an eruption of dust into the room.

'Melie my treasure, you never know when you'll need the kinds of things I've spent the best part of a lifetime turning into a fine art. Mark my words, these country skills will be a lot more use to you than knowing what to do with those computers everybody's buying down in the supermarket. You'll see.' Welly's reply, delivered as always in his broad Yorkshire accent was tinged with annoyance. 'So-called progress, I ask you! What they want to build that for anyway? What's happened to the old way of life?' he muttered. They were very much alike in their views and ideas and Melie couldn't help feeling that they must have met before, or shared some common ground in the past. But she was only ten, how could that be? Sometimes he seemed to drift off into a vague moment as if he were living in two places at once and had just nipped into the other one to attend to something important. Razor sharp one moment, vague and almost forgetful the next. He was a puzzling character that old Welly Jackson. And what did he mean by 'you'll see?' Exactly what, she wondered as she drifted home that evening, would Amelia North see?

Exploring was definitely on the menu for tomorrow, with Luke and maybe Tiny Page and a few of the Schultz kids. So it would be home, tea, finish that book at last and then bed round about ten. A little late for a ten year old some would say. But it was the summer holidays after all and it wasn't easy getting to sleep while it was still daylight. It was even harder with that annoying little firefly that had been buzzing around Melie's bedroom for the last couple of nights.

Chapter 2

Tiny Page and the Schultz Kids

Downstairs in the front kitchen, Da was trying to poke some life into the morning fire with an old toasting fork. His crumpled, blue linen jacket hung off his bony shoulders; it was at least two sizes too big for him. As a youngster Melie had loved delving into those baggy pockets and marvelling at the bizarre bits and pieces that she pulled out. Now, at the age of ten and a bit, her life was a little too full of her own diversions and adventures and she sometimes forgot the close bond she'd shared with Da from birth to the age of six. This didn't seem to bother Da too much. He'd still back her up with great encouragement in everything she did, because Melie was very much like he'd been at that age. He was adventurous, off the wall and somewhat out of step with the ordinary kind of people in the world. He was certainly different to most people round and about Powder Mill Fields. Now worn out and frazzled, with short greying hair and an attempt at a cool little goatee beard clinging to his chin, he'd certainly cut a dashing figure in days gone by. As a teenager, his hair was streaked with green dye and he wore a safety pin poked through his swollen earlobe. The punk fashions of nineteen seventy- seven which graced the streets of cities like London and Manchester had actually looked a little out of place amongst the small Yorkshire villages he'd hung around in.

'Ah, youth!' he'd sigh, over a small Irish whisky and a

pile of faded photos. Sometimes the whisky flowed long into the evening and the tales he told his daughter grew out of all proportion to reality. Then he'd fling open the front kitchen windows and bellow down the street his old code of living from days gone by, 'No passion, no power! Punk will never die!' Next, he'd tirelessly bounce the giggling young Melie up and down to the ceiling and back, all smiles and admiration for the daughter he loved. In a way, she was lucky, because he gave her two shares of his love; one for her and one for the wife and mother who'd gone away from them to another place when Melie was only two.

The toast just popped and the kettle freshly boiled, Da opened the door to the knocking visitors and shouted up the stairs.

'Melie, its Tiny Page and the Schultz kids,' he yelled, 'come on!'

Amelia North thundered down the stairs and bounced into the kitchen. Grabbing a slice of toast from the plate on the table, she hurled herself upon the little group of kids and sent them skittling across the floor. Pinning Tiny Page down whilst chomping on her toast, Melie spluttered out the gang's code of belonging.

'No passion, no power,' she cried, ribtickling him mercilessly under an avalanche of sloppy breadcrumbs.

'One life, live it!' Tiny coughed out the standard response against a barrage of laughs and giggles.

The smiling Schultz kids, Molly, short for Molybdenum, and Jam, short for James, hauled Melie to her feet. Brushing toast crumbs off her oversize, turquoise mohair jumper that used to be her mum's, she called them to attention in a mock military line up.

'So kids,' she boomed, 'where's Luke then? And, Jam Sandwich, where's Schultz two and three? Not coming today or what?'

'Yeah, they're coming. It's that twit sister of mine,' replied Molly as she prepared to do her famous vocal impression of her twin. In the opinion of most of the gang, Sammy went all dreamy and drippy whenever Luke was around. 'Luke, let's go in the loft, I've got that new game I was wanting. We can go round to Melie's later,' she drawled in an affected nasal squeal. 'Oh Luke, will you marry me, it is a leap year after all!'

'Bet she loved it when Crate Boy stayed too!' Tiny joined in. 'I can just see the two of them hogging the handsets and Sulky Sammy sitting with that look on her face! Why's she wasting her time? He doesn't fancy her!' The fact that Tiny himself fancied Sammy Schultz had been well publicised all over school at every opportunity for the past year. He'd never been allowed to forget how his cheeks had flushed to the colour of ripe tomatoes when directed to hold her hand in the Christmas play. The fact that eleven year old Luke was the blue-eyed captain of Turley Holes Primary School rugby team didn't help Tiny's case much at all. At ten years old, Tiny was already the largest of the gang by far. Some would say that he was perhaps rather too fond of the chips from Robinson and Peacock, the village fish and chip shop. Melie's gang was a true brotherhood and they accepted one another for what they were, but kids from the other two gangs from around Powder Mill Fields would pick on Tiny. He was usually pushed into being goalkeeper for the school football team on the basis that he'd block half the goalmouth without having to move a muscle. Though Tiny took it all in his stride, his protective friends, especially Melie, knew he was saddened by their fun poking. The mysterious loss of his dad when he was seven had deeply affected Tiny Page, so hurtful jibes were the last thing he needed.

Da looked over from behind his pint mug of tea with immense pride at the way his daughter and her friends were so at ease with each other and the world.

'Hey there, Amelia North,' he yelled, adopting an officer's manner and taking a stab at a public school accent. 'Rally your squadron and go out there to take on the world today! Da will be right here when you come home!'

'Bye Da!' she whispered in his ear as she bounced up to kiss him on the cheek. 'Love you, and see you later.' The four heroes trooped out into the small back garden and dropped into the shed for the supplies they'd need on their adventures that day. None of the gang noticed, but following on behind was the little firefly from Melie's bedroom.

Chapter 3

The Hole in the Hedge.

In the sunlight filtering in through the window a billion specks of dust hovered and glittered in the air.

'What do you think's biggest then, a billion or a trillion?' pondered Luke, who'd joined them en route to the shed. Following on behind were Schultz two and three; Sammy, short for Samphire and Alexander which was never shortened. The twin girls had long since given up trying to explain their cumbersome given names to school friends. What's more, they had given up trying to work out why their parents had chosen them in the first place; the words seemed rather extraordinary as names. The shortened versions were preferred, unless it was Teasing Time.

'Well that'll be a trillion,' replied Sammy, 'but I couldn't be sure about it. Who cares anyway? There's loads of dust and that's that.' The kids loved hanging out in there. Unlike many other places in their young lives, it felt reassuringly real. It was obviously quite old. It stood there at the corner of Da's vegetable patch in the back garden and it seemed as if it had always been there. As a productive allotment, the patch had had its day. It was almost completely choked with rye grass now and the dreaded mare's tail. Apart from one clump of struggling rhubarb right in the centre, nothing of any significance grew there at all. From time to time Da would cut some stalks of the spectacular red plant and, as a random act of kindness, bundle them up with newspaper and string before plonking them on a neighbour's doorstep as if they were a longed for treat. Sure as not, they'd end up living on the kitchen shelf in the newspaper for a month before being deemed too rancid to be of any use. Then they'd be plonked somewhere else in their wrapper, ideally the compost heap but often the dustbin. Another thing about the shed was the smell. A musty, fusty mixture of dusty old rope and mouldy daffodil bulbs infused with a hint of dark creosote. But best of all was the amazing array of tools, old baskets and bags, gardening and do-it-yourself paraphernalia, lost toys and general items of an assorted nature, all set out on wonky shelves or swinging from the walls and eaves on sisal strings. A haven for several species of spider and countless creepy crawlies, it was a jumble really, a collection of bits and pieces that had passed through Da's hands on his journey from young punk to homebuilding dad. Once, these bits and pieces were important indispensables, necessities of life if one was to get along smoothly. But like the box of vinyl records on the top shelf, now only occasionally used as brilliant Frisbees, they were the relics of a bygone age. Sometimes remembered but mostly forgotten about ... unless you were a kid! From out of this wonderful jumble, Melie and the gang could conjure up just the right equipment for any adventure they could think of.

'Let's take these with us,' said one, as out came seven straight hazel staffs all a good stretch taller than the kid wielding it.

'Here's your Bag of Tryx,' said another as a brown leather bag with a long shoulder strap and a few hippy beads was produced and draped over Melie's shoulder by Alexander the Crate. It was an iconic piece of regalia for the gang and possibly the key symbol of leadership in the otherwise casual organisation of the group.

'Here you are Melie, a couple of candles. Even you could manage to get a fire going with these. I'm not sure you could light a match though, what do you think? Still, raw sausages might be ok!' Jam Sandwich Schultz was joking; it was Teasing Time.

'We'd be safer with a bunch of bananas and some monkey nuts; at least we wouldn't starve or die from food poisoning!' Tiny Page pitched in with his own little dig at Melie's expense, straightening his red framed glasses, which had slid down to the end of his nose as always.

'Okay, okay,' she sighed with upturned palms and a smile of mock sarcasm, 'you lot light the fires, I'll just lead the way!'

Their ages ranged from Luke's eleven down to Jam the smallest Schultz at seven. Sticking together through thick and thin, they'd shared many adventures and excursions into places where the boundary between real and imaginary had sometimes been hard to see. One time they'd lost Molly down a dry well near the Powder Mill's ancient water wheel and had had to lower her brother Alexander down to her on the end of a long rope. To get them back out, the gang had bravely rounded up a cow from the next field and somehow cajoled it across to the rescue site. Melie had tied the rope around its neck and persuaded Luke to ride it across the yard at a run, Sammy luring it along with handfuls of fresh grass. The lost Schultz was out in no time! In spring, they'd discovered what they thought to be a pirate chest half buried in the sludge at Powder Mill Pond and then held a running battle with both other gangs of kids, using mud balloons and catapults to defend their property. As it turned out, the chest wasn't brimming with pirated pieces of eight from a seventeenth century Spanish galleon. But the wooden crate itself had been worth defending. From that day forwards it came in useful in the shed as the catapult box. For a while afterwards Melie and the kids became known as Les Catapultiers, the Spanish link having accidentally evolved into a version of French. Alexander, in recognition of his bravery during the battle, became known as Alexander the Crate, which time eventually devolved into unflattering Crate Boy. But the adventure of a lifetime they all longed for had continued to elude them until now. Later that day outside their new den and after they'd dined al fresco on Luke's perfect campfire sausages, Melie gathered the troops.

'There's this weird hedge over by the Nidd,' she said. 'Let's go have a look.'

'What's weird about a hedge?' Molly asked her. 'Anyway, it's miles away and I can't be bothered. Let's just hang around here.'

'It's not miles away Molybdenum! Anyway, I reckon it'll be worth it,' Melie ventured. 'When we were playing hide and seek yesterday I saw this hole. There were these butterflies. I know it sounds stupid, but ... look, you'll just have to come and see.'

Half an hour later, the weather beaten explorers from Turley Holes were watching bright blue butterflies disappearing into the hole near the top of the hedge and not coming back out. The day was changing from late afternoon to the onset of early evening and shadows were beginning to stretch eastwards down the hill. It was warm and it was quiet; there seemed to be no one around. Hovering above their heads, the little firefly watched the proceedings with growing anticipation of what was about to happen. Melie looked at the kids in the gang and a strange understanding that couldn't be explained seemed to pass between them, as if they'd been here before, together on this very spot or one very much like it. They must have sensed that this was a special moment.

'See that hole?' Melie said, 'I'm going in.'

Chapter 4

A Firefly on the Wall

It was unusual to see a box hedge towering so high. This one dwarfed the kids and was interwoven with razor sharp firethorn dotted with plump, orange berries and shiny leaves in two shades of green. Only the foolhardy would attempt the perilous climb onto the branches of a monster such as this and expect to walk away unscathed. But Melie was determined to reach the hole at the top. Tiny suggested building a human pyramid, something they'd practised many times before, but with kids of all shapes and sizes this wasn't going to be easy. No-one wanted to be on the bottom tier, but after a few failed attempts, Melie eventually managed to make it work and she cautiously clambered to the top, tottered unsteadily on Luke's shoulders and looked into Butterfly Hole.

'What can you see?' Luke managed to ask, shuffling underneath her.

'Come on Melie, hurry up, my knees are killing me!' Molly shouted, 'come on!'

'What's she doing? Melie!' joined in Sammy as she began to crumple under the weight of the kids up above. They were all becoming uncomfortable and were growing seriously impatient with Melie for taking so long at whatever she was doing up there. She seemed to be peering into the hole and then craning her neck, trying to look over the top into the field of barley that lay on the other side of the hedge. Tiny, on the second tier with Luke, was firmly focused on the bristling firethorn spines that threatened to pick his nose for him. Alexander's shoulders were killing him and he wished he were not right at the bottom. It was no use, collapse was inevitable and with shouts and some unpleasant scratching, the whole structure crashed to the floor with Melie North on top of the pile. After a moment, they began to extract themselves from the tangle. Tiny Page was first to his feet and once he'd found his glasses he gingerly pulled two nasty looking spines from his left cheek and turned grumpily to point the finger of blame at Melie. But he thought better of it. As the rest of the kids began to ease up from the ground, Tiny noticed that for once she was lost for words, obviously dumbstruck by what she had seen in the hole in the hedge.

'What's up?' Tiny eventually asked, dabbing at the little spots of blood with a dirty hanky.

'Melie, what is it?' joined in Jam Schultz. 'Don't tell me you saw something weird in there.' Melie sat stunned on the grass, shaking her head to compose herself.

'It just can't be ...'she whispered.

'What can't? Oh come on Melie, what's in there?' asked Alexander. 'Look, are you having us on or what?'

'Melie, tell us!' Luke was the eldest and he felt responsible. Had she seen something unpleasant? Melie looked up at Luke and finally spoke.

'It was me,' she said. 'I saw a face looking straight back at me out of the hole and it was definitely me; same jumper, same six plaits, Bag of Tryx, the lot.'

***

Lost in her own thoughts on the walk back to Turley Holes that evening, it wasn't until she turned into Mill

Square and said goodbye to her gang that Melie noticed she was being followed. It could just be coincidence, but a little firefly, probably a lesser Glow Worm by the look of it, seemed to be hovering behind her every time she glanced round.

'Strange to see you this far north, you lost?' She delivered the question as if expecting a reply; it came as something of a shock when she received one. This was turning out to be quite a day. The firefly spoke with a high-pitched male voice that didn't quite fit at all.

'Amelia North, child of Maeva,' it whined, 'you must go back, you are welcome, you are needed. It is your eleventh year in Theirworld.'

'Me?' asked Melie, looking first at the firefly and then scanning the street. People would think she was talking to herself. 'You ... you spoke!'

'I spoke to you. Either you are the child of Maeva or you are not. Speak it plain and speak it true, time is short, time is nearly gone.' The firefly buzzed once around her head and settled on the palm of Melie's upturned hand. Like her Da, Melie was an open-minded individual able to accept the unusual, but she was finding this experience hard to grasp.

'I don't know what to say. You're a firefly ...' she whispered. Again, the firefly spoke.

'I am chosen to guide you to your destiny. I take the persona of firefly only in Theirworld. A firefly is a small and conveniently inconspicuous persona, noticeable only when necessary. In Hedge, I am known as Fergus Wiseman, which I only reveal to you because you need to know of this. Amelia, time is short, time is nearly gone. You must come into Hedge where you are welcome, where you are needed. You must fulfil your destiny in your eleventh year.' Melie's mind was made up; this must be some kind of waking dream. This just could not be happening, not in Turley Holes. And whilst inconspicuous was the last word she would have chosen to describe a firefly, something deep inside told her she really ought to listen, that it was really happening and that it was somehow important.

'Exactly whose world are we talking about here?' Melie asked.

'Amelia,' said the firefly, 'I thank you for staying. Time is short, time is nearly…'

'I know, yes I know,' sighed Melie, 'time is nearly gone. Okay, so I'm talking to a firefly!' Melie was beginning to wonder how she could possibly be swept along by this impossible situation. 'I don't believe this,' she muttered as a light drizzle began to dampen the pavements in the fading light.

'Believe it my child; it is as real as you yourself.' The firefly, or Fergus or whoever, was calm as he spoke. 'You ask whose world. Well this is your world and is called Theirworld by our world which is Hedge. You must come into Hedge as you and you alone can be entrusted with the quest for The Shining Stone, which has passed between worlds and must return before the last hole is lost. The fate of Hedge is safe and assured but the fate of your world, Theirworld, is bound up with the fate of The Stone.'

'A little complex,' Melie thought to herself.

'Indeed child, complex and serious.' The firefly aired Melie's thoughts as if reading her mind.

'So let's get this straight,' said Melie. 'This is Yorkshire on planet Earth. That's one world. You're from another world, which for some reason is called Hedge. You lot call our world Theirworld. You've lost some kind of stone and you seem to want me, on my own, to get it back for you before I'm eleven and then Earth will be okay. Is that what you're saying?'

'You have listened well child,' said the firefly. 'And now you must go to seek the help of the one you call Welly. Go at once, there is no time. Explain what you saw in the hole, that you have spoken with Fergus Wiseman and that I permit you to take possession of his curiosity circlet. We will meet again in Hedge, where you will find me in Futhark, near…' The firefly stopped suddenly, as if startled and then vanished as a chilling darkness seemed to drift into the little stand of trees across the road.

'Completely mystifying,' gasped Melie, trying to take stock of it all. 'He knows Billy.' She set off running in the direction of Billy's cottage, glancing back from time to time for fear of that weird darkness. It had scared her, really scared her, with its brooding presence and dark malevolence and it had certainly made the firefly leave in a hurry. In no time, she arrived breathless at the front door of Billy's cottage, number thirty-nine, Forty Steps, a short, dimly lit side street running up to the embankment that carried a disused railway line across this particular part of Yorkshire. No trains had passed along it in Melie's lifetime. She knocked at the door and as she waited, a large hedgehog bumbled across the pathway, looked up at her and then scuttled away into the damp undergrowth.

Chapter Five

The Conversation of a Lifetime

Billy rested his elbows on the table, fingers splayed wide and fingertips touching as he listened intently to all that Melie told him. A meagre fire grizzled away in the grate, keeping both of them warm in the unseasonal chill of evening. It was getting a bit late for the ten year old to be out and about, but something big was unfolding here. Da would have to wait. She finished talking and after a while Billy shuffled in his tattered armchair, leaning forward to look deeply into Melie's eyes.

'Are you absolutely sure about the darkness?' he asked.

'Yes, it just kind of drifted into that little stand of trees in Mill Square,' she replied, a little perplexed that this darkness thing was what interested him most. Why wasn't he interested in Fergus the talking firefly and this other world or the mysterious Maeva and the missing stone?

'Melie,' Billy whispered, as if reading her mind just as Fergus had appeared to do, 'I am interested in everything you say and have so much to explain to you, but it is vital that you are clear about the darkness. How dark was it?'

'Well, what, you mean like as in shades of grey or black?' she found herself using the same whispered tones and looking intently at Billy who seemed earnest and grave. 'Okay, I would call it very dark and kind of dense. Solid almost, but definitely a mist; you couldn't see through it. It just drifted amongst the trees and hung there swirling, slowly though. Does that help?'

'Melie,' said Billy, 'if I understand you properly then I think you are very fortunate to be sitting here now, alive and just a little shaken because I believe you've seen an Air of Mystery.'

'What's an Air of Mystery?' she asked. Melie was becoming more confused by the minute.

'Melie, you are going to learn a great deal about all that you heard from Fergus Wiseman, but it is getting late and I must get you safely home to bed now. There's something I must attend to and your Da will be worrying about you and wondering where you are,' said Billy. He rose from the chair, placed an old fireguard in the hearth and picked up his hat. 'But,' he added, resting both hands on her shoulders, 'I expect you'll be straight round here at nine in the morning'. His face beamed into a smile. 'And why shouldn't you Amelia North?! If what I've been piecing together in this old mind of mine is true then you are in for one grand old adventure!' Then he whispered quietly to himself, 'Quite as I had been expecting.'

***

Da was waiting in the front kitchen when Billy delivered Melie safely home that night. A few friends from the village were seated comfortably around the kitchen table, with whisky, mugs of tea from the huge teapot nestling underneath its stripy tea cosy and a pile of digestive biscuits on a plate.

'Here she is folks, my wonder child!' Da cooed, oozing an obvious pride in his daughter. 'Taken on the world today?' Da strode towards her, scooped her warmly into his arms and planted a kiss on her forehead, before whispering, 'Bit late love, you okay?'

'I'm fine Da,' she replied. 'Been sort of busy today; been round at Welly's. Can I have a biscuit?' Melie asked, remembering that she hadn't eaten since Luke's campfire sausages.

'There's tea in the oven. Grab that and a biscuit then off to bed. Oh and don't forget to clean your teeth,' Da reminded her. It seemed that ordinary day-to-day things still existed. The friends, Connell Brown, Captain Geo Schultz and Lizzie Page wished Melie a cheery goodnight as she climbed the stairs, hardly able to contain the excitement about the conversation of a lifetime that was waiting for her down Forty Steps in the morning. Once again, for Amelia North, sleep would be a long time coming.

They were all waiting for her outside the front door when she rushed out the following morning, eager to meet up with Billy at the cottage. Luke, Tiny Page and the Schultz kids had themselves found it hard to get to sleep the previous night with all the excitement at the hedge. They'd gone home feeling mystified and were eager to talk about what Melie had seen.

'No passion, no power,' said Luke. Melie paused before replying, remembering the events at the hedge.

'One life, live it,' she said, as they touched fists in their matey yet ceremonial way. 'How's it going gang?' she enquired as they all joined in with the ritual. She was trying to play down yesterday's events. She certainly wanted to avoid mentioning her conversations with Billy and the firefly until she'd had time to think it all through.

'Melie, are you sure you're okay?' asked Sammy. She was genuinely concerned. 'I think we all felt something strange was happening back there but tell us again, was it you that you saw in the hedge?'

'Sammy, I'm sure it was me,' Melie replied. 'It was my face looking straight back at me, straight into my eyes. And behind was ... well, it was not what I thought would be on the other side of the hedge. It looked amazing in there, like another place somehow. I saw the barley when I looked over the top, but not when I looked through the hole. I don't understand; it was as though I was looking at a different place inside the hedge. Weird. I just want to go back and have another look. Maybe it's nothing though. Maybe I was just seeing things.'

'Well what's stopping us going back? I want to see it too,' joined in Alexander the Crate. 'Can't we go back now?'

'Yeah, Crate Boy's right, we should go. Let's go. But are you sure you're okay Melie?' Tiny Page was worried too. Worried and excited. They all were. Their close friend had looked into an amazing place and seen herself. It was not an ordinary situation; this was big, quite unexpected.

'Well, I do want to go, course I do. But I can't go. Not just yet.' Melie skirted around the issue while she conjured up an excuse to delay matters. 'I need to go and call in on Welly. Just to make sure he's okay, you know. He's getting on a bit and they say you should go and check up on old people now and again.' Melie's efforts failed to convince the gang but even as Molly was about to challenge her, Luke silenced her with a knowing and discreet shake of the head.

'Yeah, well that's fine Melie,' he said. 'We'll meet up later; let's say eleven o' clock at the hedge, how's that?'

'Good, that's good, see you later. About eleven,' said Melie taking her chance to slope away. She called into the shed first to grab her Bag of Tryx before rushing off down the road. The kids looked at each other.

'Something's fishy here. She's onto something,' said

Tiny, airing their collective thoughts. 'We'll follow her.' This was more of a statement than a suggestion and they crept off in the direction of the Eighth Wonder of the World.

***

Melie rapped on the door of Billy's cottage at nine sharp that morning, having managed to put the gang off her trail and take a shortcut across a few back gardens to get there quicker. She scraped at the flaking pale green paint with already dirty fingernails while she waited for the old man to get to the door and welcome her in. Clearly, there was a lot more to Billy Jackson than anyone would have believed. Until last night he was just the local strange old man, tramping around the place in his odd wellies and going on and on about country lore. But now he could explain about mysterious dark shapes and with some authority on the subject. Best of all though, he believed her and all her marvellous revelations about her conversation with a talking firefly. She felt a twinge of pride in the way she had always respected the elders, especially Billy, for what they could teach the younger generations. Even so, Melie couldn't help thinking he was quite a character, living like a hermit in his ramshackle old place. He must have had his head firmly screwed on back in the nineteen sixties. As Melie recalled, he'd come into ownership in a rather unusual way after he'd found a legal loophole known as adverse possessory title. A property standing unoccupied and apparently derelict could be made secure and if no one came up to claim it within a period of years, ownership would be granted. Billy had padlocked the door, barred the windows and left it for a few years to go off wandering, then moved into his newly claimed home on his return.

And it was quite a home! He lived in just two rooms, a lounge cum bedroom and a kitchen cum bathroom. No one had ever actually seen a bath in there, but Billy was remarkably clean smelling for someone who didn't possess one. It wasn't the tidiest of places. In fact it was unofficially deemed the untidiest place in the village by Melie and any other kids who'd been in there. A coal fire, always alight even in summer, provided the focus of attention in the living room. Facing this was a mismatched pair of tattered but comfortable armchairs. There was a dusty old drop-leaf dining table in the bay window which itself was so dirty that light struggled to break through at all. Either the carpet square had been designed not to extend as far as the walls or it had frayed itself away over the years to reveal a border of greasy old floorboards around its perimeter. A huge ornate dresser in the darkest wood imaginable and with a cloudy mirror at its centre covered one entire wall. Unfortunately, the remaining walls were left clear to show off the tasteless, flowery wallpaper to anyone who dared to look at its mixture of yellows and lilacs without sunglasses.

The kitchen was even more interesting. It was sparsely appointed to say the least and piles of dead houseflies had accumulated on the windowsills over the years. Brittle old plastic floor tiles in pale yellow and black curled at the edges like crisps. A filthy sink brimmed over with unwashed crockery. A fridge lurked in the corner. Miraculously it still worked despite its great age; for all anyone knew it may well have been one of the earliest ever made. There was a small table with a chair and countless cardboard boxes littered most surfaces. Some of these contained old brass plaques that must have been taken off the walls outside offices and shops over the years. For what purpose other than to feed Billy's eccentricity one could only hazard a guess but there must have been hundreds of them, tarnished and stacked up there in that kitchen. They read like a who's who of Yorkshire trades from days gone by: solicitors, chiropodists, farriers, dentists, painters and decorators, turf accountants, funeral directors, bookbinders and more.

Strangest of all there didn't seem to be a bed. Did Billy sleep in his armchair? He certainly didn't sleep upstairs because every single bedroom door handle on the landing was tied with a length of old washing line to the central banister, giving the impression that no one had ventured into those rooms for years.

'There's a lot to tell girl, a lot to tell and there is no time. Time is short,' said Billy as he settled himself into the armchair next to Melie's in front of the fire. 'Where to start though Melie, where to start, I wonder? You saw yourself in the hole. If this is true then it means you are welcome in Hedge.'

'It was definitely me,' Melie confirmed as she slid the bag of Tryx off her shoulders and placed it on the floor. She took care to avoid squashing Billy's cat, Nettle, which had settled by her feet as always. Billy began to explain.

'Right then Melie, listen well,' said Billy. 'Now this may be a bit of a shock, but I am not from here. I'm from Hedge. It's a completely separate world from this one and believe me Melie, it's so, so different.'

'Hang on, hang on,' gasped Melie, 'what do you mean you're not from here? I thought you'd always been here. You were here when Da was young.' Billy was right; this was a bit of a shock. 'And how's it different and where is it? And how do I get in? And why's it called Hedge? That's a strange name for a world isn't it?' Melie's excitement was beginning to bubble over as the conversation of a lifetime unfolded right there at number thirty-nine. She was on the edge of her seat, wanting more.

'Amelia, child of Maeva, just listen,' said Billy. He paused as he shuffled forwards in the chair. 'Look, I'll tell you as much as I can. I don't know how there comes to be two worlds, there just are. It's quite a place, and yes, I think Hedge is an unusual name. But it's always been called that, always. There is what you might call a hedge surrounding our world, or so they say; I don't suppose anyone has ever journeyed around the entire boundary. That would be unlikely; it's an extensive world. And the hedge is endlessly wide, from our side. Here and there are connecting holes and some of these lead to your world, which is Theirworld. So Hedge, where I come from, is literally through the hole in the hedge where you saw yourself yesterday. I mean that's just one way to get in.'

'So you mean I can actually get in there through that hole?' Melie was simply brimming over at the prospect, visualising that crossover.

'Please listen to me child,' said Billy. 'It is quite unusual to be able to get into Hedge and especially rare to be invited, as it seems you have been. But please, hear all that I have to say. Save your questions until the end. Two worlds, Melie, two worlds exist side by side and yet they are so different. The one is brimming over with love and happiness, harmony and goodness; the other, yours I'm afraid to say, has too much unkindness, disloyalty, greed and a great sadness. In Hedge there is abundant good fortune, great respect for nature, warmth and light and colour, whilst Theirworld, which is your world, suffers misfortune, chokes the essence of the Earth, squashes the spirit and divides people.'

'Billy, do you mean like how we are taking everything out of the Earth and not giving anything back? I mean having to be careful with the environment and all that?'

30

Melie asked. 'But we're not all like that are we? And there are good things about our world too, aren't there?' Melie was actually quite upset to hear Billy speak like this.

'Melie, you're right. It's not all like that. It's just that it exists and it's getting worse quicker than it can get better, no matter how hard people with insight are trying,' Billy explained. 'Anyway, Hedge looks different too, as you'll find out when you go.' Melie beamed, thrilled at this, but remained attentive as Billy continued. 'So the two worlds are quite different. Hedge citizens want the benevolence of their world to spill over into yours Melie, to share their happiness and it could happen. It could happen soon. It could simply pass, as if by... what's the word ... osmosis, yes that's it, osmosis. Benevolence and happiness and everything else of that nature passing from my world to yours through the connecting holes and remember, there are many of these around and about. Your world, Theirworld, would be saved from the fate that otherwise awaits and would last forever in a state of complete harmony. No more greed, no more conflict, no more hunger. Just peace and it could happen in our time Melie.' Billy sat back and contemplated the glowing embers in the grate for a moment, allowing Melie time to take it all in and then he said, 'But time is nearly gone, time is short. Until The Shining Stone returns to Hedge the harmony will not flow and one by one, hedgerows and the like in your world are being destroyed to feed the greed. Fewer hedgerows; fewer holes, until one day...'

'So this is where I come in,' said Melie, rising and pacing, focused and very clear. 'I have to find this Shining Stone, on my own Fergus said, and return it to Hedge before it's too late. If not, Theirworld...' Melie surprised herself by using that name, '... will burn itself out.'

'That is so,' Billy confirmed. 'Find The Stone before the few remaining holes are lost Melie North and you will save your world from its doom. Sound easy? I think not.'

Melie settled back in her armchair. It did seem rather unbelievable; ten years old and expected to save the world! As far as she knew, she was the only one who knew anything about it all. Would anyone know if she just didn't go through with it? Why not just walk away now and pretend none of this existed at all? Then again, her Da was always telling the world that she'd change it one day...

Appearing once again to read her mind, Billy said, 'And there is a choice. You will or you won't. The future of my world, Hedge, is safe and assured; it's for the good of your world that you'd be doing all this.'

'He would say that, wouldn't he?' A man's voice from behind them joined in the conversation and they both spun round. It was Connell Brown.

Chapter Six

Malevolence

The knife sliced easily through the bitter red stalks as Da cut the large crinkly leaves off the rhubarb on his allotment square. Fanning his face in the morning sunshine with each leaf, he tossed them aside one by one onto his disorganised compost heap. He breathed in deeply, relishing the sweetness of the fresh warm air and then flung his beloved jacket onto the prickly little holly hedge that bounded the square on three sides. It was getting a bit warm for Da. His rainbow braces were worn for decorative effect rather than practicality; his long, battered khaki shorts were a little tight around the waist but he wouldn't get rid of them. The bulging side pockets were stuffed with a mystifying assortment of things he'd picked up around the place and his punk pink sunglasses rested on top of his head. He'd worn these every summer since Melie's mum gave them as a Christmas present back in their punk days in nineteen seventy-seven. He was quite a character, as were most of his friends. Teaching for a living in Turley Holes primary school, his entertaining style held Year Four in thrall over endless hours of learning by discovery.

'You still a teacher Da?' they'd ask in The Half Dead Tree from time to time.

'I'm not a teacher! I'm Da North and I teach,' he'd reply. The distinction was subtle, but in Da's opinion, it was a definite distinction.

He'd been plain David North at school, but round about the time of his last big summer holiday something had happened that marked a wind change in Da North. At sixteen, he baked in the record breaking summer temperatures and started to pulse in tune and in time with the new sound of punk rock that spread up from London, via Manchester into the Yorkshire cities in the mid nineteen seventies. Da the punk was a charismatic, green haired, party animal. He quickly became a teenager intent on keeping a step ahead of the crowd. His old pop records were relegated to the dustbin and he filled his mind with the energetic new bands that were showing how it was possible for everyone to live the rock and roll dream. Da North reinvented! Until then, plain and unadventurous Da seemed destined to a school life overshadowed by the other kids at school. They'd take off on flights of fanciful extrapolation, perfecting the art of taking the humour in a situation to the limits of possibility. Da sat by and watched. But it all changed during that summer. Da North was now the life and soul of the party. He'd grown, met his love May, in May as it happens when the trees are at their best and spent his life with his artist love through boom times and lean. They'd seized the world, infused it with their own brand of colourful crankiness and made a lot of people smile. They'd smiled themselves and seemed to share a secret both special and unfathomable until the day she went away to another place when their daughter Melie was only two.

Wrapping the rhubarb and tying up the parcel with a length of sisal string from the shed, he shouldered his jacket and wandered off to find a likely recipient, reading the old headline on the uppermost paper, *Council Approves Parish Hedgerow Removal.*

'What are they up to now?' Da muttered, annoyed at the

Council's apparent contempt for nature. 'Bet there'll be no hedges left before long. Morning Connell.'

'Morning Da. Is it going to stay like this all summer then? Nice holidays you teachers!' Connell's reply was friendly but somehow he seemed edgier than usual. Connell Brown was anything but usual. He'd spent years working to save the whale on ships patrolling the Southern Ocean. He'd worked the streets of London as a juggling sensation able to balance almost anything he chose on his chin, including a bicycle. He was quite a character with his thin plait, but always suspicious and sometimes mistrustful, cautious perhaps, as if something unsavoury had befallen him in younger days. They did say he'd lost a sister when they were kids of about twelve or thirteen and they'd never found any trace of her, dead or alive.

'What you up to then?' Da asked, parcel in hand and walking backwards down the road in the opposite direction to Connell to keep the conversation going.

'Well, just off to see an old mate,' he replied. 'Something's not feeling right. It wants sorting.' Connell marched on.

'See you then. No passion, no power!' Da called out down the street after the purposeful figure of Connell, who did reply but Da couldn't quite make out what he'd said.

They were true characters: Da, Connell, Captain Geo Schultz with his eye patch, vest, red beret and camouflage trousers, Lizzie Page and Luke's mum Posy. The Captain worked as a very gifted and highly respected chorographer, making historical maps that seemed to combine a scientific rigour and attention to detail with an astonishingly artistic flair. The nickname referred to his six-month tenure of the chess club captaincy back at school and somehow it had stuck with him. He'd made a lot of money in recent years from high profile commissions by the Hoi Polloi, as he called them when holding court in The Half Dead Tree.

'Basically rich grown up boys and girls,' he'd say, when explaining who his customers were. 'Nothing better to spend their inheritances on than pretty maps of places they'll never think of going. That's the Hoi Polloi. I set them up as armchair travellers, although mine are historical maps. That's the fundamental difference between what I do and the cartographers of this world.' It was a mutually beneficial arrangement. The deal done, they could sit and ponder while he could spend his growing fortune on travelling in the real world as opposed to the world of maps. And Captain Geo had certainly travelled, having thoroughly explored and absorbed many interesting places around the globe over the years. He'd met his wife Beezy on a visit to the rainforests of Suriname where they fell in love, Geo entranced by her South American beauty and gentleness. A wonderful mother to their four amazing children, she was much younger than her husband and was currently travelling back to her roots as photographer on a research project into rainforest wildlife.

Melie and the kids would sometimes watch the less extraordinary grown-ups trudging through Mill Square, aiming to be home from work in time for tea at five thirty. The Lost Souls, as these became nicknamed, looked exhausted and flattened, grey skinned, grey haired and dark eyed. The energy had been sucked out of them by the demands of modern living. The kids exchanged pitiful glances as these Lost Souls drifted past and the little gang were adamant that this fate would definitely not be waiting in their own adult lives. Completely different from Da and his friends, The Lost Souls seemed to lack the colour, the zing and the smiles. Yet even The Enlightened Ones, as Melie called Da and company, seemed unsettled. They shared a certain mysterious common ground and their friendship had remained enviably strong since childhood. They appeared at ease with the world and comfortable with themselves. But they were searching for something more, and sometimes it showed.

***

Melie wanted to feel annoyed with Connell for barging in on her conversation with Billy, but something told her he was meant to be there.

'Connell!' cried Melie, 'What are you doing here? You made me jump!' He'd obviously been eavesdropping but how much he'd heard was anybody's guess.

'Melie, I think you should be careful here,' he said. 'He won't have told you everything. What's he said about Malevolents?' They were treating Melie more like a grown up than a ten year old.

'Connell Brown,' growled Billy, 'I have explained to Amelia North all she needs to know for now about the situation. You will not help matters along by talk of such things and I respectfully ask that you leave this place at once.' Billy spoke with a clear, calm authority completely out of character with the way he was seen by everyone around Powder Mill Fields. Almost everyone; Connell Brown seemed to see Billy differently and he clearly knew about Hedge.

'What's a Malevolent?' Melie's question was calm and direct. Connell knew something about what was going on. There was no point dancing around the issue.

'Sit down Melie. Please sit down.' Connell's tone was insistent and she did as he requested. 'Listen, you know me and your Da go back a long way; we were at school together. I like him, I like you and I'd do anything to help you. That's why I'm here. I do know about Hedge and I know what you have to do. I know of Fergus and I know who Billy here really is. I understand it all and I've been there.'

'You've been there?! When have you been there? What's it like?' asked Melie, eager for information and reaching for the Bag of Tryx as if preparing to leave immediately. Before Connell turned up, Melie had wondered whether Billy was making the whole thing up, or at least embellishing the facts. He was definitely capable of that with his eccentric nature.

'Well let's just say it was an astonishing place,' said Connell, 'and it was a long time ago. And Melie, I'm not the only one round here who's been, although the others can't remember anything about it, not really.' Connell paced slowly around to the large bay window and fell silent for a while as he surveyed the overgrown garden beyond. 'I don't fully understand why,' he sighed, 'but somehow all sorts of news and information from the place just seems to pour into my head overnight, as though I'm being kept informed. I can't go back though. It's nearly impossible for Theirworlders to return to Hedge a second time.' He paused and looked at Billy before continuing. 'Well we know of one person who has but it's not for me to tell you about that.'

Melie hung onto every word Connell spoke, transfixed by his revelations, which were intriguing to say the least. It was tantalising to assume that the others who'd been into Hedge like Connell were his friends; Da and company. Melie thrilled at this prospect and wished Da was with her now so he could share in the excitement. She was deeply involved in something extraordinary, which only yesterday she knew nothing about.

'Yes,' said Connell as Billy stared into the grate shaking his head slowly from side to side, 'it's hard to see how you could become so involved in something so big so quickly.' Uncanny, she thought, here's someone else who seems to be able to read my mind. Without speaking, Connell transmitted his own thoughts straight back to her; *'I can.'* Melie stood up, startled and shocked, but was quick to react.

'Can you really?' she thought straight back to him.

'Yes I can Melie. I don't understand how but I have worked out why'. She dropped back into the chair, dumbstruck, as Connell continued, but speaking this time.

'Melie, I can read your thoughts and you can read mine,' confirmed Connell, moving across to lean against Billy's dresser. 'I think that's because with all that's heading your way I've have been given these abilities so I can be some kind of communication link between you and Hedge. You know, in your quest for The Stone. Well that's what I think anyway. Look, I know it's all hard to take in, but just accept it Melie. It seems there's no time.'

'So come on then, what's a Malevolent?' Melie asked for a second time.

'It's not all perfect in Hedge,' whispered Connell. 'Billy would agree wouldn't you Billy?'

'It's true,' he confirmed, nodding wearily as Connell continued.

'Mostly the people are good and true, most of them,' he said. 'Some though, well … let's say they've taken on ways that are more like the bad bits of Theirworld.' Connell resumed his pacing and spoke as if he were a detective piecing together a hypothesis, using his hands to emphasise each point. 'They've been twisted by the contradiction of living in a world like Hedge yet feeling … evil. Yes, let's call it evil. So they drifted out of solid form and became nothing more than mists cast out into Theirworld never to return. Thing is, they know that if they can find The Shining Stone they can use it to reverse the flow between worlds and they'll pour the badness into Hedge.'

'I've seen one,' Melie said abruptly. 'I saw it last night just after Fergus, when he was a firefly if you know what I mean, vanished into thin air. Billy thinks it was an Air of Mystery.'

'She's right Connell. She said it looked very dark and it was right here in Turley Holes last night,' Billy confirmed, nodding.

'An Air of Mystery?' Connell mused, shaking his head. 'They are the worst of the Malevolents, they really are. They'll take all hope and leave you in despair forever if they, what's the word ... if they enshroud you.' He shuddered slightly, as if imagining that unsavoury prospect. 'Stay away from the Malevolents Melie. If you see one just run; there's no other way.' Connell was clearly shaken and concerned for her safety.

'The worst; that means there's more than one sort,' Melie surmised, showing a maturity and insight beyond her ten years. Billy joined in now.

'Yes Amelia, there's a few,' he sighed. 'An Air of Intrigue will lure you inside by preying on your curiosity. An Air of Superiority will have you cowering and humble for the rest of your life. An Air of Excitement will shock you instantly. A bit like a heart attack I suppose you could say.'

'But what about an Air of Mystery, if they are the worst what do they do?' Melie asked, a vague memory stirring somewhere inside about a dark mist during a lightning storm which somehow caused the disappearance of Tiny's dad in Mill Square a few years ago. The mystery disappearance was big news back then, scaremongers having stirred up an alien abduction frenzy in the absence of a more concrete explanation. But then the fuss had died down. The reporters and television cameras had left and Turley Holes returned to normal for everyone except Lizzie Page, a newly installed single parent with a young child to bring up on her own. Billy looked at Connell, who in turn looked at Melie with his piercing blue eyes.

'Well,' he said gravely, 'it's like I was just saying, an Air of Mystery will consume you slowly and you'll vanish without trace to who knows where. You can bet it won't be anywhere pleasant.'

Melie shuddered at this thought. She stood and walked over to the window, still carrying the Bag of Tryx and gazed at the peaceful morning outside the Eighth Wonder of the World. She inhaled deeply and blew slowly out through pursed lips, feeling the weight of the world on her shoulders. Why did all this have to happen? Stones, vanishing without trace, talking fireflies, it was just too much. She wanted to be out there as normal exploring with the kids in the sunshine. That instant she was startled to see Luke, Tiny Page and the Schultz kids creeping about amongst the bushes below the window ready for adventure as always. Had they heard anything through the dusty glass of Billy's front window? With a sharp presence of mind, Melie managed to think of anything but what she had seen as she knew Connell could tune in to her thoughts. And then on impulse she spun round clutching her bag in the bay window at thirty-nine, Forty Steps.

'I'll do it,' she said, 'but I'm taking my gang with me.'

Chapter Seven

Sanguinella Couch

Next morning the house was quiet when Melie woke up in her untidy bedroom. Through the ever-open window, she listened for a while to the sound of summer birdsong, testing her identification skills. She heard blackbirds, starlings, chaffinches and a magpie. Not her favourite robin though, for at this time of year they'd all be sulking somewhere about their moult. She yawned and sat up in bed, stretching and enjoying the moment, before wakefulness reminded her of the amazing couple of days she'd had. At the start, she'd been just an adventurous ten-year-old girl, a tomboy some would say and leader of one of the three gangs of kids round and about Powder Mill Fields. Her striking, ginger hair hung in six plaits down to her shoulders. She favoured oddly assorted, rather bohemian clothes. Her nature was impulsive yet at the same time composed and she was mature for her age, extraordinarily so. The natural world was her first love and her expertise in country lore was legendary. That she was perhaps a little disconnected from the rhythm of the modern world did not worry Melie in the slightest. But now she stood on the verge of great adventure, apparently carrying the fate of two worlds on her shoulders, charged as she was with the overwhelming task of returning The Stone. There were puzzling questions to be answered; not least, why she was the one Fergus had chosen.

After a quick visit to the bathroom, she dressed while she mulled a few things over. She was supposedly the child of Maeva. Well who exactly was that? Whatever was a curiosity circlet? How was she supposed to recognise this lost Stone if she ever saw it? But above all, how could they expect a ten year old to succeed? Couldn't they have picked a grown up instead? She wouldn't do it alone, she was taking the gang. And what would she tell Da?

Sitting down on the bed to tie her rainbow laces, she noticed the Bag of Tryx lying on the bedroom floor instead of hanging on the shed wall as usual. She picked up the pale brown leather shoulder bag and twiddled her fingers through the hippy beads hanging from it. The lovely fat turquoise and the long, thin, creamy ones were her favourites, reminding her of Indians in America, or Native First Nation or whatever they called them in Geography. They were just people as far as Melie was concerned. Tipping out the treasured contents, she inspected her favourites one by one, serious and purposeful as though preparing for a great battle to come. She picked out her folding pruning knife with its curved blade in Sheffield steel and a rosewood handle. She opened the knife and carefully ran her thumb along the edge, testing the sharpness of the steel. Not the useless safety knife as Luke often joked at Teasing Time, this was the tool of the true explorer and she imagined its usefulness in the days ahead. Next Melie picked up a treasured family heirloom; the brass compass which once belonged to Da's grandfather. He'd travelled amongst the Navajo in north-western New Mexico, who presented him with a beaded turquoise pouch in which to store his compass. Melie watched, entranced as the ornate needle swung around to North. Yes, this would be coming along for sure. Her precious tourmaline crystal which

Lizzie Page had given her, saying it would help Melie think outside the box, gleamed slender and black in her hand. She took solace in the familiar feel of these few items, handling them with respect and expertise, yet still the thought of the road ahead made tears well in her eyes. Tears of trepidation, tears of excitement and tears for a sense of great loss from her younger days that rarely surfaced in Melie. Replacing every item into the Bag of Tryx and finishing the lace tying she dragged a sleeve across her face and then went off downstairs to meet the day, leaving the bed unmade as always.

In the front kitchen Da was fiddling with the rusted clasps on an old brown leather suitcase on the table, where she noticed Geo Schultz's beret still sitting there from a couple of nights ago. Unfinished beans on toast, probably Da's tea from the previous night, slowly congealed and crusted in the warmth from the window. Several stalks of freshly cut rhubarb still bore their leaves, which hung over the edge of Da's usual chair waiting for bundling and handing over to some neighbour. As he probed at the clasps, Da hummed along to an obscure tune on his tape player by a favoured band of Da's from long ago. Orange Juice or something like that, Melie recalled.

'Rip it up and start again ... rip it up and ... start again...' mumbled the focused Da. 'Oh Connell, it won't budge, I'll get to it later on.' Melie hadn't noticed Connell Brown leaning on the battered pine dresser against the back wall.

'Morning, Melie.' Connell's first communication was spoken, but then, *Don't tell him, he just won't get it and won't let you go. And Melie, we need to get moving. Powder Mill eleven thirty.'* She'd almost forgotten the telepathic relationship she evidently shared with Da's mate but she stayed cool and transmitted her thought straight back to him.

'We'll be there.'

'Meaning what exactly?' was Connell's reply. *'You can't bring those other kids. For a start, James Schultz is only seven. They haven't been invited either.'*

'His name is Jam Sandwich Schultz actually,' replied Melie, *'sometimes known as Shultz Number Four and sometimes known as The Observant Jam Sandwich. He's coming, along with the other kids if you expect me to go at all, so you can take it or leave it.'* Melie felt in control of the situation and furthermore was pleased that the telepathic conversations were quick or else Da might have begun to wonder about the long silences. 'What's in the case Da?' she asked, reaching for a spoonful of the dying baked beans and chewing them back to life.

'It was in the loft,' he replied. 'Been there a while and I can't remember what we put in it. Your mum used to stash things away in there and I'm hoping she stashed a few bundles of pretty green inside. Pretty green; cool, crisp cash. Have you seen the state of our gas bill?' Da was clearly trying to maintain something of a brave face as he handled his lovely May's old suitcase but the grief still broke through from time to time. 'I'll have another go at it in a while. What are you up to today Melie N?'

'Actually Da, I'll have to be off, things to do, people to see', said Connell Brown, slipping quickly off the dresser and heading for the door before stopping. In a way that seemed unusually profound in Da's eyes, he squeezed Da's shoulder and whispered, 'No passion, no power.' Da's strained response startled Melie.

'I think punk's dead Connell,' he sighed. They parted, Da back to his chair where he scooped up the rhubarb and held it against his chest like a baby and Connell down the road to the Powder Mill. Melie sat down across the table from her Da, feeling awkward in the tense atmosphere. She put it down partly to Da and his longing for May and partly to Da knowing what was going on. Did he know? How could he know? Had Connell told him? What should she say? She fingered the tourmaline crystal inside the Bag of Tryx, leaned towards him.

'Tell me what you're thinking Da,' she said, 'because I can't read your mind.'

'Melie, something's bothering me,' whispered Da. He placed the stalks on the table between them and began to slice off the leaves using a knife just like his daughter's. The leaves dropped to the floor in a pile, and as he spoke he punctuated the air with his knife as if conducting an orchestra. 'I've had these dreams. Loads of dreams where there's a young girl calling out a name as if she's searching for someone she's lost. I never get to see her face and she's upset. Now I'm upset because ...' and he reached across the table to take her hands in his, '... I think it's you looking for your mum.' There was a silence and unspoken feelings wove a closer bond between the two of them. 'Another thing,' Da said, after a time, 'whenever I see Connell or The Captain or Lizzie, Posy Schofield too, Luke's mum, I feel there's something we all shared when we were young, something big you know, but I can't remember what it is. I just can't remember.' He folded the knife and tossed it onto the table where it clattered to a standstill. 'And there's this big desire to go back somewhere. Who knows where? I don't. I can't explain it really. I sometimes think I see it in The Captain's eyes too. It's as though there's another place waiting for us.' Melie stood and walked around the table, coming up behind him, lovingly wrapping her arms round his shoulders and pressing her cheek against his greying hair.

'You know what Da?' she said, in tune with his feelings, 'about the sharing thing. I felt something just like that a couple of days ago too. We were playing hide and seek over near the Nidd, by this hedge ...' She stopped short, mindful that she might be about to give the game away, then continued. 'Well after a bit, we all felt like we'd been there before or something. It just felt weird, like, none of us could quite understand what it was about, a bit like something travelling between us all, kind of inside.' Melie remembered the puzzled looks that had flitted across the faces of her friends that time. There was so much that Melie wanted to tell her Da, but would he stop the job before it had really started? He just wouldn't let her go through with it at ten years old. The child in her wanted her Da to sweep her into his arms, tell her it was all ok and take the burden instead of her as dads do. But as well as all that, this rather unusually mature ten year old understood the magnitude of the task and if she was taking it on then nothing at all would be allowed to stand in her way. There were so many questions! Where would Da think his daughter was for the next few days or weeks or even longer? How could she put him through the worry? Would he understand or ever forgive her for the hurt? Although with the way he was talking, she did begin to wonder if he knew something. And apart from all that, who would look after Nettle if Billy came along?

***

Luke pressed the rusted doorknocker flat, trapping his note against the peeling paint of the Powder Mill's huge wooden door. The lion's features, cast in iron years ago were blurring into one with weathering and old age, but it still held the heavy ring of the rapper between its jaws with an unyielding ferocity.

'That'll keep the folks guessing gang,' he said as he turned to face the assembled explorers in the overgrown courtyard. 'So, you all remember the plan?' And then he stopped short and by the look on his face, the kids reckoned he was trying the old trick of getting them to look behind themselves.

'Oh come on Luke, you don't expect us to fall for that one,' said Molly with mock sarcasm and arms splayed out, 'I mean I know it's only half past eight, but ...' She tailed off as Luke shook his head slowly. As one, the Schultz kids and Tiny Page turned around and what they saw brought gasps of astonishment. Standing before them with a beautiful grey cat in her arms was Sanguinella Couch.

'Children,' said the woman in a refined tone. She paused. 'Hello! Look, I am sorry to startle you, but I do seem to have that effect whenever I drop into your world, which is, of course, Theirworld.' A short awkward silence followed and then she continued. 'I'm Sanguinella, Sanguinella Couch from Gush, in Hedge. I am delighted to meet you all.' She took a pace towards them and stretched out one hand in greeting whilst scooping the cat onto her shoulder with the other. She paused once again. 'You don't really know what I'm talking about, do you?'

All six children stared at Sanguinella, marvelling at her glorious outfit in various shades of green, grey and lilac that reminded them of old Robin Hood films. She wore a length of grey cloth with silver stars wrapped around her head as a kind of cross between a bandana and a scarf. And then as if suddenly remembering numerous parental warnings about talking to strangers, they stepped back as one, for Sanguinella was strange indeed.

'No, no, children!' said the stranger, 'there is nothing to worry about, nothing at all. I'm from Hedge, Gush as a matter of fact, and I have been called in by Fergus ... you do know Fergus I presume ...' They nodded dumbly in response, although Jam, the youngest, shook his head at first until he remembered the extraordinary things he'd heard through Welly's window the previous morning and then he too nodded. 'Good, good!' she exclaimed. 'That is good.' Another pause, then she held out the cat towards them. 'Look, Fergus wanted to be sure we'd be safe on our search so he wanted me to come along with Lavender.'

'No offence, but it's just a cat', said Luke.

'No, no, it's not a cat. It's a healing cat; Lavender the healing cat. She will look after us when times get a little hard to bear on the journey ahead,' Sanguinella seemed to purr in a profound and cat-like sort of way as she stroked Lavender. Events were become quite extraordinary and as Luke looked around at the others, he could see they were just as puzzled as he was. Turning and regrouping a few paces back towards the door, the six kids huddled together to discuss the situation, like American footballers discussing tactics.

'Right,' said Sammy. 'You could say this is not a typical morning. Not particularly run of the mill. Unusual, in fact. Extraordinarily so.'

'Too right', joined in Molly, her identical twin. 'The woman's a weirdo. And do any of you really know who Fergus is?' Weirdo was turning out to be a very timely replacement of fundamental as Molly's favourite word. While Sanguinella fussed over Lavender and strolled around in the little lane leading up to the Powder Mill, the six kids in Melie's gang speculated with mounting excitement. Luke took a long drink from his water bottle and replaced the stopper with a slap.

'Look,' he said, 'I caught a bit of what they were saying in Billy's house but I couldn't make out much. It seems like Melie is going back to the hedge and she wants us with her. The rest was just beyond me.' He turned to sneak a glance at Sanguinella, before taking up his bottle and draining it. They broke off a little to look across at the woman. Tiny Page pushed up his glasses and calmly stated the obvious.

'Okay, we're all going searching for something with Catwoman,' he whispered. 'There might be trouble ahead, but luckily, Fergus the mystery man has sent a cat to look after us. We're off back to a magical hedge and the great adventure begins. Pardon me but should I expect to see a yellow brick road under my feet?' This brought a giggle from a couple of the kids, especially from Sammy Schultz, Tiny was pleased to notice.

Then Alexander piped up, expressing everyone's subconscious question in the process.

'But how long are we going for,' he said, 'and come to think of it, where will our parents think we are?' At this, the group walked into the sunshine towards Sanguinella the catwoman.

'Let's just say they know already ... in a manner of speaking ... although they don't realise it,' she purred in a reassuring tone. 'They won't be worried, trust me. I think they have somehow been expecting something like this to happen. When you're gone one of them will understand and he will ... sort it out with the others.'

'So they won't be needing this then.' The kids and the catwoman spun round on hearing Melie's voice, just in time to see her extracting Luke's note from the iron grip of the lion's jaws. She unfolded the paper and quickly read its contents before stuffing it into her Bag of Tryx with her other bits and pieces. She then continued, addressing Sanguinella, 'I'm Melie North by the way, Amelia North. Have we met? No, I think I'd remember. And don't tell me, I'll bet that cat is going to start talking in a minute.'

'Melie, look, we're all here and ready to go. Thanks for telling Mr Brown you're taking us with you. Shall we go then? Oh, this is Sanguinella Couch and that's her cat, Lavender. We're ok; it's going to keep us safe!' With this Luke lightened the proceedings somewhat and all seven kids grouped up again and excited chatter began, Melie filling them in about the amazing events that were unfolding right there in Turley Holes, the smallest of the three villages. Sanguinella and Lavender the healing cat basked in the sunshine and held a whispered conversation as if such things were commonplace in Yorkshire between an oddly dressed woman and a cat. Right there at the heavy wooden door of the Powder Mill, six excited explorers were being primed by their leader for the adventure of a lifetime. Then together with their strange guests, they made their way to the hedge to meet up, as arranged, with Connell Brown and Billy, who had arranged that Nettle would be lodging at number thirty-seven until such a time as the adventurers returned to Turley Holes.

Chapter Eight

Pearls of Bog Rosemary

It was getting towards the middle of the afternoon when the explorers gathered below the mysterious hole, an entry point into the world of Hedge as Melie now knew. The sun was still hot, the air quiet and calm and Luke was regretting having drained his water bottle back at the mill. At the foot of the grass bank, the River Nidd worked its course Eastwards to its ultimate destination in the Humber estuary and a cloud of butterflies flitted along the greenery round and about the hedgerow.

'So,' said Billy, 'this is it then, we're going in. I expect Melie has told you kids everything she knows about Hedge which is my world and your world which is …' Melie cut in, interrupting Billy's flow.

'Billy,' she said, 'I've told them all about the two worlds and all about what needs to be done. I've even told them time is short, like Fergus was so keen to point out, so let's get on with it. We just want to get in there.'

'Well there's a slight problem really,' said Connell.

'What's that Mr Brown?' asked Alexander.

'Well,' Connell replied, 'it's going to be easy for Melie to get in and for… actually while we're at it, can we drop the Mr Brown? Please, it's Connell. Like I was saying, it's easy for Melie, she's invited. As for Billy, Sanguinella and Lavender, well Hedge is their home so they'll get straight in. It's a bit more difficult for me. I just assume it'll be ok. They wouldn't have been sending me messages for years if I wasn't welcome. It's just the rest of you, that's the problem.' Collective dismay settled amongst the kids; the possibility of not getting into Hedge was unthinkable. The Observant Jam Sandwich was about to suggest that thwarted was the word until he thought it might just add to the disappointment and annoy people. There was a time and a place for being clever with words and this was certainly not it.

'What about the pearls?' suggested Sanguinella, who'd been silent ever since they left the Powder Mill. 'We could tell them The Secret. After all, it's relevant to the whole thing isn't it? I mean, if there are more of them in the quest then there is a greater chance of finding it isn't there?' She directed this last question at Billy who seemed to be pondering the sense in sharing this Secret. Sanguinella seemed anxious that the gang should not miss the adventure.

'What pearls?' Melie asked. 'What's secret about pearls?' She was wondering why Sanguinella seemed to think that more kids meant more chances of finding The Shining Stone. Fergus had said that she and she alone could find and return it to Hedge.

'Okay, I think it's okay to tell them,' ventured Connell, who had been staring ahead as if listening to a voice from afar. 'Yes, it's okay; I'm getting that message from Hedge. You can tell them about the pearls.' Connell's direct telepathic link with his mysterious contact in Hedge was working in the gang's favour. He had no idea who was sending these messages and keeping the channel of communication open, but it always seemed to be a woman's voice in his head.

'It's those orange berries on that pyracantha isn't it?' Luke speculated on seeing the mass of fruits on the hedge.

'Well if by pyracantha you mean firethorn, you are almost

right,' said Sanguinella. 'The orange berries, as you call them, of firethorn mixed with box at entry points between the two worlds are the key to getting through the holes.'

'*Strange for a box hedge to be so high,*' Melie mused as she looked up to the hole, twenty feet above.

'*Yes it is, isn't it?*' came Connell's telepathic response, reading Melie's mind as before. '*The voice tells me that where high grown box and firethorn meet and orange berries thrive, that is where entry portals survive.*'

'*Thanks, Connell, I'll remember that,*' Melie replied by airing her own thoughts. Even though Billy and Sanguinella should have intercepted the messages, it seemed that the exchanges were so swift that they passed undetected by others.

'So,' said Sanguinella. She placed Lavender on the grass, at which the cat strolled up to the nearest leg, Molly's, and rubbed herself against it as all cats, even talking cats, do. Molly couldn't resist directing a whispered, 'hello … weirdo,' at the cat.

'Children,' continued Sanguinella, 'look at these berries just here,' and she gestured grandly towards the bright fruits of the hedge as if addressing a much larger audience. 'You will see they are orange, but if you look closely can you notice anything about the berries chosen by the butterflies which manage to enter the hole?' True enough, Melie noticed that as before, only the bright blue butterflies were entering and leaving the hole. It was just possible to make out a subtle variation in the appearance of the berries they landed on before going in, and those the unsuccessful butterflies selected.

'Is it the sparkles?' asked The Observant Jam Sandwich. 'I mean, some have a kind of sparkle to them if you look closely, and those are the ones the butterflies land on.'

'Yeah, that's right,' joined in Tiny and Sammy at the same time, 'Jam's right, there are some sparkly ones!' Sanguinella continued with her lecture.

'Excellent observations! Excellent! Some of these...' and again, she swept her hand flamboyantly towards the hedge, '... are not just firethorn berries, they are pearls of bog rosemary. Eat a fresh pearl and you will get through the holes into the world that waits beyond.'

'Brilliant, that's brilliant! Come on, what are we waiting for? Let's go!' Most of the children piped up at once, eager to get the adventure underway, all except Melie and Luke.

'Wait,' Melie ordered quietly.

'What you thinking Melie?' asked Luke. 'Same as me?'

'Same as you.' Connell echoed Luke's question by way of a reply, but telepathically. Luke looked at Connell.

'How did you know what we were thinking?' gasped Luke. 'Melie, he knew what we were thinking!' Proceedings had just taken another unexpected turn and Luke wanted to pinch himself just to be sure he wasn't dreaming.

'Yes Luke,' said Melie, 'Mr Brown, Connell I mean, can read thoughts, but I thought it was just me and him and other Hedge people.'

'It's ok Luke', Connell messaged the boy. *'Don't ask me why it happens but it just does. Not sure why I can suddenly link with you though, it was just Melie before.'*

'Fine, that's just fine, he can read my mind! It's all getting a bit serious now isn't it? I mean what if I'm thinking something I don't want anyone to know?' Luke asked the group indignantly.

'Something about me maybe?' asked Sammy hopefully.

'Oh come on Samphire!' sighed Melie. 'Get real! Look, let's get this sorted out. It just can't be that simple. There's no way you'd get in just by eating a berry. Not even a pearl of bog rosemary or whatever they're called.' Melie paused, lingering on the curious notion of a marsh plant growing on a hedge. 'Sanguinella,' she said, 'I don't quite get how a bog rosemary can possibly have pearls. I really don't. And I'm pretty sure it's poisonous. Should we really be eating these things? Where's the catch?'

'Pearls of bog rosemary,' replied Couch, 'are peculiar to Hedge; in your world they are found nowhere other than around and about the connecting holes. Not the plant itself though, only the pearls, that's the curious thing. And you've got to eat them when they're freshly picked. Try them as a ... what is it you call it out here ... a takeaway and you'll get more than you bargained for. Eat pearls when they are fresh and you can enter my world. Eat them just moments after they've been picked and there's no saying what your destination will be. It's a way of preventing just anyone from getting in. You could end up anywhere ... and I mean anywhere.' She reached out, picked a magical pearl with a delicately precise twist of her fingers and held it up for a moment to glisten in the late afternoon sunlight. 'Just one more thing,' she added, 'it has to be picked and fed to you by someone from the world of Hedge.' At that, Sanguinella Couch deftly placed the pearl into Molly's nearby mouth, which had been conveniently gaping open in wonder at the magic and mystery of the bog rosemary story. Before any of the kids could take in what was happening, in the blink of an eye really, the catwoman slapped Molly heartily on the back causing her to swallow the pearl and she vanished with a whoosh straight through the hole in the hedge twenty feet above their heads.

'Molly!' shouted her twin. 'Okay, so where's she gone Sanguinella or whatever you're called. Bring her back, now!'

'Yes, come on,' said Jam as he grabbed the woman's arm, 'She's my big sister!' Connell Brown stepped in now, placing his hand on Jam's shoulder.

'James, it's alright, she's just gone into Hedge,' he said. 'We're all going in there, right now. You'll see her in a moment.' Melie took control of the situation.

'Right,' she said, 'come on then, who's first? Sanguinella, another please.'

Sanguinella studied the hedge carefully, selected a second pearl and prepared to feed it to Luke. He hesitated just for a moment remembering all the advice about not eating berries unless you were sure what they were.

'Ok then,' he said, 'I'll eat anything as long as it's not tripe or porridge!'

***

Molly Schultz had landed with a bump at the bottom of the other side of the hedge and had rolled to rest on the softest, greenest grass she had ever seen. She was sitting only a few feet away from where the rest of the explorers were standing and preparing to eat their pearls of bog rosemary, just through the hedge. But Molly was in a completely separate world from where she'd spent the first ten years of her life. She could hear nothing of the commotion she had just left when Sanguinella popped the bog rosemary into her mouth. All she could hear was the buzz of a few insects in the late afternoon sunshine and birds chattering up on the hedge, which strangely seemed to tower a good deal higher here on this side. At least fifty or sixty feet she reckoned. It was decidedly weird and she wished the rest of the gang would hurry up and arrive, although, she supposed, there was no hurry really. She felt calm, she felt safe and felt really quite happy. Maybe there was time to explore, or why not catch that bright blue butterfly which was coming through the hole right now? But Molly could only watch, transfixed, as the butterfly in question fluttered down and then swooped with fine control. It glided to a controlled landing on the grass beside her and then walked off, having transformed in the process into a tall man in bright blue clothes!

'Good evening, I am glad to see you. You are very welcome. The others are on their way just now,' said the man in a gently reassuring voice. 'Oh, I'm Davis by the way, Davis Hedgeranger and might I just say how delighted I am to meet you Molybdenum Schultz. I'm just waiting for my sister then we'll be off.' He chuckled to himself as he folded his arms and looked upwards, drawing Molly's attention to the hole with a nod of his head.

'Hang on,' said a dumbfounded Molly, 'hang on. I mean, what happened to the butterfly? First, there's a butterfly, now there's a man. Davis. It's all very weird.' She looked up at the hole, then back at Davis who beamed excitedly. 'Don't tell me, Davis, your sister wouldn't just happen to be called Mavis by any chance would she?'

'Well as a matter of fact she is. Do you know her?' he replied inquisitively in a voice that Molly thought of as the most gentlemanly and polite she had ever heard in her life. A bit, she thought, like chocolate soufflé would sound if it could speak. It briefly crossed her mind that in Hedge chocolate soufflé probably could speak.

'Actually no, no I don't know your sister,' said Molly, by now beginning to feel a little uncomfortable being here in another world talking to a strange man. Still, just a few minutes ago, she'd been in her own world conversing with a cat.

Davis began tapping the fingers of his right hand on the upturned palm of his left very quickly as though using an invisible calculator. It looked haphazard but Molly felt there must be a purpose and order to his actions. Just a moment later a second butterfly fluttered and then swooped down to land on the grass next to Davis as a beautiful woman dressed in the same bright blue as her brother. She dusted herself down and adjusted her outfit a little before reaching out and taking Molly's hand for a firm and enthusiastic handshake.

'Hello there, pleased to meet you,' she said. 'I'm Mavis.'

'I know,' Molly replied meekly, overwhelmed by the way her day was turning out. She watched the Hedgerangers walking off hand in hand down the grassy hill towards what looked like a distant village with a wonky church spire. 'Weird,' she whispered.

'Who are those two?!' Luke's voice startled her back to reality and as she turned, she saw the whole group dusting themselves down and watching the Hedgerangers walking down the hill. Melie, Luke, Tiny Page, Schultz two, three and four (Molybdenum, Schultz one, had been born a good two minutes before Samphire and so claimed age superiority), Billy, Connell Brown and Sanguinella with her cat. Melie stepped to the front of the group and eased the Bag of Tryx over her head from one shoulder to the other.

'Well, we're here,' she whispered. A little way off, an important looking man seemed to appear from out of nowhere. He shook hands enthusiastically with the Hedgerangers and made his way towards the adventurers, who became lost in their own thoughts for a while as they took in the scene before them. Seated on the grass, Lavender and Sanguinella conversed quietly in a mixture of purrs and spoken word. Billy hopped around excitedly from one welly to the other, all handclaps and exclamations of delight that he was back in his own world after what must have been the longest time. Connell Brown stared around, one moment open mouthed and incredulous, the next alert and watchful as though trying to tune in to some important telepathic frequency. There was something fretful and unsettled about Connell now that he was in Hedge. Sitting on the grass, Tiny readjusted his glasses and strained to see the detail of the distant village, hands shielding his eyes from the late afternoon sun. From time to time, he took off his glasses and then replaced them as if he couldn't decide whether he really needed them to be able to see that far. Luke possibly didn't realise that he was holding hands with Sammy Schultz as he too gazed towards the jumble of buildings, which, he figured, lay about half an hour away in walking time. Sammy just stood gazing at Luke. Molly and Melie sat beside each other and surveyed the countryside before them, a patchwork of farm fields in varying shades of russet and green across which low walls of golden flint had been scrawled haphazardly as boundaries between plots. Here and there were clumps of trees, which Melie recognised as the same, familiar varieties from around Powder Mill Fields back through the hedge. Just along there towards the village were woods of Silver Birch swaying in the breeze. Over by that bridge was a stand of Weeping Willow, presumably marking the line of a small waterway flowing through the fields. Alexander the Crate and his younger brother Jam Sandwich Schultz seemed uneasy, gazing ahead to the new world before them yet next moment turning back to look up to the hole in the hedge through which they'd arrived as if by magic only a minute or two ago.

In Melie's opinion the whole place didn't look much different to the place they'd just come from. It just felt somehow calmer and much quieter. What she did notice as she looked around at her gang was that some of them seemed to have changed a little in the space of five minutes since coming into Hedge. Tiny's glasses were not now sitting on the end of his nose; they were in the breast pocket of his shirt. Luke's hand was not intertwined with Sammy's; his arm was around her shoulder. Molly didn't seem to be viewing Sanguinella as a weirdo now that they were in Hedge; instead, she was enjoying a pleasant conversation with the woman and her cat. In perfect English, Lavender was assuring Schultz number one that she should disregard misconceptions about humans owning cats. As far as Lavender was concerned, it was quite the opposite.

A familiar voice broke the silence, as the man who'd shaken hands with the Hedgerangers spoke up as he approached the companions.

'Amelia North, child of Maeva, you are welcome, you are needed,' chirped the man. 'I am chosen to guide you to your destiny. You may recall our conversation in Theirworld earlier today. A firefly is my small and very convenient persona when in Theirworld, which is your world. Whilst in my world, which is Hedge, I am the persona Fergus Wiseman, which I now reveal to you because you need to know of this. Amelia, time is short, time is nearly gone. You are come into Hedge where you are welcome, where you are needed. You must fulfil your destiny in your eleventh year.'

'I'm sure it wasn't earlier today, I'm sure it was the day before yesterday,' Melie quickly calculated as she thought of how to reply. It was plain to see that he held a position of some importance in Hedge. 'Fergus, erm … hello,' came Melie's uncharacteristically flustered response, accompanied by a poorly executed attempt at a curtsey.

The youngest Schultz kids couldn't resist a few sniggers at Melie's expense; she was hardly ever lost for words, whatever the company. Melie composed herself and was about to introduce Fergus to her gang, but she stopped short and wondered aloud, 'Where's Connell going? And Fergus, how come there's a weasel in your pocket writing with a quill?' All eyes followed Connell Brown as he marched off down the lane towards the village. In no time at all he was at the little bridge near the willows where he flumped down to sit on the wall, legs dangling over the water below.

'Connell!' called out Billy, 'Connell!' The kids looked at each other and then set off running towards their companion, leaving Fergus a little exasperated at the swiftness of their departure. Sanguinella appeared rather indignant that they'd just upped and left in the middle of what she took to be an important meeting. Lavender just gazed and purred as Billy, hands in pockets, sighed and scuffed the turf with his green welly.

'It's not a weasel, it's a meerkat! A meerkat, Amelia!' Fergus called after the companions as he and the other grown-ups gave chase.

Chapter Nine

Towards Futhark

Back in the kitchen in Turley Holes Da leaned back on his chair, staring at the suitcase whilst absentmindedly spinning his pruning knife round and round on the old pine table. In the otherwise unlit room the dwindling fire grizzled away in the hearth, bathing the walls with an eerie orange glow and casting shadows which danced around in time with the flicker of the flames. The clatter of the spinning knife and the ticking of the clock on the wall marked the rhythm of the room, with just the odd crackle from the fire and an occasional creak from the chair. Da stayed completely silent, considering the rusty clasps of May's old case with great intent as if trying to break the code of an ancient puzzle, and then he reached for one of his few concessions to the modern age; his mobile. Pausing for the briefest moment and then sliding it open, he keyed in the number of his best friend The Captain, thinking it strange, unfortunate perhaps, that he could easily recall the eleven digit mobile numbers of all his friends, yet couldn't remember the contents or significance of the suitcase. The phone rang a few times but then clicked over to the answering service, where the rather posh sounding recording of a woman announced that the dialled number was currently unavailable and suggested that Da leave a message after the tone.

'Oh Georgie boy, where are you?' muttered Da, exasperated at his friend's laziness in his moment of need.

Then the message tone. 'Captain, Where are you? Come on, answer your phone I know you're there, it's Da.' A pause followed. 'Okay, ring me later when you can drag yourself away from that map. Please, it's important! See you.'

Da knew that unless the Captain was out mapping, or entertaining clients in The Half Dead Tree, he'd be up in his study, the spare bedroom of his house, which just happened to be conveniently situated right next door to his treasured pub. As if his lucrative and plentiful commissions weren't enough to occupy his time and amazing mind, Geo Schultz had been working for the past ten years or so on a rather special project of his own. He'd been experiencing clear visions, almost real enough to touch, of seemingly random places at various times over the years. He'd been mapping these in painstaking detail ever since. Exactly how they were relevant and how they were related remained as unclear today as when the first vision came along back in the late nineteen-eighties. But he'd always felt able to share his obsession with Da and company, Melie's so-called Enlightened Ones, because he knew they'd take him seriously.

'Okay, Connell next then,' said Da, punching in the number with some urgency in his touch. Again, there was no reply, not even from the posh sounding woman. 'Oh come on, where are you all?' Da was beginning to feel a little frustrated. Just now when he could feel something important brewing, something that had needed talking about for years, they weren't there to talk! Standing up and moving over towards the doorway, he flicked on the light, flooding the room with a more business-like tone. While he dialled a third time he shoved a digestive biscuit into his mouth, barely noticing it had gone soft sitting on the plate out of its wrapper for the past day or so. He was hoping

Luke's mum, Posy, would be able to answer as he was sure something big was unfolding here. 'Come on Posy, come on … Posy! Hello duck, it's Da.' His words were spluttered rather than spoken, due to the biscuit.

'Da!' she said. 'You sound happy, what's to do? Desperate for someone to talk to and you finally found me. You eating your tea or something?' Posy was actually pleased to hear from her old friend.

'No, no it's just a biscuit; it's just… oh never mind, hang on a minute.' Da quickly finished and swallowed the last piece of digestive, wiped his mouth on his sleeve and continued. 'Sorry, just finished. Yeah, late lunch. Posy, can you come round to mine? I'm trying to get everyone together but The Captain and Connell are out. I'm trying Lizzie Page next. I want to talk to everyone about something really quite important.' A long pause followed. 'You still there?'

'I'm still here,' she said. 'I was just thinking about what you said. It's funny, but it's as if I've been expecting you to call. There's been all sorts of things going on in my head this last couple of days and by the way, is Luke round at your place? I haven't seen him since he went out this morning and it's getting on a bit now,' said Posy, sounding more anxious than usual at Luke being out so late.

'Luke?' said Da. 'No, not seen him. Come to think of it Melie's not back yet either.' Da's earlier conversation with his daughter came swiftly to mind now that he'd noticed she was still out quite late at night. 'They'll be alright. Out changing the world, I'll bet. I always said it'd happen sooner or later …' His voice trailed off, for as soon as he'd spoken Da North knew in an instant that was exactly what they were doing right now, along with Tiny Page and the Schultz kids. 'Posy, I know it's late but you need to get round here as soon as. Something's happening, something big, I just know it. Bring Lizzie and I'll walk round to Geo's place to fetch him. I'll find Connell too.' It was clear from the tone of his voice that Da was being serious, yet something left Posy feeling calm and reassured.

'Okay, see you in a bit, I'll drive down,' said Posy. 'I'll just put the cats out, bye for now.'

Da slid the phone closed and was about to pocket it when a couple of beeps showed a text coming through from Geo Schultz. Sliding the phone back open, Da read the message aloud. *'Da, need to see you straight away. Coming round. Many uncertainties. C.'* Da closed the phone.

'C for Captain! You and me, mate, are on the same wavelength!' he chirped.

Geo Schultz, The Captain, chorographer to the stars, was right; there were many uncertainties. But one thing was sure; Da North was gathering the troops. The mystery of their close and complex bond was about to be unravelled.

***

The kids finally caught up with Connell Brown, sitting on the wall of the little bridge near the willows in Hedge. He sounded upset for as they approached the kids heard the sound of gentle sobbing and were embarrassed. Turley Holes youngsters did not often hear a grown up crying. They held off for a few moments allowing the rest of the travellers and their host to catch up with them while they stood around awkwardly, looking at anything except Connell. The sight of Fergus, his oversized purple long coat flapping behind him as he ran and the meerkat gripping tightly at the hem of his pocket was amusing if not somewhat bizarre and it served to lighten the mood.

'Sorry we ran off,' said Melie to the gasping Fergus. He was clearly out of practice where running was concerned. 'We were worried about Connell. Oh it would start raining!' Sure enough, what seemed to be a light shower had begun to fall, but as Melie and the kids looked upwards, they saw that the rain wasn't coming from the sky; it was coming from the trees.

'Ah yes, these are weeping willows,' Fergus panted as he stood upright and checked the meerkat had survived all the excitement. He took out a large crimson handkerchief with which he dabbed his bald head before replacing it in a coat pocket. 'Weeping willows. This, you see, is the literal zone, this area between the stream and Futhark. That is Futhark over there just beyond the wood of birch. It is in Futhark that you, Amelia, were to find me when you arrived in Hedge as you will no doubt remember. I must say I was expecting you and you alone. But here you are and you have found me already I am delighted to say. Time is short, time is nearly...'

'Gone, I know,' Melie cut in. 'Look Fergus, there's loads I need to ask you about. I just think I'm in a bit of a state of shock, you know, coming into Hedge. I think we all are,' she said, looking around at the weary faces of her gang. 'A bit tired too. And there's that weasel ... meerkat I mean, sorry ... in your coat pocket. Now we've got willows that are really weeping. I'm sorry to sound rude Fergus, but I think we're all hungry too.' Melie paused. 'I thought the littoral zone was along the coast anyway, not in the middle of farmland.'

'Amelia, my child, the zone you speak of is indeed a coastal zone; you have listened well in your geography at school,' Fergus confirmed. The littoral zone is sometimes submerged, sometimes exposed, according to the tide,' he added as the meerkat scribbled away furiously in a little notebook with the quill. Naturally the creature, described by Sanguinella as a meerkat scribe and one of only four in existence in Hedge, held the kids transfixed while it beavered away, apparently writing down every word of every conversation involving Fergus Wiseman.

'Okay, we know that, so how can this be a littoral zone?' chipped in Luke, who then remembered it would have been courteous to introduce himself. 'My name is Luke by the way,' he announced. 'Luke Schofield, sorry, I'm just hungry.'

'Schofield. Schofield …' Fergus muttered to himself. 'Luke, child of Posy, I am correct am I not?'

'There's something not right here,' Luke groaned. He pointed to Connell, still seated on the wall. 'For a start he can read my mind. Fergus knows my mum's name, there's a talking cat, a nutty woman and you've got a meerkat that uses a quill. What's it writing anyway? Come on Melie, let's get out of here, I'm leaving!' Luke was in a fluster now and he made as if to stride off in the direction of the hedge, but stopped short and said quietly, 'Sorry, it's all a bit too much and I just want something to eat.'

'There will soon be food beyond your wildest imagination for you all,' Fergus announced grandly and much to the relief of the companions. 'We are close to Futhark where the food fair is taking place at this very moment. We will be there very soon, very soon. Travellers are very welcome.' This cheered everyone up and as they all began to imagine what kind of food might be on offer at this food fair, Alexander suddenly piped up.

'I've got it!' he cried.

'Got what?' 'What's he on about?' 'What?' The kids

turned to face him and all spoke up at once.

'The littoral zone; he means literal as in l, i, t, e, r, a, l. You know, the willow is a weeping willow, so here it actually weeps,' Alexander stated triumphantly. They all looked up into the trees around them and noticed that not only were droplets of water drizzling down as a light shower from the tips of their leaves, but the sobbing which they thought was coming from Connell was coming from the trees as well!

'Very literal,' said Sammy, leaning on the wall of the bridge next to Connell and looking down into the stream. 'I suppose that's why those dragonflies have scales and are breathing fire.' The kids rushed over to the join her on the bridge, pointing excitedly to where the little insects flitted about, an even mix of dragonfly, the wings, and actual dragon, except in miniature; scales, tail and fire. Tiny Page took his glasses from his pocket and replaced them on his nose, just to be sure. Meanwhile the grown-ups and Lavender stood aside from the commotion and, Melie noticed, engaged in quiet conversation that seemed rather more serious than the excited chatter about the dragonflies that passed between the kids in her gang.

The walk down into Futhark turned out a little longer than expected but with surprises of a literal nature on every corner and with the prospect of a meal at the food fair, it passed quite quickly. By the time they reached the birch wood they'd discovered the literal meaning of foxgloves, tulips, limestone and gooseberries along the way. Jam Schultz found these particularly amusing until he reached out to pick one. He was promptly bitten on the finger by the squawking fruit. It was all very exhausting so the kids were relieved to hear Billy proposing a short rest and they settled down in comfortable spots amongst the trees and shared whatever remaining drinks they had. With a gracefulness out of place in this woodland setting Sanguinella placed Lavender on the lush grass at the foot of a tree but then stumbled against it as the cat became intertwined with her flowing robes.

'See that?' whispered Sammy to Molly with a giggle. 'She'd have been on the deck if she hadn't grabbed the tree!'

'There's no need to laugh, she's alright actually, Sanguinella Couch. I quite like her now. Thought she was a weirdo before, but things seem a bit different in Hedge,' said Molly as the catwoman glanced around trying to preserve her dignified image and quickly slipping her hand beneath the folds of her dress.

'Sanguinella Cow, that's what I think!' Sammy spluttered mischievously into her drink.

Choosing a seat close to Connell, Melie tuned in to his thoughts, 'You ok Connell?'

'Ok now. I was not so good back there though. There's something odd going on and I can't quite put my finger on it; something about meeting someone in Hedge. I think you're going to meet someone too. It's funny but I just keep thinking it's my sister, you know, Polly.' Connell's reply was tinged with sadness and Melie remembered Polly was the sister who'd disappeared years ago when they were young. She'd heard The Enlightened Ones talking about it often enough.

'Look, it'll be ok.' Melie's tone of thought was comforting and she put a hand on Connell's shoulder before continuing. *'We're in Hedge and it's all a bit strange and mixed up. I mean, did you see those tulips? Talk about literal!'* Her thinking voice trailed off as she realised how trivial this must have seemed in Connell's sorry state.

'You're right Melie, I will be ok. It's just that I can feel

she's here in Hedge. When I get the chance, I'll get Fergus alone and talk to him about it. He seems like he'd know.' And then his mood lightened a little as he spoke aloud, 'Yeah, Tulips, good one! Hey, I wonder though, maybe it is Polly sending me these messages.' The companions sat around in little groups for a few minutes longer amongst the trees, chatting away about the wonders they'd seen, the prospect of what food they'd find in Futhark and the uncertainty of what lay ahead for them.

'Come on then, let's go, I'm ready to eat,' said Tiny Page as he rose and scooped up his bag. 'Let's hope walnuts are off the menu!' Alexander, who along with Jam was really taken with this literal zone novelty, added a couple of observations of his own.

'I don't think sandwiches would go down too well either,' he said. 'And you can forget hotdogs!' With a mixture of delight and trepidation, curiosity and excitement the companions made ready to continue onwards to the food fair and everything was going very well in Hedge that day until the incident with the silver birches. As Sammy reached down to haul the dozing Luke to his feet she leaned with one hand against the papery trunk of the silver birch he was resting under, for a little extra leverage against his grumbling resistance.

'Okay, okay, I'm coming, give me a chance!' complained Luke once he'd readjusted to the uncomfortable prospect of life on the vertical plane. Then he spotted it. 'Hey, what's that on your hand Sammy?' Sammy looked down at the palm of her free hand and let out a sharp squeal, which turned into more of a horrified squeak when she saw that the skin was now shiny silver, as if covered in liquid mercury. Luke shouted to the others, 'Hey, come and look at this, her hand's gone silver!' As the squeal gradually evolved into a kind of whimper, they dashed over, amazed at what they saw but not entirely surprised at the latest turn of events in this most unusual of places.

'Sammy, it's alright, look, it's fading already,' Melie reassured her whilst at the same time trying to calm the youngsters' excitement with a subtle glare. True enough, the silver was fading rapidly. As the relieved Sammy prodded and poked at her restored palm, Jam and Alexander took one look at each other and then rushed up to grab the tree, whooping mischievously. They danced around waving silvered palms in the air as one by one the rest of the kids joined in the fun and reached out for the magical tree trunks amidst shouts and cries of gleeful abandon. It was a sure sign that they were finally overwhelmed by the strangeness and mystery of their journey.

'Children!' cried Fergus, 'Amelia North you must become calm again, time is short. Okay Melie!' His shout was so loud that they all stopped in their tracks and turned to face him, brought to their senses as quick as a flash. 'Amelia, child of Maeva,' he continued, his usual tone and manner restored, 'everything is quite as it should be, these are simply...'

'Silver birches, of course!' cut in Tiny Page, 'literally!'

'Yes, these indeed are silver birches and in this literal zone the hand of one whose heart is true will take on the tone of the tree. The palm turns silver for a time until the soul is strengthened by the purity of this precious metal,' said Fergus slowly, much to the delight of the meerkat, which scribbled down his words at a more leisurely pace for once.

'So what if your heart is not true?' asked the perceptive Melie. 'Does your hand still turn silver?'

'It does not, my child,' replied Fergus, at which Melie

began to wonder just who she was the child of. 'The hand of those whose heart bears ill will take on the tone of the heart. Their dark intent will stain the palm with a mark of gloom.'

'So it'll be black instead of silver then,' said Molly Schultz as more of a statement than a question. She was the only one who had noticed the colour of Sanguinella's palm when she'd stumbled against the silver birch just earlier.

Chapter Ten

Barnaby Sticks Biscuits

It took just under an hour to reach the village from the magical birch wood. They'd left the wonders of the literal zone behind a good while ago and yet their journey remained full of interest as the light and colour of Hedge began to unfold in the gentle breeze of early evening. Lush trees rustled, clattered and creaked. Pale yellow towers of wheat swayed lazily in the fields like the dancers at the end of the evening. Dry walls of golden stone radiated a warm glow from baking in the sunshine all day long. The weary companions trudged along the stony track, Melie North and her gang of kids, Connell, Billy, Fergus and Sanguinella Couch with her healing cat. From time to time, the kids spotted a bird they didn't recognise, or heard the cry of some creature they couldn't place. Here and there wood smoke could be seen drifting across the fields, the sign of a garden bonfire or perhaps a farmer burning stubble. Swathes of sweet smelling bluebells nodded away in the shade of wayside trees. Nodded rather than jingled like the ones a mile or so back had done. The companions walked in a purposeful silence, passing amongst blankets of bog rosemary once in a while and for the troubled Connell and for the kids it gave time to reflect on all that had happened. Thoughts of concerned families, quite literally in another world, were beginning to worry the young Jam and Alexander. Melie, Luke and Tiny gave reassuring smiles of encouragement at every corner. Molly and Sammy walked nearest to the front of the group, which was led by Fergus who muttered quietly away as the meerkat scribbled with the quill. Molly seemed agitated.

'Sammy … we're in trouble,' she whispered to her younger twin. 'I've seen something that doesn't seem to fit with what's going on here.'

'What, what have you seen?' Sammy asked under her breath, moving closer to Molly and taking her by the hand.

'I think I should tell Melie. I'll tell Fergus…' Molly's voice trailed off and Sammy sensed a growing unease.

'Molly, tell me, I'm your twin,' said Sammy before looking behind at the others. She felt an unexpected chill in the air which seemed to mirror the change of mood. She felt Molly's grip tighten.

'Sammy, you know that silver birch thing back there in the wood?' Molly whispered. 'Well Sanguinella's palm was black, not silver. It should have been silver like everyone else's, but she touched a tree when she nearly fell over the cat didn't she? She slipped her hand under her dress, trying to look cool and hide it, but I noticed it was black.'

'Molly!' said her twin quietly. 'You're getting a bit freaky, I'm sure it was nothing.' With this, Sammy tried to conceal her true feelings though she was beginning to share her sister's unease. She looked around hoping for reassurance yet saw only a calculating coldness in Sanguinella's dark eyes.

'Stop looking round!' hissed Molly and she pulled Sammy sharply by the hand to catch up with Fergus, who somehow seemed aware that something was wrong. He took the quill from the meerkat and slipped it into his inside pocket, out of reach of the puzzled scribe.

'Twins, you seem troubled, how may I be of assistance

to you?' Fergus' tone was grave and serious, yet he did look a little comical as he shoved the protesting meerkat unceremoniously deeper into the pocket. The three kept walking at the front of the company as Molly explained her fears in a hushed voice as quickly as possible to avoid suspicion from prying eyes. Melie noticed of course and she came forward to join them just as they approached the first building of Futhark village.

'Something's wrong, isn't it? You okay?' asked Melie. 'What is it?' Like their parents back in Yorkshire this younger generation shared a certain intuition, each in tune with the other, each able to notice thoughts and feelings. Fergus leaned in closer to the three girls as they walked.

'It is Sanguinella,' he whispered. 'Your friends believe she cannot be trusted, as do I. Her heart bears ill.' He glanced over his shoulder suspiciously. Melie paused, considering Fergus' words.

'The silver birches,' said Melie. 'Black palm instead of silver? I was never sure of her, even back at the Powder Mill.' She turned to look back down the straggle of companions towards Sanguinella at the rear of the group. 'Keep it quiet, don't worry the youngsters.'

'They need not know of this,' Fergus said after a moment. 'I will summon the Hedgerangers who will place a Solace between the woman and the companions. Sanguinella will not pass through to Futhark.' He then keyed in a command onto the palm of his left hand with the fingers of his right just as Davis had done earlier that day at the Hedge boundary. Fergus' apparent control of the situation was of little comfort to the three worried girls, a world away from home in the company of a strange woman who'd evidently pretended to be something she was not. 'Just act naturally,' he advised, scanning the lane into the village for a glimpse of Davis and Mavis.

'That's easy for you to say,' said Luke, who'd joined the group and gleaned enough from their conversation to know that something was going seriously wrong. 'You've got an invisible calculator on your palm and a scribbling meerkat in your pocket. If there's trouble you'll just turn into a firefly and fly away!'

'Luke,' hissed Melie, 'he's trying to help us, just go with the flow! Do the sensible thing and try to get the youngsters moved away from Sanguinella. Tell Tiny. Be subtle. Be careful; she might be dangerous.'

'Hey, it's me!' Luke joked as he moved off to herd the kids to safety, although deeply worried for himself and his friends.

It was as though Sanguinella suspected nothing and it all happened with such lightning speed. From out of nowhere Davis and Mavis materialised right in front of the startled woman, each wielding a straight hazel staff with which they stabbed the ground at their feet while crying out a stern warning.

'A Solace binds your pathway in the name and in the time of Maeva!' they cried. A faint rumbling hum pulsed in the air around Sanguinella for no more than a second and she seemed to fade and soften for the tiniest moment, her outline blurring slightly as though viewed through mullioned glass. And then she simply disappeared just as her face twisted into a petrifying sneer of the darkest malice, which sent shockwaves of fear deep into Melie's soul and knocked her backwards onto the well-worn Futhark pavements.

***

'Look, just forget the fire Posy! Just leave it, we've got

to get this sorted,' cried Da, exasperated at his friend's apparent lack of interest in the proceedings. 'Can't you see what's going on here? And where's Connell? He should be here by now!' Posy rose slowly, propped the soot-blackened poker against the beige tiles of Da's kitchen fireplace and turned to face the assembled friends.

'I'm glad Connell's not here as it happens,' she said calmly. Posy joined the rest of them at the kitchen table and picked up a packet of custard creams, which she tipped out onto the plate of biscuits. The Captain immediately took one from the pile.

'Connell's done nothing, what do you mean you're glad?' he asked as he bit into the biscuit, catching the crumbs in his upturned palm and speaking awkwardly with his mouth full. 'You've not had a ding dong have you?' Lizzie Page cut in sharply.

'No, they have not had a ding dong,' she said. 'Who have you been hanging around with lately Geo? I'd have expected an improvement in the eloquence stakes with your posh clientele.'

'What's the way I talk got to do with anything Lizzie?' he spluttered, by way of a reply. 'All I asked was why she's glad Connell's not here.' He stuffed the rest of the custard cream into his mouth and slumped back into his chair, sulking.

It remained quiet in the kitchen for a while. The atmosphere seemed unusually strained between the lifelong friends. Lizzie rose and walked over to open the window wide to try and rejuvenate a sad looking African violet on the sill by picking off a few dead leaves and relieving its thirst with tap water. Outside, the clear night sky was bursting with a million stars. Da picked up his knife, which he opened and closed rhythmically while he looked down into the fire, now crackling into life thanks to Posy's poking just earlier. The Captain picked up another unopened packet of biscuits and read the label absentmindedly, Barnaby Sticks Biscuits, thinking the brand name vaguely familiar.

'This feels weird,' muttered Geo. 'You could cut the atmosphere with a knife in here,' he added gloomily.

'Yeah, come on you lot,' said Da, snapping his knife shut and spinning it to a standstill on the table. 'Let's sit down, right here, and talk; we should be sticking together. This is important. And Posy, we won't say anything about Connell, okay?' The friends were used to treading lightly on the delicate subject of Posy's one time relationship with Connell and it was rarely mentioned that some in the village believed Connell to be Luke's father. They'd been very close for a couple of years around the time of Luke's birth and Luke did share Connell's piercing blue eyes and rather brusque nature. But Connell Brown, even amongst The Enlightened Ones, was a complex character known for being a cautious type. He'd left Posy before Luke was born to live alone in a small stone house in Mill Square, keeping a comfortable distance between him and any rumours of family ties. Distressing and rather uncomfortable at the time, the matter rarely came to the surface in Posy Schofield nowadays, but the meeting in Da's kitchen that evening seemed to be stirring the emotions in all of them. The unexplained bond they shared seemed somehow more intense, as though it was about to burst into the open in a kind of eureka moment. Lizzie Page closed the window and returned to the table, bringing the plant with her and smiling.

'They're okay, you know, I just feel they're okay,' she said. 'And you know what? I've got a feeling Connell's with them.'

'You know what, I think you're right,' said Da, 'but just exactly where are they? Where in this world could they be?' It hit them in an instant as a sudden and collective realisation. The point in question was exactly which world the gang of kids were actually in and the answer was waiting inside May's old suitcase sitting there between them in the middle of the kitchen table.

'Come on then, let's get it open,' urged The Captain, reaching for Da's pruning knife and pulling the case towards him.

***

A small crowd had gathered around her by the time Melie began to recover from the ferocity of Sanguinella's departure. She'd been scooped up from the Futhark pavement by Billy with a surprising display of strength and agility for a man of at least seventy. The return to his own world seemed to have sparked a physical change in Billy, the old Welly Jackson from Turley Holes.

'Why don't we get her inside one of these shops away from this lot?' suggested Connell, feeling Melie's brow for any sign of a raised temperature. 'She just needs a bit of space.'

'Connell, she is not ill, she has just had a nasty shock,' said Billy. 'You should have seen the look on Sanguinella's face. That was pure evil. Things have changed since I was last in Hedge if people such as this are walking freely.' The meerkat resumed its scribbling as Fergus joined in.

'This is a matter of some seriousness Billy and indeed of some rarity.' Fergus raised his voice and swept his arm to include the onlookers in his audience as he continued. 'I can assure all of you that such malice, such ... wrongdoing, has not been seen in Hedge for many years.'

'Malevolence,' Melie murmured, still only half-conscious but coming round gradually in Billy's arms. 'Malevolence, I saw malevolence in her eyes. I think that's the word you're looking for.' She got back onto her feet again, stretched as if waking from a deep sleep and looked down at the tourmaline crystal in her hand. 'She's just the kind of new member the Malevolents are looking for to join their exclusive club.'

'Melie, thank heavens you're okay!' cried Jam, who leapt up joyfully and clung so tightly onto his friend and leader that she could scarcely breathe. 'You had us going there, what happened?' Melie was swamped by the gang of kids, and by all the adults except Connell who remained alert as he scanned the street, half expecting the cat woman to return. He was after all the closest thing to a responsible adult in Melie's life in Hedge, a world away from Turley Holes where Da would be anxiously pondering his daughter's whereabouts. Melie shook herself free from the huddle and took a step or two away.

'I'm okay,' she said. 'Really, I feel okay. Just a big shock that's all. We all saw what happened, but it's fine, she's gone and I don't think she's coming back to Futhark in a hurry. Did you see the Hedgerangers and that thing they did with their staffs?' She sounded shaken, although for the benefit of the youngsters she was putting on a brave face.

'Yeah, weird that!' said Molly. 'What was it Fergus, a Solace or something?' She put her arm around Melie's shoulder and drew her back into the group. Fergus, Davis and Mavis had started trying to calm down the onlookers. Most of these had just witnessed the biggest piece of news in their lifetimes and were visibly shocked. Fergus turned and replied with his usual air of calm authority.

'A Solace,' he explained. 'That is true Molybdenum Schultz. Simply stated, a Solace will bind the path and prevent progress so giving comfort in a moment of distress. It is a form of barrier, although invisible, which will prevent the traveller from continuing with the intended journey, in this case Sanguinella's journey into Futhark. Come on, move along now. Move along please!' Fergus eventually persuaded the onlookers to leave and then the travelling companions themselves were shepherded along by the Hedgerangers away from the shop outside which all the commotion had been taking place that evening. The symmetrical frontage was particularly striking, with a centrally placed door set back a little from the line of the twin windows, both of which curved inwards to meet the door. With ornate wooden frames painted in a bright turquoise with sunshine yellow detail, the windows displayed a mouth-watering array of exactly the kind of pastries and similar delicacies the travellers had been yearning for since entering Hedge. Fergus and the Hedgerangers, though, assured them that just a little further along they'd find all the sustenance and comfort they could hope for, so the shop was reluctantly bypassed. The sign above the windows read Barnaby Sticks Biscuits.

Chapter Eleven

Pink Pamela's Hospitality and the Suitcase Back Home

It had been a fantastic night in the village thanks to the wonderful hospitality arranged by Fergus at Pink Shutters; an extremely comfortable boarding house run by an eccentric woman the kids had nicknamed Pink Pamela. A delicious selection of food and drinks had been laid out as a buffet on a circular table in the middle of a large room where a log fire sparkled and warmed the bones in the chill of evening. Tempting sofas with sumptuous cushions lined the walls on three sides whilst the fourth wall was almost entirely taken up with the largest window any of them had ever seen. Had it been daylight, there would have been a super view across the rooftops because the room was located on the top floor of the house. Instead, stars in their millions painted a silvery glow onto the carpet of assorted buildings which made up the extent of Futhark village that could be seen from this aspect of Pink Shutters. The ceiling seemed to be non-existent and the actual apex of what they could only imagine to be a tall, thin cone shaped roof was so far away it simply could not be seen in the half-light provided by the fire and the outrageously fat candles dotted around the place. The overall effect was that they were in a giant tipi, although rather more comfortable than they'd ever believed a tipi could be. The exhausted companions were struggling to eat anything at all; they were far too busy yawning or else chattering excitedly about recent events.

Pink china plates were loaded with sandwiches, sausage rolls, pineapple and cheese cubes on sticks, pizza, crisps and cheese straws. It was as though Pink Pamela had taken the trouble to provide exactly the kind of party fare Melie and the gang had been enjoying at each other's birthday parties in Turley Holes for the past few years. There were also a good number of fruits for the diners to choose from; the usual grapes, bananas, pears and oranges, along with one or two unrecognisable varieties presumably unique to Hedge. Some of the drinks were equally unfamiliar, but all were exquisitely thirst quenching and perfectly suited to satisfying the taste buds, whether hot or whether cold. The whole experience in that particular room in Pink Shutters, the tipi as it became known, was just what was needed after the marathon journey that day.

As the evening wore on, the seven children draped themselves around the place, lost in their own thoughts. Some picked at the food; some were dozing off and then waking with a jolt in time to see sandwiches and sausage rolls sliding from tilting plates onto Pink Pamela's carpet. Melie stood at the window with a handful of crisps, gazing out into the starry night. Fergus and Connell, who'd been conversing in a whisper in one corner, came over to join her.

'I wonder if they're seeing these stars in Turley Holes tonight?' she mused out loud.

'Melie,' said Connell, placing a comforting arm around her shoulder, 'I just know they're all fine back there. I just feel they're okay. I'm not just saying this, but I really am certain Da knows you're alright. It's as though messages are coming in from home now as well as from Hedge … or maybe it's just something I'm imagining.' At this Melie tried to reassure Connell, who she sensed was feeling responsible for her.

'I'm fine too Connell,' she said. 'I mean I know a lot's happened ... and that thing with Sanguinella back there was really scary. But I feel okay. That's lucky with all I've got to do isn't it?' She bit into a crisp as she looked around at the kids, some of whom had been ushered out of the tipi and off to bed. 'It's just the gang, especially Alexander and Jam. It's a lot to put up with at their age. They must be feeling pretty bewildered and just a bit homesick as well.' Connell looked at Fergus with a wry smile on his face.

'You know Fergus,' he said, 'you've chosen quite a girl for this task; I feel like I'm talking to a thirty year old!'

'Ah Connell Brown,' sighed Fergus, 'it would have been a great honour to have been involved in any choice in the matter. Indeed, there was an element of choice, if you can call destiny choice. But enough for now, we must all rest. Tomorrow there will be many answers to many questions. Many uncertainties remain ... and many meetings lie ahead.' The last of the companions were shown to their rooms on the lower floor of the house by Pink Pamela, two large rooms even more comfortable than the tipi, one for the boys and one for the girls. Connell, Billy and Fergus had their own rooms whilst the Hedgerangers stayed in a small cottage at the end of the garden. Fergus was the last to leave the tipi and as he blew out the last candle, he breathed a sigh of relief.

'All is well,' he whispered, 'all are safe.' Then he looked down at the meerkat and ruffled its furry ears, smiling. 'No need to write that down my friend, come on, it is time for bed.'

***

89

'It just won't budge, no … no, hang on I think I've got it!' yelled The Captain as he prised open the first clasp on the suitcase. 'Yes!'

'Oh, nicely executed Geo!' whooped Da, taking the knife from his friend and inspecting the curved blade. He was relieved to see there was little damage to its keen edge. 'Let me have a go at the other one, I can't wait to get this thing open.' He probed at the rusty clasp like a seasoned safe cracker as the friends crowded around the table expectantly. 'Almost there … almost there,' he whispered, hoarse with excitement and mounting anticipation. 'Got it! Yes!' A flurry of excitement as whoops and cries of joy filled the little kitchen and then silence as all eyes settled on the case. Da carefully closed his beloved knife and slipped it into his pocket. This was a momentous occasion and they all knew it. The mood shifted from joyous to solemn and knowing glances passed between them. The common ground they'd shared long ago was about to be explained and yet all were reluctant to take the step of lifting the lid. Da eventually spoke up. 'Right then,' he sighed, 'we'd better have a look.' He reached for the edge of the lid at each side and slowly raised it, folding it back on itself onto the table. The onlookers remained silent; the only sound was a crackle from the fire. Da looked at Geo and the two women, raised his eyebrows in a gesture of relief and took a large key from the case. He turned it over in his hands and then passed it to Posy as he reached in for a long scroll of thick paper tied with sisal string. This he passed on to The Captain for he was sure it was a map of some description. Geo untied the string and rolled the map open, holding it to the light in outstretched arms and gasping in amazement.

'This just can not be happening,' he whispered, shaking his head in disbelief. 'It's just impossible. Impossible!'

'What's impossible?' Da asked excitedly.

'I'm not joking,' replied Geo. 'This map is the same as the one I've been working on for years! I've been mapping these places, straight out of my head, and this is it!'

'That's impossible!' said Lizzie.

'I know, I just said that,' whispered Geo. 'All I want to know now is why these places?' He sat down by the fire, eagerly examining the map with his expert eye, completely oblivious to whatever else Da might take out of May's old suitcase. While The Captain pondered over the map, Da reached back into the suitcase and pulled out a circular tin, which at one time would have contained boiled sweets, judging by the pictures on the lid. Da vaguely remembered the tin from a childhood Christmas and something told him the sweets had long since been eaten. The question was what was inside? Da sat down on his chair and carefully twisted off the lid.

'Hmm, not quite what I was expecting,' said Lizzie. 'What's with the orange powder?'

'Search me,' said Posy, taking the tin and inspecting the contents. 'Looks like ground almonds gone off. Doesn't smell like it though. This smells really sweet, a bit like fennel tastes.' Then she swiftly handed the tin back to Da, 'I'm not tasting it though.'

'Me neither,' said Da, sniffing the powder. 'Could be anything.' He put the tin down on the table and twisted the lid back on. Posy took the last item from the case, a letter addressed to 'David'.

'I guess this is for you,' she said and handed it to Da who read the name for himself, placed the white envelope on the table and turned away from his friends to look into the fire.

'In case you're all wondering, it's from May,' he announced quietly as he continued to watch the flames.

Leaning forwards in his chair, he picked up the poker and prodded the dwindling fire. 'And yes, I'm going to open it in a minute.' Just as the Enlightened Ones kept an unspoken silence about the true nature of the relationship between Connell and Posy in days gone by, they were equally tactful when it came to the matter of Da and May. Though it was as long ago as the year two thousand when she had left her husband and young daughter and gone away to another place, hardly a day went by without Da thinking of his beautiful May. There was a cruel poignancy in tales he'd heard and mocked as a younger man about the enduring quality of true love, sometimes against all odds and across the decades. The young pistolero running with the punks in the late Seventies would never have believed it possible to love someone truly and deeply almost ten years after they'd gone. His parents would have called it holding a candle for someone. Da had run the gamut of emotions since May's departure; shock, despair, anger, bewilderment, resignation, sadness and hope. His friends had rallied round and supported Da and daughter Melie, partly out of love and respect and partly out of the inexplicable bond, all of them, including May, shared. Maybe now, near Melie's eleventh birthday, the solution to the mystery disappearance would be solved by a simple letter.

'Come on Da, its okay, you've got us.' Geo's tone was sincere and comforting as he carefully returned the map to the open suitcase and placed a hand on Da's shoulder. 'I think it's time you got that letter opened mate,' he said. Da slowly looked around at the assembled group, sighed deeply and then looked back into the fire once more.

'Thanks,' he sighed, '… you know … for …'

'We know. It's okay,' said Lizzie. 'Now come on, get that knife of yours working, let's see what's it's all about.'

Da unclasped his knife, slit open the envelope and unfolded May's letter. He scanned the whole page first and then read it out.

My best mate Da,

It's July 2006.

With all that has been and all that is to be, I hardly know where to begin. I left you, I left our lovely daughter and I am still at a loss to understand how I could do it. I won't blame you if you can never forgive me, though I know deep in my heart that you have, if only for Melie's sake. She'll be eight years old now, nearly nine, and I can only imagine how beautiful she must be and what joy she brings to Turley Holes. Turley Holes in the summertime, what memories!

Da, I never stopped loving you, and I bless the day that I ever met you, in the month of May when the trees are at their best. Do you remember? I can see you now charging about on that moped trying to show off outside The Half Dead Tree. The young Da, king of the punks!

Do you know, I can't even explain in this short letter just why I had to leave, but you must believe me it was not a decision taken lightly. In fact, it was a decision taken for me. The pain of our parting is the sacrifice I made and not a day goes by when I deeply regret the hurt I must have caused you and Melie. Amelia. It's a beautiful name for a beautiful girl.

There are some things – important things – which I must tell you. First, you will be wondering about the contents of the suitcase. They were placed there by a power that you will come to understand as long as events unfold according to destiny. The key opens the Powder Mill, wherein you will find the beginning of the journey. The map – which The Captain will be able to interpret – locates the places of comings and goings between worlds. The tin contains powder. It is a concentrate of Dissolution, which dilutes in spring water and transports adventurers whose cause is worthy.

Everything is preordained. I know that four enlightened souls are hearing the words you read. I know that one is journeying already and that he is with the children. I know that one was lost long, long ago but will be found again. I know that one is bound in the destiny she was born to.

And now you must go, with The Captain, Lizzie and Posy, to the Powder Mill and find the beginning of the journey. Do not delay - the fate of two worlds will depend on the success of the two generations.

Your May.

Da stared blankly at the letter for a few moments and then read it again quietly to himself, looking up at the items described as he came to them as if checking an inventory. The others kept a sober silence, The Captain standing beside Da, Lizzie seated at the table and Posy seated upon it. When he had finished Da folded the letter and slipped it into the inside pocket of his jacket.

'I haven't got a clue what she's talking about,' he said.

Chapter Twelve

Parting Company

It was rather quiet around the breakfast table in the tipi next morning. It had been a restful night and they'd all slept soundly in their beds at Pink Shutters. But homesickness was beginning to creep in amongst the gang of kids as thoughts turned once again to Turley Holes and the grown-ups back home. Connell, though, had reassured them all that their families knew they were safe and that everything was alright. But whilst the kids understood Connell's telepathic abilities and trusted him, this was little comfort to the youngsters although the toast and porridge helped.

'Porridge,' yawned Luke. 'It would be porridge. What's for pudding, tripe?'

'Oh stop moaning, Luke,' said Tiny. 'Look, I'm sure they'll bring you something else, they do seem pretty good at looking after people. You should have seen the duvet on my bed; it was like sleeping under a ton of feathers.'

'Better that than a ton of bricks. He'd have been flattened wouldn't he Alexander?' joined in Sammy, clearly intent on winding up her younger brother.

'Very funny Samphire,' replied Schultz number four, 'I know I've just woken up but I am well aware that a ton is a ton! Just get on with your porridge and then while you're at it eat your boyfriend's for him!' Sammy smiled and sneaked a look at Luke, whose cheeks had flushed to a shade of pink not unlike that of the breakfast crockery. This boyfriend business was becoming somewhat tiresome.

'Anyway,' said Sammy, 'it'll be so cool to be out and about in a different world. I love being somewhere no one knows you; a bit of anonymity for once. I might even take my sketch book and make a name for myself round here as a wandering artist.'

'Well that's easier said than done,' said Tiny Page drily. 'How can you make a name for yourself but be anonymous?' This brought out the giggles and splutters and Tiny took a low bow in recognition of his grand example of wordplay. The kids chatted away as they devoured the delicious food and drinks Pink Pamela had set out for them and as wakefulness began to kick in, they became eager to continue with their great adventure. Each one of them, even Luke, cleared their porridge bowls. He was relieved to see that hot buttered toast rather than the dreaded tripe was next on the menu. After a while Connell and the other grown-ups joined them at the table and tucked into toast and tea from a large pink teapot with a stripy cosy to keep the brew nice and hot.

'We've got one just the same back home,' said Melie, 'strange that isn't it?'

'What's strange?' asked Tiny, who appeared slightly unfamiliar without his spectacles.

'Well here we are in a different world altogether, with lime flavour stones, meerkats that can write and no ceilings, but there's the same tea cosy we have at home,' Melie replied. 'I just think it's strange.'

'Amelia, my child, there are similarities and there are differences everywhere,' Fergus joined in. 'Here in Hedge you will find many things you would consider unusual. But they are only unusual because they are outside your everyday experience. When I first visited your world, which is of course Theirworld, I was astonished to see the people travelling here and there in motor cars.' There was a pause, during which Melie visualised the roads around Turley Holes teeming with cars looking for parking places each Saturday, market day. Then Fergus continued. 'It astonished me even more when I learned that these cars were propelled by the combustion of what Theirworlders call fossil fuel. Imagine ...' Fergus' voice took on a rather quiet and sombre tone '... a people wilfully destroying the atmosphere and jeopardising the future of their world.' Though it was no fault of theirs, some of the kids felt a little guilty at this. They feigned interest in whatever came into view amongst the breakfast debris and began to sweep up toast crumbs or study the crackle glaze on the adults' teacups. Nevertheless, they knew that Fergus' words were right and were glad that they shared his concern. Molly broke the temporary silence.

'So how do people travel around Hedge without cars? I mean if it's too far to walk,' she quickly added so as not to give the false impression that they were the kind of kids who were allergic to walking.

'Molly, there is much for Fergus to tell about the ways of Hedge and its people and there is much that you will learn for yourself,' said Billy. He leaned back in his chair and twirled his beard, which seemed to be losing more of its yellow tinge hour by hour since their arrival in Hedge. 'But Fergus, why not just satisfy Molly's curiosity on this one? I'm sure they're all dying to know.'

'Yes, come on Fergus,' urged Luke, 'let's hear all about it then.'

'For heaven's sake, don't get him started, we'll be here all day,' chipped in Connell for the telepathic benefit of Luke and Melie.

'Ok, just this one explanation then we'll cut him short,' replied Melie.

'Well then, can I presume we are all sitting comfortably? Then I will begin.' Fergus seemed intent on holding audience for some time to come and the meerkat groaned as it flexed its fingers ready to scribe. 'In Hedge we walk. We were given the benefit of legs and so we use them wherever we can.' At this, he rose from his chair and paced slowly around the tipi, as if demonstrating an unfamiliar concept, using his hands to reinforce a point from time to time as he continued. 'But of course there are many towns and villages spread about the land and there are many times when walking would simply take too long.' His pacing ceased beside the stone fireplace at a pink painted door, against which he rapped his knuckles with a flourish. 'On such occasions we take the Corridor!'

'That's not a corridor. Isn't that just a door? Are you sure it was there last night?' The Observant Jam Sandwich was clearly wide-awake by now.

'Ah yes, that is how it would seem and that is how it would be if someone who shall remain nameless …' at this he took a slight bow and beamed with pride as the meerkat scribbled away and then continued, '… if someone had not seen the potential in the simple door to revolutionise the way we travel around here in Hedge. You will notice the intricacy of the decorations with which the door knob has been inscribed,' said Fergus. 'Well as pleasing to the eye as these delicate engravings may be, they do have a special and really rather unique function, if I say so myself.' Connell, along with Melie and the kids, gathered around Fergus taking great interest in the Corridor but then were rather disappointed as he said, 'I will be pleased to demonstrate but not without purpose. The Corridor is only useful with purposeful intent and so I would like to make a suggestion about the rest of the day. If you would be so kind as to return to your seats around the table…' With this, he ushered them back to their places as if rounding up sheep, to join the Hedgerangers, who had now come in for cups of tea in the tipi.

'Actually Fergus,' said Melie, 'if you don't mind I've got a suggestion of my own.' Melie had settled into the world of Hedge with apparent ease and she was somewhat less awestruck in Fergus' presence than when they'd all arrived the previous day. 'You said there would be many answers to many questions today and something about meetings, so I think I should stay here with you to talk about all that and the others should go exploring in Futhark with Davis and Mavis to look after them. What do you think gang?' The kids heartily agreed with Melie's suggestion. The prospect of being at large in another world for a guided tour with personal bodyguards was exciting to say the least. In next to no time they'd raced around Pink Shutters collecting their gear, weaving in and amongst Pink Pamela and her staff as they cleared the breakfast clutter and swept discarded toast crusts into dustpans with pink-handled brushes.

'Right then,' cried Luke, adopting an officer's tone to bring the gang to attention with their usual mock military line up. 'So kids, where's Tiny then? And, Jam Sandwich, where's Schultz one, two and three? Not coming today or what?' Then they all fell into fits of excited giggles and fun poking only to be scooped up by Connell and the other adults in readiness for the big departure.

'Now then my friends, if you please, may I have your attention once again?' Fergus almost shouted this request above the hubbub. 'We have made ready to depart and I can now show you the wonders of modern travel here in

Hedge.' He stepped towards the Corridor and reached for the handle in the middle, twisting the outer rim of the dial, which made a series of substantial clicks as it turned. 'We are here in Pink Shutters, Futhark,' he said, pointing to a red arrow at the top of the dial. 'Right here, see?' The kids and Connell crowded round to get a better view of the metallic dial with its many markings and inscriptions which they took to be place names, but the only ones they recognised were Pink Shutters, Futhark and Gush. Fergus continued, 'The destination is Greenbanks, Chowk,' and he turned the dial's inner rim so that the two locations were aligned with each other at the red arrow. The door swung open noiselessly and with a slight bow of his head, Fergus gestured towards the swirling clouds of white mist, which billowed inside the frame. 'Step this way if you please Amelia my child and you too Connell. Come on now, time is short…'

'Hang on,' said Melie, 'just a couple of things. For a start, I thought we were staying here to have a talk. I thought the others were going exploring round Futhark with the Hedgerangers.'

'The explorers will indeed be walking the byways of Futhark as soon as they wish,' said Fergus. 'Connell and your good self will be accompanying me to my home, Greenbanks in Chowk and we will be travelling by Corridor. At the end of the day Davis and Mavis will see to it that we meet together in Chowk where we can all enjoy a hearty meal and a good night's sleep before the quest for The Stone gets underway.' A pause as the companions exchanged glances whilst deciding whether this was an acceptable arrangement and then Fergus continued. 'Splendid! I think I have made myself clear. Come along then; homeward to Chowk!' and he stepped through the doorway into the mist, the meerkat scribe clinging tightly to the hem of his pocket as always. Connell and Melie looked quickly at each other and then followed, with only the briefest pause for a reassuring smile to the gang. The door closed without a sound and the travellers were gone. Billy spoke first.

'Well, I must have been away longer than I thought. I've never seen the like of that before! Fascinating!' He stepped up to the door and traced a finger around the metallic dial. 'Fascinating,' he whispered and then turned to the others, twirling the point of his beard with panache. 'But it's walking for us today. Let's go then, Barnaby Sticks Biscuits first stop I think.'

'Why there?' Molly asked.

'You've obviously never tasted them!' he replied, as he swept out of the tipi followed by the excited adventurers.

Chapter Thirteen

Exploration, Explanation and Meetings

A dewy mist clung to the streets around Turley Holes as Da and his companions set out for the Powder Mill early the next morning. The contents of May's old suitcase clattered around in a small rucsac slung across Geo's shoulder. They hadn't slept of course and had spent the past couple of hours gathering what they might need from their own homes before reconvening in Da's kitchen. Wordlessly they hurried along through Mill Square, scrambling up the railway embankment onto the disused line which they followed out of the village for about a quarter of a mile. Then down an indistinct little footpath through a maze of towering brambles and out through a gap in the rusted wire fence into a field where one or two cows grazed on the lush grass. A pause for breath and a quick moment to exchange reassuring glances and they were off again, continuing along their secret childhood route to the mill. The mist was clearing as the sun's warmth began to dry off the dew from the long grass, although just a little too late; their shoes were already soaking. By the time they reached the door of the Powder Mill where Luke had tried to leave the note the previous day, glorious sunshine prevailed. It was Da who spoke first as they rested for a few moments, sitting on one of the low walls leading up to the door.

'You all okay?' he asked. The Captain took a long drink from his water bottle and then replaced the stopper with a slap.

'I'm okay,' he replied. 'You okay? Yeah, we're all okay. You know, it must be pushing thirty years since I've come to the mill by our old way,' he mused, before taking up his bottle once more and draining it.

'Me too, just like yesterday though isn't it?' said Lizzie.

'Oh come on, stop it you lot, you're making me feel old!' joked Posy, bending to pick the burdock seeds from her dew dampened jeans. Da straightened himself up from his seat on the floor at the foot of the wall and allowed himself the luxury of a long yawn and stretch against the tiredness from the sleepless night.

'Right then,' Da said, 'let's have that key out G Schultz, we'd better have a look inside.' The Captain picked up the rucsac from the wall and took out the key, which he offered to Da. 'No, go on, be my guest,' Da said, gesturing towards the huge wooden door with its lion's head knocker.

As The Captain grasped the handle ready to insert the key, an uneasy stillness seemed to descend on the trees, which moments earlier had been rustling gently in the light wind. A few startled wood pigeons clattered noisily amongst the upper branches as they took flight. The shadowy undergrowth amongst the tree trunks seemed to darken in places. The companions shared the distinctly uncomfortable feeling that they were being watched by someone … or something … intent on knowing their business. An indefinable malice hung in the dark spaces amongst the bushes, stirring slightly as though poised to rush out and attack the group. The Captain lowered the rucsac to the ground and Da deftly unclasped the knife in the pocket of his blue jacket; they were preparing for a fight. Lizzie fingered the tourmaline crystal in her pocket and Posy took a step forward to peer intently into the darkness. After a few extremely tense moments the feeling faded as swiftly as it had started. The mood lightened and the breeze stirred up the trees once again, although the pigeons did not return to their roost. Relieved, they turned their attention to the Powder Mill and the mysterious key, which slid into the lock and turned effortlessly. With a satisfying clunk, the door swung open. The Captain slotted the key into the other side of the lock, shouldered his rucsac with a flourish and rubbed his hands together gleefully.

'Well then,' he said, 'what are we waiting for? Onwards and ... ah ... downwards?'

'What do you mean downwards? Asked Lizzie. 'I think the phrase is onwards and upwards Geo, just who have you been fraternising with in that precious pub?' She pushed past him to look through the open doorway. 'Ah,' she said, 'see what you mean.' All four crowded around and peered into the gloomy interior. Sure enough, the floor inside the Powder Mill was a good deal lower than the ground they were standing on, about thirty or forty feet lower in fact. It was a weird arrangement and it triggered a vague recollection in them all of a similar situation years ago, something to do with a hedge.

'This is weird!' exclaimed Posy in a whisper, 'I don't remember this before. We just used to walk straight in.'

'Yeah I know,' said Da. 'I mean I know we were just kids last time we were in here but even after all this time I'm beginning to remember it plain as day. The floor wasn't down there back then.' He clung to the doorframe and leaned into the void, straining against the dim light to try to gain a clear view of the situation. The floor was definitely well below ground level and just visible in the gloom.

'Hey, there's a rope!' said Posy excitedly, 'we're in!' Lizzie stepped up to the threshold and tightened the straps of her own small rucsac.

'I'll go first; I can do this kind of stuff,' she said. Reaching around to the left of the doorframe, Lizzie grasped the thick rope which hung from a metal ring secured to the woodwork and then eased herself down the series of knots along its length with some expertise. In a few moments, she reached the floor and then called up to her companions above, 'I'm there and it's easy. Who's next?'

'How did she learn how to do that? I didn't know she could do that!' exclaimed Posy, amazed at her friend's rope work skills. 'Lizzie, you made that look easy!' she called down to her friend.

'Almost anything can be easy if you just straighten your mind out first,' Lizzie shouted back up to them, grasping her tourmaline crystal in her hand and smiling to herself. 'Come on Posy, just go for it!'

Not one of them found the descent as easy as Lizzie Page had made it look. Posy was nervous and struggled against the fear of falling, gripping the thick rope with all her might and consequently weakening rapidly as she went. Geo wanted to look the part with his camouflage trousers and red beret but was getting his legs all tangled in the flapping rope and ended up going down arm over arm, tiring quickly. Da managed to close and lock the door with great difficulty whilst hanging onto the rope with one hand, dropped the key down to The Captain and then tried to go too slowly, searching for footholds on the wall and almost falling off backwards in the process. But before too long they had all reached the foot of the rope and were safely inside the Powder Mill.

'Now, if I remember, there's gas lighting in here,' said Posy, feeling her way along the wall in the pale light filtering in from the few windows which were not boarded up, forty feet or so above their heads. 'Yes, I thought so, here it is! Got a match anyone?' Da reached into the chest pocket of his blue linen jacket, tossed her a box of matches and next moment Posy began firing up the wall lights around the large room one by one. As the gloomy interior grew brighter, the friends took stock of their old childhood headquarters. They were shocked to see what had happened to the walls since their last visit. They were painted with incredible illustrations of quite extraordinary people and places, all of which seemed strange yet at the same time inexplicably familiar to the group. A portrait of a rather small man with an oversized purple long coat would have given the impression that he was of some importance, magisterial perhaps, were it not for the small animal peeping out of his pocket. Several taller people were pictured wearing bright blue clothes, which resembled some kind of uniform. Two women, one very elegantly dressed and holding a small grey cat stood beside another who seemed much older and somewhat troubled. This one was holding a long clay pipe in her hand as though she were a smoker. Another group looked like a cross between pirates and travelling people, their clothes practical and flamboyant and each looking rather serious. One of these in particular looked very striking with a red cap, a small blond beard twisted into a single plait tied with a black ribbon and an eye patch. Underneath each portrait, the artist had penned the name of each character and this one was Mungo Cheeseman. One entire wall had been covered in a meticulously detailed painting of a box hedge intertwined with firethorn, each branch, leaf and each orange berry appearing almost real enough to touch. Way up near the top of the hedge there was a large hole, about the size of a manhole cover, around which bright blue butterflies were painted flittering around and about. As the others examined the hedge painting, The

Captain turned his attention to the wall opposite the door.

'Impossible! I don't believe this!' he cried. He swung his rucsac off his shoulder and took out the map they'd found in May's old suitcase the previous evening, unrolling it on the floor in front of him.

'Geo, what is it?' Posy asked as they knelt beside him excitedly.

'I think we all know what it is don't we?' suggested Da who remained standing beside the group, 'and I don't just mean that the map on the wall is the same as Geo's and May's.'

'It's the hedge isn't it?' said Lizzie. 'We went through that hole when we were kids didn't we? We went into that other world and met those people didn't we?'

'Mungo Cheeseman. Fergus Wiseman. Sanguinella Couch and her sister and all the rest,' joined in The Captain. 'Funny how Mungo has a red hat and an eye patch … or should I say it's funny how I have?' They sat down together around May's map on the floor of the Powder Mill sharing a few silent moments of recollection and then Da stood and walked up close to the map. Turning to face them, he took May's letter from his pocket and held it up for them all to see.

'I've worked it out,' he said. 'It's May. I've had dreams about a young girl calling out a name as if she's searching for someone she lost. I never get to see her face and she's upset. I used to think it was Melie looking for, you know, May. But it's not; it's May looking for Polly Brown.' He turned to face the map, running his hand across the detailed drawings. 'May did these paintings, it's her style.' After a moment he continued, still facing the map. 'We went into Hedge when we were young and I thought it was quite by accident, but in fact we were meant to go and Polly was meant to get left behind so that May went back to find her. She leaves me and Melie, then gets back in there and ends up as some important person; you heard the tone of her letter. It's as though she's set us a pre-ordained mission, you know, this journey she mentions.' He stopped and turned back to them, then continued gravely, quoting from May's letter, *'I know that one is bound in the destiny she was born to'*, it says here. Well guess who that is, that's Melie, that's who. She's off on this adventure and the rest of the kids have gone with her haven't they?' His friends stood and joined him by the map on the wall and once again, they became silent for a moment, taking it all in. Lizzie broke the silence.

'We'd forgotten all about those incredible times hadn't we?' she said. 'And what about those times when we've sometimes looked at each other over the years and felt something we couldn't explain? I know we've all felt it. I know I felt it again when I saw these floors on different levels. I mean do you remember how the ground seemed much lower in Hedge than here? This feels like a bit of an outpost of Hedge.'

'You're right,' added The Captain, rolling May's map and putting it back in his rucsac. 'And don't you sometimes wonder how we've all turned out to be slightly extraordinary people, at least compared to most of the rest of Turley Holes? It's because we've been into Hedge. Something like that is going to leave its mark on you. Tell you one thing though, if the map shows entry points to Hedge like May says, then it must be a big place. Look at where some of them are.' They studied the detail on the wall and saw places in many parts of the world. A couple of locations in Malta were on there, one spot in central Sardinia too, the Hunza valley in Pakistan and the Japanese island of Okinawa. Da was pleased to see

The Mojave desert in California and the French city of Lille featured on the map, as he'd visited these on his travels over the years. Closer to home, Kettlewell in Yorkshire's Upper Wharfedale was marked prominently, in there amongst the more exotic locations.

'Well I'll tell you something else,' joined in Posy. 'Connell was in on this with us too, and I'm sure he's the one in the letter who is already with the children, *journeying already* or something I think May wrote.' She paused for a few moments while she worked things out and then continued. 'That's what we've got to do now, join up with them and help with whatever they're doing, wherever they are.'

'Well how are we going to do that?' asked Da. 'How can we get to them in Hedge, assuming that's where they are of course.'

'What about that Dissolution powder from the suitcase?' suggested Lizzie. 'She said you just dilute it in spring water and it takes you where you want to go.'

'Lizzie's right,' said The Captain, 'look at this.' They walked across to where Geo stood before an inscription in the corner of the map on the wall, which he read out. 'Dissolution: Dissolve a pinch of powder in spring water, state your destination and drink immediately. Well I've got a bottle of spring water so what are we waiting for?' He took out the water and the tin of Dissolution powder from his rucsac and carefully added a pinch of powder for each of them.

'Tell you what G, add one for luck because boy we are going to need it!' joked Da, which lightened the mood a little. Once the mixture was prepared, they checked they'd picked up their belongings, turned off the gas and then one by one took a drink from the bottle.

'Oh no!' exclaimed The Captain.

'What is it?' asked Lizzie, starting to feel faint under the influence of the potion.

'We didn't state where we wanted to go before we drank it,' gasped Da wearily, feeling light headed.

'Quick somebody, say it before it's too late!' cried a swaying Posy. The Captain frantically scanned the wall map for inspiration.

'Grab each other,' he yelled. 'Sardinia!'

Chapter Fourteen

Meetings, Exploration and Explanation

It was obvious that Fergus preferred a comfortable lifestyle. Melie leaned back in the rocking chair at Greenbanks right in the centre of Chowk. Whilst the journey by Corridor she'd just taken with Connell and their host hadn't exactly been long and tiring it had caused great excitement and a rest in these sumptuous surroundings was quite in order. She looked into the garden through the large French doors at an extensive lawn covered in drifts of fallen pink blossom from a row of ornamental cherry trees along its edge.

'Actually they're probably not French doors in Hedge because they haven't got a France here have they?' she wondered aloud.

'Good point Melie,' was Connell's telepathic response. *'Actually I wonder if they have any countries or whether it's just one big place.'*

'Or one small place. Or medium sized. I dunno, maybe Fergus will tell us,' Melie mused in her thinking voice as a breeze brought down a fresh carpet of blossom onto the lawn. 'It must take billions of petals to cover that lawn. Hello Fergus.' He had just joined them in the room.

'Hello Amelia my child, I am so pleased, so pleased to have you here at last!' Fergus enthused. 'You too Connell. There are many answers to many questions … and many meetings lie ahead.' He placed a circular tray onto a table between their three chairs and poured glasses of what appeared to be fruit juice for his guests from a jug before taking one himself. His guests couldn't help but notice his edginess and the tray of glassware had rattled gently in his unsteady hands. 'Juice of the cherry infused with essence of cinnamon and warmed. Enjoy!' Then he took a long drink from his glass, placed it back onto the tray and sat down, mopping his brow with his handkerchief. The meerkat was not in his pocket as usual, Melie noticed, it was fast asleep on a sheepskin beside the fireplace, its quill and notebook neatly beside it on the floor. 'You will have many questions, but please allow me to speak and save your questions. There is much to explain,' said Fergus, standing to remove the purple coat and reveal a crisp white shirt with yellow brocade waistcoat. His trousers matched the coat and he wore a large yellow bowtie in a shade that clashed with everything else he wore. Connell shuffled uncomfortably in his rocking chair feeling slightly under dressed for once. He was usually considered something of a dapper dresser in his cream linen suit over an olive green tee shirt. Truth was it was just about the only outfit he possessed which possibly explained why it always looked fashionably crumpled.

'I will start at the beginning,' said Fergus, seated once again. 'You do know of course that The Shining Stone is lost and must be returned, by you Melie and you alone, in your eleventh year. That your companions have accompanied you on your quest is now by the by and water under the bridge as they say in Turley Holes. You may be wondering two things. First, how was it lost? Well The Stone has been lost for a long time, about one hundred and sixty of your years. It was stolen by one Mordechai Fern, the very man appointed to its safekeeping. It is unclear why he committed this unforgiveable wrongdoing and I suppose we will never know, but of one thing we are certain ...' At this Fergus rose from his chair and moved over to the large marble fireplace where he absentmindedly ran a finger along the mantelpiece as if inspecting for dust. He paused for a moment and then continued. '... I am afraid to say that Mordechai Fern was murdered by a fellow citizen of Hedge, someone whose identity remains a mystery to this very day.' Melie and Connell exchanged uncomfortable glances; Fergus was clearly agitated by his revelations.

'Fergus,' asked Melie, 'how come everything seems so kind of ... well, so kind of perfect here in Hedge? I mean I know there was that nasty business with Sanguinella the other day and the murder you've just told us about, but I get the impression that those are kind of one offs.'

'Well there's the Malevolents, don't forget those,' added Connell. Fergus became even more agitated at the mention of the Malevolents and he returned to sit beside his guests.

'You are right Melie. Hedge is quite a place, quite a place.' Fergus paused as if searching for the best way to explain. 'There has always been such harmony, such happiness and such abundant good fortune,' he said. 'I mean ... a murder, simply unthinkable! And as for the theft of a sacred artefact, that's incredible! Why?'

'Fergus,' said Connell, 'it's just not like that in Theirworld. I am sorry to say that good and evil exist side by side in equal balance. Just as there are wonderful people who live by a code of loving and giving and sharing, there are those whose hearts and minds are filled with greed and malice. We just have to accept it as a fact of life, although those of us on the side of good are doing our best to lead by example.' He too now rose and walked over to the French doors to look down the blossom-covered lawns.

'What Connell's saying,' went on Melie, 'is that there's

a mix of people in Theirworld, driven by different values. I think the bad news for most of us is that some people are so greedy they aren't satisfied with what they've got and they want to take more than their fair share. That's the problem, it just leads nowhere but trouble.' Once more Melie showed an astonishing degree of maturity and insight for her age.

'Do remember though,' added Fergus, 'that in Theirworld, which is your world, there is great imbalance. There is unfairness and unevenness where many, many people have very few material comforts and very few opportunities in life, whereas for others the opposite is true. That is the root of the problem. That is why the whole ethos of Hedge is one of harmony and cooperation ... we have always striven to keep everything fair and in this way prevent a situation where malicious thoughts thrive and prosper. Always.' He picked up his glass from the table, finished off his juice and then looked down at the sleeping meerkat for a moment. 'We just want our Stone back,' he whispered.

Melie now rose and joined Connell by the window, considering using her thinking voice but stopping short as she realised that Fergus would be able to tune in to their telepathic conversation. Instead, she caught Connell's eye and twitched her head to indicate she wanted him to follow her. They walked around the room as though exploring together but just feigning interest in various items dotted around the place. On one wall hung a large painting of a box hedge intertwined with firethorn, the leaves and branches very realistically represented by the skilled artist. They recognised the hedge as the one through which they'd entered Hedge as they noticed the large hole near the top with bright blue butterflies flittering around it. The pink Corridor entry or exit point through which they'd arrived earlier, with its intricately inscribed metallic dial occupied another wall, whilst the wall opposite the fireplace was completely filled with bookshelves. Standing near the bookshelves was a wooden lectern with a large leather bound book resting open upon it. As if by magic, sentences in black ink were just appearing on the page as if handwritten by someone invisible and in a hurry. Each sentence remained for a few moments and then faded but new script was coming through continually so that there were always five or six lines on the page. It was as if the invisible writer were recording the proceedings of something happening somewhere else. From time to time, a completely separate manuscript would appear on a different part of the paper and in a different colour. In the few short moments that Melie stood beside the lectern, she noted that three different colours, indicating three different invisible writers were busily working away.

'That's totally weird Connell, look at that,' she whispered, pointing out the book with a discreet nod of the head as Fergus continued to brood over the missing Stone in his rocking chair. 'Tell you something else that's weird,' she added. 'This business about everything being too perfect in Hedge. I mean I know we're in another world but they seem to be trying too hard to keep everything squeaky clean.'

'I know. Last time I was here it was just the same,' whispered Connell as he looked at the open pages, trying to read what was being written. 'We all felt the same, well, all except my sister. She really warmed to the place and as far as she was concerned it really was the perfect place ...' His voice tailed off as his thoughts turned to his lost sister and Melie remembered that he was rather hoping she was here in Hedge. 'I'm not saying there's anything wrong with Hedge; it's just that I think they're trying to make it too perfect that's all,' he concluded. 'It's not a bad place.' They both looked at the book again, struggling to decipher the script as it came and went.

'Fergus, who are the invisible writers?' asked Melie. Fergus rose and joined them at the lectern.

'Ah yes, The Script,' said Fergus. 'Well you know I carry a meerkat scribe in my pocket, although she is resting just now.' He looked fondly at the little creature snuggled beside the fireplace. 'In Hedge we believe that everyone should have the opportunity to know what is happening at all times. There are four meerkat scribes still in existence in Hedge, as I believe Sanguinella mentioned, and these are carried by The Governance which consists of myself and three other citizens charged with the safeguarding of the people's interests.' He picked up the heavy book and pointed to the blue script as it appeared and disappeared. 'See here, this is coming through from Fooze Williamson. It looks like she is meeting with Hedgerangers outside the home of Henrietta Couch, Sanguinella's younger sister. Well I say young but she has lived for around one hundred and seventy of your years. That is considered middle aged here in Hedge. It seems that they are checking the house for any sign of the elder sister after yesterday's proceedings outside Barnaby Sticks Biscuits.'

'Oh I think I get it,' said Melie. 'Just as your meerkat was writing down everything that you said, Fooze's is writing down everything that she says, is that it?'

'That is so, Amelia North,' replied Fergus. 'In this way everyone in Hedge can be fully informed of the activities of The Governance as those activities unfold. Amelia, is everything alright?' Melie's attention had wavered just for a moment, as if she was aware of another presence. She'd felt her Da was somehow there in the room with them, looking at The Script.

'No, I mean yes,' she replied. 'I'm alright ... really. I just thought ... Da ... but it couldn't be. What was that you were saying Fergus?'

'Everyone can access The Script in their own books in their own homes at any time, although I'm not sure that everyone reads it,' Fergus continued. 'Ah look, just there in red, that's Quartz Munro coming through now. It looks like he's in Futhark. Oh dear ... '

'What is it Fergus?' asked Connell, trying to read the hurried red script.

'Lavender,' replied Fergus gravely. 'It would appear that Lavender the so-called healing cat has been seen in Futhark and a crowd are in pursuit just at this moment.'

Melie was really quite alarmed at the prospect of Billy and the gang of kids at large in Futhark. Lavender's presence would surely mean that Sanguinella was not too far away. Even so, she couldn't resist lingering on the pun of the crowd in *purr suit* of the cat and although she tried to keep it to herself, she did notice Connell's fleeting smile.

'Is Sanguinella there Fergus?' she asked. 'What does Quartz Munro have to say about that? Are they going to be okay?'

'Amelia,' he replied in reassuring tones, 'I can absolutely guarantee that the Solace placed by the Hedgerangers yesterday means Sanguinella will never enter Futhark. A Solace is binding and unbreakable and will never be lifted.' Despite Fergus' assurance, Melie couldn't help worrying about her friends and hoped the Hedgerangers were on their guard. She began, though, to turn her thoughts to The Stone and its recovery and went over in her mind a few key questions to ask. Connell was incubating one particular question to ask Fergus but he was saving that till later. It was about his sister. The three of them returned to their seats by the French window and Connell topped up the glasses with juice. The meerkat stretched out a long yawn and then settled back down to her deep sleep.

'Okay,' said Melie, 'The Stone. I understand why you need it back in Hedge, so that it's safe from the Malevolents and you can use it to pour Hedge's goodness into our world, Theirworld I mean. But what does it look like and where do you think it will be? And why is it me who has to find it?'

'Good questions Amelia, as I would expect from you,' said Fergus. 'Well it is quite a remarkable artefact. It is shaped like a large egg and ... as a matter of fact I have seen a game being played in Turley Holes on one of my visits in the persona of firefly. The players used a ball shaped a little like a ...'

'Rugby!' exclaimed Connell. 'You mean rugby. They use a ball shaped a bit like an egg. Don't like the game myself though, never did. Is The Stone about the size of a rugby ball then?'

'Somewhat smaller Connell,' replied Fergus. 'Like a rugby ball but flattened at one end so that it can stand on a surface. Or perhaps it would be best described as a large egg.' He paused as he searched for an exact comparison and then continued. 'Perhaps like that of an ostrich. I can describe its appearance but cannot be certain about what exactly it is made from. It is a kind of rock and quite heavy. Opaque yet at the same time almost translucent and transparent in places with what appear to be infusions of gold and striations of a black crystal inside.' Fergus was growing quite emotional about the lost Stone and Melie thought it must hold great power and significance in Hedge. Out came the crimson handkerchief with which he wiped a tear from his cheek before continuing, once again airing Melie's thoughts just as he had on their first meeting in Turley Holes. 'Such is the power and significance of The Stone. Please, forgive my tears ...'

'Fergus, it's okay ... really,' said Melie. 'Isn't it Connell?'

'Yes, it sure is,' he said. 'Come on Fergus, tell us more about The Stone, you're doing really well.'

'They say it glows. They say it can light up the darkest of places and illuminate the night sky,' he whispered. 'As for where it is now, well there have been great deliberations over the years and many wise citizens of Hedge have pondered that very question. There are those who say that The Stone will return and those who say it is lost forever. And Amelia, it is not for me to say why it is you and you alone who are entrusted with the quest to bring The Stone back but you will learn very soon, very soon.' He took up the handkerchief once more, wiped his flustered brow and then drained his glass in one go.

There were many other questions in Melie's mind. Why was the ground much lower in Hedge than in Theirworld? Was there a different timescale here compared to Turley Holes? Why had Billy been in Theirworld for so long? Why did Connell keep receiving messages from someone in Hedge? What wrongdoing had been committed by the people who eventually drifted out of solid form and became Malevolents? Did Malevolents cause the disappearance of Tiny's dad? What was the inexplicable understanding that sometimes passed between the kids, just as with Da and his friends? And as she gazed out of the French window, she wondered just how big Hedge was. Was it just one huge place, or did it have countries. As she looked down the blossom carpet, she saw two women walking towards the house, one of whom looked vaguely familiar.

'Fergus, who are those two?' she asked.

'Ah,' he replied, donning his topcoat once again and gently shaking the meerkat into wakefulness before placing it and the writing paraphernalia into his pocket. 'Connell, the one in violet is Polly, your sister and Melie, the one with the meerkat in her pocket is Maeva, our leader, your mother.'

Chapter Fifteen

Explanation, Meetings and Exploration

A satisfying ring from a bell on a bouncy spring announced the arrival of the first customers at Barnaby Sticks Biscuits in Futhark that morning. The door had swung open into the shop and had clattered against the little brass bell, giving a certain old-fashioned charm to the proceedings as Billy and the gang of kids trooped in. Davis and Mavis remained outside as for some reason they weren't particularly interested in the wonderful confectionary within. The Hedgerangers' diet seemed to consist mainly of tea, bananas on toast and more tea as observed at breakfast and in conversation on the walk from Pink Shutters. Once the doorbell had tinkled to a standstill, the shop was very quiet inside. The ticking of a clock was the only sound and strong sunlight from the windows illuminated a billion specks of dust, which twinkled as they hovered in mid-air. An ancient wooden counter dominated the room, its top worn smooth by countless eager transactions over the years. The shop till which sat on one end of this counter was an imposing antique with intricately patterned metal casing. It had an enticing array of black numbers set into circular ivory keys, which looked certain to resound with a hearty kerching when pressed to pop up the price in the little window at the top. Behind the counter the wall was almost completely taken up with haphazard shelves bearing glass jars of the most amazing sweets, some of which the kids had never seen before. There was a doorway which seemed to lead into a room behind the shop, with a door screen in strips of brightly coloured plastic. Most of the floor space in the centre of the room was taken up with a low table overflowing with dishes, plates and domed glass cake stands which themselves were piled high with delicacies. Dozens of varieties of biscuits, small cakes iced in every pastel shade imaginable, meringue nests stuffed with mouth-watering combinations of summer fruits, pies, pastries, tartlets and turnovers. The large windows were set with silver platters of chocolate creations so tantalisingly displayed that passers-by would find it impossible to resist. Customers flocked to Futhark's most popular shop in their droves according to Billy, who was clearly excited to be back in his favourite haunt. He just couldn't stop hopping from one foot to the other and twiddling the end of his beard, which seemed even less yellow than the previous day, as he pointed out old favourites and top recommendations.

But it wasn't just the goods on sale that made the shop so popular; the proprietor was quite an attraction too as the visitors were about to find out. The rattle of the plastic door screen announced the arrival into the shop of a very small man who stepped up onto a low wooden stool at the end of the counter next to the till. He wore a dark blue and white striped apron over a collarless white shirt buttoned up to his neck. A pair of circular, gold framed glasses perched on the end of his nose and seemed to magnify his eyes out of all proportion to the rest of his features. A bushy black moustache obscured his upper lip and the crown of his bald head gleamed as if polished vigorously with a duster. It was as though he was about to give a performance.

'Good morning!' he chirped. 'Welcome to Barnaby Sticks Biscuits, the finest establishment in Futhark if not in the whole of Hedge!' His pronunciation, along with his appearance, had a distinctly French flavour. 'My name is Fenouille. Fenouille de Groix. I am happy to be of service to you today.' He paused as if expecting applause and then almost tumbled off his stool when he noticed an old friend amongst the group. 'Can this be?' he cried, 'Gracious me, is that really you?' The kids looked around and Jam Sandwich Schultz nodded, then shook his head and then looked puzzled until he realised Fenouille was talking to Billy.

'Fenouille!' cried Billy. 'My old friend, it's been such a long time since I've had the pleasure of walking through these doors!' He strode over to the stool and gave his old friend an affectionate hug and then a kiss on each cheek. 'Fenouille de Groix! Yes, it's been years and years!' said Billy as he stood back and looked the Frenchman up and down a couple of times. 'But you're looking as youthful as ever! Tell me, what's your secret?' To Luke, Tiny Page and the Schultz kids, this seemed to be turning into a replay of an old ritual between the two men. Fenouille stepped down from his stool, shuffled over to the low table and picked up a plate of cream sandwich biscuits, which he made a show of offering ceremonially to Billy with a low bow.

'It is these,' he cooed dramatically, as though imparting a slice of top secret inside information. Breakfast on three of these every day and you too could look like me!'

'Barnaby Sticks Biscuits, my favourites,' Billy drooled. He took one and bit into the crunchy biscuit with obvious delight. 'Fenouille, I almost forgot! You must forgive me, I haven't introduced my friends.' One by one, the gang of kids were ushered before Fenouille who shook their hands enthusiastically as Billy spluttered out their names between mouthfuls of biscuit. He explained they were just visiting Hedge as guests of Fergus Wiseman and were friends of

Amelia North who was about to embark on the search for The Stone.

'Ah yes, Melie North,' said Fenouille, 'that poor girl from yesterday. I read all about it in The Script, you know, the incident with Sanguinella Couch and the Hedgerangers. Nasty business, and right here in Futhark and in food fair week too! I must say I have been wondering about that woman and her cat for some time now. Never really trusted her you know. She's nothing at all like her sister. Very much like her mother though.' He turned his attention to the table full of delicacies once again. 'Children, do forgive me, how rude! What would you care to try this morning? Help yourselves!' The gang made their selections and settled themselves down on the floor to eat as Billy followed Fenouille into the back room for a chat and a cup of tea.

'We may be some time children. Lots to catch up on and lots of biscuits to sample,' said Billy. 'Why not have a wander with Davis and Mavis and I'll see you back here in an hour or so?'

'Yeah, that's fine,' replied Tiny Page. 'We'll be okay, see you later.' After they'd eaten, the gang of kids left the shop and went off with the Hedgerangers down the street, now a hive of activity as the town's inhabitants buzzed about their daily business.

'I'd forgotten about the food fair,' said Alexander. 'Fergus told us about it when we came through the hole, remember? Wonder if they'll have any Jam Sandwiches?'

'Yes of course I remember, Crate Boy!' replied his brother Jam, a little miffed at his brother's teasing. 'Anyway, it looks like that's it over there.' He pointed along the street to a widening in the road where masses of colourful tents had attracted a large crowd of Futhark townsfolk. The tents reminded the kids of circus big tops, although much smaller but just as brightly striped. Amongst these larger tents were a number of tipis draped in canvases, which radiated white in the morning sunshine. Wood smoke drifted lazily skywards from the openings at the top of every cone, each of which was festooned with brightly coloured ribbons just waiting for a breeze to come along and set them flapping. To the visitors Futhark presented an amazing spectacle. For a start, it had something of a medieval feel to it. The houses and buildings were mostly timber framed with upper storeys that jutted out into the street, almost touching in one or two places. Sammy noticed a pair of neighbours sharing a cup of tea across the small gap between their upstairs rooms, one reaching across to refill the cup of the other from a large teapot as they chatted. Houses and shops were placed alongside each other all along the street in a haphazard arrangement, which gave a real sense of community. It occurred to Molly that this was not as weird as it seemed, you wouldn't have to walk far to the shops. And you'd be happy to do just that for shops like these, with their colourful, enticing windows and welcoming open doors. There were cake shops, grocers, clothes shops, toyshops, cafés and shops selling fruit and vegetables which spilled out onto the pavement in magnificent displays on low shelves and wooden barrels. There were shop windows where people were seated on little stools knitting away furiously to make the colourful mohair jumpers which were sold there.

'Hey, Melie's got a jumper a bit like that,' observed Jam Schultz. Some shops seemed to specialise in the most wonderfully imaginative hats, which came in all shapes and sizes, displayed in the windows on life-like porcelain heads. There were feathered hats and bowler hats in any colour except black. There were wide brimmed hats of straw, tall top hats, short top hats, hats with veils and hats with flowers.

Hat makers stood at the doorways, some wearing hats and some not, but all were busily stitching adornments onto their creations with all the panache of true artisans. As if that wasn't enough, every single one of the porcelain heads was alive with conversation, smiles, grins, nods, winks, frowns and grimaces, exchanging pleasantries with anyone passing within earshot or gossiping about passers-by just out of range. The kids were transfixed by the commotion in the hat shop windows; it wasn't the kind of thing they'd grown used to in Turley Holes!

Customers and residents teemed in and out of these shops and houses; no one seemed in much of a hurry. Up and down the street they walked, chatting away to each other or in some cases to themselves. One woman was loping around the place in a comical fashion as if imparting the latest news to seemingly randomly selected listeners. She wore an old cream overcoat down to her knees and buttoned up to the collar, long light blue football socks and brown shoes. Above the hubbub, the kids could hear her French accent loud and clear as she babbled on.

'They are not going to arrest me yet. Oh no, they will never catch me, not this year and maybe not the next. But who knows, eh?' She danced across to another startled pedestrian and leaned over to whisper in his ear. 'I will see you tomorrow, as long as they don't arrest me. Arrest me, Skittish Matilda! What do you think of that? Anyway, I will see you again tomorrow.' She twirled around graciously towards yet another bemused shopper and made sure he was well aware that her arrest was not imminent either now or in the future, just in case he had any doubts on the matter. The children were quite bewildered by all this.

'What's she going to be arrested for?' Tiny asked Davis.

'Oh, don't worry about that,' he replied. 'Skittish Matilda

has been behaving like that for years and years. We all think she's lost her marbles somewhat. It's probably down to her diet; she's taken to eating nothing but sprout soup since her poor husband died last month, and he himself ate it all his life. He wasn't the most popular amongst the good townspeople of Futhark; that most maligned of vegetables can have disastrous consequences, if I may be so bold.' All Tiny could manage by way of reply was a barely suppressed giggle at the image Davis had painted. Luke pointed out a very tall man in a short top hat striding along the street very purposefully indeed, taking the odd biscuit or small sandwich from platters proffered by one or two of the food sellers standing outside their shops as if waiting for him. Never once did he stop to chat or to thank them, instead he just carried on striding, craning his neck now and again as though searching for someone.

'Ah, that is Montague,' said Mavis. 'He walks everywhere and never stops, apart from the obvious bathroom necessities. Never even sleeps!'

'Montague,' pondered Sammy. 'That's an unusual name, what do you think Molybdenum?'

'You could say that … Samphire!' replied Molly, fuming. She would never let it show, but at Teasing Time Molly always wished she was the one who'd been named after a sea vegetable instead of her twin. She'd grown tired of explaining the meaning of Molybdenum to her new friends in Hedge; this was never easy at the best of times.

'Never sleeps,' added Davis. 'You will have noticed the generosity of the shopkeepers. See how they are giving him food and drinks. Well that is how he sustains himself. They all expect him at certain times and he is never late, never early. In fact if you watch him closely you'll see what I mean.' Sure enough, shopkeepers appeared in the doorways of their shops with their offerings at the precise moment that Montague arrived there and then they disappeared inside as soon as he'd swept the sustenance from the platter and carried it off. It reminded Luke of marathon runners he'd seen on television grabbing drinks from a table as they ran past.

'Children,' announced Mavis. 'You simply have to visit the chai tent, it's our favourite! Would you mind?'

'No, no, not at all,' replied Molly. 'It's the least we can do, you've been so kind to look after us and show us round. Where is it then? What's a chai tent?'

'It is this one just here at the start of the food fair,' explained Davis, 'the one with the fire.' The kids were thrilled to see a lovely log fire burning away under a large canopy striped in red and white. It was supported by a wooden pole in each corner and a longer one in the middle of each of the shortest sides so it was pitched like a roof. The fire burned on the ground right in the centre and the smoke twisted upwards and then separated into twin plumes before drifting out under the eaves to dwindle into the morning air.

'Bet Melie would have been able to name the wood they're burning to make that kind of smoke,' said Alexander who was quite taken with the twin plumes. Around the fire were what appeared to be bales of straw with tailor made covers in thick fabric and on these, the seated customers were drinking from large mugs. Two sooty and perspiring waiters in leather aprons busied themselves with tending the fire, stirring the contents of the large copper urn and replenishing the customers' mugs with the obviously popular drink. Ushered by the Hedgerangers the gang settled down beside the fire and immediately felt its relaxing influence. They were all served steaming mugs of chai and as they sipped away, each one of them decided it was the loveliest drink they had ever tasted. The fire crackled and glowed, the light smoke fuzzed lazily skywards and the children were mesmerised by the peaceful mood in the tent. They reflected a little on what they'd seen in this fascinating town and in this fascinating world so far. They'd forgotten about why they were here and about the enormous task they faced. They'd even forgotten that they were in a different world from the safety and security of their families.

'Hello children, there you are!' boomed Billy as he squashed himself into a little gap between Luke and Sammy on a hay bale, much to Sammy's disappointment but to Luke's and Tiny's relief. 'I see you have found the chai tent! Best part of the food fair, that's what I say. Look, I've brought you all a packet of biscuits.' He was just in the process of handing out the small packets when their heads were turned by a noisy crowd dashing past the tent in pursuit of a small grey cat. Luke sprang to his feet.

'Billy, we need to get out of here,' he said calmly. 'Let's get back to Pink Shutters and then on to Chowk.'

Chapter Sixteen

Demons, Revelations and Igneous Intrusions

The crackling fire in Sanguinella's hearth warmed the room and cast an eerie glow across the ornately framed portrait on the chimneybreast. After the incident with the Hedgerangers, she was glad to be back in Gush and safe within her own four walls once again. The venomous sneer she had unleashed upon Melie earlier that day had taken its toll and weakened the woman's spirit, yet as she reflected on the comings and goings of the past few days, her resolve strengthened. The Stone would come into the possession of the Couch family no matter what. Mordechai Fern's miserable life had been swept away by the cruel hand of the woman in the portrait for refusing to reveal its location all those years ago. The only killing since the beginning of time, Fern's dismissal had simply delayed the discovery of The Stone and with the arrival of this so-called Child of Destiny, Sanguinella's moment of glory grew ever closer. She was thankful that Fergus Wiseman's interference in events had brought the girl into Hedge where it was only now a matter of time before she would reunite the treasured artefact with its rightful owner. Everything was unfolding according to plan, yet if it were necessary to kill once more then that consummate pleasure could be handed over to The Malevolents who would delight in ensuring the foolish child's death was particularly slow and agonising. The fire quickened, as though feeding upon Sanguinella's dark thoughts and as it did so Desdemona's eyes brightened in her portrait and turned to meet her daughter's adoring gaze. Sanguinella reached out her blackened palm and stroked lightly across the nameplate below the frame, at which the central letters glowed a vivid red and spelled out the word *demon.*

'You have done well my faithful daughter.' The words were uttered by the portrait's unmoving lips and sounded remarkably powerful for a woman speaking from beyond the grave. 'Your reward grows ever closer as those around you play into your hands. In time The Stone will be in the possession of the Couch family and balance can be restored by my rightful heir.' Sanguinella remained transfixed by her mother's eyes, heartened by her words of encouragement and positively thrilled at the prospect of finally denouncing Maeva and taking over her position as supreme ruler. With The Stone in her possession, her long held dream would at last become an exquisite reality.

'My mother,' whispered the daughter, 'all is well and all will be well. At this very moment Lavender tracks the child's companions through the streets of Futhark and through her eyes I can see they are about to make for Chowk where she and Connell Brown are no doubt preparing to meet their long lost relatives. Fergus Wiseman has done well to disguise his yearning to possess The Stone for himself as a well-intended exercise in destiny fulfilment!'

'That is splendid, my child!' cooed Desdemona. 'And what of the Enlightened Ones, are they about to live up to their pathetic title and learn the true meaning of supreme wisdom? What turmoil have you in store for them once captured and brought to bow before you?' Desdemona's voice was brimming with barely contained glee at the prospect of the parents' looming demise.

'During the past hour of Theirworld time they have been trailed by the Malevolents from their village to the Powder Mill,' said Sanguinella. 'It is a complete mystery to me how they have successfully gained entry. I suspect some involvement on the part of Maeva and those renegades Mungo Cheeseman, Moo Gabrielle and of course my precious sister.' Sanguinella's words trailed off into brooding resentment at the thought of Henrietta's shift of allegiance all those years ago, a hatred of which their mother was well aware.

'Sanguinella, my favoured child,' she cooed, 'that woman will soon be of no further concern to you. In your moment of triumph, your sister must endure the traitors' humiliation and endure it for as long as you allow her to make the choice between banishment to Oblivion and death at the hands of The Malevolents. There is nothing in her power, nor is there anything in her possession that can stand in the way of your glory.'

'My dear mother,' Sanguinella's eyes moistened just a little as she spoke, 'my only wish is that you were beside me to share in our majesty as we, the Couch family, fulfil our birth right and rule supreme.'

'This is your time, my child,' replied the portrait. 'Grasp your destiny with strength of spirit. Let no one stand in your way. Eliminate those who would seek to destroy you and eliminate them cruelly. I will watch over you with pride in all that you do my daughter. And remember, without passion there is no power.' The demon letters faded back into her name and Desdemona's eyes resumed their silent vigil once again. All was quiet, save the settling of the dwindling embers in the grate.

***

Through the French doors, Melie watched Connell as he rushed down the blossom-strewn lawn towards his long lost sister. They stood before each other for just a moment and then hugged in a fond and lasting embrace that oozed love and affection. It was thirty-two years since they'd lost each other and they had plenty to talk about as they walked arm in arm down the Greenbanks garden.

'He hasn't cut that plait since the day he lost her,' Melie mused as she watched them walk away, perhaps subconsciously delaying the moment when she and her mother were to meet. When they did, there were no embraces and the awkwardness of the moment took both of them by surprise. Melie's childhood had been filled with expertly handled adventures of the most extraordinary fashion, not least the one unfolding in the quest for The Shining Stone. Yet this unexpected meeting with her mother Melie found difficult to come to terms with. At least proceedings would go unrecorded as May took the quill from her meerkat scribe and placed it out of reach inside her coat. The two of them smiled nervously as they met and then Melie held out a hand in the traditional gesture of friendship, which May accepted warmly without letting go.

'I remember that jumper,' said May. 'It looks good on you, but always a bit tight on me. Your Da gave it to me when we ...' She paused for a moment and looked away. 'Punks wore mohair jumpers back then.' Another awkward pause followed, during which May swallowed hard as though suppressing tears. 'We were young; kids really.' May released Melie's hand and reached out to touch her face but Melie backed away and looked down at the blossom carpet, which she scuffed lightly with her foot. May lowered her hand and looked towards the house, then back at her daughter whose arms were folded tightly around each other as though trying to keep warm on a miserable day.

'Melie, don't you want to ask me anything?' asked May. 'Look, I'll ...'

'It still smells of you,' interrupted Melie. 'You know, from before. I remember what you smelled like. But I couldn't remember what you looked like. Without a photo I mean.' She paused, looked directly into May's eyes and said coolly, 'I was young, a baby really.' Their eyes met, both welling with tears and then Melie rushed to hold her mother for the first time in nearly nine years. 'How are you here?' she cried. 'Why did you leave? I've tried to understand. I don't know who you are now, you were my mum.' Melie held on tightly as she blurted out questions. She didn't really expect May to answer, not just yet. Not now that she'd found her mum after all these years and they were holding each other and being together at last.

'I guess you're not really expecting an answer right now Melie, but I'm going to give you one. It's important.' May aired Melie's thoughts in the same way that Fergus had done so often since they'd first met in the street in Turley Holes. This came as no surprise at all to Amelia North. 'One thing I will say is this,' continued May. 'The only certainty in life is that everything exists in a state of flux and the sooner you learn that the better.' She eased away from their embrace and took her daughter's hands in her own. 'I have asked myself a thousand times over how I could have left you and Da back then. It's just inconceivable that I could have done it. No one could possibly understand. I couldn't. But I just had to go.'

'Okay,' said Melie, holding her mother's gaze. 'Why though? And what's this Maeva thing all about?'

'Well like I said, life is a constantly changing force Melie,' said May. 'You do know that when we were young we all came into Hedge. There was Da. There was me. There was Connell and his sister Polly, The Captain, Posy and Lizzie Page. We were young and we were adventurous. A lot like you and the gang of kids really, but a bit older.' The two of them walked along the blossom carpet. May continued to fill in the missing pieces of the jigsaw as she stroked the scribbling meerkat gently between the ears. 'We'd all become friends of Billy Jackson who seemed to have been around Turley Holes forever as the resident interesting character,' explained Maeva. 'It was unusual that he allowed us to befriend him as he'd always been a bit of a loner. A hermit really and most people avoided him at all costs as though he was some kind of tramp.'

'That's how most people see him now back there, with his odd wellies and all that,' Melie added, surprised that she'd referred to Turley Holes as back there and not back home. 'We call his cottage the Eighth Wonder of The World. You should see it; it's just about falling down. And as for the inside ... oh, I suppose you have seen it, I forgot.'

'I know what you mean,' said May. 'It's cosy though, beside that fire. Does he still have Nettle? She must be getting on a bit now.'

'Yes,' replied Melie, laughing aloud as she added, 'although I think it's more a case of she has him. It's like that with cats isn't it? So you'd become friendly with Billy, then what?'

'Well he seemed to take a particular shine to me and at the time I had no idea why,' replied May. 'It became clear eventually though. And that's what I mean when I say life's in a state of flux. One minute I'm just May, the punk girl from Turley Holes and before you know it I'm Maeva, hailed as the forerunner of the prophesied Child of Destiny.'

'Did you say the prophesied Child of Destiny?' Melie

asked. 'Don't tell me, that's me isn't it? Fergus keeps on telling me it's my destiny to return The Shining Stone in my eleventh year. That state of flux thing, well you can say that again! It's all happening!' They had come to the end of the Greenbanks garden now and May leaned on the low fence while Melie sat on the top rail facing out over the common land in what she took to be the centre of Chowk. A large horse chestnut tree dwarfed the surrounding cottages and a few sheep grazed around and about on the grass. Melie was startled to see a cat stretch into wakefulness on a slatted wooden bench and then sit dazed and disorientated for a moment before hopping down and walking lazily away. She had to look twice, but was relieved to see that it was not Lavender.

'I now know that Billy had seen something in me that told him I was this forerunner as prophesied in ancient times,' explained May. 'Ancient Hedge times that is. He wanted me to come with him to the hole in the hedge, which I know that you are more than familiar with Melie. There was no way I was going on any adventure that did not involve my friends, especially Da. So to cut a long story short we ended up going through the hole with Billy, who'd given us bog rosemary.'

'What happened when you got in?' Melie asked. 'When we got in yesterday ... I think it was yesterday, I haven't quite grasped the timescale here yet. When we got in we were met by Davis and Mavis and then along came Fergus ... but I suppose you know all that.'

'Yes my child, I do know of this,' said May with an air of nobility in her voice that reminded Melie of the way Fergus spoke. 'We ourselves spent time with Fergus Wiseman and indeed took great delight in exploring around and about. We certainly made the most of our visit and met many interesting characters, although we were unsure of why we were in Hedge at all and eventually we decided that we should return to Theirworld, which is exactly what we did.' May's persona, Melie thought to herself, was becoming quite different to how she had appeared when their reunion had just begun on the blossom lawn.

'You are very perceptive, my child, and I in turn am very receptive to your thoughts as you now know,' May responded telepathically to Melie's observations.

'Yes, of course, I should have known you could read my thoughts. It's just the same with Fergus and Connell. Luke too, and now you,' replied Melie, in her own thinking voice.

'It is because,' said May, 'with all that has taken place, I have become Maeva and not May. I fulfilled the prophecy by returning to Hedge to seek one who had become lost and by doing so proved that I was able to move between worlds independently of any assistance from within.'

'I suspect the one who had become lost was Polly Brown,' guessed Melie. 'The story around Turley Holes for years was that she'd just disappeared when she was about twelve. My guess is that she stayed behind in Hedge instead of leaving with the rest of you. Maybe she was so taken with the place that she didn't want to leave and then went and found that she couldn't get out. Am I right?'

'Indeed you are, my child,' replied Maeva. 'Your Da may have told you he had dreams in which a young girl was calling out as if looking for someone. He used to think it was you searching for me. He will now have realised that it was me crying out for my lost friend. I returned to Hedge as May from Turley Holes to find Polly and I remained in Hedge as Maeva the prophesied forerunner and elected member of the Governance.' She looked down at the meerkat as if seeking reassurance of her status and noticed it had drifted off to sleep.

'I'm glad this is not all going in The Script,' smiled Melie, 'it's a bit too special for that.'

'It is special for me also, my child, for me also,' agreed Maeva. Melie smiled to herself. Here at last was someone who could justify calling her my child! Reading Melie's thoughts Maeva smiled and winked at her.

***

'We'll have to suppose it worked then', grumbled Da North as he lay there uncomfortably wet gazing at the cloudless blue sky. 'I'd always imagined Sardinia to be a little more glamorous. Is this it then or what?' The Dissolution had clearly taken them far away from the Powder Mill and it had dumped them rather unceremoniously in the middle of a stagnant pool where dozens of red dragonflies whizzed around, hovered and then whizzed again. Dripping with muddy water the others stood quietly, taking in their surroundings and readjusting sodden clothing in the baking heat. The pool was an overspill from a wide stream of clear water, which flowed down the middle of a much wider dry riverbed strewn with dusty, lichen encrusted pebbles. Here and there straggly clumps of willow held on as best they could, their roots scavenging under the surface to drink in the cool water. A few withering shrubs clung to the edge of the pool, their orange berries having largely dropped off into the mud to rot where they lay. Along the distant skyline a craggy ridge of limestone stretched as far as the eye could see. Closer at hand the landscape was swathed in woodland where the rasping sound of crickets in the trees broke the silence.

'This is it,' said Posy. 'That ridge is typically Sardinian.

It's oolitic limestone. There's loads of it around this part of the world. And you see that darker cliff just beyond the trees? Well that's an intrusion and it's probably dolerite. It's a sill actually, connected with the volcanic features around Southern Italy. You know ... sill ... igneous intrusion ...?' Her voice trailed off as she realised this level of geological knowledge was way beyond them. 'Didn't you listen at school?'

'Thank you Posy,' said Da as he dragged himself out of the mire and stood dripping in the sunshine. I do know dolerite is a type of rock but I'm afraid that's as far as it goes. I thought a sill was something cats sat on to make like they wanted back in. Geology is clearly more your thing than mine. But thank you anyway. So, we're in Sardinia. Why exactly?'

'It's the name I spotted on the wall back at the mill. Well I had to say something or who knows where we'd have landed?' Geo replied.

'He's right,' said Lizzie Page. 'Anyway, Sardinia's on that map for a reason. We've no reason not to believe May. Her letter said it's a map of entry points into Hedge. So it must be that there's one round here somewhere.' They all began scanning the immediate surroundings as if expecting such a location to be an obvious feature. Da spoke first.

'I don't think it's going to be that easy,' he said. 'Let's go up to that village and see how the land lies.' They hadn't noticed until that point, but clinging to a hillside close to Posy's dolerite sill there was indeed a village, perhaps more the size of a small town. Given their bedraggled state and the wearying heat, the prospect of refreshment and the chance to take stock was just what the doctor ordered.

Chapter Seventeen

Tortue and his Rabbit Stew

The village turned out to be larger than the explorers had anticipated. In the midday heat the narrow streets were deserted and the inhabitants sheltered inside their homes, presumably enjoying a long lunch followed by a siesta. Perhaps the houses were comfortable and well-ordered on the inside, but outward appearances suggested otherwise. Most of the town's buildings, whether houses, shops or eating establishments, were rather unkempt and really quite scruffy. Some window recesses bore splendid grilles of ornate ironwork but these were rusted. Most of the doors were impressively constructed and they sported intriguing iron knobs and knockers, not unlike the lion's head on the door of the Powder Mill. But now their peeling paintwork was obscured by fading posters and they had long since lost their glory. Wherever wooden beams featured on the facades, these were weather-beaten, warped and greying after countless decades of exposure to the unforgiving Sardinian sun. The explorers felt somewhat conspicuous as they made their way along the silent streets of smooth cobbles, watched from the walls by countless pairs of eyes. The exception to the town's scruffiness and its single most striking feature was the astounding array of paintings which adorned almost every wall. Paintings of people who they supposed were past inhabitants who had perhaps gained fame or notoriety for one reason or another. On closer inspection, most of the paintings were labelled with inscriptions and several of the subjects carried firearms of various shapes and sizes.

'These people,' whispered The Captain reverently, 'they're mostly bandits aren't they?' He remembered that bandits had been operating in parts of Sardinia as late as the nineteen sixties.

'Not all of them.' Posy's reply was equally hushed. 'That one's a bandit hunter. See the inscription?' She pointed discreetly to a gable end where a large painting of a fearsome looking woman frowned down upon the group. They walked along a little further, admiring the artwork yet feeling somewhat intimidated by the characters' brooding presence, until they came to a widening in the street. Ahead of them was what might be described as a central square, a misnomer that had always infuriated Geo the chorographer as such places were rarely square at all. Town circle, though, somehow didn't sound quite right and The Captain had grown to live with this irksome issue. In the middle of the square, at the widest point, a small fountain drizzled weakly into a circular pool with a low concrete wall upon which opportunist billposters had plastered notices dating back years. Posy the geologist pointed out that the fountain must be fed by a spring and the water would be fine for drinking. Slanting off to the right a small alleyway dipped steeply downwards and was lined with grey wheelie bins, around which a draggle of scrawny cats foraged for scraps. To the left the town square was terraced widely into three or four levels connected by broad stone steps and whilst this gave a distinct amphitheatre feel to the place, it was simply because the town was built on a steep hillside. The explorers sat down on the wall of the pool and Geo reached into his rucsac for a drink before remembering he'd drained it back at the Powder Mill. He was just about to refill the bottle in the fountain, when Posy silenced him with a shake of the head.

'Don't make it look obvious,' she whispered, feigning interest in one of the posters on the pool wall. 'Up there on the middle terrace in that doorway, there's actually a real human being in this place.' Trying to be discreet, they all looked around at the spot Posy described, where they saw a woman dressed in black sitting on a chair in a doorway smoking a long clay pipe. Her dark hair was scraped back severely and tied in a bun at the back of her head. Her face, even from a distance, gave the impression that she was deeply troubled about something. She contemplated the group for a while and then leaned back into the building as if calling for someone. Almost immediately, a man appeared beside her, blinking against the strong sunlight. He looked very striking with a small blond beard twisted into a single plait tied with a black ribbon. An eye patch covered his left eye and he carried a leather shoulder bag complete with hippy beads. Just like Melie's Bag of Tryx, Da noted. In one hand, he held a bottle of beer and in the other a red beret.

'I can't believe what I'm seeing,' gasped Da. 'That's Mungo Cheeseman. And isn't that woman Henrietta Couch?' Mungo beckoned the explorers to come and join the two of them at what now appeared to be a small taverna. In the blistering heat and with the purpose of their journey in mind, they could hardly refuse. As one, they gathered up their belongings and trooped up the wide stone steps linking the terracing. To be out of the oppressive heat was such a relief and the explorers settled down at a long table with their hosts. It was a tiny room and as their eyes became accustomed to the darkness of the interior, they noticed the quirkiness of the decor. The four walls were festooned with football club souvenir pennants from all corners of the globe; it must have taken years to accumulate all of these. No doubt, the owner was a keen follower of football and had amassed the collection by talking to visitors to his taverna over the decades. Impressed by his knowledge of the sport they would have been only too keen to send him a pennant from their local team once they'd arrived back home at the end of their holiday. Da was very impressed to see the exact pennant he'd had as a boy when he'd been a keen supporter of the local stars Leeds United. Da was the first to speak.

'Drinks all round then,' he said. 'What do you say Mungo? It is Mungo isn't it. You reckon they'll have any Irish in here?' It was false bravado; Da was nervous in this charismatic company. Even though they'd all met before it was a long time ago and he couldn't quite gauge the mood in the quirky taverna.

'You'll be meaning Irish whisky, will you not?' said Henrietta by way of reply. 'Well you'll find no whisky in this town. Not Irish, not scotch, not anything, not here. It is bad for you anyway. You should to give it up Da North, if you know what's good for you.'

'It's not a problem,' Posy joined in, as if keeping the peace, 'we'll have beers. Get them in Da'. The atmosphere was tense as everyone tried to make sense of the situation. Da signalled to the waiter who folded his newspaper and put it down on the bar before shuffling across to take the order.

'You'd better get one in for Moo, she's on her way,' said Mungo as he pulled up a chair which he sat on the wrong way round, resting his arms on the back.

'That's seven beers please,' said Da, 'and food all round, whatever you've got cooking.' The waiter, who must have been at least seventy or eighty years old shuffled back towards the bar in his carpet slippers with a grunt of acknowledgement.

'There goes a man of few words. Let's hope he understands English,' said Lizzie, trying to lighten the mood. 'Hello, I'm Lizzie. Lizzie Page. I don't know if you remember, but we have met before, in Hedge.'

'Yes, of course we remember you all,' confirmed Mungo. 'And I must say Geo Schultz; I have to admire your look. I think you borrowed it from someone I know very well!' They all looked at The Captain and then the entire company burst out laughing, for of course the two were dressed in an almost identical manner. As they waited for the refreshments to arrive, the visitors from Turley Holes explained how they had come to be in Sardinia. It felt somehow appropriate in the presence of Mungo and Henrietta to describe the events leading up to their departure from the Powder Mill earlier that day. After all, they'd all once been in Hedge and the two esteemed characters were citizens of that world. Dissolution powder, detailed wall maps and May's transformation from Turley Holes punk girl to a mysterious figure of some importance were matters the pair would believe and take seriously. It was when Da mentioned his daughter Melie and her gang on their journey into Hedge with Connell and Billy that Mungo became particularly interested.

'Da, your daughter, Amelia, do you understand the significance of her journey, the quest you speak of?' Mungo's tone was quite serious. Da was about to reply when Henrietta cut in.

'Your daughter, Da North, is the prophesied Child of Destiny,' said the old woman. 'Maeva, your May, is the forerunner and as such is now supreme leader of our world, which is Hedge. Time is short Da North. Time is nearly gone. Your daughter is embarking on a quest to return The Shining Stone in her eleventh year. That is the reason she is journeying with her companions.' A silence followed and hung in the air as the explorers pondered over Henrietta's explanation. The waiter shuffled over to the table and despite his old age had managed to carry seven bowls of rabbit stew balanced along his arms. It was good timing. Moo Gabrielle had just breezed in through the door to join them.

'Hello, everyone, I'm Moo. Moo Gabrielle,' she announced, buzzing around the group shaking hands with the visitors. 'Moo. It's short for Moutarde and Moutarde's mustard in French so I do prefer Moo. Actually, I get called Keys too, but that's another story. Pleased to meet you!' Moo was certainly a bundle of energy and seemed a good deal younger than the other two. Her appearance, though, was equally striking. Her faded jeans were fashionably ripped and barely held together by strategically placed safety pins of various sizes. She wore a blue and white hooped sailor's shirt that reminded Posy of the kind of thing burglars wore in storybooks. Her hair was plaited into one thick auburn pigtail that hung to the left. Her scruffy pinstripe suit jacket of the kind traditionally reserved for stockbrokers or politicians was now well past its best, but looked cool with a dazzling array of mismatched replacement buttons in all colours and sizes imaginable. Clipped to the leather belt around her waist was a huge bunch of keys that jangled as she danced around the room. A pair of odd trainers completed the picture. 'Looks like I'm just in time! Pass me the bread Da. Mmm, rabbit stew!' she spluttered as she blew onto a large spoonful to cool it down. 'I'll pay, I've got myself plenty of Euros,' she declared grandly and then, noticing the quizzical looks on the others' faces, added quickly, 'don't ask!'

'The kids would just love to meet you!' Da thought to himself as she slurped and dunked away contentedly.

'Well that might be sooner than you think Da North.' Henrietta had clearly read Da's thoughts and had replied in her own thinking voice, much to his amazement.

'You can read my mind! How can you do that?' Da thought straight back.

'You will find that it is not uncommon between citizens of Hedge and some from Theirworld. It can be a useful and conveniently secret way of communicating when the spoken word is less than appropriate,' was Henrietta's response as Da tuned in, intrigued. Here he was, miles from home joining in this grand adventure with friends and associates who shared common ground through experiencing the world of Hedge. He could communicate telepathically with a woman who must be at least a hundred and fifty years old. As if that were not enough, his lost wife had been revealed supreme leader of an entire world and his daughter a prophesied Child of Destiny! Da had clearly taken to the idea of telepathic communication like a duck to water, as he kept the telepathic communication going.

'Tell you what Henrietta; this is turning out to be the weirdest summer. Don't you think?' The woman didn't reply. Instead, she just smiled to herself as if to say she'd seen some weird summers of her own over the past century or so, journeying around the place with her companions looking for The Stone.

They savoured their meal and enjoyed the refreshing beer. Geo realised it had been a while since they'd eaten and was glad to be tucking into the delicious stew. As they dined, the visitors chatted freely about recent events and their hosts gave their interpretations as best they could. Henrietta showed grave interest in the moments leading up to their entry into The Powder Mill, especially the eerie silence and dark shadows in the trees. She seemed to shudder inside as if reminded or reconnected with something horrible from her past. Amongst the most intriguing explanations was that the waiter, who had looked very familiar to Geo, turned out to be a Watcher. Like Billy Jackson who had been round and about Turley Holes for as long as anyone could remember, Tortue de Groix was one of a dwindling number of Hedge citizens posted out into Theirworld to watch over the entry points to Hedge. They simply kept an eye on things and made sure the secret places remained secret and undisturbed. Tortue had been here in this village for a long time watching over the very pool from which Da and the others had emerged that morning. More than just a link between Theirworld and Hedge, reasoned Geo the chorographer, such locations could be part of an interlinked travel network. But like all crossover points between the two worlds this was slowly dwindling into non-existence and now the once crystal waters were reduced to stagnant mud. It wouldn't be long before this location was lost forever. Lizzie, who had been cradling the tourmaline crystal in her hand during these conversations now rose and walked to the small window, the only window in the room. She smiled as she noticed a vibrant African violet sitting there on the sill in a white pot.

'Connections,' she mused. 'All this is about connections isn't it?' She turned to face the group at the table. Tortue had come to join them and he sipped from a bottle of orange juice as she continued. 'We are all connected because we've been into Hedge as youngsters, where you all come from. We even met you when we were there. I mean just look at The Captain, it's not just coincidence that he's dressed like you Mungo is it?' She returned to the table and sat down next to Posy. 'All these places on the map in the Powder Mill and yours too Geo, are all connected. I guess you just need Dissolution Powder to make the journeys.' She fingered her crystal as she went on with her summation. 'You Da, May, Maeva I mean, or whoever, Melie, Billy, us, our kids, Connell ...' At the mention of Connell's name Lizzie directed a reassuring smile at the blushing Posy. 'You Mungo. Henrietta and Moo. You too I suppose Tortue. We are all connected. The Powder Mill as well. It's all one big web of intrigue but here's the big question; exactly what is the connection?'

'See this?' said Mungo as he held up a thick circle of glass framed with an ancient brass rim. 'This will help you to see why we're all in this.'

'And what exactly is that?' enquired Da.

'That,' replied Tortue in a distinctly French accent, 'is a curiosity circlet and it doesn't even belong to him, isn't that right Mungo Cheeseman?' Mungo held up the circlet to the few rays of sunshine that managed to filter in through the window. A billion specks of dust hovered and glittered in mid-air.

'No. I mean yes, you're right. I took it from Billy in Turley Holes last time we passed through there,' he admitted. 'Maeva was with us. We filled up that old suitcase in your place Da and gave The Powder Mill a bit of a makeover with ropes and paintings.' Mungo despatched Tortue off to the bar with the crockery and empty glasses. 'I mean, I know I shouldn't have taken it but Henrietta and I were onto something. We were about to get busy on a quest of our own and thought it be might be useful to take this little treasure along with us.' He handed the circlet to Da who examined it reverently before passing it to Posy for inspection. Of course neither one of them knew what to do with it. 'As a matter of fact,' Mungo continued, 'I'm pretty sure that was the night when ... well, forgive me Lizzie, but I think that was the night when your husband disappeared.' He paused, looking first at Moo then at Henrietta who took over.

'I am afraid to say Lizzie Page that it was not aliens who abducted your husband as we've heard tell about over the years here and there. In truth I am not even sure what aliens are, but that is by and by.' She paused, looked at her two companions and then carried on gravely. 'Tell me, have you heard of The Malevolents?' She went on to explain to Lizzie and her friends all about the terrible Airs and the fate of those unfortunates who got in their way. She told them they had probably been followed to The Powder Mill that morning by Malevolents who had spied on them from amongst the trees. These revelations did not sit well with the visitors. As the stark reality of real danger came to the fore, the warmth and cosiness of Da's kitchen seemed to fade into distant memory.

'With any luck,' joined in Moo Gabrielle, 'they won't have managed to work out your destination was Sardinia.' She absentmindedly spun the breadknife around on the table and watched until it clattered to a standstill. Moo seemed genuinely worried.

'That's a risk we can't take,' said Mungo after a while. 'Chances are they'll know. They'll have told her. They'll be on their way, and soon. They might even be here now.' The mood was taking a sombre turn in Tortue's small taverna. Just earlier, they'd been enjoying rabbit stew, laughing about the mysterious similarity in appearance between Mungo and The Captain. Right now, the revelations about Malevolents was putting a serious slant on the whole adventure. Henrietta was beginning to take control of the situation.

'We cannot leave,' said Henrietta. 'We must wait. My sister has many faults but she is very clever. She will not act; she will only follow until Amelia North leads her to The Stone. We sleep here tonight.'

The visitors were increasingly baffled by the conversation. Stone, what stone? And how exactly was Henrietta's sister involved? Was she one of The Malevolents? When was Melie going to lead them to this stone? Where was it? Not surprisingly, though, the chilling prospect of Melie at large somewhere in one world or another with Malevolents creeping around was weighing heavily on Da. Where exactly was his daughter right now? Reading his mind Henrietta aired Da's thoughts.

'You are wondering where your daughter is now,' said Henrietta. 'I think it is time for you to look into the curiosity circlet Da North.' She glanced at Posy who handed the circlet to Da. He grasped it in both hands and looked into the glass, beaming to himself as he saw his daughter with Connell in a sumptuously furnished room, standing beside a large book on a lectern. Beside them was a small man wearing a yellow brocade waistcoat. Da recognised him as Fergus Wiseman. He'd met him before, in Hedge and seen him in May's painting in the Mill. Da was sure he heard him say something about a crowd pursuing a cat. His joy on seeing Melie quickly dissolved as he sensed a looming danger through the glass, which shuddered violently and grew ice cold in his hands. For what felt like the first time ever, Da North was seriously worried for the safety of the gang of kids, especially his daughter. Without a word he handed the circlet back to Mungo and sat down at the table once more.

Chapter Eighteen

Circlets and Snorers

Fergus managed to accommodate the entire group at Greenbanks that night, although the sleeping arrangements were rather less comfortable than at Pink Shutters. Once they'd been delivered safely back to the tipi by Davis and Mavis, Billy and the kids had wasted no time in taking the Corridor and heading for Chowk. The adventure was rapidly taking a serious turn and everyone was hopeful that the Hedgerangers would manage to put Lavender off their trail. It was becoming clear that the quest had to get underway as soon as possible. But how to get started on a quest was something upon which none of the assembled company could seem to agree. Where to go first was the sticking point. Fergus was all for returning to Theirworld and looking for clues back at Melie's house. For some reason he seemed certain that they would find a crucial piece of the jigsaw right there in Turley Holes. Billy was not keen at all to leave Hedge now that he'd returned after so many years away. Connell flatly refused to go anywhere without Polly just when they'd become reunited. The Observant Jam Sandwich pointed out that the grown-ups were the ones wanting to have the final say. Luke and Tiny couldn't take their eyes off The Script. From time to time, they called out key points scribed by the meerkats in the pockets of Fooze Williamson and Quartz Munro. Luke found it amusing that Fergus' comments were appearing in The Script when he was right there beside them in the room. Molly found this a weird, childish attitude, whilst Sammy felt thwarted. She wanted Luke's attention all for herself but he only had eyes for the stupid book. The only ones who seemed to be making any serious progress were Maeva and Melie, who cradled the tourmaline crystal in her hand. The pair had settled themselves at the table near the fireplace and Maeva was sketching out a map on a large piece of paper. Much to the annoyance of her meerkat, she had borrowed its quill for this purpose.

'... And these points here, here and ... yes, here,' whispered Maeva, 'are some of the European entry points.'

'So it could be any one of these or any of the rest around the world,' Melie pondered. 'That's quite a lot to go at and like people keep saying, time is nearly gone. What do they look like, these entry points? I got the impression that they were all holes in hedges.'

'Well,' replied Maeva, 'most of them are. Some are just near hedges. Remember, it must be a mix of box and firethorn. The points themselves take many forms.' She remained in silent contemplation for long moments, and then continued. 'But of course many of these places are dwindling ... time is so short.'

The rest of the group continued to grumble away and the prospect of any agreement being reached grew less likely with each passing minute. Sammy had finally given in and was standing beside Luke trying to look interested in The Script. Tiny had decided to escape the indecision and he now sat cross legged in front of the French doors. Totally bored with proceedings he was reduced to breathing on one lens of his glasses and then holding it up to the sunlight. It was apparently much more fun timing how long the condensation from his breath took to clear from the glass.

Molly and her brothers were fiddling with the fire, loading it up with logs and prodding away with Fergus' poker. Melie was bursting to address Maeva as Mum but somehow this didn't seem right in the circumstances. She'd realised that they hadn't really talked much about Da, although she sensed that Maeva felt connected to him now that her daughter was here. Finally, she plucked up the courage.

'Mum,' she whispered, 'Da's okay. You know, he's alright. I mean to say, he does miss you.' She paused and looked up at her mother. 'You are my mum ... I just wanted to call you Mum.'

'I know, my child, my Melie. Amelia. A beautiful name for a beautiful girl,' said Maeva. She reached across and placed a hand on Melie's shoulder. 'I do so wish he were here so we could all be together again, you know that don't you?'

'I know,' replied Melie. 'It's just with all this going on and this map and these places. It all seems such a big deal. Why can't it just all be about getting our family back together? Why do we have to save the world?' Melie slumped back in her chair. She wanted to change the subject and talk about something else. Something that children all over the world had been talking about with their mums since time began; troubling dreams. It was a recurring dream that had been plaguing Melie from time to time in the weeks leading up to the quest. A mysterious man seemed to be looking for a hiding place on a rainy hillside. Dark shapes loomed out of the mist as if crowding in on him, only to be swept away by the storm. Then he was running through a long tunnel and a woman's laughter echoed all around. She wondered if the man was Da looking for his May, or maybe Connell looking for Polly. She even wondered if the laughing woman was Maeva. Maybe she would talk about it some other time.

She straightened up in her chair and looked intently at the map.

'You know, it's a bit weird,' said Melie

'What is?' Maeva asked.

'Da. Yesterday I was looking at The Script with Connell and Fergus and I felt that Da was there too,' Melie replied.

'You felt it? You're missing him aren't you?' whispered Maeva.

'No, well I mean yes of course I'm missing him,' said Melie. 'But it was more than just that. There was this weird vibration kind of thing, you know, just in the room. I don't think the others felt it.' Maeva sprang to her feet, beaming.

'That's it! Melie, that's it!' she cried, at which the rest of the party stopped what they were doing and turned to look. 'You say there was a vibration? And you say you felt Da's presence in the room?'

'Yeah, that's right,' replied Melie, 'Have I said something wrong?'

'No,' cut in Fergus. 'No, no, no Amelia North; you have said something absolutely right! Why didn't we see it before? It is preordained that Da and his companions are travelling already. I am right, am I not Maeva?' Maeva nodded enthusiastically. Melie was now on her feet with the rest of them.

'What, what is it?' she asked excitedly. Even the bored Tiny Page had jumped up to join them. At last, they seemed to be getting somewhere! Maeva smiled at Fergus, shaking her head.

'Why haven't we thought of this before?' said Maeva. 'Da has looked into a curiosity circlet and seen you Melie,' she said. 'That is what the vibration means. I don't suppose you've ever felt an Earth tremor, but that is what it feels like.'

'Right,' said Melie, 'so, if he's seen me … can we see him? Billy, have you got a curiosity circlet for me? Fergus told me to tell you I could take possession of one or something, but with all that stuff with the Air of Mystery I forgot all about it.'

'What? You've seen an Air of Mystery?' cried Maeva. 'Do you know how dangerous that could have been Melie?'

'Mum, don't worry, I got away,' Melie replied. 'Billy, have you got one then or what?' Melie was taking calm control of proceedings. All eyes fell upon Billy and though the awkward silence lasted only moments, each of the companions sensed something was wrong.

'Well,' he said, 'it's like this …' And Billy went into a long winded explanation of how he'd had it one moment and then he couldn't find it and maybe it had got mixed up amongst his boxes of plaques. He'd just decided to keep quiet about it because he knew how rare these things were and he was just a bit too embarrassed to tell anyone. Maeva looked at Fergus who raised his eyebrows.

'I think we can guess who has it, so it is fortunate that I myself and Maeva possess our own circlets!' announced Fergus, much to the relief of the group. Each one of them had already worked out that a circlet was a direct line of communication with Da. They were just one call away from a rendezvous with The Enlightened Ones!

***

'Will, you please do something about that snoring?' hissed Da when he could finally stand it no longer. In the half- light of the early hours, the dreadful sound seemed to amplify out of all proportion to a simple snore. It had been a very uncomfortable night in any case. Despite their tiredness from the rigours and revelations of the previous day, the travellers had hardly slept. If mattresses had featured on the primitive bunk beds rather than just plywood sleeping platforms, it might have been a different story. Still, at least it had been a rest. The sound didn't stop. Through the gloom, Da could just make out the dozing form of Moo Gabrielle seated in an armchair by the window here in the upstairs front room at the taverna. The woman had obviously managed to drift off to sleep once she'd finally realised that Malevolents wouldn't be stalking them just yet. The others were clearly having an uncomfortable time of things. The sound of creaking plywood, exasperated sighs and restless shuffling filled the room and just made things worse. Da was at the end of his tether. To add to his frustration he could now hear Tortue De Groix, clattering around in his kitchen and orchestrating as much noise as possible from the breakfast crockery and cooking paraphernalia. He was clearly an early riser, unlike Da. It felt more like bedtime than time to be getting up.

'Oh, please! Will you just shut up?' Da broadcast his plea around the room, in the hope that the snorer would receive it loud and clear. But still the snorer continued and with such a force that the whole bunk bed seemed to vibrate. That meant it must have been coming from up above! Mungo Cheeseman was the culprit! Da leapt off his platform, relieved to be on the vertical plane once more and he was just about to shake the sleeping Mungo into wakefulness when he realised the top bunk was empty. Empty apart from Mungo's bag on the rumpled bedclothes and this seemed to be the source of the annoying vibration. It wasn't snoring, it Mungo's curiosity circlet and someone was trying to make contact! Glancing around to be sure his companions were still asleep Da reached into the bag and gingerly pulled out the circlet. By now, he was wide-awake with anticipation, hopeful that it might be Melie on the other side of the glass. He glanced around again, just to be sure. This was important. Too important for any mistakes and it might be the only chance of finding out where in which world his daughter was waiting for him. The circlet's brass rim vibrated in his hands, but this time the metal remained pleasantly warm to the touch. Da steeled himself and then looked inside. What he saw took him completely by surprise. He saw a face looking straight back at him through the glass and it was his own. It wasn't a reflection, but an exact likeness, a twin almost, looking back and smiling.

'Not completely unexpected.' The voice from behind brought Da to his senses and he turned to see Mungo standing there. 'I always thought you'd be welcome in Hedge,' said Mungo. 'You and Maeva are alike in so many ways.'

'What do you mean welcome in Hedge?' Da asked, a little confused yet more awake than ever.

'You've seen yourself,' replied Mungo. 'That means you're welcome in Hedge. That means you could choose to live there, coming and going freely like a Hedge citizen. Well, for as long as the holes remain open anyway.' For long moments, Da looked into Mungo's deep blue eyes, trying to make sense of all that was happening to him. Then he remembered he was holding the circlet.

'That's all very well,' said Da, 'but what are we going to do about this? Maybe somebody's trying to make contact. It might be Melie. Will you have a look?' Mungo took the circlet and looked into the glass.

'Fergus Wiseman. I wondered if it might be you.' He glanced at Da, raising his eyebrows and subtly jerking his head towards the glass where Da supposed Fergus' face was staring out at the speaker. It was as if Mungo was trying to make some kind of unspoken comment about Fergus. The disdainful, eye-rolling kind of comment teenagers often reserved for unreasonable parents. Da felt a burning mistrust in Mungo's subtle gesture.

'I guess you'll be wanting to know where we are, am I right?' Mungo was wasting no time. He was getting straight to the point. 'Tell you what Fergus, why don't you let me have a little look-see who's there?' Fergus must have complied, because Mungo started craning his neck from side to side, having a good look around the room in which Fergus was standing. 'You'd better have a look at this Da. I think you might be pleased with what you see.' He handed the circlet to Da whose face lit up with joy when through the glass he saw Melie smiling back at him from the sumptuous room he'd seen her in yesterday. Standing beside her was his May, wearing a long dress in shades of green that oozed elegance and nobility. An entrancing array of simple jewellery adorned her ears and seemed to sparkle as though part of her being. The finely woven scarf around her shoulders was adorned with a single silver safety pin that harked back to the fashions of youth. Her golden hair, that remained just as short and spiky as Da remembered it, now seemed to radiate a silvery glow. Yet in Da's eyes she looked just the same as when they'd ruled the world around Turley Holes in their punk days. May the gentle artist and beautiful, adventurous young woman. He'd never stopped loving her since the day they met. Across the years of separation, Da North had always known they'd meet again somehow. Melie, their daughter, had brought them together at last in her quest for The Shining Stone. Neither spoke, content just to gaze and make some sense of what was happening. Mungo broke the silence, looking over

Da's shoulder into the glass.

'Maeva, it's good to see you my friend.' He nodded towards Da. 'Sorry about this bloke, he seems lost for words. Any idea who he is?' Mungo's joke was designed to break the ice and nudge the pair into action.

'I don't know what to say,' said Da. 'It's okay May. Everything's going to be okay. We're going to get to you. You're in Hedge aren't you? We went to the Mill. Melie's with you isn't she? We're all here. Well, not Connell; he's there too. How can we ... you know ...' His voice trailed off as he realised he was garbling. In contrast, Maeva remained just as calm and reassuring as she had always been when she replied.

'Da, I'm sorry,' she said. 'I think you understand how I feel and why I had to go. Nothing stays the same. I've missed you and wished that things could have stayed as they were a thousand times over. But that's all done now and we're moving on.' She ushered a smiling Melie into the picture and placed one arm around her shoulder. 'We're going to be together again, the three of us.' Mungo, who had tactfully stepped aside during these few tender moments cut in once more.

'Maeva, the time has come now hasn't it?' he said. 'Your daughter Amelia North is The Child. Time is short. We've searched for many years but there's been nothing. We need to work together. We can help. Henrietta's got something important. The girl has to get here and get here fast, to Sardinia. Tortue's place. Use powder, the hole's just about still open.' He took the circlet from Da who seemed to be in a happy daze and he looked deep into Maeva's eyes. 'And Maeva, be careful,' Mungo added. 'There are those whose hearts bear ill and who are not what they seem. I advise you to stay in Chowk and watch carefully. Keep Polly Brown with you, there's a reason.' The glass clouded over and the communication was at an end. The rest of the companions were beginning to wake up around the room, stretching and yawning in the early morning light. They were oblivious to all that had just happened. Mungo shouldered his bag and slotted the circlet back inside, taking Da by the arm and leading him downstairs.

'Tortue! What's cooking? Big day today.' Mungo seemed happy at the prospect of what the day held in store as he and Da sat down. 'Up already Henrietta? I guess you've twigged what's happening. Ah, coffee! Colombian I hope. Thanks Tortoise.' Henrietta, who looked less troubled than usual, was seated by the window smoking her long clay pipe. From the papers on her lap, it looked to Da as if she'd been reading some kind of old letter. She looked across at Mungo and smiled.

'She is coming,' was all that she said. In dribs and drabs, the rest of the company came downstairs to join the breakfast table. They helped themselves to the food on offer and tucked in contentedly, most of them bleary eyed and not quite awake. After a while, the delicious Colombian coffee served by their host began to work its magic and Geo was the first to speak.

'Can't believe we're up and about at this time!' he yawned. 'What is it, five o'clock or something?'

'Or something,' joked Da. 'It's four thirty.'

'Four thirty?' groaned Posy. 'What's going on? I thought sleeping was a big deal around here judging by yesterday's siesta. Pass me a biscuit Geo.' The Captain reached across and took a half-eaten packet of biscuits. He was just about to hand it to his friend when he noticed they were Barnaby Sticks Biscuits.

'That's where I recognise you from Tortue!' he chirped,

you must be Fenouille's brother; Fenouille De Groix, in Futhark, at that shop! I remember now, he makes these fantastic biscuits. You tuck in Posy, they're great!' At the back of his mind, Geo thought he'd seen another pack of the biscuits not that long ago. But he couldn't remember where, it didn't matter really. Lizzie had been right though; there were connections of all shapes and sizes in this adventure.

'Anyway, who was that snoring last night? And why are we up so early?' Lizzie asked, rising and joining Henrietta by the window. 'What's going on out there? Have we been invaded or something?' The town was buzzing with activity. The drab fountain in the square had been festooned overnight with flags and bunting which transformed it into a majestic centrepiece, as though a big celebration was in the offing.

'There's lots to tell Lizzie, lots to tell,' replied a jovial Mungo Cheeseman. 'Isn't that right Da?' Excitedly, Da went on to explain all that had happened with the curiosity circlet and The Enlightened Ones hung onto his every word. Naturally, the parents were overjoyed that the kids were on their way to meet them and could hardly contain their excitement. Moo was thrilled to hear that the quest for The Stone was about to take a turn for the better and she couldn't wait to meet Melie North. Mungo filled in all the details of how the three from Hedge had searched in vain for many years, hoping to retrieve The Stone. Mungo's apparent mistrust where Fergus was concerned was explained by Henrietta, who had joined them at the breakfast table.

'There are those who are not what they seem,' she said gravely. 'There are those who covet The Stone and would keep it for their own. We concluded long ago that someone in an office of trust in Hedge held such ambition. Yet he would have the world believe his intentions to be honourable. He has cleverly given the impression that his purpose in life, his destiny, was to watch over The Child and bring her into Hedge in the quest.' She sighed deeply, troubled once more and fell silent as Moo Gabrielle took up the story.

'There were four of us,' she said. 'Quartz was the fourth, Quartz Munro. You'll probably meet him. He's crazy. You'll like him. We could see it; something desperate in his eyes. Fergus Wiseman's. We couldn't trust him. We had to do what we could to find The Stone ourselves and place it in Maeva's care.' Then Mungo continued.

'We had the map,' he added, 'and we had the Watchers around the world, Theirworld I mean. Forgive me Tortue; the Watchers have been of little help to us. They have given news here and there. News of anything unusual around the holes. Anything. We were up against it. What's that thing people say in Turley Holes, something about a needle and the haystack?'

'Looking for a needle in a haystack,' explained The Captain. 'I guess you've been searching round and about these holes then. They're a bit like portals aren't they? Like I was saying, I bet there's this big travel network and I suppose these holes would be like stations of some sort. Stations where you could hop on or off the network. That's what I think anyway.'

'What you suppose is true enough Geo Schultz,' said Henrietta. 'And we four travelled far and wide along the secret byways, but it was to no avail. Quartz returned to Chowk to watch over Fergus. And it is unfortunate ....' here she paused for a moment and looked towards the window, '... unfortunate that there are others who seek The Stone and would kill to obtain it.' Lizzie thought she could detect a hint of tears in Henrietta's normally inscrutable dark eyes. A hint of great sadness and regret for something dreadful from the woman's past. Da noticed this too and for a moment, he thought about mentioning the old letter Henrietta had been reading earlier. Lizzie seemed to sense this and stopped him in his tracks with a subtle shake of the head. Henrietta looked him straight in the eye with a knowing smile. She'd clearly been reading his mind. Everyone fell silent as they mulled over the proceedings, until at last Mungo lightened the mood.

'And just in case you're wondering why everyone and his cat are up so early today, it's the parade.' The Captain smiled, amused at Mungo's near miss with the adage. Little did any of the company realise how innocently portentous that near miss would prove to be later that day. 'Come on,' said Mungo, 'drink up and let's get out there. I hope the Chowk contingent get a move on, there'll be two hundred horsemen on the street by noon.'

Chapter Nineteen

Two Hundred Horsemen

If it hadn't been for the dead cat under the horse chestnut tree, Melie would have never even suspected that Lavender had been on the prowl in Chowk. The poor creature she'd seen waking up from its catnap the previous day now lay still and lifeless on the grass. Its left ear had been cruelly ripped and a trickle of blood oozed from one side of its mouth. The small pink tongue remained sticking out at an awkward angle and the upper lip was curled into an absurd sneer. All around lay clumps of fur, a sure sign that a vicious catfight had taken place between two of these fearsome predators. Some of the fur was a deep grey and brought back uncomfortable memories of the incident with the Hedgerangers just outside Futhark. Without a doubt, the victor in this fight to the death was none other than Lavender, the so-called healing cat. Melie had returned with Tiny Page to the fence at the end of Fergus' garden, for one last look at the beautiful tree before they all departed for Sardinia. Tiny shared Melie's discomfort at the ugly scene.

'That's not looking good,' he said when he saw the unfortunate creature. 'Do you know what I think?'

'Well I reckon you're thinking the same as me TP,' replied Melie. 'Lavender's her spy. You've seen them talking. I just know they're in cahoots right now, Kitty watching our every move and Sanguinella rubbing her hands together as the inside information floods in. She knows what we're up to, you mark my words.'

'It wouldn't surprise me at all,' suggested Tiny, 'if she could actually see through Lavender's eyes. I mean I know that kind of thing only happens in stories, but I bet I'm right.' He climbed over the fence and bent to stroke the limp body. 'I suppose Davis and Mavis will clear it up, poor thing,' he sighed.

'You know what?' said Melie, climbing up to sit on the fence, 'something's not right here. I've been feeling it for a while now. All that stuff Fergus was telling me about The Stone helping to flow goodness into our world from Hedge. Well Connell reckons the Airs want to flow badness back into Hedge, reversing the flow so to speak.' She reached into her Bag of Tryx and cradled the tourmaline crystal as she spoke. 'I think there's something Fergus isn't telling us.'

'And I think you're right,' agreed Tiny, climbing onto the fence beside her. 'I think he's more concerned with keeping the badness out than sharing the ... you know, whatever Billy called it ... the benevolence.' They sat in quiet contemplation for a while and then Melie summed up her fears.

'Fergus is a bit mixed up,' she said. 'I think he just wants The Stone for himself, never mind all that rubbish about goodness, badness and benevolence. Come on mate, let's get back. We'll be leaving soon.'

'Hang on a minute,' said Tiny. 'Melie, be careful. I think all eyes are going to be on you from now on with all this Child of Destiny stuff. Just be careful, that's all. And Melie, I know this sounds a bit ... but ... well, you know ... I'll be there for you, that's what I'm trying to say. It's going to get dangerous.'

'Sure thing TP,' chirped Melie, 'No passion, no power!

Come on you blind bat!' Tiny could only manage a hint of a smile at her matey jibe because he was troubled by a hazy vision. In an otherwise dimly lit room, a roaring fire bathed the laughing Sanguinella Couch in an eerie glow. Her cat-green eyes burned with evil intent as she stared at the demonic woman in the portrait above. He was sure he heard the woman whisper *Tortue.*

Back at Greenbanks, preparations were well underway for the journey. They'd be travelling by Dissolution and Maeva was running through the basics for the benefit of the novices. She was emphatic that Melie would be the one to state the destination. This was after all her daughter's big moment and Maeva was leaving nothing to chance. Tortue's involvement had been explained, so at least they'd arrive in the right part of Sardinia. It was the second largest island in the Mediterranean and according to Maeva, there were at least four known holes spread around the place. As the group was particularly large, they'd be setting off from the lawn and everyone had been clearly briefed on who they had to grab hold of and when. It had all sounded very straightforward at the time, but Alexander was struggling to remember whether he was grabbing Molly or Melie. Sammy was trying to swap with The Observant Jam Sandwich who had been allocated Luke. Polly was quick to point out that they should get it sorted out as it would be such a shame if anyone were left behind, a comment that her brother was quick to notice. Once the Hedgerangers had dealt with the dead cat and had joined the rest of the group Maeva called for attention

'Well, this is the moment we have all been waiting for,' she announced grandly. 'We all know the destination to be Sardinia. Mungo Cheeseman is adamant that the hole you will arrive at remains open, although it is dwindling fast. Time is of the essence. We cannot delay.' At this, she squeezed her daughter's hand and smiled, whispering softly, 'No passion, no power, my love.' Connell was preparing himself for the big moment. When Maeva had announced that she, along with Fergus and Polly would remain in Hedge he had flatly refused to budge. It had taken all of Maeva's persuasive skills to make him understand that it was for the best and the success of the quest may well depend on it. But he was not entirely happy. In the end, he reasoned that he still held a degree of responsibility for the rest of the kids at this stage in the quest and so he accepted the inevitable. Polly was staying, but he was definitely coming back for her. Melie understood completely that her mother had to stay in Hedge. This group of adventurers were not the only ones Maeva had to think of; the entire population were under her protection. Melie rather hoped the person she'd be protecting them from would be Sanguinella. But it was likely that because of Lavender, Sanguinella would be following on to Sardinia with the Malevolents in tow for company. Melie and Tiny suspected that was the very reason Fergus had elected to remain in Hedge, but out of politeness they didn't say anything. Billy was clearly disappointed to be leaving his own world so soon after getting back in but he tried his best not to show it. As they were making their way through the French doors, Luke, still fascinated by The Script, called them back.

'Hey everyone, hang on, there's a message coming through. It's red so it must be Quartz Munro.' The others paused in the doorway.

'Come on then,' said Melie impatiently, 'what's it say?'

'He's just taking the Corridor from Pink Shutters; he'll be here in thirty seconds,' replied Luke, visibly excited at the prospect of meeting a third Script contributor. Next moment the pink Corridor flew open and Quartz Munro burst into the room. He was certainly a striking figure and Luke was most impressed. He wore a battered old nautical jacket in navy blue with three gold braids around each cuff and a meerkat squashed into the chest pocket. Underneath was a pink jumper that seemed to be knitted from sparkly wool and his weather beaten face was half covered by short, grey stubble. It was impossible to judge his age, but he was an irresistible personality. Completing the outfit was a crumpled, white sailor's cap adorned with a gold braid anchor and a shiny black peak.

'That was close, nearly missed you!' he boomed. Munro slammed the Corridor behind him and scanned the assembled company. 'Ah, some new faces! I'm Munro, Quartz Munro. Don't mind me; I'm always leaving things to the last minute. We going then or what? Can't wait to get back to my old shipmates, it's been too long, far too long!' He winked at Maeva who smiled in agreement, pleased to have a seasoned explorer tagging along with the adventure. They regrouped hurriedly on the lawn, scattering cherry blossom in all directions as they formed their circle ready to depart. Mavis handed out the powder and Davis followed on with little cups of spring water on Fergus' circular tray. Quartz produced a tiny bowl from an inside pocket for the meerkat to drink from. When all was ready they waited for Melie's signal.

'Sardinia, Tortue!' she cried, as they downed their Dissolution and grabbed their allotted partners. In the few seconds while the mixture took effect, Tiny just had time to hope he'd misheard the woman in the portrait.

***

The expressions on the faces of the painted bandits seemed even more disdainful than the previous day. It wasn't surprising really. The town over which they kept their silent vigil had been invaded by hundreds of visitors who had come to see Mungo's parade. Exactly where they had come from was anybody's guess. The surrounding area wasn't exactly a bustling metropolis. Most of these people must have travelled miles to get to the town, so the parade must be something worth seeing. Even though it was still early, there was a certain carnival atmosphere and people were already seated outside cafés trying to get the attention of the waiters. The locals didn't feel any need for urgency in their work; after all, they'd probably witnessed this spectacle dozens of times. Da and the rest mingled with the crowds and made their way along the cobbles back down the route they'd taken the day before. Today was completely different. Noise and laughter boomed all around, echoing from the walls. Families with young children jostled for the best vantage point and settled themselves in readiness. It occurred to Da that the children would never last; it was hours until the horses were due to arrive. Without fail, they'd be crying out for drinks or ice creams before too long. The town had sprung into life. Tattered doors and boarded windows had been flung open and the streets transformed into lively bazaars. Striped canopies shaded windows and enticed customers into the tiny shops. Stalls and tempting displays spilled out into the street, laden with souvenirs and assorted trinkets meticulously arranged with the purpose of attracting a quick profit. The traders wrung their hands and checked pocket watches in anticipation of the bulging purses they hoped to empty before the day was over. Waiters bustled around tables, serving drinks and snacks to chattering customers. Crowded under a wide archway a huddle of musicians tuned their brass instruments, which gleamed in the sunshine. Excited onlookers glanced up and down the street, looking out for friends they expected to meet, or hoping for the first glimpse of the parade.

Outside the bars, groups of horsemen stood beside their mounts, drinking beer and swapping tales. Horses' hooves clattered and stamped impatiently on the cobbles and children gathered around, plucking up the courage to proffer handfuls of grass. Here and there, deals were done as horses of all shapes and sizes changed hands. Da and the rest listened intently as traders made offers and counter offers, pondering, bargaining, deliberating, then spitting on hands and slapping to seal the deal. It was a time-honoured practice and all parties walked away feeling they'd grabbed a bargain. At a little café, the companions stopped and sat around a couple of small tables under the shade of a wizened maple, ordering drinks and settling down to watch and wait. It wouldn't be long until the parade started and Da was hoping that his daughter would get there in time. Henrietta busied herself with pipe tobacco, which she kept in a leather purse hidden in the folds of her dress. Moo Gabrielle quizzed Posy and Lizzie about life in Turley Holes and explained that she was next in line to be Watcher once Billy came to the end of his tenure. The three were excited at the prospect of friendship and happy times together round and about the Yorkshire villages. The Captain picked Mungo's brains about the connecting holes and scribbled down notes on Maeva's map with a pencil. He was bubbling with excitement at the prospect of creating an updated map and using it to extend his travels. Da just sipped his coffee and waited patiently for Melie to arrive, looking at his watch from time to time as though it would make a difference. By mid-morning, the crowd could hardly contain their excitement. Then suddenly Mungo leapt up onto his chair.

'Here they are!' he shouted. Every head turned in unison to look towards the end of the street, where the first of the riders, came cantering round the corner. The spectators cheered wildly and hundreds of hooves clattered on the cobbles. Hats were thrown into the air and toddlers hoisted onto shoulders as the crowd surged forwards to welcome the strikingly rugged, white shirted Sardinian horsemen. It was barely controlled chaos. Wave after wave of excited horses, three abreast, squeezed along the narrow passageway between jubilant onlookers lining the walls six deep. Horseshoes skidded and scraped along the ground as riders grappled with reins to maintain control and keep the parade passing by. The visitors from Turley Holes could not believe their eyes. This wild abandon just would not happen back in England; here was an accident waiting to happen!

'Look!' cried Da, 'over there near the railings!' He leapt up onto the chair beside Mungo and started waving his arms above his head.

'Where?' shouted Posy. 'Is it the kids, have they made it?' She cupped her hands to her mouth and screamed at the top of her voice, 'Luke! Over here!' The rest of them were on their feet now, waving and shouting in the direction of the group who had found their way to Sardinia from Greenbanks in Chowk. Moo Spotted Quartz Munro who from somewhere about his person had produced a short hunting horn, with which he was announcing his arrival with gusto.

'He's crazy isn't he? I told you, he's a complete madman!' cried a smiling Moo who had unclipped the bunch of keys from her belt and was waving them in the air. 'Don't you just love that nutcase?!' She was clearly very taken with Quartz Munro. With the exception of Davis and Mavis who remained ever watchful and alert to unseen dangers, both groups were waving and shouting out greetings across the ebb and flow of the parade. The excitement was at fever pitch. Melie was overjoyed to see her Da at last, whirling her turquoise mohair jumper round and round above her head and grinning from ear to ear. Connell signalled to the parents with double thumbs up; he'd delivered the kids safe and sound. Or so he thought. Down the steep little side street, dark mists swirled around the grey wheelie bins, unseen by all save the unmoving eyes of the painted bandits, powerless to cry out a warning. A grey cat arched venomously and hissed its deadly warning at the local feral scavengers. Suddenly, it was as though open warfare had broken out in the tightly packed street. The nearby horses, spooked by the brooding presence began to panic, rearing onto hind legs and whinnying with fear as they flailed wildly in the air. Riders held on, wrestling for control of the reins but barley managing to stay in their saddles. The crowd, hemmed in by the walls on either side jostled and screamed as they tried in vain to dodge the terrifying onslaught. It was like a domino effect as pandemonium swept along the parade and sent horses and spectators scattering in every direction.

Melie and the Chowk contingent were cut off from Mungo's crowd. Only a madman would have tried to weave between the surging horses. Quartz Munro raised his hunting horn and trumpeted loudly as he marched into the melee with apparent contempt for danger. The horn's piercing tones spurred nearby horses into frenzied retreat and their riders could do little to prevent them backing away. This opened up a kind of no-man's land across which Melie and the travellers sprinted in the hope of reaching the café where Da and the rest were anxiously waiting. They were half way across when the towering horses began to surge back towards them, eyes wide with fear and threatening to trample everyone underfoot. In the blink of an eye, the Hedgerangers raced in front, waving their staffs and shouting to keep the horses at bay. Their intervention held off the inevitable just long enough to allow safe passage, but at the last moment the brave duo were caught by thrashing hooves, knocked to the ground and trampled violently. There was little hope. Nothing could be done to save Davis and Mavis who had sacrificed themselves to save their companions. In a state of shock, Melie and her friends staggered towards their parents who had pushed through the crowds. The younger kids were terrified, some crying pitifully. Molly, who had become very friendly with the Hedgerangers, was fighting to get back amongst the horses in a vain rescue attempt. She was held back by Connell and Luke, who themselves were holding back the tears. Da scooped Melie into his arms and rushed back to the relative safety of the café. Geo, Posy and Billy gathered the rest of the kids and ushered them aside. The chaos looked set to continue. Shell-shocked spectators battled towards the town square hoping to find some respite where the street widened around the fountain. Still the horses charged around, many having thrown their riders, who grappled with reins or lay motionless on the ground. Waiters and shopkeepers had joined the fray and were dragging the fallen onto the terracing near Tortue's place and out of harm's way. The travellers backtracked towards the square with Mungo and Henrietta in the lead, making for the taverna where they hoped to regroup and make sense of what was happening. Alexander and The Observant Jam Sandwich were shouldered aloft by Quartz and Connell and Melie clung on tightly round Da's neck. Luke and Tiny bravely battled on with the adults in front, whilst Molly and Sammy were carried by The Captain and Lizzie. Billy, Posy and Moo Gabrielle brought up the rear. As they reached the fountain they became stuck in the logjam; there must have been a thousand people crowding the square. It was impossible to get through to the steps leading up the terracing and as they looked, Melie cried out in horror.

'Up there, it's Lavender!' she screamed. All eyes fell upon the grey cat bounding up the steps towards the top terrace where a tall, elegantly dressed woman was just emerging from the taverna. Close behind, a gesticulating Tortue de Groix was remonstrating with the woman, who had clearly upset him deeply. The onlookers watched horrified as out of nowhere a swirling dark mist, which Melie recognised instantly as an Air of Mystery, enshrouded the poor man. His scream faded into oblivion and he was no more. Lavender leapt into the woman's arms and they both disappeared into thin air. For the first time since the Malevolents had turned the parade into a disaster zone, the meerkat popped its head out of Quartz's pocket, realising this was something it really ought to be writing down. Most of the words Quartz had uttered during the struggle for safety were a little too earthy for The Script; especially those shouted at the height of the confusion as he'd punched his way through unyielding crowds.

'We're getting out of here,' announced Mungo Cheeseman, 'right now. Geo, move it, powder, quick. We'll use water from the fountain.'

'But I thought we had to be near a connecting hole for it to work,' cried Da.

'Dwindling holes have a stronger pull. Maybe over

a couple of miles with Dissolution, we're fine, it's cool Da, don't freak!' replied Mungo. Geo and Posy hurried amongst the group, doling out Dissolution from the tin. They all popped it into their mouths and then leaned over the concrete wall to scoop handfuls of water. Just as they were about to take their drinks Mungo shouted, 'No need for passports folks, just grab hold, we're going to Valletta!'

Chapter Twenty

Mungo's Hideaway

Despite their hunger, the meal that Quartz and Posy had managed to concoct from the meagre larder in the Valletta hideaway was hard to stomach. The horrors encountered earlier that day had left an unsavoury taste in their mouths. With one or two exceptions the companions had never witnessed anything quite like those awful scenes, where two of the company were left dead on the street, trampled by the horses. Duty bound to protect the travellers in the quest for The Stone, Davis and Mavis had given their all to provide safe passage. Quartz retold the terrible events for the benefit of the meerkat scribe who had spent the entire episode trembling with fear deep inside the breast pocket. No doubt at this very moment Maeva, Fergus and Polly Brown would be receiving the grave news through The Script in Greenbanks. Billy could hardly bear to think of his friend Fenouille, by now grieving in the back room of the shop. He would have read of his brother's demise at the hands of Sanguinella and her Airs from Quartz Munro's contribution earlier that day. They had made it to Malta's capital; they were safely hidden away for now. But each one of them felt burdened by the magnitude of the task, especially Melie North.

'It's my fault,' she spat, and she stabbed into the food with her fork. A rage burned deep inside. 'I didn't have to bring you with me. He said I had to do it alone. Why didn't

I listen? I've put you all in danger.' She could hardly bring herself to look her gang in the eye. 'What's so special about me, why me?' The large wooden wall clock struck ten, absurdly loud in the gnawing silence. As if startled by an unexpected intruder, the enormous chandelier hanging from the ceiling trembled a little on its rusty chain at every chime, the crystal pendants tinkling softly. Melie slammed her fork onto the table and held her head in her hands. She was not tearful. Her despair transcended simple tears. If only the gang were adventuring round and about Powder Mill Fields with their catapults. Playing the explorer on home ground suddenly seemed a more attractive proposition than the real thing just now. Still, this was no ordinary adventure, not when there were two worlds to save and people were being killed. Tiny broke the silence.

'I know how you're feeling Melie,' he sighed. 'Bring back Powder Mill Fields and the other two gangs. This is getting a bit much. Did you see the way she just disappeared? Did you see that horrible woman and that cat of hers! That was just a freak show. It's getting a bit serious now, all this.' He stood up and moved around the table to where Melie was sitting. 'Look, come on,' he whispered, 'no passion no ...' He was interrupted abruptly by Luke, who had jumped to his feet, clattering his chair back onto the floor.

'... No power! Well, there's plenty of passion!' He was clearly irate as he yelled, 'but we're pretty low on power aren't we? Aren't we?!' At this, he turned to face Connell, who had been pushing the same piece of bread around with his fork for almost the entire duration of the meal. 'And just who are you?' demanded Luke. 'Are you my dad or what?' An awkward silence fell, in which Connell did not look up from his plate.

'Luke, don't ...' said Da, but before he could continue,

Luke interrupted once again.

'Shut up. Just ... shut up will you?' He turned to Posy. 'Well is he? You should know, you're my mum, aren't you?' He sank back into his chair, sobbing with frustration at all that had happened. The trauma had unlocked something in Luke that he couldn't explain. His anguish reflected the way they were all feeling. Even seasoned campaigners like Mungo and his gang were struggling to come to terms with the way the quest was unfolding. In the end Mungo, the natural leader of the group, tried to bring them all to their senses as he stood at the head of the table and cleared his throat.

'Look,' he said, 'this is where we're at. No one expected anything like that insane stampede. We all knew Sanguinella was bound to be following along. She wants The Stone and she'll stop at nothing to get it. You saw how she snuffed old Tortue out just like that.' He clicked his fingers to reinforce the point. 'Well that damned Air of Mystery anyway.' He paused for a moment, conscious that most of the kids might not know much about the Malevolents. He was leaving that one to their parents. Moving towards the only window in what Melie took to be a basement room, he looked up into the starry night. 'Stars,' he laughed. 'All that lot up there, it's running like clockwork. It's all preordained. You could work out what's going to happen, and when.' He turned back to face the group. 'Isn't that right Geo, you're the mapmaker.' For a brief moment, The Captain considered drawing the distinction between mapmaker and chorographer but thought better of it. Mungo was in full flow, this was not the time. But Melie thought otherwise. Without budging from her seat and still cradling her head in her hands, she calmly stated the obvious.

'We all know this quest is preordained,' she groaned, 'We

don't need reminding of that.' Now she too rose and moved to the head of the table, with Tiny Page following behind in solidarity. The wise old Henrietta was keenly watching, anticipating a shift of leadership. 'The point is we've got to find this stone. I know it's important to you Hedge citizens, but to me it's just a stone. I want to find it, get it back there and then get on with my life. As far as I'm concerned, the best part of this whole thing is that it's bringing my family back together. That's me, Da and my mum, May. Not Maeva, May.' She glanced at Da for the briefest moment and sensed his support. 'So,' she concluded, addressing relevant team members in turn, 'you can philosophise all you like about stars, you can blow your stupid hunting horn and knock people out if they get in your way and you can put all the stuff about benevolence in your clay pipe and smoke it for all I care! You can even dream your life away poring over maps and wishing you were somewhere else. But we all know how appealing Kansas suddenly became once the long and winding road petered out don't we? Well maybe you lot from Hedge don't. Do you have televisions? Anyway, let's just get up in the morning, make a proper plan and get the job finished. We've lost three already.' She cradled the tourmaline crystal in her hand and glancing at Lizzie, she had a distinct feeling that she was doing the same. Next, she turned her attention to the perennial matter of Posy and Connell. 'Oh and by the way,' she said, 'why don't you two stop messing about? You love each other, so just get on with it. Life's too short and all that.' This last observation had the desired effect on the dumbfounded companions. Rather than taking offence at Melie's assertions, the entire company just looked at each other and burst out laughing. Connell and Posy grinned contentedly, flushed with embarrassment and relieved that the ice had at last been broken. Moo Gabrielle leapt for joy, her keys jangling at her waist.

'I knew I'd like you. Nice one Melie! She's something else, isn't she Munro?' she whooped, slapping him on the back so hard that the meerkat dropped its quill on the floor. Billy beamed with pride that his young protégé was indeed turning out just as he had been expecting. Da just beamed with pride for pride's sake as parent's do. As they rose to disappear off to bed, Henrietta surprised them all by adding to the joviality. Stooping slightly like a fairytale witch, she strengthened the collective resolve with a timely observation.

'We'll get you ... and your little cat too!' she croaked, in a plausibly executed American accent.

The next morning Melie awoke to blistering Mediterranean sunshine streaming in through the tiny window of the room she shared with the Schultz girls, still fast asleep in their bed. Lizzie Page snored in the corner, which Melie found amusing rather than annoying. Posy's bed lay empty and undisturbed beside the wall. It was a beautiful room. In keeping with the rest of the house it was sparsely furnished, with walls of solid limestone glowing like warm honey in the soft light. The stone ceiling featured a remarkable arrangement of arched buttresses, which gave Melie the impression she'd been sleeping in a secret crypt hidden away beneath a church. A heavy tapestry covered the entire wall opposite the window and apart from a square of carpet was the only concession to comfort.

'Cosy,' groaned Melie as she stretched into a huge yawn, 'very cosy.' She reached for her Bag of Tryx, which lay on the floor beside her jumper and eased it quietly up onto the bed. Once more, she inspected its contents one by one, as she mulled over the horrors of the horse parade. The tourmaline crystal. Her trusted knife. 'Useless safety knife, yeah right,' she whispered, smiling to herself at Luke's usual jibe. She unclasped the turquoise-beaded pouch and took out her great grandfather's brass compass, watching the needle swing around to North under the glass. 'You've been around a bit,' she whispered. Getting up quietly she moved across to the window to study the intricate dial in better light. She loved to focus on something detailed in the morning and when eating breakfast at home, she would read the print on the cereal packet. Melie could, if pressed, regurgitate the text word for word from most of the well-known varieties. She could at the very least name the vitamins contained within the most popular brands. As her roommates slept on, Melie gazed out across the impressive harbour of this fortified city on the sea. The place simply oozed history and she could see why it had gained a reputation as a maritime stronghold over the centuries. With limestone ramparts and solid walls as wide as roads, any would-be invader might just as well lift anchor and head for home. Yet in spite of this outward show of muscle Valletta was certainly picturesque, with fantastic sunshine and cloudless skies of the deepest blue. Once she'd sorted out the here, there and everywhere of North, South, East and West, she placed the precious compass on the windowsill and then set about waking the others. For Sammy and Molly this involved the uncomfortable prospect of being jumped upon and shaken mercilessly. 'Come on you sleepyheads!' Melie yelled. 'Can't lie around in bed on a day like this; we've got things to do and people to see. We're playing hunt The Stone today!' Melie felt a sudden twinge of guilt at the way she'd dismissed the precious treasure as simply a trinket to be found, during her outburst the previous evening.

'What? What time is it?' drawled Sammy, shielding

her eyes from the light. 'It can't be time to get up already; we've only just gone to bed.'

'No way, José, can I just have ten more minutes?' Molly yawned. 'I was just dreaming about blue butterflies turning into people ... oh, yeah, I remember ...those weird horses ...' Her voice trailed off as the reality dawned. She really had met those blue butterfly people. They really had become her friends, especially Davis and they really had been trampled to death. Molly, more than any of the companions, was finding it hard to accept that the crumpled bodies of the Hedgerangers had been left where they lay. The authorities would have to deal with all of that; any awkward explanations by the companions may have jeopardised the quest. 'Yeah, we'd better get up, come on.' Lizzie slept on.

Downstairs in the basement room Da was seated at the table with The Captain, Connell and Posy. Alexander and Jam Schultz were dozing on a worn leather sofa that looked like it had been there in that room for hundreds of years. The boys looked like they'd be content to doze there for the next hundred. Tiny and Luke were searching around the place, looking in every possible hidey-hole for breakfast ingredients. It was a fruitless search. Mungo's larder had been emptied the night before and given that he was always out adventuring with his companions, it seemed unlikely that he kept much in the way of provisions.

'Luke, stop slamming those cupboard doors will you?' groaned Posy, who clearly hadn't slept much.

'Who rattled your cage?' replied Sammy on Luke's behalf. 'He's just hungry that's all. Actually, he's always hungry.'

'You won't get any sense out of these two,' chipped in Da, nodding his head towards Connell and Posy. 'Been up all night talking, haven't you?' He raised his eyebrows at

Connell whose cheeks flushed a deep pink.

'Which two?' asked a sleepy Lizzie Page who'd just surfaced. 'Any toast or anything?' She noticed Posy's cheeks tinged with the same rosy glow as Connell's. 'Ah, you two,' then she winked at her friend.

'Excuse me,' Geo chipped in, 'do you mind? Some of us are trying to work here. Good morning by the way, I'm Captain Geo Schultz, as if you didn't know, chorographer to the stars. Right now I'm onto something, so please, keep it down.' To illustrate the point he held up the map, which he'd been poring over with a large brass magnifying glass for the past couple of hours or so. 'If there's tea going, count me in,' he added before continuing with his inspection.

The Turley Holes explorers were gathered on their own for the first time since this whole adventure began. They were hungry and somewhat disorientated with the whirlwind comings and goings under the influence of Dissolution. Above all, they were still smarting from the sad loss of their companions at the Sardinian horse parade and painfully aware that Sanguinella and her deadly allies were on their trail. It was a chance at last to talk about their recent experiences; the paintings in the Powder Mill, Skittish Matilda, gooseberries, May's suitcase, Pink Pamela's hospitality, the silver birch incident and mohair knitters in the shop window. All these wonders and still more were enthusiastically recounted in intricate detail, some with nods of recognition from the grown-ups who'd seen the same things when they themselves had visited Hedge. Each one of the assembled company marvelled at the special relationship they shared through having visited that amazing place. They were a collective unit connected at a deep level that transcended the usual bonds between parents, children, friends and neighbours.

'So,' said Melie as they silently pondered this last unspoken truth, 'where's Mungo and his mates?'

'Out foraging,' replied Da. 'They do have supermarkets in this place and Moo's not short of cash, believe me. You should have seen the wad she pulled out to pay Tortue for the stew the other day. Don't suppose he'll ever get paid for the breakfast now, poor bloke.' Another short silence followed.

'Well I hope they're back soon,' moaned Luke. 'All I want to do is eat these days; must be all the excitement.' Melie rose from her seat at the table and moved across to the window, as if preparing to address the troops once again.

'Well they seem to know how to live around here,' she said. 'I mean, this is one heck of a place. Just look at all this limestone. It's not going to fall down around their ears is it? An earthquake wouldn't budge this lot!'

'Oh, yeah,' said Da, 'I was just going to mention that. I hope you've all noticed it's oolitic. Isn't that right Posy?' He giggled as Posy smiled in mock sarcasm at his jibe. 'I suppose you'll be telling me it's full of oolites or something any second now,' he added.

'Da,' she whispered triumphantly, 'that's exactly what it's full of, unlike you!' They all enjoyed the joke at Da's expense; he clearly had no idea what oolites were and had just plucked the name out of thin air.

'Okay,' he conceded, 'you're the geologist! What I do know is these Mediterranean houses have these thick walls and tiny windows to keep it cool on the inside. There, I do know something. Trust me, I'm Da North and I teach!'

Next moment Mungo and the others returned and brought in the shopping. In no time at all Moo, Quartz and Billy had rustled up a hearty breakfast, which to Luke's relief did not involve anything resembling tripe or porridge. Once they had eaten their fill, Melie raised the pressing matter of the quest for The Stone and pointed out that had Fergus been present he would have been sure to remind them that time was nearly gone. Melie could sense the general unease amongst the grown-ups at the mention of his name, but she thought better than to pursue it in the presence of the younger kids. Another silence followed. Henrietta spoke first.

'Indeed; the quest for The Shining Stone.' She pulled out her long clay pipe, which she set about filling with tobacco whilst explaining how they came to be in Valletta. 'Many generations ago and I mean many generations in Hedge time, people first spoke of another place. It was a yearning for great adventure, for exploration and for new discoveries, which would benefit all citizens of our world. Far and wide throughout our lands the adventurers roamed, searching for a connection to what they hoped lay beyond.' The mysterious Henrietta held the companions entranced as she relayed the tale, pausing from time to time to smoke her pipe. In the background, Moo Gabrielle quietly made tea for everyone in a large pot, which she covered in a stripy tea cosy. Melie couldn't help but think it impossibly coincidental, for it was exactly like the one at home and the one in Pink Shutters. 'In the end, their search took an unexpected turn,' whispered Henrietta. 'Quite how it came to be there is a mystery that has engaged the greatest minds for centuries, but they found a treasure of unsurpassed beauty; The Shining Stone. It became a symbol; a symbol of purity, a symbol of harmony and a symbol of unity.'

'We've had one or two symbols like that in our world over the years,' remarked Connell, with a hint of sarcasm in his voice that was clearly intentional. 'But most of the time they don't seem to work. They just cause nations to fall apart.'

'Of this we know,' continued the wise old woman. 'If only the benevolence of Hedge could to flow into Theirworld. But perhaps that is not to be.' At this Quartz joined in the conversation.

'Well it strikes me that it will H,' he said, 'just not in the way you'd think. Give it a few years, Theirworld years. I think you'll see what I mean.' He looked at Melie who winked back at him, indicating that she knew exactly what he meant. Tiny knew too and he reached under the table to squeeze Melie's hand before he realised what he was doing and yanked it away, blushing. Ever alert, Sammy noticed this little exchange, which she immediately filed away in the depths of her memory for later use at Teasing Time. Mungo now took over the explanations.

'But The Stone was more than that,' he added. 'It turns out that those who'd handled it just seemed to know where to go to find these connecting holes between worlds and travel through them.' The Captain's ears pricked up every time the alluring prospect of travelling between connecting holes was mentioned. He just wanted to get this quest over with and then get started, hopefully taking Beezy with him if she ever got back from Suriname. 'Not many people got to handle it though,' said Mungo. 'Those in charge around the place made it their business to appoint these Stone Guardians. They were just trustworthy citizens duty bound to look after The Stone and keep it safe. Just sitting on it and keeping it safe, nice work if you can get it. They managed to be true to their word, on the whole.'

'On the whole, what do you mean?' asked Melie.

'Well there was this one Guardian who spent a little too much time travelling around from one place to the next, finding all these connecting holes,' replied Mungo. 'He'd show up from time to time in between expeditions to who knows where and every time he'd be trying to change things. It seems he's the one who kick started the whole nasty business about the Malevolents.'

'You mean he became influenced by the bad bits of Theirworld and brought that back into the harmonious world of Hedge. That's how Malevolents come about isn't it Billy?' Melie asked, remembering how he'd explained the Airs' origins beside the fire in the Eighth Wonder of The World. It seemed so long ago. Billy nodded, confirming what Melie had asked.

'That is so Amelia my child,' said Billy. 'Citizens with unnatural leanings towards evil drifted out of solid form and became nothing more than mists cast out into Theirworld never to return.'

'What was his name?' asked Melie, noticing how Henrietta had shifted uncomfortably in her chair when Mungo had started speaking.

'Well, it was ...' he paused and looked at Henrietta who remained impassive. Billy was struggling to get the words out. 'It was ... Fitzwilliam Couch. That was ... well ... what I mean to say is that was Henrietta's great grandfather. Couch, you know, as in Sanguinella.'

Chapter Twenty-One

The Secret Letter and a Food Fight to Remember

The companions were uncomfortable with the connection between Henrietta and Sanguinella. With the shared surname it had been plain for all to see, but as Henrietta was clearly part of Mungo's gang they'd thought nothing of it until now. An element of doubt had begun to creep in. It was left to Henrietta to explain herself.

'It is true that I am Sanguinella's sister,' said Henrietta in a measured tone. 'Yet you must believe me when I say this is in name only. I wish that I had never been part of the Couch family and when you know the truth, you will understand why this is so.' She looked first at Melie and then at Lizzie. 'There are those amongst you who know that what I say is true.' It was as if Henrietta could sense that the two were secretly cradling their tourmaline crystals, which they carried with them always. 'You possess the power of insight to a degree that is rare amongst those of your world, which is of course Theirworld.' Henrietta placed her pipe on the table and reached for the teapot as she continued her explanations. 'My great grandfather neglected his duty to safeguard The Stone. He travelled constantly and because of this, he brought malevolence into Hedge. His great friend Bombardo Cheeseman ...' at this all eyes turned to Mungo, who simply smiled and nodded, '... shared his love of exploration. Quite by accident he unlocked the mystery of how to journey between worlds without the need to touch

The Stone.'

'I guess he just got hungry and picked a few bog rosemary pearls' chirped Luke. 'He sounds like my kind of guy.'

'That is so Luke Schofield,' said Henrietta. 'He developed the use of Dissolution by powdering pearls of bog rosemary and combining with spring water. Bombardo was another Stone Guardian. Naturally, he himself began to travel, yet unlike my great grandfather he remained pure of heart and untarnished by his journeys through Theirworld. It was on such a journey that he arrived here on what you would call the island of Malta, the cradle of your ancient civilisations. He studied the ways of Theirworld and became a great friend of an old sea captain, who lived in this very house here in this noble city.' She looked around the room, admiring its impressive stonework and feeling its magical quality. 'When his friend eventually died, at the age of two hundred and eleven I might add, the house came into the possession of Bombardo who used it as a base for all future explorations. The two men must have been drawn together by destiny, for it is quite remarkable that this room is actually a connecting hole.' She drank more tea as the others considered all she had told them. The adventurers from Turley Holes gazed around in wonder, each one beginning to feel the unmistakable aura of a magical place. It was very much like the feeling the grown-ups had experienced in the Powder Mill at the start of their journey.

'So we know why we're here, I guess it actually belongs to Mungo now,' said Melie. 'But what became of Fitzwilliam and how come The Stone went missing? And how come the old sea captain lived so long?' she asked. Billy Jackson took up the story.

'Anyone from Theirworld coming into close contact with a Stone Guardian will live for a very long time Melie,' he confirmed. 'Anyway, it seems that somehow the Couch family... forgive me Henrietta ... possessed the ability to resist the deterioration into mist form. That is to say, they did not become Malevolents. They lived on, disguising their evil intent and using it to elevate themselves into a respected position amongst the citizens of Hedge. They gained the trust of The Governance whilst plotting in secret to wrest control of The Stone and use its influence to rule supreme. If ever this came to be, then needless to say Hedge would become a world apart from the harmonious place it is today. It is unfortunate for our quest that the Couch family came to possess the ability to travel between worlds without the need for Dissolution. Fitzwilliam was a mere mortal, just like the rest of us of course and he eventually died of old age. It comes to us all sooner or later.'

'What Billy is saying,' said Quartz, 'is that they were pretending to be nice but all the while they were cooking up a takeover behind the scenes. We realised this, the four of us and Billy, but no one would listen. They were all being fooled.'

'Then when Maeva came along,' added Moo, 'we thought here was someone at last who'd be able to see straight through them. But no, even she couldn't see them for what they were. Desdemona, that's Henrietta and Sanguinella's mother, was the worst of the lot. Nasty piece of work until the day she died, but they couldn't see it like we could and would they listen? No way; they thought we were crazy. With her mother dead and buried, Sanguinella really started smarming her way into the good books of The Governance. She was really put out that Maeva, the so-called forerunner of the Child of Destiny, was top dog. We think she thinks Melie will lead her to The Stone and then that's it. Hasta la vista baby! Game over.'

'I believe that also,' said Henrietta. 'But not all in the Couch family seek to possess The Stone. It was many years ago that I renounced my association with Sanguinella. She was no longer a sister to me and I have spent my lifetime working against her.' Henrietta reached into the pocket of her dress and took out the old letter that Da had noticed in the Taverna. She seemed agitated and fiddled with her pipe on the table. 'As a young girl I witnessed the only killing since time began. It happened in Futhark. The victim was the author of this letter and the killer ... was my mother.' To Mungo, Moo and Munro, this news was a bombshell of staggering proportions. In all the years they'd known Henrietta, there had been no hint at all that she held the secret to the second most sought after piece if information in the whole history of Hedge; the identity of Fern's killer. They were visibly shocked, but understood completely why she had kept it from them. Henrietta had been saving it for the ears of the prophesied Child of Destiny. She let the news sink in for a moment and then continued. 'I stole the letter and I have kept it hidden for a hundred years and more, until now. I believe that Mordechai Fern, last known Stone Guardian, stole The Shining Stone and concealed it secretly in Theirworld only to face death at the hands of my mother.' She waved the letter for all to see. Tears welled in her eyes just as they had done in Futhark all those years ago. 'This letter is the start of our quest and now that Amelia North has joined us The Shining Stone is within our reach at last.' She handed the letter to Melie, who opened it and started to read aloud, becoming more excited as she reached the last passage.

Mordechai Fearn my dear friend,

I have taken a great risk because I want to do some good in your world, to ease the suffering and the difficulties faced by you and the miners around you. I have hidden a treasure of immense value in a place where you should be able to find it. As I write, I am filled with sadness because I know that when I visit you to present this letter it will be the last time we meet. The power to cross over from my world to yours is dwindling and will soon be lost forever. In the name of secrecy, I cannot tell you the location of The Shining Stone, your treasure, so I give you this clue:

Namesake's old providence lies behind Futhark on a whim

Your dear friend,
Mordechai Fern

Afterwards the room remained silent, although it was almost possible to hear the cogs whirring in The Captain's mind. Locations and clues were essential ingredients of the chorographer's work and he was already processing the riddle. Posy too seemed to be wrangling with the finer detail of Fern's clue as though she knew something the others didn't.

'Namesake's old providence lies behind Futhark on a whim,' repeated Melie. 'It's a bit confusing with their names being nearly the same, what are the odds of that?!' She passed the letter to Da and then continued. 'But I've already worked out one thing. When he says namesake's in the clue, he's just referring to that very fact. They have the same name, just about. So he really means the other Mordechai's old providence lies behind Futhark on a whim.'

'I don't want to state the obvious,' said The Observant Jam sandwich, 'but Futhark is in Hedge, where Pink Shutters and the biscuit shop are.'

'Wow, now that's what I call a brilliant mind!' cried his brother in mock sarcasm. 'Why didn't I spot that?'

'I wonder why, Crate Boy,' was Jam's friendly retort.

'So what we need to do,' said Da after he'd read the letter and passed it on to Connell, 'is solve this clue and we'll find The Stone. Shame we've all ended up here then when we have to go back to Hedge.'

'What do you mean go back to Hedge?' asked Moo Gabrielle.

'Well it says here,' replied Connell, 'something about ... where is it? Here look, behind Futhark.'

'Yeah, that's what we all thought at first,' said Quartz. 'We've been puzzling out this riddle ever since Henrietta first showed us the letter. I mean, we're not stupid but we've been on the case for years. Just can't crack it. But old Mordechai Fern does make out in the first part of his letter that he's been visiting another world and hidden a treasure where the other bloke should be able to find it. And everybody in Hedge seems to think The Stone's been stashed in Theirworld, so who are we to argue? A world overflowing with concerned citizens can't be wrong.'

'Or can they?' pondered Tiny Page. 'You know, something that you said Billy has got me thinking.'

'What's that TP?' asked Melie. 'Actually, come to think of it, I bet you're thinking the same as me.' This was getting to be quite a habit with the two. They were clearly becoming the closest of friends, a fact that was not lost on the ever-watchful Sammy.

'Well, we must all be on the same wavelength, that's what I say,' added Molly. 'It's about the old sea captain living over two hundred years isn't it?'

'I guess so,' concluded Luke. 'The same thing might have happened to Mordechai. I mean the one the letter was supposed to go to.'

'He could still be alive,' said Melie. 'If we could find him, he might be able to interpret this riddle.'

'Or indeed give us The Stone if he's found it and given it pride of place on the mantelpiece in some residential home for the elderly,' quipped Connell.

'It's possible,' said Mungo, 'but unlikely. Think about it, he never got the letter so he's never seen the clue, thanks to Desdemona Couch and her handiwork.' Henrietta was keeping very quiet.

'Right,' said Melie, 'if I was organising this I'd ...'

'Melie,' interrupted The Observant Jam Sandwich, 'you are organising this, remember?'

'Well I would start with finding Mordechai Fearn,' she said. 'This might sound stupid, but let's try looking him up on the internet. I mean I'm not that good with it myself, but that seems to be the way to find stuff out these days.'

'No computer,' said Mungo. 'No need. We've got a library in Valletta packed with reference books going back years. I mean there's got to be something in there, you know, some kind of mining history or such like. He was a miner; it was in the letter, right at the beginning.'

'That suits me,' said Posy. I'm a geologist ...'

'As if we didn't know,' quipped Da, winking at The Captain.

'Yeah, right,' she replied. 'So I'm kind of on home ground with mining and all that. Let's go and have a look then.'

'Hold it,' said Billy. 'I've lost track of the days, what with one thing and another, but I reckon today is Sunday.

The library will be closed.'

'Well they don't call me Keys Gabrielle for nothing,' said Moo, jangling her bunch of keys. 'Believe me, we're in. Let's go.'

'Just wait a second,' said Mungo. 'Melie, I think I should be giving you this really.' He reached into his bag and took out the curiosity circlet. 'Well, you know, Billy was supposed to give it to you, but I'd ... well I suppose I'd stolen it so he was a bit stuck wasn't he?' He handed the circlet to Melie. 'Sorry, but ... you know ... well you've got it now. Oh and look after it, don't go losing it or anything.' He raised his eyebrows at Billy who looked away sheepishly.

'Thank you Mungo,' said Melie. 'I will.' A long pause followed, as she put the circlet into her Bag of Tryx, slipping it inside the empty compass pouch. 'For once I don't know what to say, but thanks. Right folks, let's find this library then.'

The stone staircase from Mungo's basement room led up to a weathered oak door studded with iron, which swung heavily outwards into a small courtyard bathed in hot sunshine at the back of the building. It felt like stepping into another world. Almost. Not surprisingly, the plants that had managed to survive the Mediterranean summer so far were looking bedraggled to say the least. Those clinging to the wall around the door, however, were an exception. Despite the drought, the vibrant combination of firethorn and box remained as healthy as ever and shone with sparkling pearls of bog rosemary. This didn't surprise Melie at all and for an instant a yearning for the grassy bank beside the Nidd swept over her. This whole adventure had started back there as she watched the picnickers and pondered the mystery of Butterfly Hole. How tempting to reach for a pearl and return to Powder Mill Fields, leaving the quest to look after itself.

Out of the corner of her eye, she caught Connell looking at her with arched eyebrows.

'Just don't go there Melie, we've got a job to do. You've got a job to do and we can't do this without you!' His gentle reproach reminded Melie that certain members of the company were able to communicate telepathically, although by now she was losing track of who could and who couldn't.

'It's okay Connell. It's a thought though isn't it? I mean quite an amazing thought. We could just zoom off somewhere else. It beats queuing with your passport only to find the flight's been cancelled due to shortage of staff or something, doesn't it?' Melie replied, in her thinking voice, adding, *'don't worry, I'm not leaving,'* for good measure and much to Connell's relief. As they trooped out of the courtyard to make their way to the library The Observant Jam Sandwich pointed out that Mungo had forgotten to lock the door. Mungo eased his worries, pointing out that as this was Valletta and not Turley Holes, there was really no need.

They were a startling group and attracted curious stares at every turn. Even on this quiet Sunday morning, the streets of central Valletta were alive with tourists and with locals going about their business. It was quite a contrast to the morning they'd arrived in the Sardinian village, with only painted bandits for company. The lack of cars was very refreshing and the distinction between pavement and road seemed somewhat blurred; people just wandered everywhere. The clatter of feet and bubbling conversation was all but drowned under the ringing of church bells in this deeply religious community. The only other sounds were the echoing cries of city birds and the odd rasp of a motorcycle engine in the distance. A few shops were open here and there, but even in midsummer, churchgoing and sightseeing were top of the agenda. Mungo led them up and down the steep little streets, weaving an intricate route across the city and before too long they arrived at a large plaza, which was almost entirely taken up with café tables shaded by enormous parasols. It occurred to Melie that their guide had purposely taken them on a contrived route in order to put anyone following off the scent. It didn't take a genius to work out that Sanguinella would have had no problem extracting the group's whereabouts from the Sardinian locals. Like all the others, Melie was painfully aware that dozens of stunned onlookers would have heard Mungo shout *'Valletta'* the instant before the group disappeared right before their eyes. Sanguinella could easily have reappeared and terrorised the required information out of any number of these unfortunates. Mungo's precautionary tactics seemed to have paid off; there had been no hint of danger between the hideaway and the café square.

'So, here we are again,' The Captain sighed. 'Another town square in another square town. I guess you'd expect the chorographer in me to notice the layout of this place. It's all set out on a grid. Some of these planners have no imagination.'

'Well they did have a lot to squash in, Geo,' said Lizzie. 'There's sea on all sides, just about. What did you expect, spirals?'

'Yeah, maybe spirals would have worked,' he mused. 'Maybe spirals or maybe concentric circles. Oh, never mind; let's just put it down to progress. Sixteenth century progress, if you know what I mean,' he grumbled. 'Come on, sustenance beckons.'

'Count me in,' chirped Luke, heading for the nearest table and slumping down in the shade of the parasol. 'Do they have chips?'

'Or Maltesers,' joked Alexander, resuming his fascination for the literal. The companions gathered chairs from nearby tables and settled down in Luke's chosen spot, relieved to be out of the heat. While they busied themselves with menus, Melie and Da took in the surroundings. It was a large square bounded on three sides by towering buildings, which were far more imposing than those surrounding the Sardinian fountain. These had a delightfully faded grandeur, which hinted at an important past. It was almost as though they had always been there; with their ornate architecture and flamboyant metal grilles or other such embellishments, they oozed a certain aura of nobility. A statue of Queen Victoria presided over the comings and goings in the square from a large plinth right in the centre. The third side opened out onto a wide street, along which generations had wandered, unwittingly providing subject matter for people-watching café clientele. The perimeter was dotted with tall trees, which had been conscientiously pruned over the decades so that they now resembled cuboids of greenery on long, snaking stalks. They served as convenient perches for the city birds, but contributed little to the shady comfort of customers; hence the need for the far more effective parasols. Once they had chosen and been served, the companions made a show of enjoying their refreshments whilst plotting how to get into the closed library without being spotted.

'That big one at the back is the library,' whispered Moo Gabrielle. 'It's that one with the Maltese flag on top. Impressive or what; those pillars are like giant redwoods.'

'You mean the one with the big sign that says National Library of Malta stuck on the wall?' said Quartz. 'Good job we've got you tagging along, we'd never have found it! How are we going to get in, through the door?' he teased.

'Very funny,' said Lizzie, quick to defend her friend's faux pas. 'Actually that's not such a silly question. Will we be going in through the door? It's a bit obvious isn't it?'

'Well we could create some kind of diversion couldn't we?' suggested Tiny Page. 'I mean we don't all have to go in, there are seventeen of us after all. How many does it take to find a book?'

'That is a good suggestion Tiny Page,' said Henrietta. 'Exactly what kind of diversion did you have in mind?'

'Well, not that I'm wanting us to get split up or anything,' replied Tiny, 'but the kids could stay out here and make some big fuss about something. Maybe knock the table over or start some kind of food fight.' The younger gang members were visibly excited by the prospect of a legitimate food fight and general opinion seemed to be that as simple as this idea was, it might well have the desired effect. In the end, it was agreed that Melie should be with the adults. The rest of the gang would provide the said diversion while Billy, Lizzie and Connell would secrete themselves and keep watch over proceedings. In dribs and drabs, the adults filtered themselves away from the group and loitered inconspicuously near the library until at last just the kids remained. Luke stuffed the handful of Euros Moo had given him into his pocket. The impressive wad would no doubt cover the bill and any damages the kids were bound to cause. This would be a food fight to remember!

Chapter Twenty-Two

Capital Confusion

Keys Gabrielle. Apt, very apt, thought Da as the bunch of keys was expertly whittled down to find one that fitted the ancient lock in the library door. Mungo kept a watchful eye on the café customers and one by one, the companions slipped into the cavernous vestibule and out of sight of prying eyes. They needn't have worried about being spotted. Luke and the gang of kids held the attention of the café customers with no trouble at all as the food fight raged on right in the centre. As pastries and sandwiches rained around the nearby tables, the café proprietor and waiting staff battled for control under a deluge of jeers and delighted cries from the onlookers; they were clearly enjoying the spectacle. The pandemonium had the desired effect. The grown-ups had managed to enter the library and Henrietta closed the door behind them, leaving Luke to deal with the furious Maltese.

It was quiet inside. Tall marble pillars gleamed in the light from the windows high above the stone floor. Every footfall threatened to betray the intruders' presence and they expected security guards to leap out at any second. At least that would have brought some excitement into their intolerably mundane Sunday shift, Da reasoned. Why spend the day snoozing in a favourite corner or flicking through one newspaper after another when you could be chasing an oddball collection of adventurers up and down the corridors? There were a couple of doors leading off the entrance hall, newly painted in glossy black with gleaming brass handles. Otherwise the only way out was up a wide staircase, which led up one flight and then split left and right. Mungo looked at Melie. She looked from one door to the other and then opted for the stairs.

'Up there,' she whispered. 'It's a big library so it must be up there. There's no room down here, come on, let's go.' She adjusted her Bag of Tryx and beckoned the group to follow. Cautiously they crept upwards and took the right hand branch, which brought them out onto a long corridor skirting the front of the building at first floor level. There were windows all along the length of this corridor, but these were coated with so much dust and city grime it was hard to imagine how daylight could break through. Melie was reminded of the bay windows in the front room of the Eighth Wonder of the World although Billy's were not partially covered in steel mesh on the outside. It was very much as Melie imagined a prison would be except that people would want to break out rather than breaking in.

Exactly half way along the corridor above an ornate double door, a sign in both English and Maltese marked the entrance to the first floor reference library. Before entering, Henrietta and Posy leaned against the door, listening intently for signs of life within. Just the sound of a scraping chair or even a single cough from a guard would have jeopardised the mission. After anxious moments, Posy gave the all clear, Henrietta opened the door and they all sneaked inside. It was a huge and imposing place. The ceiling was a long way above their heads, indicating this room must actually take up at least two storeys. The four stained glass domes in the roof gave a surprisingly airy feel to the place, completely at odds with the dingy corridor and its dirty windows. Wooden parquet flooring stretched from wall to wall and smelled as if it had recently been varnished. Much of the floor space was taken up with neatly arranged rows of desks, each with a reading lamp with a green glass shade. This was a library intended for research. The silence was agonising and even the large clock seemed to be ticking quietly on purpose, afraid to disturb over-serious readers in this most serious of places. On a central, raised vantage point, a circular counter presided over the room and Melie could just imagine bespectacled librarians seated behind it shushing anyone who dared to breathe, let alone drop pencil sharpenings onto the floor.

But the single most spectacular feature was the book collection. Arranged on impossibly high wooden shelves, there was every chance that some of these ancient volumes had not been touched by human hands for decades. Stretching the full length of the room, the books on the lower shelves were caged in with wire mesh, either to deter prying fingers or to stop them jumping out, Melie surmised. The intruders marvelled at the prospect of what lay contained amongst the billions of pages stored within the four walls of this inspiring place.

'There must be something about everything in here,' whispered Moo. 'I mean, don't you get the feeling they've all been brought here because they're important?'

'Or maybe they've been shoved in here because no-one knows what else to do with them,' joked Quartz in a hushed tone. 'No need to write that one down chum,' he added, for the benefit of the meerkat whose quill had been poised in readiness for some important scribing ever since Moo's key had clicked in the lock.

'Where to start though?' added Melie. 'There's so many. What do you think Posy? Is there a mining section?' She was beginning to wish she'd stayed outside with the gang, throwing sausage rolls around. The companions began to scout around the lower shelves, searching for clues as to the organisation of the books. Da provided the solution straight away.

'This might not have occurred to anyone,' he said, 'but libraries do have cataloguing systems you know. Usually computerised but I get the impression it'll be a manual system in this place. It must be round here somewhere.'

'How about this?' suggested Melie, crossing the room to a wooden cabinet with dozens of small drawers just the right size for index cards. They gathered round Melie's cabinet and searched the drawer labels for inspiration. 'Let's try this one,' said Melie reading aloud the faint typescript, *'mil* to *mis.'* She opened the drawer and flicked through the cards. 'Millionaires, millstone grit, mimicry in tropical birdlife, Minnesota, misericord. What's a misericord? Never mind, miniature poodles ... here we are, mining. Mining History.'

'Well it's a start,' sighed Mungo, 'but I was somehow hoping one of these cards would say Mordechai Fearn, address and telephone number. So what number's Mining History then Melie?'

'Three seven four two six point nine one two,' she replied. 'Let's get cooking, we want anything to do with records of miners, come on.' She moved across to the books, scanning the reference numbers on the spines of those behind the mesh until she found the thirty-seven thousands. This section occupied a narrow column of shelving which soared towards the ceiling in tiny increments. 'Oh no,' groaned Melie, 'guess where mining history is going to be!' Each of the companions looked upwards in dismay; they were somehow going to have to reach the uppermost shelves. 'There must be a way. I mean, I guess they don't have flying librarians in this adventure do they? Talking cats and fireflies I can just about cope with,' joked Melie.

'Over there,' said Da, 'look, there's one of those sliding ladder things.' At the far end of the wall of shelving was a very long metal ladder, attached to rails along the top and at several points along its length. 'Don't look at me,' said Da, 'heights is not my forte. You've got to be a mad man to go up that thing.' All eyes turned to Quartz Munro. Thirty seconds later, he was at the top of the rickety ladder being slid along the rails by Mungo, Posy and Moo Gabrielle. Unfortunately, the wheels on this ingenious contraption hadn't been oiled for a very long time and threatened to attract the unwanted attention of dozing security guards with every squeaking turn. Inch by heart stopping inch they rolled Quartz along the shelving until at last he reached the thirty-seven thousands.

'There's loads about mining history,' whispered Quartz. 'Must be a dozen at least. I'll bring them all.' The meerkat scribbled furiously, not daring to look down from such a great height. It was a precarious squeeze in that pocket at the best of times.

'Wait,' said Henrietta. Not one of them had noticed, but she had been sitting for some time at one of the desks reading the letter she had carried around for the past hundred years or so. 'Blue. Bring the blue one.' She folded the letter and pressed it to her cheek like a mother cradling a child.

'Blue one?' whispered a puzzled Da North.

'Just do it Quartz,' said Posy. 'Henrietta is onto something. And hurry up about it, our luck can't hold out much longer.'

'Okay,' said Quartz, 'there's three. I'll bring them all.' He manoeuvred the three volumes that had any hint of blue on the spine off the shelf and then carefully climbed down the ladder balancing the books on one upturned hand.'

'Oh, come on Munro,' hissed an exasperated Moo Gabrielle. 'Stop showing off, you look like some kind of waiter.'

'Shut up, I'm nearly down Moutarde,' he replied, and seconds later he was on the floor beside her. 'Right then Henrietta, here's the blue ones. There's Nineteenth Century Pits in South Yorkshire, Open Casting: a Concise History and Sulphur Mining Essentials. What do you reckon? It's not looking that promising is it?' He handed the three books out amongst the group and then joined in the search for clues about Mordechai Fearn. It wasn't going to be easy. These were sizeable volumes and after several minutes scanning indexes and contents pages, not one of them had spotted any reference to the elusive Fearn or any other individual for that matter.

'Well then, Henrietta,' said The Captain, 'three blue books and no miner. Any other gut feelings?' There was a touch of sarcasm in his tone and he was just about to suggest that they find a computer somewhere and start again when Henrietta spoke up.

'Blue John,' she said. 'There is a strong connection with Blue and now I sense Blue John. Please go back up there Quartz Munro and try again.'

'Who's he?' asked Da.

'Who's who?' replied Posy. 'No, don't tell me you think Blue John is a person! Come on Da, everybody knows what Blue John is, don't they?' She looked around at the blank expressions on her friends' faces. 'Okay, I know, I'm the geologist. Well Blue John is a mineral, a version of fluorite and a lot of it was mined in Derbyshire hundreds of years ago. Still is now and again.' Their blank expressions suggested her friends were none the wiser. 'Right, let's just leave it at that shall we? Come on Quartz, up that ladder.'

A short pause followed, in which Posy could sense they were all silently affirming that they did know quartz was a mineral too.

'I'll go,' said Melie and she sprang up the ladder to resume the search. 'Here we are, look, Blue John Mining in Derbyshire, I'm coming down.' Within moments, the group were crowding around Henrietta's desk as Melie searched through the index for clues. 'Right, how about this, lifespan, pages three two three to three five seven, let's try that.' She flicked through to the relevant pages and they all began scanning for information. 'Wait a minute, wait!' she cried. 'No, you are just not going to believe this! Listen, its right here ... Mordechai Fearn. This is him ... where was I? Mordechai Fearn. Still mining in Derbyshire aged ninety-six. Ninety-six, it has to be him! Most people didn't live past thirty back then.' She passed the book to Posy, who took over the running commentary.

'Yeah, but not everybody had been hanging out with a Stone Guardian had they?' Posy added, excitedly. 'What else does it say? Hang on, yeah, there's a typescript of some letter he left, wow! Listen ... *and so I leave you for good my grandchildren. No longer will my longevity shame and burden you.* Oh just listen to this, you are not going to believe it ... *in Malta's ancient capital I shall end my days.* Did you hear that? Malta's ancient capital!'

'That is unbelievable!' exclaimed Da. 'He's right here in Valletta! This can't be coincidence. Things just have to be preordained haven't they? I wish I'd listened at Sunday school! There just has to be a God!'

'Da North, teacher at Turley Holes Primary School, don't you know anything?' asked The Captain. 'Malta's capital is Valletta now, but that's now. The ancient capital was Mdina, also known as the Silent City for the past few centuries.

Look in Valletta if you want, but you'd be looking in the wrong place.'

'This is brilliant!' added Melie, as if they needed telling. 'We are so close. Find old Mordechai and ask him all he knows about his namesake. I mean there must be something that'll help us with the puzzle. Come on, what are we waiting for?'

'Let's hope he's still alive,' said Mungo. 'He can't have been and gone and died, not after all these years, that'd never do!' Henrietta stood up from the desk and placed the letter in the pocket of her dress once more.

'He is alive,' she said. 'I feel it. Let us go and join the others. We must find the old miner in the Silent City without delay.'

'What about the book?' asked Posy, as if excited at the prospect of taking it along for a spot of holiday reading.

'Leave it here on the desk,' replied Mungo, 'it'll give the librarians something to wonder about tomorrow. I can just see them,' he said, adopting a mock continental accent that was rather more French than anything resembling Maltese, 'ah yes, no doubt about it, somebody broke in here yesterday looking for clues about Blue John, that crazy English miner who lived into his hundreds and moved to the Silent City to get away from it all. He'll be the one who can help them find an old stone and take it back to a talking firefly!'

***

They sneaked out into the square as discreetly as possible just as the commotion from the food fight was dying down. Luke was in the process of paying the disgruntled proprietor for the damage and the rest of the gang were sheepishly helping to restore order to the scene. Tables were repositioned and dusted down, whilst food debris was swept up into dustpans and tipped into bin liners held open by scowling waiters. Melie was bursting to share the news about Fearn with her gang, but a giggle from Da stopped her in her tracks. He had just noticed Luke's hair, now stained red as if one of the other kids had emptied the dregs from a bottle of claret all over it.

'Hmmm, seems punk is not dead after all then!' joked Da. 'Although I always preferred green hair back in the good old days, I must say. It suited my complexion, or so I'm told!' This brought a smile to Melie's lips and as she looked up at her beloved Da, she felt a warm glow deep inside; it wouldn't be long now until he and May, her mum, were back together at last. As much as she wanted to find and return The Stone, the delightful prospect of a reunited family was Melie's driving force. Nothing in this world was going to stop her now.

Right then, an uneasy stillness settled on the trees dotted around the square. Moments earlier, they had rustled gently in Malta's famous Mediterranean breeze. Startled birds flapped noisily amongst the branches or launched themselves skywards from window ledges with a jarring cacophony of birdsong. A strange darkness descended as though a heavy shower was brewing over Valletta. Once again, the Turley Holes companions shared that same uncomfortable feeling they had at The Powder Mill. Someone, or something was snooping around the square watching the group, only this time they knew exactly who was responsible for the unwelcome attention. Da pulled Melie close and the whole group quickly gathered in the library doorway, unconsciously forming a protective shield around the pair. Mungo and his seasoned explorers scanned the trees and the café tables, where a few unwitting customers sat and puzzled over the sudden change, oblivious to the looming danger. Melie wasn't sure why, but she had immediately reached inside her Bag of Tryx where she felt the curiosity circlet vibrating gently, just as it had done ever since Mungo had handed it over in the hideaway. She felt a great comfort as she caressed the glass, as though someone somewhere were watching over her. Out of the corner of her eye, she noticed Billy's hand reaching into the pocket of his greatcoat and for the briefest moment, sensed that he too was handling a circlet, until she remembered that he didn't possess one any longer.

'We're leaving,' stated Mungo. 'We'll have to walk. Come on, back to the hideaway.'

'No, wait,' said Lizzie Page. 'Not there. This is Sanguinella's doing. She's watching us. Well Lavender's watching us and she's seeing through the cat's eyes, that's what I mean. It's too dangerous.'

'Lizzie's right,' Melie added. 'Let's not be hasty, we can't give any clue about where we're going. Just stay put. They won't hang around, they'll be gone soon.' She had switched her attention from the circlet to the tourmaline crystal inside her bag and she sensed that Lizzie too was cradling her own talisman. 'They won't attack,' she said. 'Cat woman needs us to lead her to The Stone. She's not stupid, but you'd think she could have sorted it so the Malevolents had less conspicuous methods, wouldn't you?'

'Yeah, weird that,' added Molly. 'She's making a fundamental error there. She might as well put up posters: Big Sister is watching you. Well, little sister anyway,' she said, glancing at Henrietta and suddenly realising she should have kept her thoughts to herself. 'Sorry, Henrietta, I was just ...'

'No matter, Molybdenum Schultz,' interrupted the old

woman. 'But what you say is true; my sister is making it clear that our movements are being watched. We must be continually on our guard. As our quest moves towards its conclusion, she will become ever more impatient ... and ever more ruthless.' Her watchful gaze settled on the pitiful sight of a pigeon's torn and bloodied body lying at the foot of one of the trees. None of them had noticed the unfortunate creature before and thoughts turned immediately to Lavender's own ruthless streak, just as the darkness lifted and the leaves of Valletta rustled once more.

'Right, we're going to Mdina,' Melie announced, 'straight away. Mungo, Dissolution won't work unless Mdina has a connecting hole.' At this, she raised her eyebrows as if asking the question. Mungo shook his head by way of an answer. 'Okay, so how are we going to get there?'

'We could always get a bus,' suggested Alexander, 'it's the only way to travel,' he joked.

'Actually, Crate Boy, that's exactly what we're going to do,' said Melie. 'Nice one! You still okay for Euros Moo?' she asked, smirking openly at Luke's red hair. He smiled sarcastically back.

'No problem,' replied Moo, patting her bulging pocket, 'we're practically there!'

Mungo led the companions on a complex route through the sunny streets and alleyways, each of them alert and ever watchful as they scurried along like mice stalked by a dangerously persistent cat. They soon reached the terminus at the City Gate, where dozens of brightly painted yellow and white buses chugged around, jostling for position in readiness for departure. Once in place, however, the drivers seemed content to switch off engines and settle with a newspaper in the sun-baked front seats or else step outside to smoke a cigarette whilst checking for any leaks. The whole scene resembled a circular racetrack, with gigantic statues of mermen above a fountain pool right in the centre. Passengers milled around searching for their buses, most of which had seen better days and would probably pass for museum pieces back home. That they were still running at all, let alone providing a timetabled service, the kids found hard to believe. As though reading their collective minds, Henrietta assured them all that despite appearances these buses and their drivers were reasonably reliable when it came to transporting the Maltese from one place to another. Uncomfortable, but reasonably reliable.

'Which one then Mungo, any ideas?' Moo enquired. 'Which way is Mdina, anyway?'

'It's not too far from here,' replied Geo on Mungo's behalf. 'I'd say it's about fifteen miles and roughly South West. Shouldn't take long.' Years of chorography had turned The Captain into a walking atlas of the world, able to recall locations, directions and distances with consummate ease. He collared one of the drivers returning to his bus carrying a paper cup of coffee and a little bag of pastries. He didn't look very well. Sammy had spotted him earlier and had turned away disgusted as he spat out a string of heavy green mucus he'd gathered in his mouth via blocked nasal cavities.

'Excuse me matey,' chirped The Captain, 'which bus goes to Mdina? We need to get there quick as possible.' The driver nodded in the direction of a particularly ancient looking bus at the outer edge of the racetrack alongside a sweep of parched shrubs. Geo's heart sank as he noticed a definite leak of some kind staining the road under its passenger side rear wheel. 'Yeah, well, thanks mate,' he said. 'Are you sure it'll get us there?' The driver spat on the ground once again, dangerously close to Geo's foot, Moo

Gabrielle noted with relief. Things might have turned nasty if it had been Munro's foot.

'Ten minutes,' the driver replied. He eyed the group suspiciously and then made a show of the fact that he was just about to eat the pastries and drink the coffee before he would even consider leaving.

'Yeah, ten minutes then,' said Quartz. 'Ten minutes, okay?' This came out as something of a mild threat, which was no doubt intentional. The driver shrugged his shoulders and walked across to his vehicle where he settled himself in the sunny driver's seat to eat his lunch. 'Yeah well we might as well go and sit on the bus instead of standing around here in full view of little Cattykins,' suggested Quartz. 'A bit of shade would be useful; anyone would think it was summer or something. Come on.' They trooped across the bus terminus, mingling with the other would-be travellers, towards the Mdina bus. As they crossed, the engine of a nearby bus clattered into action and coughed out a cloud of black fumes, signalling to anyone interested that it was just about to depart. The companions stepped back off the road as it pulled out to leave and as they did so, Melie noticed the single passenger seated on the back seat at the kerbside window. It struck Melie that he looked somehow familiar. He looked old and frail, and decidedly unwell. There was something unusual about the way he fixed Melie with his quizzical, staring eyes. She looked away and then back again, only to notice he was still looking, craning his neck to look at her as the bus drew slowly away along the road.

'I know.' Connell's telepathic message took Melie by surprise, as though pulled back from a momentary time warp. *'I think so too. We're heading for the wrong bus. We've got to get on this one haven't we?'* Melie looked at her friend and confirmed his hunch in her thinking voice.

'You're right. We have to move fast. I don't know why, but that's the bus we need. That man ...' A short pause followed, and then, *'Connell! That's him! I just know that's Mordechai Fearn!'*

Chapter Twenty-Three

The Silent City

'Follow that bus,' yelled Melie, 'come on!' She'd already started running. A second bus screeched to a halt as Melie dashed into the road, stopping just in time. If Connell hadn't grabbed the strap of Melie's Bag of Tryx and hauled her backwards it would have hit her. The driver was not pleased. He leapt down from his seat to take the matter up with the crazy man in the cream linen suit and the ginger haired girl. It took a swift intervention from Quartz Munro to defuse the situation before it had even begun. He gave the driver a hefty shove with his shoulder as he stormed towards Melie and knocked him flat.

'Want some friendly advice?' Quartz asked the startled driver. 'Don't get up; you might live to regret it!' The driver looked as though he was about to spring to his feet and challenge this impudent idiot in a sailor's cap when he noticed the meerkat and the small army of allies who had gathered around. He remained seated on the road, rubbing the back of his head, which he'd clattered against the kerb on the way down.

'That stupid kid, what did she think she was doing?' he yelled at the assembled group. 'I nearly hit her. Is she alright? What's the hurry anyway? You English are always in a hurry.' He stood up, making it clear that he wasn't looking for any trouble.

'Yeah, well we've got a bus to catch,' said Da, not really

understanding exactly why they had to catch it at all. 'And the bus in question is the one that's just disappearing down the road. Look, mate, we'll pay you to follow it, won't we Moo?'

'Yeah, course,' she replied. 'We've got cash and we'll make it worth your while, how about it? Can't hang around though, so are you up for it or what?' She pulled out a handful of Euros and waved it ostentatiously, just to help the driver make up his mind. Then she looked at Melie. 'Why are we following that bus Melie?' she asked.

'He's on that bus. I just know it's him, Mordechai Fearn I mean,' she replied with some urgency. 'Look, we're just wasting time, are you taking us or is Quartz going to knock you down again and drive the bus himself?' It was a bullying tactic and though Melie was not exactly comfortable with such behaviour, she was prepared to make an exception in this instance. 'Come on, how does a hundred Euros sound?' she added.

'Get on!' said the driver without a moment's hesitation, 'we're leaving now. I must be crazy, what am I doing? A hundred you say?'

'A hundred,' replied Moo Gabrielle, quickly counting the cash into the delighted driver's palm. He folded the notes, slid them into his shirt pocket and with another glance at Quartz's meerkat he leapt onto the bus and into his seat. The companions quickly followed and without further ado, the chase was underway. The bus screeched away from the kerb in pursuit of Mordechai Fearn. Melie had been certain it was him. His expression as he'd returned her stare suggested they had met before somewhere or at least shared some common ground in the past. Yellowing, grey hair, which hung lank and greasy under a battered trilby, suggested a lifetime spent smoking cigarettes. Something about the deeply lined, careworn complexion told Melie that lifetime had been particularly long. His stained dark brown suit jacket and mismatched trousers gave the impression he'd long since given up caring about how he looked, as did the ridiculously loud, flowery tie in shades of yellow and lilac. It reminded Melie of the wallpaper back at Billy's house in Turley Holes and in less desperate circumstances, she would have been quick to share her observation with Tiny Page and the other kids. As it was, keeping up with the bus in front was all that really mattered now.

'So how do you know that's Fearn, Melie?' asked Da. 'You've never seen him before, it could be just some old bloke who doesn't get out much.' He clung to the backrest of the seat in front of him as the driver careered round a sharp bend at top speed. The hundred Euros were clearly burning a hole in his pocket.

'It's him Da, I just feel it,' she shouted over the roar of the straining engine. 'Don't ask me why or how, but it's him, trust me. Come on driver, move it! We just can't lose that bus!' urged Melie.

The excited adventurers clung on to any available surface as the rollercoaster bus ride sent pulse rates soaring; this was just the kind of escapade the best heart-in-mouth adventures were made of. The lack of a door on the bus added to the overall excitement factor. A small bust of The Virgin Mary in a glass case above the driving seat gave the distinct impression that nothing short of divine intervention had been responsible for keeping this bus on the road for so long. The driver on Fearn's bus was obviously relishing the challenge of staying in the lead, a position he was not going to relinquish without a fight. He was clearly a Maltese national, as Mungo was quick to point out at the top of his voice. After many years based in Valletta he'd grown to accept that most local drivers had never paid much attention to a highway code; their apparent contempt for the rules of the road was legendary. Unfortunately, the roads in the immediate area were notoriously busy with like-minded drivers behind the wheels of their own vehicles. Some of these were not about to miss this opportunity to practise their racing skills and gradually the numbers involved in the chase swelled out of all proportion to necessity. Before long, seven small cars, two mopeds and an ancient Land Rover piled precariously high with building materials of every description had joined the buses on the main road westwards out of Valletta. Horns blared, pedestrians dived for cover and cars screeched to a halt as their drivers cursed loudly and engaged in vigorous fist shaking or similar gestures of a more damning nature. It would have been an easy task for any police cars to follow the procession. The wobbly Land Rover had been shedding small bags of plaster at intervals along the way as it floundered along and these had burst open on the tarmac marking the trail with piles of pale pink powder.

The kids were thoroughly enjoying every minute and every mile of the pursuit, as indeed were the grown-ups. Even the reserved Henrietta was grinning from ear to ear as she gripped tightly onto a metal handrail and Quartz was blasting out the hunting horn with gusto. Sammy was making the most of the opportunity to cling tightly onto Luke, especially after he'd planted a kiss squarely on her lips as the excitement went to his head for one crazy moment. As far as Sammy was concerned, things were definitely going to plan! Luke couldn't help noticing that his mother was using the wayward driving as an excuse to cling onto Connell Brown, although she probably didn't need one. Alexander and Molly were standing on their seats, holding onto the edge of the luggage shelf and whooping with joy, accompanied by Lizzie and Moo Gabrielle on the seats behind them. Billy was grinning out of the rear window at their pursuers, whilst The Captain was straining to hold May's map under control in the rush of wind from the open door and sunroofs. He was already thinking ahead to how they were going to escape from Mdina if Sanguinella and her Malevolents should pay a surprise visit. There was always the possibility, of course, that he was contemplating the exquisite prospect of future travel between connecting holes. Such was the alacrity with which his brilliant chorographer's mind could switch forwards from one exciting prospect to the next, even at times like these! Melie and Tiny Page were up at the front with Mungo and Da, urging the driver along like jockeys in a steeplechase. They needn't have bothered. With his hundred Euros tucked into his shirt pocket, this driver was definitely in the business of providing value for money. He drove his ageing bus past the limits of endurance, intent on closing the gap between leader and follower. As The Observant Jam Sandwich noted, this was definitely happening inch by hair-raising inch.

'We're catching up!' yelled Schultz number four at the top of his voice. But just when things were going well a pickup truck overloaded with bales of freshly cut long grass pulled onto the roundabout that lay ahead, effectively cutting the companions off from Fearn's bus. There was no way this glorified hay cart was going anywhere fast. The driver's three very young children were enjoying the ride, clinging to the topmost bale and brandishing the very sickles used to hack down the grass. Mother was leaning right out of one window yelling into a mobile phone and the driver's view was largely obscured by an enormous brown Alsatian sitting on his lap and barking furiously.

Despite a barrage of horn blaring and desperate shouting and bawling the pickup driver remained oblivious to the problem and chugged along at what felt like a snail's pace down the narrow road. Slowly but surely Fearn's bus pulled away and the mission seemed doomed to failure with every frustrating second stuck behind the one driver with any regard for speed limits.

'Oh, no!' cried Melie. 'This just can't happen, we can't lose that bus! What are we going to do?' For one brief moment, those nearest to Quartz Munro had the distinct feeling that he was considering climbing out of the open sunroof and doing something about the problem in his usual heroic fashion. Perhaps he was going to run along the roof of the bus and leap onto the truck, like a cowboy attempting to hijack a train and then pull over onto the verge. The meerkat felt it too and slid down inside the pocket with one paw over both eyes. It didn't happen. The truck also began pulling away; the bus had run out of diesel.

It seemed pointless complaining to the driver. For one hundred Euros he had done his best to catch up with Fearn's bus. He was no doubt hoping the woman with the plaited pigtail and wacky buttons wouldn't be asking for any change now that he'd failed to deliver. The companions stepped down off the bus and watched the grass truck disappearing into the distance, blocking their view of the bus in front which was probably at least mile away already. Melie looked at their surroundings. They had left the built up area around Valletta and were now standing in open countryside. Fields stretched away on all sides, dotted with farms, a few vineyards and swathes of prickly pears. In the distance, Melie spotted an imposing walled town standing high on a hill in a commanding position.

'Look,' she said, 'up there. Please let that be Mdina, the

Silent City.' A collective sigh of relief followed. If Melie was right, their destination lay only about a mile away across the fields. Mungo climbed back onto the bus to ask the driver if the walled town was indeed Mdina. He had remained in his seat as the bus rolled to a standstill when the fuel ran out. It was almost as though he sat in a stupor, a gnawing disbelief creeping over him as the reality of what he'd been doing for the past thirty minutes or so began to sink in. He pulled out an oily Manchester United towel from underneath his seat and wiped the sweat from his forehead. Chasing another bus around the roads of mid Malta was definitely not on the timetable and he was beginning to fret about how he would explain all this to his superiors. Would they believe him if he said the bus had been hijacked by a crazy sailor with a meerkat in his pocket? Perhaps not, so maybe he could say he was rushing a ginger haired girl to hospital having accidentally nudged her with his bus. His mind whirred. Above all, he was wondering how he would be able to hang on to his hundred Euros, which he'd transferred into his shoe for safekeeping. He reasoned this was the last place anyone would choose to look for evidence of any misdemeanour given the fact that he hadn't changed his socks for at least two weeks. In the end, Mungo had managed to extract the necessary information from the bewildered driver through a series of nods and shakes of the head in response to simple questions.

'Talk about trying to get that needle out of the haystack again,' exclaimed Mungo as he stepped down from the bus. 'It was like talking to a wall. Isn't that one of your sayings in Turley Holes?' he asked.

'Yes,' replied Connell. 'Talking to the wall. You're nearly right with the haystack one. But next time try this; it's like getting blood out of a stone. I think you get the picture. So is that Mdina or what then?' He shaded his eyes with one hand and looked towards the hilltop town.

'That's it,' replied Mungo. 'It's near enough to walk, but we'll have a job on our hands trying to find old Mordechai now won't we? Ah yes, it'll be like trying to find a needle in a haystack, I see how it fits now!' He chuckled with satisfaction.

'Yeah, well,' muttered Melie, 'Here's another one; you wait all day for a bus and then two come along at once.' She was visibly disgruntled at being thwarted by an empty fuel tank and a pickup truck just when everything was falling into place. It certainly reinforced her disdain for the weekend traffic crowding Mill Square on market day back home. Home. She was actually beginning to question just where exactly this was, with the way events were unfolding. 'Well, there's no point hanging around here,' she sighed, 'we'd best be off. I know we'll find our miner when we get there. After all,' she added, with an out of character air of sarcasm, '... everything is preordained.'

The assembled company climbed over the dry stone wall at the side of the road and set off across the fields. They were making a beeline for the Silent City, sweltering in the midday heat as they trudged along through the parched grass, Melie and Mungo in the lead and Billy Jackson bringing up the rear. As the jeers and whistles of the drivers who'd joined the chase back in Valletta faded into the distance, the companions were able to enjoy the warmth of the sun and reflect on recent events. Things certainly seemed to be happening in a hurry. Melie counted the days since Sanguinella had fed them the bog rosemary pearls at Butterfly Hole.

'You could be right,' said Tiny as the pair walked along beside a low wall of golden limestone blocks. 'It's a bit tricky though. I mean the timescale in Hedge was a bit hard to get your head round wasn't it? But yeah, I think it was four days ago that we got into Hedge and met up with Fergus.'

'Wonder how many more it'll take?' asked Melie. 'I just hope Mordechai can shed a bit of light on this for us.'

'If we ever find him,' said Tiny. 'I mean just look at the place, it's not some little village is it? He could be anywhere in there.' They looked up at the towering walls on the hill. Someone had certainly chosen a good spot for a capital city back in the old days. From this side it looked more like a castle. 'No way would anybody want to try and conquer that place,' mused Tiny. 'They probably did that boiling oil thing to keep them out. You know, pouring it onto the invaders' heads from the battlements. Gruesome or what?'

'Too right,' replied Melie. 'Anyway, it's like Mungo said back at the hideaway, Mordechai never got the letter so he's never seen the clue. So what exactly is he going to be able to do for us? Something I hope, because this isn't just a game is it? People have been killed ...' She paused as the awful memory of Davis and Mavis sacrificing themselves to save the others from the stampeding horses lingered. 'He'd better be able to help us, that's all I'm saying,' she sighed.

Luke walked along just behind his mum and Connell, trying to appear disinterested in their conversation whilst actually straining to hear every word. It was looking like Connell might actually be his father after all and he was suddenly glad that he'd confronted the pair with his suspicions back in Valletta. After all, Melie had said that life's too short and Luke was growing to understand the truth in those words. He just hoped his mum and Connell, his dad, felt the same. The fact that they held hands in a loving way as they walked suggested they did. The sun was shining in a clear blue sky. The gang of kids were out adventuring in paradise and the unmistakable smell of pizza ovens drifted on the air from some café in the hilltop town. Things were definitely going well for Luke Schofield!

It didn't take long at all for the companions to reach the gate of the Silent City. They had left the fields of prickly pear behind and walked along a road that grew ever steeper as it curved around the hillside. The smell of horses alerted the group to the possibility of another attack from the Malevolents; the Sardinian incident remained painfully fresh in the collective memory. As it turned out, however, these horses were part of the local tourist industry and pulled little carriages full of sightseers around the town. Cars were evidently banned unless you lived within the walls or were going inside to do business. And the walls were certainly impressive. It was hard to imagine how anyone intent on invasion would stand a chance of breaching the defences, even if they managed to cross the cavernous moat. There was no water in there nowadays, just a few orange trees dotted around and numerous feral cats scavenging around for food.

'Well, we made it,' said Melie. 'Let's get in there and find him.'

Chapter Twenty-Four

Eighteen Forty-One

Mdina was clearly a popular stopping off point on the Malta tourist trail. Even though late afternoon was turning into early evening, the town was alive with sightseers and souvenir hunters. Customers filed in and out of the few shops, although most were content to browse around the goods on display rather than commit to a purchase. A reverential quiet hung in the air; this was the Silent City after all. People seemed afraid to communicate in anything more than whispers. Were it not for the towering old buildings on either side of the narrow streets off which the whispers echoed in a gentle hubbub, it would have indeed been silent. There were only a few cars around, no doubt belonging to the lucky residents. Who wouldn't have wanted to live here in the Silent City, Malta's ancient capital? Steeped in history and swathed in a medieval beauty, the only drawback was the seasonal influx of tourists by the hundred thousand armed with cameras and guidebooks translated into every conceivable language. Market day in Turley Holes was nothing like this. The only way to escape the crowds was to turn off down one of the little twisting alleyways, which curved enticingly away from the main drag.

The companions soon decided to investigate along one such alleyway and they trooped along, led by Melie, Da and Mungo, although a sense of hopelessness had begun to creep in. Just how did one go about finding a two hundred year old miner from somewhere in the North of England in a hilltop town in the middle of the Mediterranean? On and on they wandered, looking at door numbers, street names and even the odd stray cat just in case. It was a lost cause and was very much like looking for a needle in a haystack, as Mungo was keen to point out.

'He could be anywhere,' groaned Melie, leaning back against a wall in exasperation. She slid down to a sitting position and craned her neck skywards. 'It's bloody hot too! Come on Fearn, where are you?' Melie was beginning to doubt that her hunch about the man on the bus was anything to get excited about. She was actually feeling a little embarrassed at having dragged them up here to Mdina on a whim, hence the swearing. This was not in Melie's usual nature at all. 'Whim!' she chuckled. 'I've brought you up here on a whim. Maybe that's what Fern meant in the clue. A whim's a wild idea. It doesn't make sense.' Tiny was quick to reassure his friend.

'Yeah, maybe Fern could foresee that we'd all be snooping up and down an alleyway sometime in the future looking for his long lost mate, on a whim!' he chirped. 'I don't think he meant your hunch about the miner on the bus though Melie, it must mean something else.' Tiny slumped down beside Melie on the ground and they were quickly joined by the other kids and some of the adults. It seemed like a good excuse for a rest. 'For a start,' Tiny went on, 'he's on about Futhark. Behind Futhark on a whim. Not Mdina.'

'You know what I think?' said Luke. 'I think we should go back up to the main street where those shops were and have something to eat. The last food that went anywhere near my mouth was a croissant and that was only because Molybdenum threw it at me. I'm starving.' Molly pulled a face at her friend, her standard reaction at Teasing Time. They all agreed that food would be a good idea. They'd at least be able to sit down and try to think of a plan that would lead them to Fearn. The thought of a bite to eat and a cool drink hauled the weary adventurers to their feet and one by one and they set off, retracing their steps back down the alleyway. The Observant Jam Sandwich, youngest and smallest, ambled along at the back of the group. He was quite taken with the fact that even though the houses in Mdina appeared quite plain and characterless, their doorknockers were remarkably interesting. They came in all shapes and sizes. Many seemed as ancient as the town itself, yet some were in much better condition than the ramshackle doors with their faded, peeling paintwork. As he lingered behind, he couldn't help feeling that he'd seen one of the knockers before, although he couldn't quite place it. It was cast in the shape of a lion's face, the iron features blurring into one with weathering and simple old age. Someone had painted it recently, in a pale green gloss. It held the heavy ring of the rapper between its jaws with an unyielding ferocity.

'Wait a minute,' he whispered. 'I know where I've seen you; the Powder Mill!' He called out to the group, 'Hey everyone, hang on a minute, I think I've found something!'

Within moments, Melie and the explorers were gathered around the low doorway. The doorknocker was indeed almost identical to that gracing the huge door of the Powder Mill back in Yorkshire. Maybe hunger and tiredness were clouding their collective judgement, but each of them was convinced this was no mere coincidence. As far as they were concerned this was a definite lead in the search for the missing miner! Some of the group began scouring the facade of the tall townhouse, searching for further evidence. It was very narrow, perhaps only three or four metres wide and the doorway was particularly low, with a curious step down at the entrance. Across the top of the door recess lay a heavy limestone lintel, although like the rest of the frontage this was partially obscured by flaking concrete rendering. At some time in the past, someone had obviously decided that the house would look much better with a smooth layer of concrete applied over the limestone. They hadn't applied it very well, for it was now crumbling away to reveal the beautiful natural stone underneath. It was just possible to make out some numbers scratched into the lintel above the door.

'Eight, four, one,' said The Captain. 'It says eight, four, one. What's that then, the house number?' The Captain tried to make sense of the inscription. 'It can't be though,' he added. 'There's nowhere near eight hundred and forty-one houses on this little alleyway. More like about thirty I'd say.'

'You're right,' Posy agreed. She traced her fingers over the numbers. 'Hang on though, what's this?' She picked away at a small piece of crumbling concrete just next to the number eight. It came away easily in her hand, about the size of a saucer. 'Look at this!' she cooed, 'another number. What we have now is one, eight, four, one. Now in my book that's not a house number it's a date.' She was about to toss the saucer down onto the floor but stopped herself just in time, remembering this was the Silent City and the clatter could have drawn unwanted attention to their discovery. She placed it gently on the ground.

'Now I'm not trying to get anyone excited,' said Da, 'but let's just suppose that it is a date and let's just suppose it is eighteen forty-one. That's quite a long time ago isn't it?' He picked up Posy's saucer and held it up, showing it to the group. 'Well obviously it was carved into this lintel before someone had the bright idea of smearing this concrete all over it, wasn't it? A long time ago ...' Da took his time, slowly building up to making his point like a barrister in a courtroom somewhere, using the teaching skills that had made him a favourite with the pupils year after year at Turley Holes Primary School. 'You know what I think?' he teased. 'It's a date of birth.' At this, he paused and tossed the saucer back onto the floor. The clatter echoed around the alleyway, threatening to give the game away to the sightseers and browsing shoppers. 'Well it might just be wishful thinking,' he added, 'but who would we really like to bump into down a dark alleyway who might have been born round about eighteen forty-one?'

'I know Da,' said Melie. 'Mordechai Fearn, that's who!' She traced the numbers etched into the lintel and then turned to face the group. 'Well spotted Schultz number four! Lion's head doorknocker just like at the Powder Mill and a possible date of birth of someone who's lived longer than most. It's him, I just know it is. He's right here in this house. Imagine that! Just behind this door!' she exclaimed. 'I think we're just one tiny step away from finding The Shining Stone! Let's give him a knock then, come on.'

'Wait,' whispered Henrietta Couch. She pushed her way through the others and stood directly in front of the door. 'I think it would be prudent to exercise caution Amelia North. This is important, too important for any mistakes.' She placed a hand on Melie's shoulder and looked into her eyes. Melie couldn't help feeling that Henrietta's words sounded familiar, as though they had passed through her mind many years ago. But how could that be? After all, she was only ten years old. Melie was about to voice her thoughts but was interrupted by Henrietta who was tuned in to Melie's thinking. *'I know, my child. It is indeed puzzling.*

Yet I have believed for some time now that your destiny in the quest for The Stone transcends your mortal years. I believe that there is some connection between yourself and Mordechai Fearn. Inexplicable and swathed in mystery, but a connection nonetheless.'

'*Henrietta,'* replied Melie, thankful for their shared telepathy, *'I've felt that too. When I saw him on the bus back there, it was as if I knew him. I mean really knew him as though I'd met him before. And now these words you've just said. They're so familiar and something to do with The Stone. Someone was feeling that they couldn't afford to make any mistakes. It's vivid, really vivid. I can feel it right now and ... well it's raining on a hillside somewhere. I've no idea what it means ...'* She stopped her train of thought and looked around at the group. From previous experience, she was well aware that these telepathic exchanges were fast as lightning. The others, with the possible exception of Connell, had no idea that anything had taken place between the two and remained poised and ready for Henrietta's explanation of why they should be exercising caution. Connell just winked at Melie and smiled. He knew.

'And ...?' The Captain prompted, adjusting his rucsac and moving closer to the old woman.

'Yes. Caution,' she continued. 'We should not all go inside. It will be too much for the old man. He will be overwhelmed and fearful.'

'He will,' said Quartz Munro, 'overwhelmed, fearful ... and maybe dead. I mean who's to say your sister and her shady amigos haven't got to him first? That nutcase bus driver blazed a trail to the Silent City with half the lunatic fringe of Valletta following on behind him. Think that cat of hers wouldn't have noticed? No offence James,' he said, looking down at the youngster, 'but if a seven year old can find the one door in town we were looking for, then I'm sure Catwoman can too.'

'Just hold it right there Quartz Munro,' snarled Melie with an air of authority. 'For a start his name is Jam Sandwich Schultz, also known as Schultz Number Four but most often known as The Observant Jam Sandwich. Observant, get it? Don't underestimate the kids in this gang, or one day you might just live to regret it!'

'Sorry, sorry,' said Munro, holding up his hands as a gesture of apology. 'I just meant ...'

'We know what you meant,' interrupted Molly. 'Just ... well just don't, okay?'

'People are always thinking we don't know anything because we're kids,' added Alexander, moving close to his siblings to show his support. The one remaining Shultz said nothing and sidled closer to Luke who by now had either warmed to the constant attention or just accepted it as his fate in life.

'No, really, I am actually sorry, it just slipped out,' said Quartz, looking at Moo for moral support. She just shrugged her shoulders as if to say *it's like I've been saying for years, you should learn to think before you speak, Munro.*

'Look, just shut up all of you,' hissed Tiny Page, who had replaced his glasses as if this would help him to think more clearly. 'Henrietta's right. Some of us should stay out here anyway to watch out for Catwoman and friends. Melie, it's your show, who's doing what?' Melie looked up at the house, scanning the walls as if expecting to find inspiration for the next move. She fingered the tourmaline crystal and sighed deeply.

'Right, listen to me,' she said. 'I think me and Henrietta should go in. I mean, we wouldn't even be here without her letter. What do you think Henrietta?'

'Yes Amelia,' replied the old woman, 'I would like to go inside with you and meet the man befriended by the victim of my mother's cruelty.' She stepped over to stand beside Melie.

'Okay,' said Melie, 'well I think Quartz ought to come too, you know, just in case there's any trouble. What do you think Quartz, you coming?'

'You can bet your life I am,' he said, 'just try and stop me!' He smiled as he imagined that stopping him from doing anything at all was probably the last thing any of the assembled company would ever contemplate.

'Tiny too,' said Melie, taking her best friend by the arm and pulling him into the group. Tiny's cheeks reddened and he automatically reached to push his glasses back up his nose before realising they were back in his shirt pocket. In the end, Melie's chosen company had grown to include Da, The Observant Jam Sandwich, Posy, Mungo and The Captain. The remaining companions stationed themselves around and about the alleyway to keep watch for any sign of Sanguinella's spies. Melie took the rapper of the lion's head doorknocker in her hand and tapped three times. The whole company paused expectantly, waiting for the door to open. A fat pigeon flapped about in the gutters above the topmost window and then flew off to settle on a rusted television aerial on the roof of the house opposite. The door remained closed. Melie looked at Henrietta and raised her eyebrows as if seeking permission to knock once more. She needn't have bothered. Quartz Munro strode up to the door and delivered half a dozen resounding hammer blows with his fist.

'What are you looking at me like that for?' he asked the frowning Henrietta. 'If you're going to knock on a door, you're going to knock on a door. Never mind pussyfooting around. If he's not dead, he's half-asleep in there. He wants waking up, that's what he wants.' He glanced down at the meerkat and was slightly embarrassed to see it scribbling away, broadcasting an accurate description of his bullish behaviour to The Script's avid readership back in Hedge.

'Yeah, fine, well you've probably scared him half to death,' hissed Moo Gabrielle. 'I mean he's no spring chicken for a Theirworlder, is he? He'll be hiding under the kitchen table now with all that banging and clattering! He'll think the house is falling down.'

'Okay, okay!' said Munro sarcastically, 'I was just trying to do something positive, Moutarde!' She bristled openly at the use of her full first name and was about to take the matter up until Melie cut in.

'Look, just shut up will you?' she ordered. 'He'll never come out with all this commotion going on. And can we keep it quiet?' At this, Melie realised she too was speaking a little too loudly and adjusted the shoulder strap of her Bag of Tryx before continuing in a low whisper. 'Let's keep it quiet; there may be a certain little grey cat on a hot tin roof.' Looking upwards, she was relieved to see the fat pigeon still in one piece, sunning itself on the rusted aerial opposite. 'Right, let's try again.' Melie reached out to rap again but stopped in her tracks. Turning slowly round to face the assembled group she put her hand to her mouth, blinked and then looked again. All heads turned to follow her stare. Standing at the back of the group was a small man with long, yellowing grey hair, holding a battered trilby in one hand and a stalk of Brussels sprouts in the other. Under the circumstances, it was easy to assume he was at least one hundred and sixty years old.

'Can I help you?' he croaked in a cosmopolitan accent that had a definite hint of Yorkshire about it.

Chapter Twenty-Five

The Last Words of Mordechai Fearn

'Look, look at this! Would you believe it? They have found him, Mordechai Fearn! He is there with the companions at this very moment!' Fergus hopped excitedly from one foot to the other as he relayed Quartz Munro's vivid red contribution to The Script when it appeared in the Greenbanks book. 'He has a stalk of Brussels sprouts!'

'I hardly think that's relevant Fergus, although I must say I share your excitement!' said Maeva as she rushed over to join him at the lectern. 'Sprouts or no sprouts though, if Melie thinks that's Fearn then believe me, it's Fearn. Where are they?'

'Malta,' replied Polly Brown. 'It looks like Mungo's been sitting right on top of him in that hideaway of his in Valletta. How long have the fearsome foursome been searching for The Stone? And all along the biggest clue in years is sitting right there under their noses!'

'Not quite,' added Fergus, 'remember, they are all in ... where does it say?' He stooped to scrutinise the text as it appeared, lingered and then faded. 'Yes, here it is, Mdina; Malta's ancient capital.' He reached down and lifted the quill from the meerkat in his pocket before continuing. 'Where is Malta then, any ideas? Here you are old friend,' he said as he returned the quill. 'Just didn't want them all knowing about my hazy Theirworld geography, that's all. No offence is intended.'

Greenbanks was buzzing with excitement at the latest news from Quartz Munro. The three of them had been following the story ever since Quartz first conveyed the dreadful news about Davis and Mavis. That had saddened the three of them. Davis and Mavis had been faithful servants of The Governance for years and would be sadly missed. Similarly, the news about Tortue's misfortune at the hands of Sanguinella and the Airs had left them horrified and fearful for the companions' safety. The excitement of the library break-in, however, had the readers glued to their seats and the information about Mordechai Fearn's involvement in matters held them transfixed at it unfolded right in front of their noses. They'd laughed at the image of the bus race through the Maltese countryside and could almost taste the pale pink powder as it exploded onto the tarmac off the back of the Land Rover. The news about the only killing since time began, courtesy of Desdemona Couch, had been hard to swallow. Henrietta's hatred of her sister was reassuring, but an air of mistrust remained even so. The Couch family were clearly a malignant force to be reckoned with. Without a doubt, the entire citizenship of Hedge would be following The Script and sharing the collective revulsion at the news of the killing. Perhaps only Fenouille De Groix had given up reading the news. His brother's dismissal would have been hard to stomach and he was likely to have given up the ghost and retired to his kitchen to grieve in private, just as Billy had imagined.

***

Melie and the explorers were quite simply lost for words in the presence of the old miner. As far as the Turley Holes contingent was concerned, speaking to a one hundred and sixty year old Theirworlder was definitely a new experience. Minutes ticked by and the meeting began to feel like one of those awkward times when no one knew quite what to do. Melie eventually broke the stalemate.

'I'm Melie North. Amelia really, but Melie's short for that. I've ... well ... we've been looking for you.' She approached the old man and proffered a handshake. He shoved the stalk of sprouts under one armpit and placed the battered trilby on his head. Stepping forward to meet the girl, he took her outstretched hand in both of his and shook vigorously. Still the uneasy silence lingered. Melie glanced over her shoulder at Da for reassurance and then turned once again to look at Fearn. 'Look, let's get straight to the point here. Are you Mordechai Fearn? We're from Yorkshire you see. Turley Holes actually. Do you know it? There's a market on Saturdays...' Her voice trailed off as she realised how unlikely it was that he'd have heard of Turley Holes or its market, or indeed, whether he'd be at all interested if he had. 'Sorry,' she added, extracting her hand from his grasp and adjusting the strap of her Bag of Tryx. 'It's just that we think you might be able to help us find something we're looking for.' Still the old man remained silent and focused on Melie.

'Well,' said Quartz Munro as the silence lingered, 'you can take your pick folks, overwhelmed, fearful or dead. Look mate, there's nothing to be scared of, we're not going to hurt you, but please, prove you're not dead and say something ... please. We haven't got all day!' Moo Gabrielle frowned at her friend and moved alongside Melie.

'Look, never mind him,' she said, 'he's crazy. But you can't help liking him can you? I'm Moo by the way, Moo Gabrielle. I think we should all go inside and explain why we're here.' She indicated the door and waited for a response and when none came she too began to wonder whether Munro had been right after all. Was he dead on the spot or just overwhelmed at being faced with this motley group of adventurers outside his front door. 'Come on,' she cooed gently, 'let's go inside. I'll cook us something. How about sprout soup? 'At this, Fearn's ears pricked up and he spoke at last.

'I had a cousin once who died,' he croaked. 'All his life he ate nothing but sprout soup. Nothing else at all, can you imagine that? Not the most popular around the town, if you know what I mean.' He bustled through the group towards his front door turning briefly to look at the commotion up in the gutter opposite as a grey cat clattered along the tiles in pursuit of a rather fat pigeon. Only Tiny Page, who couldn't help thinking he'd heard the sprout soup comment before somewhere, noticed the cat up on the roof. As it stalked the fat pigeon, he quickly ushered Fearn up to the unlocked door and held it open for the entire group to pass through before anyone else had time to notice. He closed the door as he too entered and locked it with the large key he was relieved to find in the lock on the inside.

'Yes, yes of course,' said Fearn, 'come in; do come in ... although I see you already have.' He shuffled over to a very large wooden table in the centre of what the visitors took to be an enormous living kitchen. Da supposed the old man probably spent most of his time in this room, very much as he himself did in the kitchen back in Turley Holes. How distant that cosy little fireplace seemed right now. For all of its unkempt and untidy state, Da's kitchen was his home. A plate of stale digestive biscuits seemed suddenly quite appealing right now. As their eyes became accustomed to the darkness of the interior, the companions saw that they were in a high ceilinged room with a short kitchen range against one wall. There was a wooden dresser littered with old papers and assorted bric-a-brac against the opposite wall and a fireplace in which the remnants of a fire lay cold and powder grey. A sink piled high with dirty crockery lay underneath the only window in the place and on the sill an African violet struggled for survival in its pot. The uncanny similarity to Da's kitchen back home was plain to see and the presence of a battered old suitcase on the table just added to the intrigue.

'Now that's what I call almost impossible,' gasped The Captain. 'This just cannot be happening!' He slumped down in an armchair next to the fireplace and immediately sprang back to his feet when he realised he'd been sitting in an almost identical chair at Da's place just a couple of days ago.

'Yeah, weird all this Dad,' said Molly.

'You can say that again,' added Alexander as he bent down to gauge the temperature of the ashes in the grate with an outstretched palm. 'You got anything to eat Mister, we're hungry?'

'Crate boy!' exclaimed Luke. 'Don't be so rude! Have you though? Anything will do. As long as it's not tripe or porridge,' he added. Fearn handed his sprouts to Moo Gabrielle and gestured towards the kitchen range. It seemed that her offer was being taken seriously. As she went off to prepare the food, Fearn lifted the suitcase and placed it on the floor against the wall, indicating to the group that they were welcome to sit at the table. As they moved to take their seats, it came as no great surprise that there were enough seats for each of them. Twenty chairs. Two remained empty and the visitors couldn't help wondering if these had been destined to accommodate Davis and Mavis. Moo was trying her best to make as little noise as possible as she rummaged around in cupboards to find the cooking paraphernalia she would need to prepare and cook the food. It was hard to keep it quiet. There was a definite awkwardness about proceedings and it was as though the atmosphere could be cut with a knife as each of them waited for someone else to break the ice. Quartz Munro was visibly annoyed by all this and he shuffled uncomfortably in his chair once or twice before getting up and setting about lighting a fire. Melie eventually spoke up, clearing her throat and smiling at Fearn.

'Well like I was saying, we've been looking for you,' she said. 'There's something we need to find and we think maybe you can help. We've been looking for it. We were hoping you might know where it is.' Melie couldn't help feeling that she somehow knew this man. The bus station at the city gate in Valletta couldn't be the first time she'd seen him; he was much too familiar for that. Mungo Cheeseman took up the story.

'We ... well some of us, are from ...' He stood up and moved to the window where he propped himself up against the sink. 'Some of us are from a different place,' he said. 'You know, a different place to this.' He looked across at Henrietta and raised his eyebrows in encouragement. She took the letter from the folds of her dress and placed it on the table, looking the old man directly in the eye. Fearn stood and went over to the fireplace where Munro was just coaxing the first few flames of the fire into life. From the mantelpiece, the old man took a dirty old piece of garden hose the length of a recorder, which he put to his lips and used to blow a stream of air into the fire. Instantly the kindling burst into flames and he piled more kindling into the flames before handing the hose to Munro and returning to the table. Melie was seated right beside the old man.

Whilst Moo and Munro attended to their domestic duties, Fearn looked deeply into Melie's eyes. The rest of the companions waited patiently, expecting him to pick up the letter and read it. Instead, he reached out and took Melie's hand in his own.

'My girl, I don't know who you are. I don't know who any of you are. You're from Yorkshire you say. Well it's a long time since I've been there, a long time indeed. Yet I do know something, though I don't know how I know.' He looked around at his guests, his gaze lingering on each of them as though assessing the situation. He nodded and smiled when he looked at Da North who couldn't help thinking the old man knew he was Melie's father. 'What I do know is this,' he turned once again to Melie, 'they won't let you back in without it, you know, this thing you're looking for.'

'What do you mean they won't let me back in?' whispered Melie, visibly shocked. 'Won't let me back in to ...' She stopped short as Henrietta invaded her thoughts telepathically once more.

'He means The Shining Stone. Being the chosen one is not without its disadvantages Amelia. Do you understand what I'm saying? You cannot fail if you want to reunite your family'

'I understand. Believe me, I will not fail. That's the only reason I'm doing all this, I'd have thought you'd have worked that one out Henrietta,' Melie replied in her thinking voice and then she continued aloud. 'Yeah, like I was saying, you say they won't let me back in. Where won't they let me back in to?' Fearn looked at the folded letter in the centre of the table and then he leaned back in his chair.

'Do you have any idea how old I am?' he asked. 'Any

idea at all? Well I was born in the year eighteen forty-one. Eighteen forty-one, can you believe that? That makes me one hundred and sixty-seven years old. One hundred and sixty-seven years old!' He seemed taken aback that his guests were not surprised. 'For a very long time I have somehow been expecting this visit, because the place you speak of Melie North is a place I know of, a place ...' Henrietta Couch interrupted.

'...a place from which you had a frequent visitor a very long time ago when you were a young man,' she said. 'The visits suddenly stopped and no explanation was ever given. You have no doubt wondered, Mordechai Fearn, how it is that you have lived to the age of one hundred and sixty-seven. Well each of us knows the answer to that.' She pushed the letter across the table, gesturing for him to read it. 'This by rights belongs to you. I have concealed this letter for over one hundred and fifty years.' For once, the inscrutable woman seemed agitated. 'I took it from the writing table of your namesake, Mordechai Fern after he had been killed by the hand of ... my mother.' At this, she sighed deeply and her eyes welled with tears. Lizzie Page placed a comforting arm around her shoulder and cradled the tourmaline crystal in her hand. Fearn took up the letter and read it aloud. When finished he folded it once again and placed it into the inside pocket of his jacket.

'Mordechai Fern,' he whispered. 'I remember it as clear as day. I was a teenage lead miner up in Yorkshire at Providence. They were hard times, hard times indeed. Prosperous they called that vein. That's a laugh!' The hearty fire bathed the room in a golden glow. The forgotten soup cooled in the pan as the companions listened intently to Fearn's story. 'He'd come and see me out on the levels. Come from nowhere it seemed and he himself seemed ...

well, not like the rest of us, not what you'd expect. He had an old man's head on a young man's shoulders and he said he was from another place.' He traced the wood grain in the old pine table with a finger as he spoke. 'Another place, imagine that! All I'd known was the mine and the village. And he saw the suffering. Oh yes, he saw it alright.' This particular memory seemed to stir anger deep inside and he slammed a fist against the table. 'Well what was I working for; for me, for my family? No!' He stood up and began to pace the room as he continued. 'We were all doing it. Slaving for the toffs to build their bloody castles, shove out their boundaries even further and then keep us out. Lucky if you lived past thirty down those passages every hour of daylight. And then he came along, Mordechai Fern. Funny that. Of all the names ...' He moved back to sit beside Melie once again, lost in his own thoughts.

'Go on,' Melie urged, what happened?'

'Well,' replied Fearn, 'it's funny, but every time he'd been visiting it's as though I felt stronger, youthful even. He said he wanted to help, you know, to give something back because he'd learned a lot from me. From me, I ask you, what could a man like that learn from me? And then he was gone.' He took out the letter and held it up for all to see. 'And now we know why, don't we? Don't we Henrietta Couch? And before you ask me how I know your name, I don't know. I just know it. And don't worry; I somehow know that you are not like your mother. She must have been a real demon that woman.'

'Indeed she was,' added Henrietta. 'As is her elder daughter, my sister Sanguinella.'

'Her sister who's on our trail right now to beat us to The Stone, this thing we're looking for that you can help us to find,' cut in Quartz Munro who was becoming as impatient as Fearn was being long-winded. 'So can we all just get to the point and get out of here. What's this clue mean in that letter, namesake's old providence lies behind Futhark on a whim? We haven't got all day you know. Time is short, time is nearly ...'

'Gone, I know,' said Fearn calmly. 'But really, there is no hurry. You can't expect a man who has seen the best part of two centuries to start hurrying.'

'You've probably seen the worst part of two centuries too,' said Jam Schultz, an observation that intrigued Da and the kids. Fearn was living history personified.

'There is some truth in that my lad,' said Fearn, 'but we will have to talk about that later. Our friend Mr Munro is eager to hear about more pressing matters. Well as I was saying, he disappeared. Dead, as we now know. I grieved for a while but worked unrelentingly season after season. Yet while my companions perished under their labours, I continued to thrive, although I did not prosper. I'd almost forgotten about the visits of Mordechai Fern and the tales he told me of another place until I heard about those girls and their fairies. I was seventy-six by then and had moved to Derbyshire, working the Blue John in the Matlock area.'

'What girls and what fairies?' asked Melie.

'It was in all the papers and there was a big song and dance about it; girls seeing fairies in the woods and setting everybody talking. The Cottingley Fairies, that's what they called them. It was in the West Riding, not far from Bradford. I don't believe in it now though, but back then, it made me think. Think that maybe there really were other places. Different places, different things. For the next twenty years, I plotted to move away. Move away from the mining. Move away from Derbyshire. Get completely away. It was looking odd, to say the least, that a man pushing eighty could still be alive, let alone mining the Blue. Hard times they were.'

'So you came to Malta?' Geo asked, anxious to know more about Fearn's travels.

'I walked,' said Fearn. 'At ninety-six, I walked to Liverpool and jumped on the first ship I could find, without paying of course. A stowaway at ninety-six, I ask you! Well I ended up in Italy and walked around for a while, got into a bit of a pickle with some young men from Sicily and managed to waltz away with some money they'd given me to look after.'

'What, you mean you stole it?' asked Molly, 'that's weird!'

'Oh, no my dear,' the old man replied, 'I didn't steal it. They gave it to me to look after for a while and then I never saw them again. Those were strange times in Europe in the late thirties; all sorts of unpleasant episodes were beginning. So after a while I boarded a ship to Malta. I'd heard they spoke English there and worked out that I could start a new life. Truth is I was ashamed to go back to England. I think my family thought I was a freak. Ninety-six and still working you see. It wasn't an easy time in Malta back then. Well, it's not easy now, but back then there was a war going on and Malta was just in the wrong place at the wrong time. They took a real pounding.'

'And you've been living here ever since,' said Melie, 'wondering whether one day you'd be visited by a bunch of adventurers asking for information about Hedge. That's where he was from, Mordechai Fern,' added Melie. 'Hedge is another world and we've got to find this treasure that he wrote about and return it fast. All sorts of things depend on it. So can you, will you, help us?'

'I will help you all I can. You know Melie; I can't help

thinking that I've met you before, although I can't see how that can be possible. In fact...' said Fearn, 'it's as though I've met you all before or at least shared some common ground in the past. But we must sleep now. I am old and I grow tired quickly. We can continue this in the morning.'

'Wait,' said Luke rising from his chair. All eyes turned to look at him. 'What about the soup?'

'Eat your soup young man,' replied Fearn. 'There's plenty for all. I need little food nowadays. I am old, very much older than I have felt for some time. I have enjoyed your company. Good luck in your adventures ... and Melie North remember, without passion there is no power, no power at all. Goodnight.' He slipped out of the room and up a wooden staircase that creaked as he shuffled off to bed for the night, taking Henrietta's letter and the battered trilby with him.

'No passion, no power, eh?' said Luke. 'How freaky is that? Come on then, soup all round.'

Chapter Twenty-Six

Of Runes and a Close Shave for Connell Brown

'Do you know what's worrying me?' asked Tiny next morning as he scraped at last night's soup pan with a wooden spoon.

'What,' teased Sammy, 'can't get Fearn's pan clean, is that it?'

'No, no not that. Anyway just shut up if you can't be serious,' said Tiny. 'It's not a game this Samphire; it's got to be sorted. Just listen will you? What's worrying me is this. If Quartz's meerkat is writing down everything that goes on round here, then it's appearing in The Script in every household in Hedge.'

'And?' asked Molly.

'And Sanguinella lives in Hedge,' observed Jam, 'in Gush as a matter of fact. So she can read all about where we are and what we're doing.'

'That's right,' said Tiny. He thought back to the previous day when he'd noticed the grey cat stalking the fat pigeon, hoping that it hadn't been Lavender poking her nose in where it was most certainly not wanted. 'So it seems to me we shouldn't be letting it scribe. It could be leading Couch and company right to Fearn's doorstep.'

'What could?' Melie yawned as she entered the kitchen. Tiny explained his concern about The Script and by the time the rest of the group had gathered in the kitchen, it was being debated as a rather worrisome matter.

'Well,' said Mungo, 'I think Tiny's right. I mean, I hope she is in Hedge, I really do; better there than here. But if she's in Gush, she'll have up to the minute intelligence on everything that Fearn said last night. Where is he by the way? I must say, he looked worn out when he went to bed. But I suppose your lot would at a hundred and sixty-seven.'

'He did, didn't he? Wonder if he's ok?' Lizzie was concerned for the old man. Mungo was right. He really did look his age as he left the room.

'He'll be ok,' said Quartz. 'He's lived through plenty that old fella. So what we gonna do about you my old matey?' He lifted the meerkat out of his pocket and stroked it's forehead with a dirty fingernail.

'Quartz,' asked Alexander, 'can I ask you a question?'

'Be my guest son,' replied Quartz, 'ask away.'

'Well I was wondering,' said Alexander, 'the meerkat scribes spend most of their time in people's pockets. So I was just wondering, what do they do about, you know, going to the toilet."

'Alexander!' cried The Captain, 'what sort of a question is that to be asking? I mean it's not as if we're short of a little stimulation for the grey matter at the moment, you know, with all that's going on.' Geo settled himself back down in the armchair beside the fireplace and continued to pore over the map. 'Going to the toilet, I ask you!'

'No Geo,' said Da, 'actually that's just the kind of stuff the kids are interested in. At school, I mean. All the nitty gritty stuff about how people actually lived. Real things that happen every day, that's what they want to know about. Let's face it, understanding spittoons is a bit more interesting than ten sixty-six, don't you think? I mean, what use is it knowing a date?'

'Ah yes,' joined in Billy, 'spittoons, now you're talking.

And I heard that ...'

'Okay, okay, let's leave it there shall we?' said Posy. 'I thought we were talking about The Script. It is quite important you know. What are we going to do about it? Any ideas Connell?'

'Well,' he said, 'if Quartz's contributions stop appearing they'll just worry. They'll think something's gone wrong. We don't want that.' He was clearly thinking of his sister tucked away in Greenbanks with Fergus and Maeva. The last thing he wanted was to cause her any distress. He was also worried that he hadn't received any messages from Hedge for some time now and he hoped his sister was alright.

'You're right, they will worry,' said Lizzy. 'And besides,' she added, 'we could only do it if Quartz says it's okay.' She looked at Quartz. 'I mean you must have some kind of position of responsibility if they've given you a meerkat scribe.' She paused and went over to the windowsill to pull a couple of dead leaves off the African violet.

'Can't think who in their right mind would give Munro a position of responsibility,' joked Moo, 'unless it was responsibility for introducing bulls into china shops!'

'Very funny Moutarde,' he snapped. 'Well they did and I have and really, it's fine by me. Why we didn't think of it before now though I'll never know.'

'Okay then,' said Luke, 'so tell me one thing, about the ...'

'If it's about meerkat scribes,' cut in Munro, 'they don't go to the toilet, don't eat and don't drink. Hardly sleep too. End of story. Now, let's get on. What are we gonna do?'

'We've got to let them know,' said Mungo after a short silence. 'Connell's right, they'll fear the worst if the little red sentences just stop. I just hope the little blue ones are still coming through. The last I heard, Fooze Williamson was out and about around Gush trying to keep tabs on Sanguinella. Rather her than me.'

'So how do we let them know? Curiosity circlet by any chance?' asked Melie. 'That's it I suppose really isn't it? We get in touch through the circlet and tell them what we're not going to be doing. By the way, I hope the meerkat isn't writing this down!'

'Worry not Chosen One,' quipped Munro, 'I thought of that. I relieved him of his quill in the middle of the night. Tickling my nose so much I couldn't sleep. Maybe I should start keeping him in a different pocket.' He waved the quill for all to see. 'See, no quill, no questions. Sorry little mate, you can have it back later.' He tickled the creature on the forehead once again and it settled down for a snooze in the pocket.

'Wait! It is not safe.' Henrietta had been listening intently to their conversation. 'Using the circlet will betray our whereabouts,' she warned. 'Sanguinella may be in Gush but we cannot be certain of that. We will endanger our advantage if we use the circlet, for if she is nearby she will detect the vibrations.'

'Detect the vibrations?' asked Melie.

'Yes,' replied Henrietta. 'My sister is powerful and dangerous. The vibrations may be delicate, but my sister will find them as loud as that hunting horn you carry around Quartz Munro. Only a madman would risk using a circlet when she may be nearby.' Once again, all eyes turned to Quartz, but before anyone could say anything, Connell piped up.

'I'll do it,' he said.

'Do what?' asked Posy.

'I'll take the circlet out into the city,' he replied. 'Contact

Maeva, tell her what we're doing, or not doing, then that's that. As we've already stopped doing it the sooner we contact them the better. So can I have the circlet Melie please so I can get it over with?'

'Yes but are you sure it's safe Connell?' asked Posy. She was worried. Given the recent revelations about their past relationship, this was not entirely surprising. 'Why don't I come with you?'

'Look,' said Tiny Page, 'I know the timing's not fantastic but I think I noticed a grey cat out there on the roof yesterday. It was after this fat pigeon. I'm not sure, but it might have been Lavender.'

'Yeah well that's just a might have been,' said Connell. 'Anyway, I'm doing it. I just have a feeling that I was supposed to come along on this expedition, well maybe this is why. You know how I was not keen on leaving Polly when I'd just found her, remember? Maeva persuaded me I had to come along. So what are we waiting for? Don't all just stand there looking worried. Believe me, if anyone's got motivation to get through all this right to the end and get back to Hedge it's me. I thought my sister was dead and gone until I got to Greenbanks. I'll be back, trust me.' An uneasy silence followed. Melie reached inside her Bag of Tryx and took out her circlet, which she passed to Connell without a word. Just for a moment, she felt sure that Billy's hand slipped inside his jacket as if to conceal something from the group. As he noticed her looking at him, she tried to cover up her suspicions.

'Oh dear,' she said, 'I think I left my compass at Mungo's place, the pouch is empty.' Connell, not one for great pomp and circumstance, winked at Posy, nodded at Da and then made for the door. He was almost out in the alleyway when he turned back and smiled at Luke in a way that settled any doubts in anyone's mind about parentage issues.

'Where's Fearn anyway?' Melie asked once Connell's mission was underway.

'He's dead,' was The Captain's sombre reply as he entered the kitchen. 'Dead in his bed so he must have died in his sleep. I thought he should know what was going on so I just nipped up there to tell him to get up. He's cold as ice; must have been dead for hours. He was holding these.' Geo passed Melie a book and an old identity tag of some description.

'He's dead?' gasped Lizzie. 'I'll go up and take a look.'

'Hang on,' said Moo, 'come on Posy, let's go with her.' The three women climbed the staircase up to Fearn's room and returned moments later to confirm what Geo had told them. He was definitely dead. There were no suspicious circumstances. He was just dead from old age and weariness. He was one hundred and sixty seven years old after all.

'I thought he looked a bit fragile when he went to bed,' said Posy. 'Poor old thing. I'm not being awful, but I thought we'd better keep this, you know, for the clue.' She handed the letter to Melie, seated at the table with the book and the identity tag.

'I suppose we're just going to have to leave him,' said Quartz, more as a statement than a suggestion. 'I mean, it's sad and all that but we just can't get any authorities involved. Not now that we're on the home strait. We'll just have to leave him.'

'He's right,' said Da. 'How about we just slip a note under the next door neighbour's door? They can sort it out. I mean I know that sounds a bit off, but what else can we do? Poor old guy.'

'Hmmm,' Billy pondered. 'I suppose we could do that. They won't know anything about us and we'll be long gone before they even read it. Come on, get me some paper, I'll write it.' No one moved. 'Look, I know it's a dreadful thing, but it's coming to us all one day. Because of his namesake, he's lived a long life. He's been in the presence of a Stone Guardian. The time was just right for him to move on to another place. Think of poor Tortue, where's he ended up?' As Billy settled down to write the note, the others gathered around the table where Melie was puzzling over the relevance of the book and the identity tag.

'Well the book's about runes, whatever they are,' said Melie, 'and the tag says ... it's a bit rusty but hang on ... two, three, seven. That's a number.'

'Really?' joked Luke.

'Yeah, ok,' quipped Melie. 'Then it says eighteen sixty; a date. Then it says Old Providence. Old Providence, what's that? Hey that's in the clue!'

'Why didn't I see it?' cried Posy. 'I'm a geologist and I didn't see the link! The Old Providence lead mine in Yorkshire! That must be where he worked. It's an important old lead mine, well it was in its heyday. Near Kettlewell, I'm sure of that, you know, Kettlewell in Wharfedale. Not that far from Turley Holes really.' Posy was brimming with excitement at the geological slant that the quest was taking.

'So,' said The Captain. *Namesake's old providence.* That bit means Mordechai Fearn's workplace, the lead mine, *lies behind Futhark on a whim.* Thing is if it's in Kettlewell how can it be behind Futhark? Futhark's in Hedge. It doesn't make sense.' He rolled out the map on the table. 'I mean look, Kettlewell's marked but there's no mention of any Old Providence lead mine or Futhark.'

'I was thinking,' said Tiny Page, 'that by old providence he meant the treasure. The Stone was some providence for his namesake, providence as in good fortune.'

'Well I suppose it means both really,' said Melie. 'That makes it a bit clearer. Fern was referring to the treasure as providence and he was also meaning the location at the Old Providence mine. It's a kind of clever double meaning. '

'But what about this *behind Futhark* business?' asked Mungo, 'I just don't get that bit.'

'Try getting this then,' said Posy, barely able to contain her excitement. 'The geologist in me has finally woken up. I've remembered what a whim is. In mining terms, a whim is like a winding mechanism. They called them gins too. They were winders for a winch that used to haul the lead ore up the shaft. And they were for grinding the ore too, on a circular track a bit like a circular railway track, but just one rail. The horse turned a grinding wheel round this track to crush up the ore. So we are getting warmer are we not? Find the mine workings, which will be easy, look for the remains of a whim and we're nearly there!'

'Yeah, just the Futhark bit to sort out then,' said Quartz Munro. 'Will that be easy too?'

'Namesake's old providence lies behind Futhark on a whim. Namesake's old providence lies behind Futhark on a whim,' Melie repeated the clue. '... and a book on runes ... we'll just have to try it. It's all we've got. We can use Dissolution to get us to Old Providence. I know it's not on the map so we'll go to Kettlewell.'

'Melie is right,' said Henrietta. 'When Connell returns we must go. Billy, have you finished the note?'

'All done Henrietta,' he replied.

'Gather up your belongings,' said the old woman, 'we will be leaving soon, very soon.'

An anxious Posy looked through the window out into the midday heat. For a busy tourist town it seemed eerily quiet. On the sill, she noticed that the African violet had shed a petal.

***

The moment Connell Brown stepped out into the sunlit Mdina alleyway he began to think this wasn't such a good idea after all. Why was he risking his neck like this? There could be a whole swarm of Malevolents just waiting to pounce. Worse than that, what if he ran into Sanguinella? He'd seen her handiwork back in Sardinia and it was enough to put anybody off, probably even Munro. It was a mission fraught with danger, he knew that. But waiting back in Hedge was his long lost sister and as far as he was concerned, he would stop at nothing to make sure the quest ran to its conclusion so that the two of them could be reunited once more. He'd come along for a reason. This was it.

On the rooftops across the alleyway, he noticed that the old television aerial was leaning over to one side. Its rusty frame had finally conceded to the daily perching habits of Mdina's pigeons, fat on tourist titbits. Littering the roof tiles were dozens of pigeon feathers, a sure sign that one of the local feral cats had managed to secure a supper during the night. Or at least he hoped it was one of the local feral cats. There was always the possibility that it could just have been Lavender snooping around. He looked left and right and then checked that the circlet was safely tucked away in his jacket pocket. Taking a deep breath, he turned to the left and quickly trotted off up the alleyway, which seemed eerily quiet for this time of day, even in the Mediterranean. After a few minutes, he emerged onto a wider street running at right angles to Fearn's alley. Shops were open and a handful of tourists busied themselves along with guidebooks and shopping bags. Here and there, a shopkeeper would peep out of the doorway to glance up and down as if wondering why all the customers had disappeared. To Connell it was almost as if he had cotton wool stuffed in his ears and it was growing hotter by the minute. By the time he reached the end of that street he had to remove his jacket, which he slung over his shoulder. Checking around for landmarks to speed his return he turned right into a large square with shiny cobbles underfoot. He hurried diagonally across it and under a low stone archway, which brought him out into a second, smaller square. Here café staff dozed under parasols waiting for customers to arrive whilst the manager fretted around the place looking at his watch from time to time. He raised a hopeful eye at the strange man with the plait, but Connell had no time to stop for refreshments now, though he could have done with a drink. It was getting even hotter. Across this second square, he came out beside the fortified wall that ran along perimeter of the city and he climbed up onto a promenade that ran along its length. He was sure that if he followed it to the left he would get back to the street full of empty shops and puzzled shopkeepers. He peered over the thick stone ramparts. It was a sheer drop to the fields, a couple of hundred feet below. In the distance, he could see the road along which they'd chased Fearn in the bus the previous day and he picked out the route they had taken across the fields. Sitting down with his back to the wall, he had a commanding view across the café square. All was well; no sign of the enemy in front and no chance of attack from behind. This was the place. He carefully took Melie's curiosity circlet from his jacket pocket and wiped the sweat from his brow with the sleeve of his olive green tee shirt.

'Yeah, need a shower,' he whispered before settling himself for the job. He paused. It had suddenly become even more deathly quiet than before. Sound seemed blurred in the same way that vision could sometimes blur. Even the birds were silent as they hopped along pecking about for crumbs. 'Weird,' he whispered. 'Right, here goes.' Rubbing the glass in the centre of the circlet he immediately felt the brass rim starting to warm up, vibrating gently in his hand. Then he whispered again, 'Maeva, Greenbanks in Chowk.' Nothing happened. He waited a few moments, deliberating whether to say come in, do you read me and then smiling as he realised this would be taking things a bit too far. Instead, he repeated his request, 'Maeva, Greenbanks in Chowk.' The circlet continued to vibrate its warmth in Connell's grasp and then there she was. Maeva's face had appeared in the glass.

'Connell,' she said, 'we were not expecting this. But we have been anxious to hear news of the quest in The Script. What has happened?'

'Maeva, good to see you, is Polly there?' Connell was anxious to see his sister.

'She is here beside me,' replied Maeva. She had adjusted the glass so that both of their faces were in view. 'Again Connell, I ask what has happened.'

'Polly, we're okay,' said Connell. 'I am coming back for you, no matter what. Maeva, you will know where we are and that the quest is going very well. But we are close now, very close. We think we should stop letting Munro's meerkat contribute to The Script. Sanguinella may be in Hedge. She may find out where we are and what we're doing, so there'll be no more Script for a while. Just to be safe. This is important, too important for any mistakes.'

'That is wise,' said Maeva. 'But I must warn you Connell. We do not think Sanguinella is in Hedge. She is certainly not in Gush. Fooze Williamson has been tracking her and keeping us informed through her Script contributions.'

Maeva turned to look briefly at Polly and then continued. 'We believe she must be following your trail. You must realise how dangerous she can be, she may be able to detect ...'

'Yeah, I know, detect the vibrations,' Connell cut in. 'That's why I'm not with the others right now. I'm out on the streets. Can't help wondering whether this is why it was such a big deal that I came along with the rest of them. You must have known something like this would come up. Anyway, I've got to ... Oh no!' He shoved the circlet back into his jacket pocket just as Polly was shouting out her brother's name. The café square had erupted in pandemonium as the dozing waiters and kitchen staff leapt to their feet and scattered in all directions, knocking over flimsy aluminium tables in their haste. An indefinable malice hung in the darker spaces amongst the parasols. It was time to get back to Fearn's alleyway. Connell leapt to his feet and put on his jacket, despite the heat. There was no way he could get back through the square. He backed up against the wall and looked to his left. There was no escape. The wall ended against the side of a high building, which towered over the surrounding countryside. Turning to his right he set off running along the promenade with the intention of getting back to the shopping street further along. The circlet clattered against his hip as he ran and he could still hear Polly shouting out his name, although the sound was muffled. Along he ran, turning from time to time to make sure The Malevolents were not gaining ground as they swarmed after him. This was not going to be easy. He stepped up the pace, panting hard, and just then he saw her standing right there up ahead on the promenade in front of him. It was Sanguinella Couch, with Lavender purring in her arms.

Connell skidded to a halt. He was trapped between the Malevolents, the woman and the thick stone ramparts! Anxiously he looked around, scanning the walls and doorways for a possible escape route. His heart pounded in his chest, the sound amplified by the eerie quiet that hung over the city. Back in his Greenpeace days he'd run a few risks and been chased by the authorities in all corners of the world. But this was serious. Being caught was unthinkable. He had to get away. He climbed up onto the rampart and looked from The Malevolents to Sanguinella. He looked down to the fields far below. To jump was impossible for that would mean certain death. The only way was to climb down, but the rocks seemed so sheer with only a few ledges and cracks to give any footing. Polly had stopped calling his name. Maeva had clearly had the good sense to end the communication. Fastening up his jacket, he sat on the outward edge of the wall and swung himself round until his feet were dangling down to a small ledge that ran the length of the wall on the outside. Gripping the edge, he traversed along in the direction of The Malevolents until he could jump down to a wider ledge two body lengths below. As he landed, he grabbed two large handfuls of the ivy clinging to this part of the wall and held on tightly. He was now on the actual cliff face upon which the rampart was built. Once he'd found his footing he looked back up the wall. Sanguinella was standing directly above him and Lavender stalked around at her feet. It was a fearsome sight. She looked like an evil giant swathed in grey against the blue summer skies. Lavender resembled a laughing hyena encircling its prey before an attack manoeuvre. Connell feared the worst. All he could think of was the way Desdemona has disposed of Mordechai Fern all those years ago, as retold by Henrietta back in Mungo's hideaway. Just as he was thinking it couldn't get any worse, Malevolents appeared beside the woman on the wall and gave the distinct impression that they would be able to drift down the ramparts with no trouble at all. Connell was in danger. He leaned out as far as he dared to peer downwards, searching for a foothold that would allow him to put some distance between himself and impending disaster. Right at that moment he drifted off into a trance like state as once more a message from Hedge came through to him. This time he was in no doubt at all that it was his sister.

'Look to the left brother, it will be safe, it will be safe.'

As he turned to look, he gasped with relief as he saw a long crack snaking downwards, about the width of a boot. It seemed to lead towards a part of the cliff face where thick matted ivy bulged out, blocking out the view of the precipice below. He worked out very quickly that he would have to risk making one or two very delicate climbing moves down to meet the top of the crack, using a few small bumps and crevices as hand holds. This would not be easy, but as he scanned the cliff above he realised he would just have to get on with it; an Air of Mystery was drifting slowly down the rocks towards him. Connell gathered his courage, took a deep breath and then slithered down over the edge of his resting place. It had been quite a narrow perch, but now that he was leaving it felt like a ballroom floor. Hanging onto the sharp edge with his fingertips, he looked down and located a couple of footholds. Then steadying himself he reached across to his left and curled his trembling fingers around a sharply incut fold in the rock. His heart was racing. There was no turning back from this exposed position near the top of a two hundred foot, near-vertical cliff. He found a hold for his right hand and then carefully shifted his weight across to the left once more. The top of the crack was now at the level of his feet and moments later, he'd managed to slither down to wedge as much of his left leg and left arm as possible into it. Up above he could still see Sanguinella prowling back and forth angrily on the rampart. The Air of Mystery was still drifting down the wall and was bringing three of its fellow Malevolents along.

There was no time to lose. Connell inched down the crack, fearful of slipping to his death at any moment. It was hard work. Every move sapped his strength and his ears pounded with each desperate heartbeat. After what seemed like an age, he arrived at the bulging ivy and as The Malevolents drew closer, he just made a fearful lunge for the greenery, clattered straight through it and landed with a bump on a wide ledge. Groaning with discomfort, he hauled his aching body to its feet and looked around. He was inside the massive clump of ivy in near darkness. He groped around with grazed hands, pushing his way through the stubborn fronds. To his delight found that the ivy covered the entrance to what seemed to be an opening running straight into the cliff face. He could sense the presence of the dark forces above and he blustered through the last of the ivy and into the cave. Once inside his heart leapt in fear. Standing before him was a startled teenager, dressed in a kitchen apron and holding a paraffin lantern in one hand.

'Who the hell are you?' screamed the shocked Connell Brown.

'Never mind who I am, how the hell did you get in here?' The lad screamed back at him. They both looked back out of the entrance as the gloom descended.

'Look, no offence mate, but I need that,' cried Connell. He snatched the lantern and smashed it against the outer rocks of the cave entrance. The blazing paraffin instantly mushroomed into a giant ball of flame that engulfed the bone-dry ivy.

'Into the cave, run!' he screamed.

Chapter Twenty-Seven

The Clappitt

It hadn't been that long at all. In fact, the companions barely had the time to gather their belongings and reconvene in Fearn's kitchen before Connell was pounding on the door. He was clearly agitated.

'Let me in! Come on, open the door, and hurry up!' he hissed, 'quickly!'

'Okay, okay, I'm coming,' said Da, striding across the room and turning the key in the lock. Connell tumbled into the room and slammed the door shut behind him. He'd obviously been running fast, for he was panting hard and smeared with grimy sweat. His beloved cream linen jacket was ripped at the shoulder and his trousers were speckled with muddy splashes as though he'd trotted through a few puddles. He handed the circlet back to Melie and then made straight for the table. Slumping down on a chair, he cradled his head in his hands. Posy sat down beside him and placed a comforting arm around his shoulder.

'Don't ask; we've no time,' he wheezed. 'They were after me and I had a lucky escape. It wasn't easy. Let's just say I did the job but we have to get out of here, right now.' He craned his neck to inspect the ripped jacket and then stood and moved over to the window to check the alleyway. 'I mean it; we have to go, now!' Connell was desperate and adamant.

'Right,' ordered Melie, 'we're leaving. Mungo, Valletta?'

'Valletta,' he confirmed. 'My place. From what Connell's saying, they're prowling around out there so we'll have to be quick. We'll have to be careful. It might sound ridiculous but I reckon we'll have to get taxis. Faster than the bus and there's no way we're walking. Got cash Moo?'

'Plenty,' she replied. 'The taxis are at the city gate so we'll have to watch it; trouble could be waiting around any corner. You ok Connell?'

'Fine, I'm fine,' he said, already standing beside the door. 'Can we just get going? Where's the old man?'

'Upstairs, dead,' stated Quartz Munro. 'Died in the night and there's nothing we can do about it. Billy's going to put a note under the neighbour's door. They can sort it out.' He smiled and shook his head at the absurdity of the situation.

'Oh no, the poor old bloke,' sighed Connell. 'Did you find anything out?'

'Plenty,' said Melie. 'But look, let's talk about all this on the way back to Mungo's place. Billy, you got the note?' Billy nodded. 'Right, we're off. Stay together and keep your eyes peeled. Once we're in the alleyway we're sitting ducks if they block us off at both ends.'

'Is that so?' said Quartz. 'I think we've worked that one out Melie. Now can we all stop pussyfooting around? I'll go in front and Mungo's at the back. Okay Mungo? Trust us, we can do this stuff. Follow me.'

They sneaked out, closing the door quietly behind them. After Billy had deposited the note, Quartz led the way out of the city like a soldier on a mission, pausing at street corners, checking the route was clear and then waving the group on. In minutes, they were squeezing into four taxis and racing away in the direction of the capital. En route, those in Connell's car were treated to a blow-by-blow account of his close shave with Sanguinella and the

Malevolents. He could hardly contain his glee when telling them how he'd met the young kitchen porter at the end of the tunnel running from the café in the square to the cliff face. What a stroke of good fortune! That tunnel had been used for decades to dump waste from the café straight down the cliff face! They sat open mouthed as he relived the daring descent and his inspired incineration of the pursuing Malevolents. Luke was captivated by the vision of the huge fireball blasting out from the cliff face. He couldn't help imagining the city under attack from invaders centuries ago, invaders who would have bombarded the walls with firebombs hurled from huge catapults. What a spectacle! Billy twirled his beard and listened intently to Connell's tale, whilst Polly snuggled against her hero. She was well aware that despite the bravado he was quivering inside.

The Silent City was soon far behind them. In the front taxi, Melie cradled her tourmaline crystal and tried to take stock of the twists and turns in the quest for The Stone. If they were very lucky, Sanguinella was still searching in Mdina. It was to be hoped she didn't chance upon Fearn's house; it certainly wouldn't have been very pleasant for his neighbours if they were in there sorting out the body. Poor Fearn, it was almost as though he'd been hanging on all those years on to fulfil his part in the quest. Now he lay dead thousands of miles away from his Yorkshire roots and probably forgotten by his descendants. He'd certainly given the companions plenty to think about though. They were now squarely on the trail of the elusive Stone. Old Providence mine had to be their next port of call and then just the puzzling matter of behind Futhark to resolve. As Melie leaned against her Da in the back seat, she pondered once again over how it could be that Fearn seemed so familiar. In the front passenger seat, Henrietta smiled. She knew what was puzzling Melie and she had finally worked out what the connection could be. Mungo remained vigilant as ever, craning his neck to look out of the rear window, keeping a watch for any hint of pursuit. Compared to the bus ride this return journey passed without incident and within the hour they were back at the fountain outside the gates of the capital. Picking up several bags of savoury pastries and some drinks from a kiosk, they scuttled along though Valletta's gridlines and soon made it back to the hideaway. Bottled spring water had been top of their shopping list; they wouldn't be hanging around here for long.

'Come on everyone, eat,' said Melie. 'We're off to Kettlewell in a minute. Things might get pretty hectic from now on.' At this Connell raised his eyebrows. *'Yeah, I know,'* she thought, and gave him a knowing wink. As far as Connell was concerned, things had already been hectic. She looked exhausted. The burden of responsibility was beginning to take its toll on the ten year old. Da took the reins on behalf of his daughter.

'There's no point trying to make straight for the mine; it's not on the map,' he said. 'We'll go to Kettlewell, like Melie says and then walk up. I don't think it'll be far. We can get a map in the village anyway. I'd rather we did that than ask someone; word spreads quickly in Yorkshire and you never know who might be listening.' He winked at Melie and then swept her up into his arms. She nuzzled against his blue linen jacket and just for a moment all her troubles melted away. She was his little girl again instead of being the leader of a dangerous expedition. 'Come on then girl, let's get going,' he whispered. They gathered around Mungo's table, each of them arranging who to grab hold of while Quartz and Moo doled out the Dissolution.

'Everyone ready then?' Mungo asked. Everyone was

ready. Now that they were at last on the trail of The Stone, the occasion had taken on an air of solemnity and the room fell silent. 'Right, let's do it!' cried Mungo. As one, they popped the Dissolution powder into their mouths and swallowed it with spring water. Just as the room began to swim, Mungo called out the destination; 'Kettlewell!'

***

It was fortunate that the Kettlewell entry point was tucked away in the corner of a steep field in the angle where two dry stone walls converged. The companions emerged into the pouring rain which had been plaguing Wharfedale for the past week. They were wet, but thankfully out of sight; had anyone seen them appearing out of nowhere they would have had a lot of explaining to do. Most survived the crossover without any trouble, but Sammy had emerged right on top of the low shrubby hedge of firethorn intertwined with box. The side of her face had been scratched quite badly by some of the sharp thorns and she daubed at her cheek to soak up the blood. Luke was most concerned and he fussed over the injured Schultz all the way into the village. By the time they reached the packhorse bridge in the centre, Sammy had cheered up and they walked along arm in arm, despite the rain.

It was a complete contrast to the comings and goings of the previous few days in great cities like Valletta, and medieval strongholds such as Mdina. Even the Sardinian mountain town seemed busy and cosmopolitan compared to this quiet Dales village. The streets were almost deserted as residents and tourists alike sheltered from the grey Yorkshire rain in their houses and rented holiday cottages. Here and there, the odd walker sloshed wearily along the road, glad to be back in civilisation after a wet day in the hills. The couple of pubs in the village looked quiet too, with just a sprinkling of customers drowning their sorrows at the bar or perusing blackboard menus. There were only a few streetlights and these were just flickering into life against the oncoming dusk. Somewhere in the distance, a farm dog barked and the post office sign creaked in the wind on rusted chains. Kettlewell had all the trappings of a ghost town, hemmed in by rain swept moorlands hung with low cloud. A comfortable night in a restaurant hotel held far more appeal than a night hike up to Old Providence mine. Eight days had passed since Melie first noticed the butterflies flittering about the hedge by the Nidd. Without exception, each of the companions felt ready for a dose of rest and relaxation so they all trooped into a cosy looking pub with whitewashed stonework called The Clappitt.

Inside, the pub seemed much bigger than they had expected, although the ceilings were quite low and it felt to Melie very much like she imagined a burrow would feel. The only lighting came from a log fire burning away in the hearth of a huge fireplace framed in age-darkened wood. Ornately carved, it totally dominated the room; it would not have looked out of place in a stately home rather than a small pub like The Clappitt. The floors were flagged in millstone grit and were polished smooth by the passage of countless boots over the centuries. It certainly seemed ancient. Oak beams spanned the low ceilings and the furnishings were a mixture of styles haphazardly arranged around the room. Some of the tables had certainly seen better times; their legs had been worn down to different heights after years of being dragged around the floor. A large grandfather clock presided over one corner of the room and a bar with a selection of beer pumps and polished copper drip trays ran the length of one wall. Surly Yorkshire men and women from bygone days glowered down from their picture frames. Who could know what stories they could tell about the comings and goings in The Clappitt? In a spindle-backed chair beside the fire, an old man wearing a flat cap snoozed contentedly and the landlord leafed idly through a newspaper as he leaned against the bar.

'Evening,' chirped Munro, taking off his cap and shaking the rain onto the flagstones. 'The sign says you've rooms here.' He sat down on a high stool at the bar and placed his hat on the drip tray. 'Seventeen of us, how're you fixed?' The landlord lowered his paper and looked first at Munro and then the rest of the companions. They certainly presented a travel-weary, rain soaked picture, obviously in need of a shower and a good night's rest. The landlord folded and then rolled the paper as though about to swat a fly. Standing tall, he pointed it directly at the meerkat.

'No pets, house rules,' he said.' His accent was pure broad Yorkshire. Munro was about to take the matter up with the landlord but Moo Gabrielle stepped in.

'Yeah, no pets,' she said, 'that's alright; we're staying, but not the meerkat. That's staying in the car. Isn't that right Munro?'

'Oh yeah,' he replied. 'It prefers sleeping in the car; doesn't like strangers. Not grumpy strangers with newspapers, do you hear what I'm saying?' Quartz was clearly finding the landlord a little tiresome with his house rules. Ever diplomatic, Moo stepped in once again.

'Yes, it's a little bit temperamental,' she said. 'Nervous disposition you see. And who can blame it when it's being carried around in his pocket all day? No, it's just seventeen people and no pets. Bet you've never seen a meerkat for a pet before have you? It beats the usual cats and dogs anytime!' Moo was struggling to think of anything to say which might convince the landlord to concede. Melie joined in with an ingenious solution.

'We're from the circus you see,' she said convincingly. 'Been working all summer and we're having a look around before we pack up for the season. It's not that unusual to carry a meerkat around with you where we come from.' She didn't see it, but she could sense the smiles from her companions. If only the landlord knew the truth in what she was saying!

'Yeah right,' the landlord grunted. 'You're in luck; there's room. Not much trade about this summer, with this rain. It'll be thirty pounds per person per night bed and full English breakfast. Nothing airy-fairy but it'll fill you up. You can pay before you leave. Let's say twenty for the kids. I can knock you up some supper if you want for six quid extra all round.' He was clearly relishing the prospect of raking in the money. As the guests worked out who would be sharing with who he opened a drawer behind the bar and took out room keys. As this was walking territory, most of the rooms were small dormitories, capable of accommodating five or six. Luke couldn't decide whether to be annoyed or relieved when Lizzie suggested that Connell and Posy took the only double room. The Captain was wondering how this was all going to be paid for. Moo Gabrielle allayed his concerns as she patted her jeans pocket to remind them all about the bankroll she carried around with her.

That night the companions dined on delicious home-made chicken casserole piled high with dumplings and crusty bread plastered with butter. They sat around the huge oak table in the back room of the pub, freshly showered and warm as toast. The Captain had slotted a folded up beer mat under one of the table legs to stop it from wobbling.

For pudding, the landlord presented them with chocolate sponge and pink custard; they wasted no time at all in cleaning their bowls. Da and Billy brought trays of drinks from the bar and they washed down their food with their favourites; soft drinks for the kids and some of the adults, local beer for the rest. Their hushed conversation centred upon the exciting morning that lay ahead; getting up to the mine and finding The Stone. As the evening wore on, they retired to their rooms in dribs and drabs, tired but happy. The quest was nearly over and as long as Sanguinella and her dark allies didn't interfere, it should be plain sailing.

Before long, the only ones remaining were Melie, Tiny, Henrietta and Billy. They moved from the table, leaving the suppertime debris behind and settling into chairs in front of the fire. Melie couldn't consider sleeping. This was important. Too important for any mistakes, so she was intending to stay up all night going over their plans until she was certain they were flawless. Tiny stayed up to support Melie. Although they were the closest of friends, Melie had been keeping something from Tiny ever since her conversation with Billy and Connell in the Eighth Wonder of the World all those days ago. It was about his dad's mystery disappearance and Melie knew that tonight she'd have to tell him what she had worked out.

Billy seemed too agitated to sleep. Melie had noticed he'd acted strangely from time to time ever since the quest had begun. Now he seemed positively anxious as though about to face a terrible ordeal. As he'd often done back in Turley Holes over the years during their long conversations, he appeared to be drifting off into vague moments as if listening intently to some invisible speaker. Then he would snap out of it and be the same old Billy, although more restless than usual.

Henrietta appeared content. She tinkered with her clay pipe, refilling it with tobacco from time to time and sucking in whatever goodness she found in the pungent flakes. She had assumed responsibility for the fire and every now and again dropped a log into the grate. The old woman was looking forward to the conclusion of a long journey that had started the moment her mother had cruelly eliminated Mordechai Fern all those years ago. Melie had given the letter back to Henrietta and it rested open on her lap. She had read its contents a thousand times over in her lifetime. Connell's beloved jacket hung on the back of her chair. Henrietta had expertly stitched up the tear in the shoulder with a needle and thread borrowed from their host.

'You seem troubled Billy Jackson,' she said, 'and I cannot work out why.' Billy rose from his chair and lifted one of the logs in the fire so that the air could get under it. Moments later, it was crackling away once more as the flames crept along its length and he sat down again.

'I don't understand this Henrietta,' he said by way of reply. 'Yes, from time to time over the years I've tuned in to conversations happening in Hedge. I always assumed they were for my benefit, so I would be kept in the picture about my role in keeping the Child of Destiny safe. But what's been coming through these last few days doesn't make sense.'

'I always wondered why you seemed to take such a shine to me,' said Melie. 'Seemed to favour me over the other kids and always telling me how all the stuff I knew would come in useful one day.' She recalled those moments when she'd felt like their views were very much alike and how she felt they must have met before. They were fond recollections; she loved her old friend as if he were a grandfather figure. Her respect and admiration for Billy was deeply rooted and founded on a firm belief that youngsters have much to learn from their elders. Once more Billy shifted in his seat, leaning forward to adjust a couple more logs on the fire.

'It's strange, you know,' he added. 'It's as if someone somewhere is telling me I will have the chance to fulfil a special destiny of my own. Me, Billy Jackson, I ask you! What kind of destiny can I possibly have other than watching over Nidd Hole and Melie here all these years?' He turned to look at Henrietta and shrugged his shoulders. 'Bewildering,' he said. 'It feels like I've got to make some sort of sacrifice, something preordained. What do you think about that? And don't ask me who's telling me this. It feels like some ancient force. Really ancient, that's why I'm troubled.' He leaned back in his chair and fiddled with his beard.

'Indeed, for some there are preordained paths,' mused the old woman. 'I cannot see what all this means, this ancient force. But of one thing you can be sure, we never know what awaits us. Everything exists in a state of flux Billy Jackson and it's not too late to learn that, even at your age.' Melie would have been surprised to hear Henrietta's words had she not become accustomed to a whole series of remarkable coincidences over the past few days. Her mum had said the same thing on the lawn at Greenbanks. Henrietta smiled as she detected Melie's thoughts, and then continued. 'On the matter of destiny Amelia North, I believe that I have worked out how it is that you feel connected to Mordechai Fearn, or at least did so whilst he was alive.'

'Go on,' urged Melie, intrigued.

'You feel that you knew him, as though you had met him before,' she whispered, 'but how could that be if you had never seen him or even heard of him until that night in Valletta?' Henrietta picked up the letter and handed it to Melie. Billy and Tiny listened intently. 'I think the connection goes beyond your mortal years. I believe that you, Amelia North, are not only the Child of Destiny chosen to retrieve The Shining Stone, I believe that you are marked to be a Stone Guardian.'

'But how does that connect her to old Fearn?' asked Tiny, eager for more information.

'The office of Stone Guardian is a venerable position,' said the old woman. 'The safekeeping of The Shining Stone is not a trifling matter and is not without its disadvantages. What I say now is important and is an enthralling yet alarming prospect.' The friends leaned in closer, desperate for the next morsel. Henrietta seemed to be delaying the moment on purpose; it was certainly having the desired effect. 'Each successive Stone Guardian can know all that the previous one has known and can see all that he has seen.' Melie sat back in her chair.

'So I know the old miner because he's known Fern,' she whispered. It was all becoming clear. The dream she'd been having. Suddenly she realised the man on the hillside was Fern. He was running through some kind of tunnel as he returned to Futhark after hiding The Stone. That was what was happening in her dream! 'Of course Henrietta!' she cried. 'The laughing woman in my dream was Desdemona, your mother. She was laughing as she killed him. Still. I suppose you would know that, you were there. Sorry Henrietta ...' Her voice trailed off; she was aware that her words might be insensitive. Then she too got up and tinkered with the fire as she continued. It was as though she was looking into the flames for inspiration. 'There's something else. I can feel cold, wet stone and I'm running my finger along some sort of markings. It's raining. There's a sense of foreboding. I don't know what it means but it must be something to do with The Stone.'

'You know what I think,' said Tiny. 'You can know all Fern has known and see all that he's seen. I suppose it would be just too good to be true if that included the whereabouts of The Stone wouldn't it.' He supposed right. Melie had no sense of The Stone's location. She just felt it had something to do with the cold, wet stone and the markings. 'Still,' Tiny added, 'it cuts both ways. I mean I bet you'd prefer not to be able to know how it felt being murdered by Desdemona. Sorry Henrietta, no offence intended.' He shuddered as he recalled his vision of the evil woman in the portrait. If his friend was feeling Fern's anguish in his dying moments, he felt sorry for her.

The four sat in silence for some time as they reflected on all that had been said. The life and times of Mordechai Fern flashed through Melie's mind as a stream of consciousness; it was as though the floodgates had been opened. Above all though, Melie thrilled at the prospect of being a Stone Guardian. If Henrietta was right, and there was no reason to doubt her given the stuff that was whizzing around her head, Melie would be living in Hedge once the quest was over. That meant the one thing she wanted more than anything else was almost within reach; her family would be reunited at last. That delightful possibility filled her with joy and she smiled into the fire, positively twirling the tourmaline crystal in her hand. But as she sat and savoured the moment, she remembered the conversation she'd been waiting to have with Tiny Page about his father. Melie reached out and took her friend by the hand. Looking straight into Tiny's eyes she explained how she'd come to believe that his dad's disappearance a couple of years ago was nothing to do with aliens. Instead, it was to do with the Malevolents. Her Da had told her about a dark mist during a lightning storm, which had caused Thomas Page to disappear in Mill Square. Melie was only eight at the time but she remembered how everyone around Turley Holes had been shocked and horrified. She could remember how her Da seemed to think he knew something about the dark mist, but couldn't quite work out what it was. His friends all felt the same too. Melie now believed that Thomas Page had been the victim of an attack by Malevolents. Having witnessed the demise of Tortue De Groix in Sardinia, she felt sure the culprit would have been an Air of Mystery. Tiny had kept a tight grip on Melie's hand during her explanation. His eyes had slowly moistened as the story progressed although he had managed to resist full-blown tears. He wiped his nose with the back of his free hand and slumped back in his chair. Reaching into his pocket he pulled out his glasses and put them on, pushing them up as usual. Melie had grown used to seeing him without them.

'So,' he said after a while, 'if all that's true ... and I believe it Melie, I really do ... my dad is probably with Tortue right now. Wherever can they be?'

'Oblivion,' joined in Billy. 'They've been banished to Oblivion. It doesn't sound pleasant but at least they're not dead like Fern and our dear Hedgerangers.' He placed a hand on Tiny's shoulder. 'There is hope, Tiny Page. Hope that one day they can be found and reunited with their loved ones.' He visualised his old friend Fenouille De Groix grieving for his brother and hoped that what he was saying held some truth. He secretly feared the mysterious business of Oblivion. As far as Billy was concerned there could be nothing worse than being banished to that place, although for Tiny's sake he was trying not to let it show.

The room fell silent once again as they pondered over the

evening's revelations. Henrietta stared into the fire. She had a foreboding about where Billy's preordained path might lead.

Chapter Twenty-Eight

Old Providence

Dawn. Melie was fast asleep in her chair beside the fire, now ashen grey in the hearth. It was the ninth day since she'd first noticed the butterflies by the River Nidd. Her journey and that of her companions was almost at an end; The Shining Stone almost in her grasp. Henrietta leaned on the sill beside an open window, breathing in the cool air of another damp Wharfedale morning. The old woman had kept a long vigil throughout the night and her bones ached with lack of sleep. Or perhaps it was age-weariness. Her personal journey had lasted over one hundred and fifty years, starting the moment her mother killed Mordechai Fern in Futhark. Desdemona Couch! The word demon concealed within that name perfectly described its owner. And as for her sister, Sanguinella had inherited all of their mother's cold-blooded malice. They would not get their hands on The Shining Stone, not as long as Henrietta had the strength to prevent it. Henrietta was prepared to sacrifice herself to ensure Amelia North returned The Stone to Maeva in Chowk. Tapping the tobacco out of her beloved pipe on the sill, she snapped the long stem clean in two and tossed it out of the window where it slopped into a puddle. There would be no time for pipe smoking; serious matters were now at hand. In dribs and drabs, the companions came down into the pub and Melie stirred into wakefulness once more. She resolved that her next sleep would be in the comfort of Greenbanks with her mother and father beside her. Yawning and stretching, she picked up her Bag of Tryx and stumbled over to her Da, wrapping her arms around him in a loving embrace.

'Morning Da,' she smiled. 'Change the world did you say? Well here goes.'

'Good morning Melie,' he replied. 'It's a big day. I'll be right beside you all the way to Greenbanks. Come on, let's eat.'

'Just a minute,' whispered Mungo. 'We've got a slight problem really.'

'Yeah, well I think I can guess what it is,' said The Observant Jam Sandwich. 'Moo's only got Euros so how are we going to pay?'

'I was wondering about that,' said Mungo. 'We need to sneak out before he gets up. I was thinking we could just leave him however many Euros he needs to cover it all. He can get it changed into English money next time he goes into town, although by the look of this metropolis there probably isn't a bank within fifty miles. What do you think?' Quartz Munro piped up. He was clearly remembering the little encounter at the bar when they'd first arrived the previous evening.

'Tell you what I think,' he growled, 'why don't we sneak out before he gets up and not leave him anything. Teach the grumpy old git a lesson.'

'Quartz!' hissed Moo. 'Where were you when finer sentiments were handed out? You can't do that; the guy's got to make a living!' She was beginning to think her affections for Munro were somewhat misplaced.

'We're paying,' said Connell. 'Over the odds if we have to. Keep him happy or else he might round up a bunch of cowboys and come looking for us. I think we've got enough on our plates keeping one step ahead of Sanguinella and her mates. Come on Moo, let's tot it up.' In the end the grown-ups worked out what they needed to leave to be realistic. He wouldn't grumble. They'd had a night's accommodation, a meal and some drinks. Breakfast would be the last thing on the landlord's mind this early in the morning and the companions would be long gone before he even woke up. They helped themselves to some food from the kitchen to compensate for this and stuffed it into their pockets. With any luck, there would be somewhere to cook it at the old mine workings as long as they could find some dry wood for a fire. Da found an envelope for the money and The Captain went outside to read the name above the door so they could address it properly.

'You won't believe this,' he said on his return. 'It just gets stranger and stranger; the licensee of this place is called Edward Fearn!' The companions were dumbfounded. Impossibly coincidental as this might be it did add a sweet and conclusive twist of fate to proceedings.

'Almost a fairy tale ending!' quipped Posy, an unintentional double meaning which Connell Brown was quick to notice. 'Come on Moo, leave him an extra hundred,' she said. 'Let's call it Teddy boy's share of the inheritance from old uncle Mordechai!'

Not one of the companions had been keeping track of the days. Had they realised this was a Tuesday they might have understood why the Kettlewell streets were deserted. Weekends were a different matter in the Yorkshire Dales. Even at such an early hour as this there would have been countless walkers setting out for the hills whatever the weather. You could hardly move without bumping into someone on Saturdays and Sundays, especially in hot spots like Kettlewell. It wasn't hard to see why people would want to come to this place, often driving miles to relax in the pretty village nestled amongst the beautiful hills and moors. But today the companions were the only ones who'd ventured outside in the miserably persistent rain. Connell was pleased to have his jacket back but even Henrietta's repair job did little to keep him dry. They were all soaking wet before they had even left the village. By the time Da led them through the little wooden swing gate which signalled the start of the path to the mine, spirits were low. He felt a little guilty at having taken the ordnance survey map from the bookshelf in his bedroom, but reasoned that its cost was more than covered once Moo had slipped the extra hundred Euros into Edward Fearn's envelope.

They plodded silently on, walking alongside a dry stone wall, which kept them out of sight of anyone who may have noticed their unusually early departure from The Clappitt. It was a little unnerving being at large in the misty conditions. In the half-light of early morning, the mind could play tricks on anyone used to watching out for dark shapes lurking around. They were hoping that their pursuers had been thrown off the trail back in Mdina. Sanguinella's rage at Connell's disposal of three of her dark allies at the mouth of the cave would have doubled her resolve to find Melie and her friends. Hopefully she was still searching up and down the alleyways, with Lavender not far behind. As terrible a prospect as it may be, they hoped the residents of the Silent City were the ones feeding Sanguinella's malicious streak. With any luck the advantage Connell had won for the companions would buy them enough time to complete the quest before the enemy worked out where they were and gave chase.

The path turned to the left and soon joined a stream, which tumbled noisily along swollen with rainwater. After twenty minutes or so, it began to climb steeply upwards and whilst there had been a few trees lower down, there were now just the odd one or two dotted around. The wall had long since petered out and the companions were in open country and open to view. It was difficult to keep the party together. The younger children were already exhausted by the fast pace Da had set for the ascent to the mine. Sodden clothes weighed them down and most of the group were feeling hungry. Geo was anxious about his map; he had stuffed it right down into the rucsac hoping the fabric would keep it dry. Mungo kept checking the lid of the Dissolution tin was firmly twisted on. It would have been a disaster if the last of the powder had become wet. He was thankful that Moo Gabrielle had had the sense to make sure three or four bottles of spring water were amongst the booty from the kitchen raid that morning. As they progressed up the path, they encountered a few signs that this had once been a mining area. Here and there, the banks of the stream had been strengthened by stone walling and the streambed appeared to have been paved with rough-hewn flagstones. For what purpose it wasn't clear, although Posy reckoned it may have been to allow water to surge through at such points, or maybe to divert the watercourse. Now and again, they would startle grazing sheep that would bolt off up the hillside or else stand and stare whilst chewing mouthfuls of short grass. It was clear from their expressionless faces that they didn't care about the rain in their waterproof woollen coats and they didn't care about The Shining Stone. They'd never heard of Mordechai Fearn but it was intriguing to think that the old miner himself would have startled plenty of sheep as he trudged to work along this very path as a young man.

After about an hour, the rain eased and the day became a

good deal lighter than at first. The path dwindled to nothing as it led into the head of the stream. All around, the hillside swept steeply upwards, giving the effect that they were in a vast bowl. The expedition ground to a halt as Da and The Captain studied the ordnance survey map.

'Up there,' said Da shielding his eyes from the sun, which was just breaking out from behind the rapidly clearing clouds. 'You can just make out that track; we have to go up there. We should be at the mine in about twenty minutes. Is everyone okay?'

'Yeah,' said Melie. 'It's been hard going but not too far now. You alright Sammy?' The companions were making the most of the welcome rest, finding temporary perches amongst the scattered boulders cluttering the head of the stream. Sammy was shivering. Her clothes were saturated and the scratches on her face looked purple and swollen. She was clearly suffering in the miserable conditions and seemed tearful and despondent. Luke had lent her his jacket and he was holding her in a tight embrace, a gesture more to do with warming the bones than romance, as he was quick to point out. The Captain had managed to find a couple of small chocolate bars in the depths of his rucsac and he shared these out between the kids. It seemed to do the trick. Alexander, Molly and The Observant Jam Sandwich were soon back on their feet and eager to go. Tiny Page dried his glasses on a dry corner of his shirt, put them on and then got to his feet. He offered to carry Melie's Bag of Tryx for a while but she declined; as a matter of policy, her Bag of Tryx was one thing she would never give up without a fight. After another thirty minutes of uphill drudgery, the companions emerged at the ruins of the Old Providence mine. The disused workings clung to the side of a broad hill on a wide platform that had probably evolved over the lifespan of the mine as excavations were made and the infrastructure expanded. Underfoot lay a mixture of sparse grass and spoil from the mine, muddy and grey after the recent rains. Large puddles steamed in the warmth of morning and all around the wet grass sparkled in the sunlight as if strewn with jewels. The weather was becoming pleasant now and each of the companions sat down on a low wall running along part of the hillside.

'It must have been an amazing place to work,' sighed Melie after a while. 'Just look at the outlines of these ruined old buildings. Imagine what it would have been like when they were newly built.'

'It would have been quite impressive,' added Posy. 'If you weren't farming you were working up here. They came from miles around to these places. You know, I've read somewhere that slate miners in Wales would walk forty miles to work, stay there all week and walk back on the Friday night. Imagine that!'

'It'd be that or starve I guess,' said Luke. 'I know which I'd choose.' No one said anything but they all knew too.

'Miles around,' mused Posy. She was in her element now. Here amongst the mine debris Posy reconstructed in her mind the comings and goings of mining business right here on this spot over the centuries. 'There would have been dozens of men, women and children slaving away,' she said, 'come rain or come shine. They'd be up here, chasing the veins deep into the hillside. Men and boys underground, women on top winching up floodwater to stop their menfolk from drowning and winching up the galena. That's lead ore Da. Like Fearn said, they were lining the pockets of the landowners whilst living on the breadline themselves.' The group fell silent as each of them reflected on the plight of Fearn and his contemporaries. It was easy to see why his namesake wanted to ease their suffering. It was not easy to see where to start looking for The Stone. The mine sprawled in every direction and most of the remaining features had crumbled away over time. Apart from a few distinct outlines of stone buildings and the odd rusted sheet of corrugated iron, the grass had taken over and covered all but a few traces of the mine's former glory. There was no sign of a whim, unless it was concealed underneath one of the huge puddles.

'Well,' announced Melie at last, 'we know what we're here for, we'd better get looking.' She stood and turned to face the rest of the companions, still seated on the low wall. It was as though she were an officer rallying her troops for one last push towards the final hurdle. Unlike their games around Powder Mill Fields though, this was for real and there was no mock military line up on this occasion.

'We'd better keep a lookout, don't you think Melie?' suggested Mungo, cautious as ever in the face of possible discovery by Sanguinella. 'What do you say me and Quartz get up on that hill and keep our eyes peeled? He can pipe up on his hunting horn if she shows up.'

'Good idea,' said Melie. 'And while we're at it how about somebody cooking some of that food we brought. I'm sure we could break up some of that wood over there and get a fire going. Don't look at me though, that's not one of my strong points.' Moo and Billy trotted off to a pile of wood leaning against the corner of an overgrown wall. It looked like a few old posts and fencing timbers that a local hill farmer had been intending to use but never got round to it. The timbers at the bottom of the pile were relatively dry and should burn without too much trouble. Before long Quartz and Mungo were in position on the nearby hill. Billy and Moo were cooking sausages, having coaxed the fire into life and appropriating a shard of corrugated iron, which they'd bent into something resembling a frying pan. Reluctantly, Da had lent Billy his beloved knife to use as a cooking utensil. The rest of the companions were dotted around the mine workings searching for the whim, which would hopefully provide the key to The Stone's location. After a while, they regrouped at the makeshift kitchen, lured by the irresistible aroma of sausages cooked outside. Moo took food up to the lookout post and sat with her friends whilst they ate. The delicious food lifted spirits and with renewed impetus they resumed their search safe under the watchful eyes of Quartz Munro and Mungo Cheeseman.

The search dragged on. By the time morning had passed into early afternoon they had found nothing at all resembling a whim. Moo and Lizzie had broken off from the search and spent some time putting together a makeshift shelter using more corrugated sheeting and a few boulders and fence posts. It was a timely intervention; the weather broke almost as soon as they'd finished and the stormy summer rain picked up where it had left off earlier. As the searchers ran for cover it lashed against their shoulders and thunder rumbled in the distance. Quartz and Mungo abandoned their vantage point and scuttled down the slopes to join the others in the shelter. It wasn't exactly comfortable. There was only just enough room for the seventeen of them to squeeze inside and the heavy rain drummed on the roof, drowning out any other sound. This all seemed somehow familiar to Melie. She couldn't help wondering if Fern had experienced something similar on this very spot. Moo and Billy doled out some bread and cheese, the last of the food, and they had managed to get the fire going again to warm up some of the spring water for hot, sweet tea all round. This took some time, as they only had one large metal drinking mug to boil the water in and the same one had to be used for drinking.

'Well if this is the easy bit, heaven help us with behind Futhark,' Quartz grumbled. 'It'll be nightfall before long and I for one don't fancy leaving without The Stone. Who wants to spend a night in this tin can? No offence Moutarde, but it's not exactly The Clappitt is it?' Munro turned up his collar against a trickle of rainwater that sluiced off the roof directly above his head.

'Yeah, well we did our best,' said Lizzie. 'But you're right. It wouldn't be much fun staying here. Even so, I'd rather stay than face Ted Fearn. Think he was grumpy yesterday? He'll be somewhat peeved at the way we left without saying our fond farewells.'

'He'll be fine,' said Connell. 'He's made enough out of us to last him a week. He won't be bothered. He's a Yorkshireman.'

'Well I'm not leaving without The Shining Stone,' said Melie. 'We've got to find it. Tell us about this whim again Posy; remind us all exactly what it is we're looking for.'

'Okay,' said Posy. 'It's like I was saying, not all whims were the same and they weren't all used for the same thing. And they weren't all called whims, but that's another story. But looking round here I'd say what we're looking for is a circle of steel. Like a steel railway track, just one rail, that would be about twelve feet in diameter. That's about four metres for you kids. It's bound to be somewhere reasonably level and they would have built it where there was plenty of space all around so they could access it properly.' Posy was clearly enjoying this. 'What you've got to imagine is a horse, or horses turning a huge millstone which would grind up lead ore delivered to the whim in push carts. We're not talking about a small area here; it's got to be quite big.'

'Right,' said Melie, 'I know it's raining and I know it's going to be getting dark before much longer. I know all that. But we came here to find The Stone and we've just got to do it. So I don't know about anyone else but I'm off out there right now and I'm not stopping until I've found it.' She immediately stood up and made ready to head out into the rain. Da and Tiny followed her example and within minutes the whole company set off to search once again. Luke and Connell took over lookout duty on the hill. They'd borrowed Munro's hunting horn and would no doubt have plenty to talk about as they watched and waited.

The search was exhausting work. Trudging around the increasingly muddy mine workings turning over boulders, rotting planks of wood and various items of mining debris was bad enough. Groping around in cold puddles of murky rainwater was even worse. It was hard to remain positive and imaginary games around Powder Mill Pond seemed infinitely more appealing to the kids than this real life adventure right now. One by one, the searchers and the lookouts returned to the shelter where Moo and Lizzie had once again lit the fire and resumed the slow process of making tea. This would have to be the last tea break. They were down to the last two-litre bottle of spring water. To make matters worse it was getting dark. Only Melie, Tiny, Da and Henrietta remained out in the elements searching for the needle in the haystack. The fading light renewed fears about the Malevolents as the four swept this way and that hoping for a clue.

Melie had wandered to the far end of the level where a tree had fallen at some time in the past. She assumed it had been struck by lightning as it lay charred and twisted, silhouetted against the pale evening sky. As she poked around amongst its dead branches, thunder began to rumble again and moments later lightning flashed all around, lighting up the hillside and the ruins of Old Providence mine. It might have just been her imagination, but as she turned away from the tree, Melie thought she saw a glint of metal on the ground in the light of the storm. It fell dark again as a clatter of thunder broke overhead, but then a second sheet of lightning flashed in the sky and she knew she had found something. As the rain hammered down, Melie dropped to her knees beside the fallen tree and scraped away at the soggy earth. Moments later, she had uncovered a small part of what just had to be the steel rail of the whim they had been looking for. It was right there underneath the fallen tree! She leapt to her feet and looked around for her friends but there was no one in sight. Climbing up onto the trunk of the tree, she cupped her hands to her mouth and screamed into the night, calling for her Da, for Tiny Page, for any one of her companions who might hear. But the frenzy of the storm drowned out her voice and the screams were carried off into the mist by the lashing wind. It was no use, she was on her own. Her saturated mohair jumper weighed her down as she jumped from the tree and looked desperately around for any sign of a hiding place near the whim. She repeated Fern's clue in her thinking voice over and again, *'Namesake's old providence lies behind Futhark on a whim.'* The last puzzle in the clue, behind Futhark, clattered around in her head. How could it be behind Futhark? That was impossible. What did it mean, behind Futhark?

She trawled back and forth, trying to determine the position of the twelve-foot diameter circle of steel that made up the whim. All the while, she searched around for anything that might be a place to conceal a treasure. The relentless rain sloshed around as she tramped ankle deep in the puddles and she began to shiver against the creeping cold. It was becoming unbearable. The Shining Stone was almost within her grasp; she could feel its presence. Once more, she was haunted by a vision from the past of a man kneeling in the rain, fearful yet resolute as he laboured. She reached inside her pocket and grasped her tourmaline crystal.

'Come on Melie, come on,' she pleaded. 'Just think clearly, it's got to be around here somewhere.' Lightning flashed again and a deafening blast of thunder erupted overhead. When the commotion subsided for a moment, she was sure she could hear another sound. The sound of metal scraping on stone and then in her mind's eye she saw him once again. He slotted tools into a bag and then disappeared into the hillside, his heavy topcoat billowing out behind him in the rain. It had to be Fern. Frantically Melie clawed at the hillside where the vision had faded. There was something under the grass! She looked around for a stone to use as a scraper. To her amazement, she found a rusted old chisel lying on the ground partly hidden by a branch of the tree. Picking it up she gouged at the grassy hillside, tearing away the thin clods to reveal some sort of stone slab. This had to be the place, but how could this be behind Futhark? Moments later, she had revealed a weathered slab, encrusted with lichen and dripping with rivulets of muddy water seeping down from the clods of grass above. Instantly another vision swept into her mind. She was tracing the markings on this very slab as if seeing them through Fern's eyes. How familiar they looked. She had seen them before, but in reality, not in a vision. She traced her bloodied fingers along the real markings now, brushing away the grime and muddy water with the palm of her hand. Where had she seen these markings?

Seconds later, she reached inside her Bag of Tryx and

pulled out the book on runes. With trembling hands, she flicked through the pages, despairing as they became immediately sodden in the pouring rain. And then she found it. The exact same markings as those Fern had chiselled into the slab one hundred and fifty years ago. Futhark! The first six letters of the runic alphabet! It was clear that Fern knew what he was doing leaving a supremely well-conceived clue such as this. The Futhark in the clue referred to the markings on the slab and not Futhark in Hedge!

'Brilliant!' screamed Melie as she stuffed the soggy book into her Bag of Tryx. 'Brilliant, brilliant, brilliant! Runes, runes, runes!' Melie's heart was in her mouth as she picked up the chisel and dug away around the perimeter of the slab. She had to get this right. It was important. Too important for any mistakes and she was glad that the constant splatter of rainfall on saturated ground masked the scrapings of the chisel against the slab. Before long Melie had managed to loosen the slab and she wiped the sweat from her eyes with the sleeve of her mohair jumper. Tears welled in her eyes at the prospect of a successful conclusion to the quest and the longed for family reunion. With bloodied fingertips, she prised away at the top edge of the heavy slab and pulled with all her remaining strength. Next moment it fell away and landed with a thud in the puddle Melie had knelt in while she worked. She had found The Stone! Inside the bone-dry recess was a parcel wrapped in waxed cloth. Melie glanced around to be sure she was alone and then reached inside and took it out. Trembling, she folded back a swathe of the cloth. Her youthful features were immediately lit by a silvery glow, which gave a magical sparkle to the raindrops falling all around. The Shining Stone's mesmerising beauty held her gaze for long moments and then she carefully wrapped it once again before placing it in the Bag of Tryx. Melie didn't feel like a thief; she felt like a Stone Guardian.

Chapter Twenty-Nine

Butterfly Hole

Her heart pounded in her chest as she raced back to the shelter, cradling the Bag of Tryx to her chest. Inside, the precious cargo radiated a warm glow giving Melie a surge of energy unlike anything she had known before. The Shining Stone had been waiting for Melie behind the slab for the past hundred and fifty years. Now it felt like part of her being and she couldn't imagine ever letting it out of her sight. One after the other Melie bounded across the puddles in the dwindling rain, overjoyed that she was so close to the final hurdle. Any time now, she would be able to reunite her family! The storm subsided as she approached the shelter and one or two of the companions had started out to meet her, rallied by her whoops of joy. First to meet her was Tiny page who immediately realised she had found The Stone and he flung his arms around her, picking her up and swinging her around. Her Da was next in line. Melie leapt right up and clung tightly onto him, planting kisses on his cheeks.

'No passion, no power!' she whooped. 'Punk will never die Da!' Such was the force of her excitement that he couldn't hold her and they both fell to the ground, squelching into a muddy puddle and laughing joyfully. Quartz Munro blasted out his hunting horn as he and Moo Gabrielle danced around and around before whirling to a standstill. Moo grabbed Quartz by the collar and pulled him towards her, kissing him passionately on the lips. After a moment, she broke away turned to the others.

'Don't you just love this madman?!' she yelled, and then she kissed him again, which brought cheers and applause from the onlookers. Sammy turned hopefully to Luke, but before she could say anything he scooped her up in his arms and swirled her round and round as she giggled away. Love was clearly in the air as the whole company celebrated Melie's triumph with hugs, handshakes and hearty backslaps. Melie jumped to her feet and hauled her Da out of the puddle.

'Come on then,' he cried, 'let's have a look at it!' Melie crouched down on the ground and opened up her Bag of Tryx. The rain had stopped and the clouds had miraculously cleared away to reveal a billion stars, which twinkled against an ink black sky. As the companions gathered around, Melie took out the parcel and folded back the cloth. Everyone fell silent as Melie showed them The Stone. It was just as wonderful as Fergus had described it back in Greenbanks. A translucent gem half the size of a rugby ball, with striations of dazzling gold, silver-grey leaf that Posy supposed could be the lead ore galena, and a black mineral that Lizzie immediately supposed was tourmaline. The Stone glowed in the darkness, radiating its beauty and energising their souls. No one spoke; instead they stood entranced by the magnitude of the moment. After a while, Melie wrapped The Stone once again and placed it back in the Bag of Tryx.

'So,' said Mungo when the euphoria had begun to die down, 'I hate to break up the party but we'd better get going. Back down to the Kettlewell entry point and straight into Hedge. Put the fire out Moo, we'd best be off.'

Half an hour later, the companions assembled in the

corner formed by the two walls ready to take the Dissolution powder. Thankfully, it had stayed dry in the tin and they had saved more than enough spring water to swill it down. When everyone was ready, they grabbed onto their appointed partners and Mungo called out the destination, Futhark. But this time the expected instant transfer didn't happen; instead of emerging into Hedge, the companions arrived with a jolt into a vast, unfathomable emptiness. Everything around blurred as though viewed through mullioned glass and sound slowed down like an old gramophone record grinding to a halt. It was as though they hung suspended between worlds, in a cavernous transition point through which journeys would usually flash at lightning speed. Some of the companions were talking, trying to make sense of what was happening, but their voices came out as a jumble of incomprehensible, slow motion sound. They could see flashes of successful travellers hurtling through the place, appearing from one point and disappearing into another. There were dozens of them, but where were they coming from and where were they going? They couldn't all be travelling on the network between Theirworld and Hedge. After some time, or possibly even no time at all, everything speeded up once again and the companions cannoned out of the Kettlewell entry point they had tried to leave by. The crossover hadn't worked! Hauling himself up from the ground The Captain looked around.

'We're back in Kettlewell!' he cried. 'What was that place we've just been to? What's happened?' He was shocked but a startling revelation was dawning on Geo Schultz. He paced around, checking that his four children were safely back. 'Henrietta,' he said. 'The letter…didn't Fern say something about the power to cross is dwindling or something? And I'm sure somebody mentioned Tortue's crossover point was dwindling too, am I right?'

'You are right Geo Schultz,' replied Henrietta. 'The Futhark entry point must have dwindled since Fern concealed The Stone at Old Providence mine.' The Captain was clearly excited. He wouldn't let anyone else speak.

'That's it, that's it!' he cried. 'I've got it, it's all becoming clear! Yes. Yes!' He punched the air and then swung the rucsac off his shoulder. Reaching inside he pulled out the map, holding it up for all to see. 'It's not just between Hedge and Theirworld ... well I mean our world of course,' he spluttered, hardly able to contain his glee. 'No, it's between lots of worlds. Lots of them! Can you believe that? Can you imagine what that means? Lots of worlds! Did you see all those people whizzing about in there?' He stopped in mid flow. 'Hang on a minute,' he said, 'how come it's daylight? How long were we in there?'

'I think I get it,' Melie cut in. 'Because the Futhark access has dwindled we came to a sort of standstill, as if we were in limbo for a few moments, well a few hours by the look of it. Then we got pulled back out here. Where we've just been is like the grand central station for all these journeys! And you're right Geo, it's not just two worlds involved in this, there must be loads of them!' Melie was just as excited as The Captain.

'How cool is that?' Tiny cooed, visualising future travel between worlds. 'This is truly exciting stuff!' He blinked in the sunlight. They'd been in limbo for a good few hours. Wharfedale was blessed with glorious morning sunshine.

'You can say that again!' added Connell Brown. 'But,' he said, 'we do have the little problem of getting The Stone back to Maeva in Greenbanks and for me that's all that matters right now, for obvious reasons.' He was anxious to get to a conclusion with the quest. Polly was waiting in

Chowk.

'You're right,' said Mungo. 'Ideas anyone?' They fell silent, trying to work out what to do. 'Melie?' asked Mungo hopefully. All eyes turned to Melie. She reached inside her Bag of Tryx and placed a hand on The Stone. Its energising force surged through her fingertips and coursed around her senses making everything clearer. It had a similar effect to the tourmaline crystal but on a monumental scale. In a matter of seconds, she had the answer Mungo was waiting for.

'Butterfly Hole,' she said. 'We have to return The Stone through Butterfly Hole, the hole in the hedge near the Nidd. It's the only way. That's why I saw myself when I looked in last week. It must be a very powerful connection. It seems to be where this whole adventure started.' She looked at Da and smiled. 'Not much longer now,' she tried telepathic communication once more. Da winked. She knew it had worked. Once again, they prepared to leave. There was just enough spring water for this final journey so it was to be hoped there were plenty of bog rosemary pearls at the hedge. As Mungo doled out the Dissolution, Melie took Tiny aside for a moment.

'Thanks TP,' she whispered.

'What for?' he asked.

'You know,' she replied, 'for being there for me. You said you would and I appreciate it. Let's just make sure we stick together and get through this last bit.' She stepped up and gave him a kiss on the cheek, which flushed a bright crimson. Melie had a feeling that she might not see him again and that worried her. As Tiny wrapped his arms around her in a matey embrace, Melie took one of the objects from her trusty bag and secretly slipped it into his jacket pocket. He didn't notice.

'Okay everyone, let's do it.' Mungo rallied the companions for the last push. They were travelling for the last time, each of them hoping that Sanguinella had given up and retreated to Gush where she belonged. It was a forlorn hope.

***

This time the transfer went as planned. Mungo shouted the destination and they emerged right beside the hedge next to the sycamore tree. They could never have expected what lay in store for them. The tree had been butchered almost beyond recognition and logs were being fed through a noisy industrial scale shredder which spewed wood chippings into the back of a pick-up truck. A team of council workers was busy with a digger ripping up part of the hedge, although thankfully not the part where the hole was located. Their fluorescent safety jackets bore the local council logo on the back. Da bristled as he remembered the headline on the newspaper he'd wrapped the rhubarb in the day he'd bumped into Connell in the street. *Council Approves Parish Hedgerow Removal.* There was every chance that if the companions didn't act quickly, the one and only way into Hedge from this particular part of Yorkshire would be scooped up by the digger and shredded. Situations such as these never failed to set Connell's cogs whirring. Putting a spanner in the works of organisations intent on spoiling the environment was all in a day's work for the intrepid adventurer. He'd sabotaged whaling operations in the South Atlantic; no little council scheme was going to stand in his way. Besides, his sister was on the other side of that hedge.

The busy workers hadn't noticed the companions' arrival and it was just as well. Quartz Munro took the initiative, using the element of surprise to his advantage. Racing towards the workers, he stormed onto the digger and grabbed the controls from the startled driver. Unfortunately, the man he'd chosen to tangle with this time was up to the challenge and they wrestled for superiority in the cramped cab. Munro's meerkat squirmed down inside the pocket and huddled trembling while pandemonium reigned all around. The other workers soon noticed the commotion in the cab and turned their attention to the companions.

'It's only a bunch of kids and weirdoes,' growled one of the workers. 'And look at that old woman, she must be seventy! Are you lot looking for trouble? Because you can have some if you want!' Each worker knew the council had it wrong about the parish hedges, but it was a job and it paid the bills. Even so, a bit of excitement was a welcome relief from the tedium of ripping up the firethorn. The workers marched up to the companions, who ushered the kids behind them. One worker grabbed Connell roughly by the shoulder. 'Why don't you lot get out of here while you can still walk?' he growled. Then he shoved Connell backwards. Unfortunately, his grip on Connell's jacket was so firm that the linen ripped right at the point where Henrietta had repaired it in The Clappitt. Connell looked down at the tear and then slowly fixed his eyes on the worker.

'Bad move,' he said and then swung a punch right at the worker's nose, sending him reeling backwards into the arms of his friends. Just as the worker rallied to launch his counter attack everything went quiet. The sky darkened a little where moments earlier it had been clear and blue. Dark shapes swirled along the hedge, converging on Connell Brown. Was this retribution for his attack on the Mdina cliff face? The mysterious shapes oozed a brooding malevolence and the terrified workers did not know which way to run. To make matters worse an evil looking woman carrying a grey cat had appeared behind the weird bunch of characters led by the man in the cream suit. Melie sensed the workers' fear and she spun round to face Sanguinella.

'Run!' yelled Melie, 'it's the only way!' Workers and companions alike scattered in every direction. Lavender leapt out of Sanguinella's arms and gave chase. The cat leapt up at a council worker and dug sharp claws into the side of the man's face. He fell to the floor cursing and grabbed the cat, flinging it high into the air so it landed with a sickening crunch on the ground. All the while Quartz wrestled with the man in the digger as it rolled backwards towards the river, gathering speed. Sanguinella and the Malevolents converged on Melie as she dodged around, weaving in and amongst the fleeing workers as if dicing with death at a Sardinian horse parade. The companions charged around, arms waving and shouting against the noise of the shredder's engine to distract the Malevolents from their swarming pursuit.

Munro at last managed to win control of the digger and he pushed the driver out of the cab. Engaging first gear, he propelled the machine like a torpedo away from the Nidd and up the hill towards the hedge, workers and companions diving for safety as he lowered the scoop. He had had an idea. Sanguinella was closing in on Melie, who raced into the path of the digger. Munro saw her just in time and swerved to the left to avoid hitting her. This was not good news for Lavender. Quartz's manoeuvre meant the huge tyres crushed her into the ground just as she was recovering from being thrown by the worker. The cat had met a sticky end at last. At this Sanguinella screamed her fury and raced back up the hill after Melie. As she neared the hedge, Melie realised what Quartz intended to do with the digger and she broadcast his plan telepathically to anyone who could receive it. With Sanguinella and the Malevolents in pursuit, the companions dashed into Munro's path and one after another leapt into the scoop at the front of the powerful machine. It was the riskiest moment of the entire quest; Munro wasn't holding back and the digger thundered forwards at full speed. Melie, Moo, Mungo, Henrietta and Da managed to scramble into the scoop, which Munro raised to the level of the hole as the hedge drew ever closer. Munro was in his element now, blasting out a succession of fanfares on his hunting horn with great enthusiasm whilst grappling for control of the steering wheel with one hand. His bullishness didn't put off Sanguinella, who streamed after the digger in desperation, howling with fury with a quartet of her darkest allies in tow. Not only did she want The Stone, she wanted revenge for Lavender's death.

The council workers had disappeared by now, having hauled the dazed digger driver out of the mud at the edge of the Nidd where he had landed after the tussle in the cab. The day's events wouldn't be forgotten in a hurry but would no doubt provide endless hours of entertainment for anyone willing to listen in the local pubs. Most of the Turley Holes contingent had been hemmed in at the hedge by a cluster of Malevolents and there was no escape. The adults crowded in front of the kids like security guards protecting dignitaries from potential assassins and they eased cautiously along the hedge waiting for the right moment to sprint away. As fear-stricken as he was, Luke's anger at being thwarted at the final hurdle was building into a surge of adrenalin; the rugby captain's survival instincts were bubbling just under the surface. It was as though he sensed his part in the adventure was fast approaching.

Munro rammed on the brakes and the giant machine skated along the muddy ground, coming to a standstill as the digger's scoop smashed into the hedge. The passengers fell painfully forwards against the sharp firethorn and rebounded, clattering against the rusted steel and collapsing in a jumbled heap. Spurred on by fear of the advancing Malevolents, they scrambled to get to their feet in a tangle of arms and legs, grappling with each other and rallying themselves for the leap across into the hole. But in her dizzied state Melie stumbled, teetering on the very edge of the scoop and her Bag of Tryx snagged against the spiny hedge. She yanked it free and in doing so ripped open a seam, watching open-mouthed as The Stone plummeted to the ground and bounded down the hill straight towards the pursuing Sanguinella. Luke's response was instantaneous. Triggered by the unthinkable prospect of Sanguinella scooping up The Stone he sprinted away from the Malevolents like a bullet, racing towards the evil woman. Seizing his chance Billy dashed after Luke and as he ran, he reached inside his coat. This prompted the others to scatter off in all directions, leaving the Malevolents floundering in their wake. Posy and Connell dashed after Luke and Billy, The Captain streaked towards the digger dragging his kids behind him and Tiny stood his ground. He picked up a discarded branch of firethorn, wielding it like a medieval mace as he lashed out, screaming his fury at the Malevolents. When he saw that the spiky weapon swung harmlessly straight through their mist-like forms he flung it to the ground and careered off down the hill. Thankfully the determined Luke reached The Stone before Sanguinella and he snatched it up, spinning round and hurtling back towards the hedge like a rugby scrum half on the counter attack. The furious woman slipped on the muddy grass but was back on her feet in an instant to give chase, the sopping folds of her grey dress slowing her progress. Each of the companions screamed desperate words of encouragement as Luke, now joined by Connell, eased away from the pursuers, willing him to find the strength to somehow return The Stone. If only Luke could somehow return the prize and save the day! This was true edge of seat action, like a last-ditch onslaught in a David and Goliath cup final. Such was the determination of the father and son rugby team the Malevolents were left trailing behind, but Sanguinella was now gaining ground. Connell saw his chance to send Luke on his way. He spun round mid sprint and dived to grab at Sanguinella's legs, bringing her down in a text book rugby tackle which sent her sprawling in the mud for a second time. It was an inspired intervention and for a fleeting moment Connell had the feeling that some invisible force from a distant place had steered his hand. He didn't move. He couldn't move. With a nod to Luke he slumped like a deflated balloon across the stunned Sanguinella. Luke hesitated for just a second but then carried on, drawn towards the hedge and almost falling over his feet in his haste to deliver The Stone.

In spite of Connell's untiring efforts to ensure the return of The Stone and shepherd the kids through the perils of the quest he'd missed his chance to reunite with his long lost sister. Billy spotted Connell's perilous position and he rushed to place himself between his friend and the pursuing Malevolents. Sanguinella dragged herself from underneath Connell's limp form and wheeled round to face Billy, who stood firm, facing the enraged woman. It looked like certain death for Billy Jackson until he pulled out a curiosity circlet from under his coat brandishing it triumphantly with two outstretched arms.

'Oblivion!' he screamed at the top of his voice, trembling with a surge of adrenalin. At this precise moment, Luke hurled The Stone towards the hedge with all the strength he could muster, like an American footballer making a long pass. It sailed through the air, describing a perfect arc before Melie caught it with both hands. At this, Munro leapt out of the cab and raced along the arm of the digger, diving into the scoop and grabbing hold of Moo Gabrielle at the back of the chain of escaping companions. Melie, at the front, dived into the hole pulling her fellows behind her. The power of The Shining Stone had ensured a safe and successful passage. Billy Jackson stood firm with his curiosity circlet as if challenging the enraged Sanguinella.

'Oblivion!' he cried once again. The Turley Holes companions watched in horror as the brass rim began to burn up in his hands while Connell lay semi-conscious and helpless on the ground at Billy's feet. The power of the curiosity circlet spiralled into a barely manageable vortex and Billy battled desperately for control, gripping the rim with an unyielding determination. Bursts of scarlet flame streaked out, threatening to engulf the stricken Connell and as Billy cried out one last time, Sanguinella and the Malevolents appeared to blur into one being as they pulsed in the air and then hurtled though the glass of the circlet, sucked in by an irresistible force. The brass rim flared up in a final blinding firestorm, as Billy Jackson himself was sucked through the circlet and into Oblivion.

Epilogue

A light rain had started to fall that afternoon but it fizzled out around teatime. Pavements up and down Turley Holes began to steam in the sunshine and an air of contentment settled on the villagers as they made their way home to their families. A group of companions returning from the adventure of a lifetime went their separate ways for now, with stories to tell and memories to cherish.

The grey and weary Lost Souls trudged homewards from their work in the neighbouring towns and cities. Along the way, one of them stopped for a moment outside Robinson and Peacock's fish and chip shop and loosened his tie. Bending to a little blue stoneware pot filled with African violets, he picked one, breathed in its sweet fragrance and then slotted it into the lapel of his grey suit. The sky was clear and blue as he smiled himself home.

Snuggled between her parents, Amelia North leaned back against the horse chestnut tree in Chowk watching the light breeze send ten thousand leaves into a scissor snipping frenzy. From out of her Bag of Tryx she pulled the empty pouch of beaded turquoise, which she squeezed lovingly and then replaced, pleased that she'd presented its contents to her best friend Tiny Page the previous morning. She hoped to hear from him soon.

Appendix 1: Inspiration.

I've always known Melie and the Companions. That's how it feels. I haven't really of course because they exist in storyland. But the characters were generally inspired by people, events and personalities from my lifetime. Tiny Page was, for a time, a best friend at school. I stole his name for the story; I know he won't mind. Luke, I suppose, has the sporting attributes that many boys of school age aspire to. I certainly did, so that's where Luke came from. Quartz is dressed just like a one-time member of a Bristol street band I've watched from time to time, although he was a drummer rather than a horn blower. Quartz's personality exists in that moment when we wish we could be straight to the point, finding freedom in the less-than-finer sentiments. Moo Gabrielle is everything joyfully positive I've ever known in anyone. Someone close to me may see herself in many aspects of Moo. Mungo is the leader we all want to be; the legendary adventurer who's been around, done it all and seen it all. Connell is the mysterious dark horse we all see around from time to time. He's the faithful brother who looks as cool as we all want to look. Jam Schultz is a kick back at all those who doubt us and who won't listen to the little voice. Posy is the love we lose, but in this story we get it back. She's a geologist and she too knows her oolites. Billy Jackson is based upon Oddwelly, well known to those from the Spen Valley as the odd welly wearing wandering man. We were always sure there was more to him that met the eye. Maybe he was a Watcher, who knows; anything's possible. Maeva is the mother figure. And she's the first love from our childhood days, lost to us as we grew into grown-ups and existing only in the imagination as a serene being. Skittish Matilda really existed and she was exactly as described. Henrietta evolved from my great grandmother Henrietta Hardy. According to family legend she always wore a black dress, scraped back her hair and smoked a clay pipe. With all manner of potions and poultices in her repertoire she was renowned as a natural healer. Some believed she was blessed with otherworldly qualities, but that was no doubt a matter of opinion.

The Clappitt was inspired by a certain public house in Hardraw with a hint of a famous watering hole in Beverley thrown in for good measure. The name was fashioned from that of a hostelry high above Haworth. Football pennants are draped around the walls of a wonderful little café bar tucked away down a side street outside the Silent City's fortified walls. I am sure that none other than Tortue de Groix himself served me with rabbit stew in there on more than one occasion. The Old Providence lead mine above Kettlewell did exist and traces of it remain for all to see. But it wouldn't be very pleasant falling down any old holes up there would it? Kettlewell's included just for the name; who could resist? Go sit beside the Wharfe at Bolton Abbey if you want to experience exactly the kind of summer picnic described at the very beginning. I'm sure that excellent picnic spots are to be found beside the River Nidd too. The painted bandits adorn the walls in Orgosolo, Sardinia. That the region can boast a high concentration of centenarians and supercentenarians is purely coincidental – or is it? Valletta and The Silent City have long been sources of inspiration to me. These ooze the grandeur, atmosphere and sense of history I was looking for through which to describe the search for Mordechai Fearn.

The Powder Mill was, for a time, the home of my grandparents and their children; my mother and her siblings, who lived in paradise watched over by Henrietta.

I first found Mordechai through his initials scratched into the wall of a Peak District lead mine. He too really existed and he really did live to an unusually great age for his time. When I first heard of him, this story was born.

As for Melie, well you'll have to find her for yourself.

Appendix 2: Timeline of key events:

1841: Mordechai Fearn is born.

1857: Mordechai Fern conceals The Shining Stone at Old Providence mine and is murdered by Desdemona Couch.

1917: The Cottingley Fairies come into the public consciousness.

1937: Mordechai Fearn arrives in Malta.

1960: Da North is born.

1976: Da's generation get into Hedge by eating Pearls of Bog Rosemary fed to them by Billy. They soon return to Turley Holes with Billy, using Dissolution. Connell's sister Polly, May's best friend, is left behind.

1998: Amelia North is born, the daughter of Da and May. She is the prophesied Child of Destiny.

2000: May leaves, returning to Hedge.

2008: In July Melie looks into Butterfly Hole and the quest for The Shining Stone begins. In September Melie and her parents sit under the Horse Chestnut tree in Chowk.